POLYMATH

A Novel

Written By

M.B. SHANNON

Tellwell Talent
www.tellwell.ca

ISBN
978-0-22887-169-9 (Hardcover)
978-0-22887-168-2 (Paperback)
978-0-22887-170-5 (eBook)

For my children

PROLOGUE

1988

It is surprising how little we know about our mothers. So much of our lives we pass in common space, yet rarely do we ever earnestly look at them, see them. Inside our mothers' wombs we purge their bodies for nutrients. Tumbling in the warm protective cave, we are soothed by the thumping of their heartbeats. Fortified by the blood drawn in the last pushes of labor, our unwritten story begins. We suckle sustenance from their breasts drained to the end for the rich, fatty milk that helps us grow.

In early days they are mere shadows that come and go in response to our cries. Soft voices that sing to us. Strong arms cradle us; nestled in close to their tired, warm bodies we lull.

Selfishly, when we learn to walk and talk, we demand more than just their bodies. We want what is most precious: time. Uninterrupted attention toward serving us, teaching us, caring for us. Vehemently we fight to explore the world, expecting to return whenever we choose to a home of plenty, where we indulge in safe rest, nourishment and more play.

Our curiosity is limited about who this woman was prior to bearing the title "mother." The details of a life, before we rudely interrupted and were the cause of halted ambitions and stalled dreams, never seep into our minds. Instead, we judge. Tired eyes that do not sparkle with the idea of possibility. Dry, red skin from years of cleaning and going without gloves in the cold winter because we forgot to bring our own. A body stretched and sagging, unimaginable to have been an object of desire or to have felt passion. "I don't ever want to be like her," we say when she reminds us to tend to our selfcare, and cautions us about keeping good company. The sighs she releases, unaware that she was holding her breath, annoy us deeply.

Perhaps those whose mothers never had a presence in their life wonder, who was that woman, what was she like? For many of us, she is just "mother," an archetype of a woman who exists only in relation to ourselves.

I did not know my mother well. She would humbly tell you, "There isn't much to know." If you stumbled upon a piece of her history, she would brush it away as being part of another time. She was a remarkable woman, whom I came to appreciate much too late in life.

Grandmama called her a "clever and stubborn child, who needed to learn things the hard way." She said these things with a forlorn look on her face. Hanging over the conversation was always the sentiment of an "if only" thought. Grandfather never spoke of her much, other than to caution not to become like her.

Many would call her a feminist. A statement she would denounce if she ever heard it. She believed she ran away from the world rather than plunged into it. Others would call her talented. Most would call her ambitious, tossing the word out with that sour-lemon pucker reserved for women who have a compunction for work, as if it is a terrible thing.

Friends remember her with kindness; they toast with a nod her contrasting naïveté and bravado. To somebody, at some point, she was a lover, a confidante, and always a puzzle. The one thing rarely said about my mother was her genius—a word reserved for men, and for a few notable women only with the distance of time and death. Marie Curie, Hypatia of Alexandria and Elizabeth I are the rare women who sit among the hundreds of men honored with the title.

I have come to learn that my mother should sit among them. Post-mortem space has brought to light her imbued talents across multiple but unrelated areas. This is her story as I have come to know it. The life of a girl, a sister, a friend, a mother, a teacher, a wife, and a true polymath.

CHAPTER 1

1937

Her fingers plucked at the strings with intentional delicacy. Behind her closed eyes, colors of moss green, dank blues and heather gray cascaded and swirled. Paulina saw music as much as she heard it. Max Bruch's Scotland came alive in her mind with the same amplitude as her bow movements when she played this Opus 46. Reverberations were created along the wood that funneled toward her chin and star-burst out to her limbs. Never had she seen Scotland, or any part of the world other than her tiny town of Kingston. She imagined the shores of the island continent to be similar to the moody waters of her own Lake Ontario. It was the expanse of the Great Lake, contained by the massive rocks that outlined the divide between land and water, that she thought of when she played.

"Beautiful, Polly! I so enjoy listening to you play." Her father sat on the stiff-backed couch, upholstered in a cream-colored fabric with clusters of small pink and yellow flowers. His papers were scattered about him on the arm rest, the oak coffee table and the faded ornamental rug.

"Thank you, Papa." She cherished his praise. "Shall I perform another?" she asked eagerly.

"Yes, Paulina. You sound so lovely. I could listen to you play that piece again and again," her mother said from the armchair embellished with intricately carved wooden legs and trim to match the tables. "Try not to scrunch your face so much when you play. It will make wrinkles."

"But I scrunch my face when I concentrate," Paulina retorted. Her spine bristled in that way only her mother could draw out of her.

"Well, try to concentrate less," her mother responded casually, never taking her eyes off her knitting. Her usually well-masked Eastern European accent was harsh, revealing her frustration.

"I do declare, Polly, your playing is so beautiful, it even makes your mother's limestone heart weep." Her father chuckled.

As he leaned over to offer his wife a playful kiss, she picked up her ball of yarn and tossed it at his nose. Kasia's smile illuminated her face, which began at her large gray eyes, exquisitely highlighted around the pupil with flecks of yellow and blue. Her skin was pale, her cheekbones high and her heart-shaped face was framed by her thick blond hair. Polly understood people saw her mother as beautiful by the way their gaze settled on her a bit too long. When her father recounted the night they met he would say, "She lit up the party with her beauty so that we could not see the stars that night." He was smitten immediately.

"You jest, but a wrinkled face does no favors for a woman, Andrew."

Paulina gently set down her Bergonzi violin, a gift to her from her music teacher when she graduated from her introductory one. At twelve, she was taller than most adults, with big hands now able to handle a full-sized violin.

"A maestro needs an instrument of equal magnificence to their talent," he had said. When her father respectfully declined the elaborate gift, Professor Randall insisted that he would never match the talent of Paulina, and could never bring life to the instrument as she did. "Violins are delicate pieces of art that need to be loved and appreciated through the hands of the player in order for them to fulfill their purpose." He insisted she take it. "As a permanent loan then, if not a gift."

"How about something on the piano instead?" Paulina offered.

Her parents could not afford to indulge her desire for a piano on her father's meager salary. The town existed around three main industries: the limestone quarry, the university, and the penitentiary. A few years ago, Queen's University opened their new Engineering Department. When her father left his position as an engineer at the mine to take a position as a professor, a small cottage home on the campus was provided as part of the package. The pay was not much better, but the work conditions were more civilized and safer. With time he would work his way from associate professor to full professor, and perhaps even someday an endowed tenure professor.

Here, she had her own room at the side of the house. Her window overlooked the parking area and garage. The room had no closets and just enough space for her single bed and a narrow tallboy dresser in the corner. Nonetheless, she was pleased to no longer be sleeping on a small mattress with a makeshift bed frame in her parents' bedroom.

Paulina was thrilled to leave the small one-bedroom attic apartment that her parents had rented since moving to town. The owner, a cantankerous old widow who lived with her adult son, kept increasing the rent while turning down the heat and refusing to change the lightbulbs in the steep staircase leading up to their flat. When Mama had enough of the woman's complaining that they made too much noise, she would move from her usual stocking feet and quiet talk to wearing her high-heeled shoes and dancing the Charleston with the radio turned up, always making Paulina laugh.

The way the owner's son stared at Polly out of the kitchen window when she played in the yard made her uneasy. Her mother called her in quickly whenever he would ask to join her in a game. Timidly, she would climb up the fire escape stairs into their apartment and all the while he would stand and watch.

"Hold your skirt tight when you climb up those stairs and do not let that man touch you, ever," her mother would scold.

Paulina, in full earnest and with a ribbon of guilt for something she had not done, would assure her, "I won't, Mama."

Her mother would embrace her in a tight hug and provide a soothing kiss on her forehead.

"Be careful of men. They can be unkind to girls," she would say intensely, her deep stare burning the warning into Paulina's memory.

Paulina found the cottage delightful, most of all because the previous residents left behind an upright piano. At ten years old, when they first moved in, she hesitated to press the slightly yellowed keys—she felt that all her life's dreams had now come true. There was nothing more she would possibly ever want from the world other than this piano.

"Yes! Something on the piano," her father encouraged. "How about *Children's Corner?*"

She closed her eyes, intuiting the location of the keys on the piano. Her fingers massaged the sleek ivory rods with raindrop touches. Into the second movement, she punched the keys like a typewriter, which drew a carousel of fuchsia and magenta across her mind. She rushed through the trills, racing to the end of the exhausting fifteen-minute composition.

"That was lovely, Polly, but why so melancholy? Debussy imbued this piece with playfulness, not sorrow."

"Oh, Papa. I just don't feel very spirited today." She stood up from the bench and leaned lazily against the instrument.

"Why not play something on the violin again, *minushka?* The piano is so pedestrian." Her mother never hid her opinion or predilections.

"I prefer the piano, Mama." Paulina strode to the large windows that opened up onto the front yard. She drew back the heavy damask drapes to let in more light. A faint spray of dust billowed out. Dust was made of shed skin cells, and she briefly pondered about the people who had lived here before whose remnants she had just released back into the air.

"Every girl around can play the piano. The violin will set you apart when you entertain someday. Your husband will be very proud of the unique experience you'll add to the evening when he invites his colleagues over for dinner." Kasia always had a way of stating things as facts to close a conversation before it even began.

"Polly, you play whatever inspires you." Her father ignited his pipe, the sweet smell pleasantly infusing the air.

She accepted the opportunity. With her feet planted on the ground, she moved her hands down an octave, arching her palms like a cat. The ball of her foot came to a comfortable rest on the dampening pedal. She played. Slow, drawn-out, deep notes that sprouted from her soul. Minor chords, laying a drowsy foundation from her left hand, clashed against the spirited runs of her right hand. Navy, ruby, and black zigzagged in front of her eyes. As the beat picked up and her pace grew livelier, Polly brought the whole piece to a celebratory conclusion.

"Oh goodness, Paulina! What noise is that you are playing?" Her mother exclaimed and set down her knitting, a look on her face as if a skunk had just sprayed the room.

"It's jazz!" The excitement of the melody was still pulsing through her.

"Jazz? Where did you hear such a thing?" Her mother's accusatory tone felt like a slap.

"I heard Professor Randall listening to it at the university before one of my lessons," she defended.

"Well, I appreciate that he is offering you free lessons, and I should be careful of what I say to him so as not to appear ungrateful. But I would prefer he stick to the classics in what he teaches you." She marched toward the kitchen.

"But, Mama, he didn't teach me this." Her mother was already through the door; Polly was unsure if she had heard her.

"If Professor Randall didn't teach you this, Polly, then who did?" Papa asked. Paulina noted a hint of doubt in his voice.

"Nobody, Papa. I just heard it the once and loved it so much that when I came home, I started to play it."

"All by yourself? No sheet music?" her father questioned.

"No, Papa, I swear. I learned it all on my own." Polly pleaded, "If you don't enjoy the music, it really isn't Professor Randall's fault. He was unaware that I was at the door listening."

Her father let out a big laugh. "Oh, my little Polly. Nobody is in trouble." He stretched out his arms, inviting her over. "You played it beautifully. I am so impressed that you were able to replicate it by ear alone after hearing it only once."

She nestled into her father's side, breathing in the luscious smell of his cologne mixed with the intoxicating smell of his pipe. His V-neck wool sweater scratched her cheek slightly. Her legs, now too long for the couch, hung uncomfortably over the edge. Despite the awkwardness of the position, she would not move from her favorite spot.

"It is actually quite easy. The music seems to float through me. So long as I let myself see the colors, the music part comes naturally."

"Ah yes, the color of music. It must be so beautiful inside your head." He pulled on her long braid, then smoothed back the fringe of hair over her forehead and replaced it with a loud, strong Papa-style kiss.

He returned to marking his papers, drawing large red arrows and circles on the pages. Each mark that he drew elicited a sigh or a shake of the head.

"I don't understand why these boys cannot get anything right. I know them to be clever and competent. Why do they struggle so much on these tests?" The exasperation in his voice spread a tension in the room.

Polly sat upright. She scrutinized the formula on the paper in front of her while her father moved through the lines guided by the tip of his pen for a second time.

"Here." She pointed to the middle section of the page. "He forgot to square the formula here—that is why he ended up with the square root rather than the right answer."

Her father scanned the page again, stopping at the exact point she noted.

"I wouldn't want to drive across a bridge built on that formula!" She laughed. "It would tip right over!"

"Polly, how does a twelve-year-old girl know that?" her father marveled.

Hesitantly, she answered, "Last week, Papa, when you forgot your lunch and Mama asked me to bring it to you, I snuck into the back of your lecture. I am terribly sorry. I know I am not to disturb you when you're teaching. I was just curious." Her speech quickened. "I was so very quiet that you did not know I was even there. I stood at the back in the shadows and listened."

"Polly, you learned this formula from listening to part of my lecture? That seems impossible!" He shook his head, while stacking the papers from his lap into a tidy pile on the table.

"You are a very good teacher, Papa!" She was relieved that he did not seem angry. "I don't understand why the boys in the class are so distracted, drawing little pictures, playing tic-tac-toe. One was even reading a novel that was hidden inside his notebook." She covered her mouth, embarrassed that she might have divulged too much and made her father feel bad.

"Oh, my little Polly, you never cease to amaze me!" Another kiss on top of her head, then he stood, gathering his papers and pens. "Would you like to attend more of my classes at the university?"

"Could I?" Delight fluttered through her body.

"Could you what?" Her mother entered, a tray of afternoon tea and scones in hand.

"Attend some of the classes at the university with me?"

"Oh, don't be silly, Andrew." She smiled kindly toward Paulina. "I don't doubt, *minushka*, that you are clever—after all you are half Andrzej, as well as half Williams." She shared a flirtatious look with her husband. "It is just that scholarly work for women makes them less marriageable. You are better off finding a smart man and helping him make the best of himself than pursuing these things yourself."

"But Mama," Polly implored, "I really want to do."

Mama's face pulled into a tight pucker, darting a warning stare at her daughter not to push this further.

"Oh, Kasia, she is still young and rather quite brilliant." He winked encouragingly at Polly. "She'll have plenty of time to think about marriage. No harm in furthering her academic and cultural development until then." As he wandered toward the door, he added for good measure, "After all, if she is blessed by God with intelligence, who are we to dismiss His gift?"

"Ah!" Kasia shook her head. "I suppose, then. But you must keep up your violin and help me around the house." She poured a cup of tea for her husband to take into his study, then prepared another for herself, which she left on the side table to cool, and resumed her knitting. "How about another violin concerto, *minushka*? It is certainly a better way to spend your time."

With reluctance, Polly retrieved her violin, and positioned it between her chin and shoulder. Choosing Locatelli's Caprice in D Major, she started right into the core of the piece. Her mother's knitting needles clicked together like a metronome. Paulina played the high-pitched ends of the jig-like music with increasing rapidity. Her fingers squeaked as they moved across the strings. The knitting needles clanked together faster. The middle bars, which repeated for three lines, drew on an increasing tension in the piece. Her mother's weave grew tighter on her needles. In the final bar, Paulina drew out the quiver of her last note longer than required. It created an irritation, like a growing sneeze that would not climax, until finally her mother threw down her knitting needles declaring, "Enough, Paulina!" To which, she immediately brought the note to a soft end. "Go outside and play!"

"Yes, Mama." Paulina hid her celebratory smile as she packed away her violin.

Autumn was Paulina's favorite season. Its beautiful colors marked the promise of newly learned things in the academic year. That excitement, contrasted with the sadness of nature's annual decay, always made her contemplative.

She meandered out into the backyard, and made her way between the boxwood hedges to the creek that ran between the houses. It was more a drainage slope for the rain than a creek, but at this time of year it ran continually. Her heart light, she mused about the animals she saw playing chase or nip-the-tail with each other: squirrels, chipmunks, blue jays. Their squeaks and chirps filled the air with musicality that even the most accomplished composers could not emulate. The occasional lonely gray squirrel, slow and skittish, would dart past her to hide against a tree, unable to safely climb it in time for her to pass. The idea of getting old troubled Polly. There was so much she wanted to do in life. Adults seemed content to simply manage chores and read the newspaper, too tired to do anything else. It was excessively mundane, and she wanted none of that.

During these walks she always made lists of the daytime creatures who seemed playful and safe, and then of those mysterious animals that skulked outside at night. She set for herself a mission to find those nighttime visitors during the day, so she could observe what they did while the rest of the world was awake.

"Polly!" a boy's voice called from down the path.

It was Oliver, a friend of her brother's, whose father taught chemistry at the university.

"What are you doing?" He walked through the mud in his galoshes. His hands were in his pockets and he was wearing a brown wool fisherman's sweater and short pants. He wore no cap over his disheveled brown hair, which he kept longer than most boys his age, allowing the natural curl to be evident.

"Looking for skunks," she said plainly.

He cocked his head to the side, scrunching up his face as if he was studying her. "You're strange." His comment was a simple statement, absent of any judgment.

"Well, you're funny-looking," she shot back with regret. Oliver was not the least bit funny-looking. In fact, Polly thought him to be the most interesting boy at school and rather handsome. His broad forehead and thick bushel of hair suggested he was smart, while his long nose and recessed chin gave him an air of nobility.

"Where's Petar?" he asked, not seeming bothered at all by her rude comment.

"Fishing for walleye at the lake." She turned her back to him and continued to walk along the path.

"Hey! Wait up." He jogged up to join her, his boots making guttural suction noises along the way, which made her giggle.

"You sound like mollusks when I pull them off rocks!" She laughed.

"Like what?"

"Never mind." She shook her head in dismay. Two years older than her and he didn't know what a mollusk was.

"Want to race?" he challenged. "I bet I can beat you to that tree at the end of path."

"But I'm wearing my Mary Janes." Kasia did not believe in play clothes. White tights, mid-length pleated skirts with collared blouses in floral prints, and large-buttoned sweaters were Polly's usual attire. Truthfully, Polly preferred these clothes herself.

"You afraid you'll lose?" he goaded. "I am wearing these terrible boots that slip around in the mud and apparently sound like sloppy snails."

He did know what a mollusk was after all, she noted. "You have at least three inches on me, so your stride is longer," she replied.

"I'll give you a three-stride lead for my height, and because you're a girl," he offered.

She soured. "No advantage. I'll beat you fair and square. To the tree and back. Winner makes the other do one dare," she said, upping the ante.

Before accepting, Oliver took a long moment to think. "Deal!" He extended his hand for a gentleman's agreement before they marked the start and finish line by digging an inch-deep trench across the mud.

"Ready, set, go!" they shouted in unison. Polly took off with long strides. Mud sprayed up onto the backs of her legs, speckling her like a hyena. The image motivated her to run faster, keeping pace with Oliver right up to the tree. She rounded the trunk tightly to minimize her distance traveled. Oliver simply spun in place and darted back along the same trajectory from which he came.

He gained two paces on her with that move. She pushed to keep up. A burning sensation filled her lungs. Her heart pounded intensely. She tried to focus on her breaths. Determined to win, she picked up her speed, stretching her stride longer. Gaining on his heels, she felt the strain on her calves and wished for a moment that she did more activities. She reached the finish line just behind Oliver by one leg length.

Breathless, they both hunched over panting. "You run pretty fast for a girl," he said. She bristled at the comment.

"Well, you run pretty slow for a funny-looking, long-legged kid." She was disappointed that her retort lacked more sting.

"Okay. Dare time." Oliver stood tall, a defiant challenge in his tone and look.

"Okay," she acquiesced, despite feeling duped and a little nervous about what was to come.

He stepped closer to her; his height even more pronounced as he looked down on her. "Dare," he declared, the smell of caramel on his breath. "I dare you to kiss me." He smiled wryly.

She recoiled in surprise. "Kiss you?"

He stepped one half foot closer. "Kiss me," he demanded.

"How about I climb that tree over there instead? Or do your math homework for you for a week?" She had never thought about kissing before. She had seen her parents kiss, and it always seemed long and warm. Petar teased her about the possibility of going her whole life without being kissed because she was scary to boys. But surprisingly, the idea of kissing Oliver was not revolting to her. In fact, there was an intriguing appeal to it that warmed her belly, opening her up to the idea of actually kissing him.

"You shook on it, Polly. If you back down, nobody will ever take your word on anything again. I'll tell everybody that you didn't follow up on your promise." He reduced the last bit of distance between them with a final step. "And, I'll still tell everybody that you kissed me anyway."

She narrowed her eyes. The warm feeling extinguished itself as if somebody had doused water on it. "Okay. I'll kiss you. But if you tell anybody, you'll live to regret it, Oliver." As idle as it was, her threat still empowered her with strength.

She draped her arms around his neck, as she had seen her mother do with Papa many times. He shifted in a clumsy way. She leaned in and gave him a quick peck on the cheek, then pulled away.

"That doesn't count!" His frustration with being fooled was evident on his face.

"You didn't specify the details of the kiss." She began to march away backwards, still facing him.

"Polly! You wait. Someday I'll get my proper kiss." His voice cracked, at the same time his face flushed pink.

"Maybe, Oliver. Maybe someday. When *I* choose to, not when I'm dared." She sent him a coquettish kiss blown from her hand, then she skipped back home to help her mama prepare dinner as usual. She was quite content with herself.

"One day, Polly! One day you'll kiss me," he teasingly called after her.

CHAPTER 2

1938

Polly languished across the cotton-candy pink duvet embroidered with lavender butterflies and golden buttercups. Her best friend Dorthey's room was an oasis. Imported Parisian wallpaper in a mint-green hue layered with grass-green stripes made the room feel like a garden, where the girls sought escape from the blustery winter snow blowing outside. Dorthey had a fireplace that kept them warm, and the iron slats over it allowed them to toast a few thick slices of bread that they then coated with butter.

"I can't believe you are going to university, Polly!" Dorthey exclaimed. She handed a piece of slightly browned toast over to Polly. Each crevice was filled with salty goodness that oozed onto her fingers when she bit into it. Careful not to soil her friend's immaculate bedding, Polly quickly sat up, dribbling a line of butter right down her floral blouse. Committed to not losing a single morsel of the delicious treat, she finished the rest in one big mouthful.

"I'm not there yet." She indulged in a gentle suck of each fingertip before she took to dabbing at the oily stain with a napkin. "I have finished all of my equivalency exams and entrance submissions. Now I just have to pass the interview panel."

"You'll do wonderfully, Polly." Dorthey clapped her hands together in delight. "Just think of all of those handsome boys you'll get to see every day. While I shall remain in secondary school with all the immature boys in our class. Oh, to be a fourteen-year-old prodigy," she dramatically swooned.

Dorthey was a beautiful girl. The whites of her large almond-shaped eyes were alabaster, against which sat shocking blueberry irises. She had a sun-kissed glow year-round that she attributed to her father's Mediterranean heritage. Her plump rounded lips, also a gift from her father, gave her a perpetually ready-to-kiss look. All the boys in the class fawned over her, though she never seemed to notice.

Dorthey set to preparing tea for two. Before sitting down, she primped at the mirror, brushing her fringe and smoothing her dress.

Polly never paid much heed to her appearance. Always more concerned with the development of her character and her intellect, she never seemed to meet her mother's expectations of physical beauty. "Dorthey is always so thoughtfully put together," her mother would say to her every time Dorthey came over. "You could learn a few things from her, Polly, like better posture and how to tame that hair of yours." If her best friend was not such a generous, kind soul, Polly would dislike her just to spite her mother. Instead, she adored her dearest friend.

Polly moved over to the table. She took a sip of the warm tea sweetened with honey. She held the delicate cup by its handle, with her small finger pointing outward, mimicking Dorthey's elegance.

"I want to marry right at the end of high school. Have three children in series while I'm still young and have the energy to keep up with them. Plus, the younger you are, the better your body is able to handle the pregnancy and bounce back to normal size." Dorthey was absolute, which Polly always admired. She never seemed to worry about things like Polly did.

"I don't know when or if I'll ever get married," Polly lamented.

"Don't you want to be married?"

"I do." Polly lost herself in a river of moving thoughts.

"But . . .?" Dorthey coaxed, very familiar with the intense deep-in-thought stare of her friend.

"I do, but I am not sure if anybody will want to marry me. Boys don't seem to pay much attention to me—I think they're scared of me. And my mother always says I am stubborn and difficult." She looked at her big hands. A working man's hands, somebody had once commented. She was acutely aware of how her thighs spread to twice their standing diameter when she sat, the outsides pressed against the sides of the chair, leaving indents in her flesh.

Dorthey's laugh eased the sadness in her heart. "Polly, you aren't scary to anybody." She set her tea cup down and stood behind her friend, giving her a squeeze of the shoulders and kiss on the side of her head. "Don't trouble yourself with these boys, Polly. They know you're too smart for them so they stay away."

"I still wish they would notice me." Her sullen heart sank a few inches deeper. "Can I not be smart and loved?"

"Oh, Polly, someday we'll both be married to wealthy men and we'll travel the world together in luxury with our children. I'll have homes in Paris and London! You'll have found love with an incredibly smart man who adores you and supports you in all of your wonderful successes. You will each win a Nobel prize, and your brilliant children will go on to discover cures for diseases and ways to save the retched simpletons like me!"

Dorthey glided through her room, arms splayed out like a dancing bird. She grabbed a crocheted blanket that was draped over her dressing table. She placed it over her head like a veil and marched down the side of the room.

"And we'll be each other's bridesmaids! We shall live close to each other, and our children will grow up like brothers and sisters. It will be perfectly splendid!"

Polly stood from the table and glided somewhat clumsily toward her friend. Even when she tried, she could not emulate Dorthey's grace.

"You promise?" she asked. She knew Dorthey was magic. Whatever Dorthey set her mind to, she usually got.

"Promise." They intertwined their pinky fingers, sealing the deal.

A gentle knock on the door broke their giggles. Dorthey's mom poked her head in the room. "Sorry to disturb you, but it is getting late and Polly should probably start to head home." Her voice was quiet. Like Dorthey, Mrs. Papineau was delicate. Unlike Dorthey with her toast-colored complexion, her mother's skin looked like it never saw the sun, not a freckle nor a blemish marred her face. There was something about the way she moved, barely taking up any space, a translucent frame that made her almost invisible.

Polly quickly began to gather the plates and cups to carry to the kitchen. With all the time she spent at Dorthey's house it felt like a second home to her. Careful never to overstay her welcome or become a nuisance, she always made sure she left things as they were before she came. She was never too loud and helped where she could. "Thank you for having me, Mrs. Papineau."

"Always a pleasure, Polly. It is awfully dark out, dear. Would you like Mr. Papineau to drive you home?"

"No, thank you. I'll be fine."

She rinsed the dishes before placing them in the sink. "Leave those," Dorthey insisted, as Polly stacked the remaining dishes. "I won't have my dearest friend soak her hands in lye, cleaning up. You have more important things to do in this world." Dorthey walked her toward the door.

As Polly bundled up her scarf and secured the buttons of her heavy coat, Dorthey gave her some last words of encouragement. "You don't need a handful of suitors, Polly, just one true love. He'll find you when the time is right." Dorthey tied the ear straps under Polly's chin in a perfect bow to secure her winter cap in place.

Waving goodbye to her friend, Polly stepped into the empty street, illuminated only by the light from the moon. The flurry of snow danced about her like a wild tango. Wind penetrated through her coat, making her bones chatter and every sinew and ligament tighten to stabilize them.

With her head bowed against the torrent of nature's anger, Polly trudged forward. Her lonely footprints erased quickly behind her, filled in by newly laid snow. Calculations ran through her mind: her current weight against the depth of the snow. Factoring in gravity and tensile force with the approximate rate of snowfall and the area of her footprint, it would take approximately fifty-three seconds for each footprint to be refilled, and a mere twenty minutes to fully erase any indication that she had been there.

Polly searched her pockets and found a dried raisin from yesterday's snack, a beautiful pebble she retrieved from the pond with gold flecks, and a hair pin that had fallen out while she was excavating the rest of the root vegetables from the garden before the early winter storm. She selected the hair pin and intentionally dropped it as proof she had been there.

Ribbons of smoke curled from the chimneys as she passed by. Oliver's mother, she could smell, was baking bread. The rector's house only had a dim light on in the study—reading, as usual. She delighted in the idea of someday being old enough to not have chores and be able to spend her days however she liked, taking long walks and filling her mind with words and ideas.

A gentle whistle whipped by her ears as she made her way through the neighborhood. The cottages here were spaced closer together, creating paths for the wind to speak. A melody of indigo and red plum entered her mind. Melancholy violin sounds rose in her ears, slow and yearning. A welcome feeling of awakening, like a stiff body and heavy head following a long restful sleep. The long stretch of arms and legs bringing the tingle of life back into each limb was reflected by the added flutes and other wind instruments. She imagined rolling over and into the embrace of a lover, a quiet dialogue summoned by the addition of trumpets and trombones, tickles and giggles of a harp overlaid to set a frolicky mood.

The colors jumped through her mind, turning to navy blue, teal, and finally fuchsias and blood reds, as the piano solo dominated her mind with the underlying Latin passion of the snow tango. She felt the crescendo rise from her toes and wash over her.

"Polly!" Petar's voice interrupted her thoughts. Quickly, she closed her eyes, trying to stamp the music into her memory. "Mama was worried—she sent me to fetch you. Are you all right?"

She stood like a statue, staring into the world, disconnected from reality.

"Music?" Petar asked knowingly. He danced up and down in front of her trying to stay warm, his patience waning quickly. "Come on, Polly. It's cold!"

He snatched her hands, pulling her out of the moment. They walked in silence until he was sure she was reconnected to the world again. "How's Dorthey these days?" he asked.

"Her usual, funny, dreamy self." Polly smiled.

"Is she scared of the war?" he asked. This was a topic they often discussed. Petar had graduated high school now. Tuition was reduced due to Papa's being on faculty, so he'd tried a year at university, but he struggled greatly. The impact on his self-esteem was noticeable.

"We didn't really talk about it. Dorthey likes to think about other things, like getting married and having children."

Petar slowed his pace. His big hands dug deeper into his pockets, while his head hung low. With the trepidation of a child, he asked, "Do you think Dorthey would ever consider marrying a simple fella like me?"

She rested her head on his shoulder. The density of the homes now offered them a barrier against the racing winds. The natural heat from their previous fast pace kept them warm with an internal furnace.

"Petar, you may not have a university degree but you have something even better. You're resourceful, hard-working, and kind. She would be so lucky to have you." Polly selected her words carefully, never wanting to be untruthful.

"You really think that, Polly?" She sensed the slight straightening of his shoulders. "Do you think maybe you could invite her over a bit more, instead of going there all the time?"

The innocent ask was a huge sacrifice for Polly. It meant subjecting herself to the constant scrutiny of her mother, and the loss of the fine delicacies that Dorthey's family could afford.

"Of course." She offered her brother a small peck on the cheek. She could do it for her big brother who always looked out for her, defended her when others called her strange, and covered for her when she was wanted by Mama, so she could secretly try to finish a book or a music score.

Racing into the house, she stomped off the snow from her boots and hastily hung up her coat, hat, and mittens. Before putting on her knitted slippers, she stepped into a puddle of cold slush. With frustration, she pulled off her socks and headed barefoot up the stairs leaving wet footprints behind.

"*Minushka*, what are you doing?" her mother called after her. "Look at the mess you are making. Come back and tidy this up."

"In a minute, Mama. I need to do something first," Polly called back as she hurried down the hall and into her room.

"Dinner is in thirty minutes!" She heard the disapproving voice of her mother trail behind her.

Against the dim light of her table lamp, Paulina wrote musical staffs and treble clefs. The sounds in her head were pouring out of her faster than she could keep up. After the first page, she no longer bothered to draw the lines but simply kept track of the notes by their spacing alone.

Ink smeared under the edge of her hand. The half notes at threat of looking like quarter notes, she forced herself to slow down. Each page filled emptied her mind and her soul slightly, allowing her to breathe easier. Engrossed in her work, she drowned out the rest of the world, lost to the sounds and colors in her room.

A light tap on the door drew her out of her trance. "Paulina, you've missed dinner and it is well past bedtime." Her father's voice was intentionally gentle to avoid disrupting her work.

"I'm not hungry, Papa," she replied.

He quietly stepped into her room, taking one long stride to reach her work station. Standing over her in silence for a few moments, he just as quickly and quietly left without a word. A gentle stroke of the back of her head let her know he understood.

Swiftly, she poured every note onto the pages, dripping ink from her fountain pen along the way. Though Dorthey had given her as a birthday gift a new type of pen—a ballpoint—she found it did not sit as nicely in her grasp. It slowed down her work, even though it may have been tidier.

Well into the next morning, Polly finally finished. Feeling both exhilaration and hunger, she took her pages downstairs with her, still percolating the dialogue between violin and piano in her mind.

In the kitchen her dinner remained on a covered plate. Cold chicken and broccoli never tasted so good.

Over the coming weeks, Polly would play and rework the composition several times. The final clean pages were now complete. With careful precision, she inscribed the title at the top of the page: *A Winter's Tango, Concerto in D Major*, by P. Andrezej.

"Who is that?" asked Dorthey. She had loyally listened to the various structural changes Polly had made over the last week, graciously sharing her opinion whenever asked. "They all sound so beautiful, Polly! I'm sure that whichever one you pick will be perfect," was her usual reply, as she and Petar amused themselves with card games, waiting for Polly to finish.

"P. Andrezej is me. *P* for Paulina, and Andrezej is my mother's maiden name. It is likely the adjudicators will take the submission more seriously with a name like that than something composed by Paulina Williams, don't you think?" She felt a sense of betrayal to her own self but knew a woman would never be taken seriously in the competition.

Dorthey shrugged. "Are we ready to take it to the post office? Petar, will you come?"

Paulina worried about the growing affection between them, hopeful that it was just fleeting during these confined winter months.

In her best cursive writing, she labeled the envelope to the *Concours International d'Exécution Musicale*, the newly founded Geneva International Music Competition.

"Every opportunity not taken is a loss. You only win if you try," was the encouragement she'd received from Professor Randall. She affixed the stamp, and gathered her friend for the walk, grudgingly accepting Petar's company as well.

CHAPTER 3

1940

By age fifteen, Polly had already broken two thresholds: being the youngest person to register for a second-year program at Queen's University, and the only woman to be permitted into the mathematics and physics program. Though the university prided itself on allowing admission to women since 1869, it was to programs "best suited to the delicate grace and beauty of a woman." Literary classics, religious philosophy and natural sciences were deemed to be benign enough to preserve the gentleness of women. Nursing was open to them, as it aligned with their natural maternal instincts. The Faculty of Medicine, though it initially accepted women in the late 1880s, was later closed to them due to protests from the male students and faculty. This was based on claims that it called upon one to deal with grotesque human ills; hence, women would be unable to maintain the composure and objective deductive reasoning required of the profession.

None of this mattered to Polly. She did not set out to plow any new ground. She simply wanted a home for the restless ideas in her mind. She dreamed of numbers. At night, before falling asleep, she solved formulas in her mind over and over: some simple and already solved, others yet unknown to the world, and many mathematically incorrect and insolvable. Those frustrated her the most because she knew, even in her dreams, that they were wrong.

Only by filling her days with the intellectual challenges in class did her mind quiet enough at night to allow her to rest.

"I am very proud of you, *minushka*." Mama had cautiously softened to the idea of further education. "When you were born you did not cry like other babies. You simply took in the world around you with fierce interest." Her mother looked intently at Paulina, scanning her face as if trying to predict what future lay ahead for her. "Be careful, *minushka*. The world can be very hard."

Father agreed on the grounds that she went to the university for lectures and study only, and did not associate with any of the boys, except Oliver, who was tasked as her chaperone since they shared many classes.

Professor Proust stood behind the walnut lectern at the base of the hall, before the cascading rows of fully occupied seats. His tenor voice ricocheted through the space, flooding the students' ears like that of a preacher, despite the poor acoustics. The white lab coat he wore, a misleading label of authority, suggested that he was something more than a regurgitator of other people's ideas.

"And so, the reality of particle B can be conclusively determined by the objective measure of momentum and position of particle A, without having to observe particle B at all."

Over his glasses, poised on the tip of his nose, he looked out upon his audience. Half were asleep, the other half were perplexed. "Any questions?" The challenging note in his voice divulged his frustration and apathy about his work.

Polly raised her hand immediately. Sitting tall, she reached skyward. Straight-backed and oozing enthusiasm, she bent forward over her small lap desk. Surely the new trajectory of her grasping hand would not go ignored, she thought.

Proust scanned the room from left to center, up and down, avoiding the front right section in which Polly regularly sat. She began to wiggle her hand impatiently, slightly rising from her seated position. Oliver nudged her left side. "He won't call on you, you know that." His voice was sympathetic. Polly scowled with determination.

"Excuse me, Professor Proust." Her voice carried through the quiet room. Slight groans rumbled from behind her.

The professor removed his glasses and rubbed his eyes. His fingers squeezed the bridge of his nose. "Yes, Ms. Williams, I see your hand."

"Sir, how can we determine an objective reality when our calculations are built on assumptions that the human mind has determined to be true, and whose truth is limited by the flawed nature of human observation, which in its nature is subjective, *and,* in being subjective, is restricted by the current thinking and mathematical calculations understood, but has not allowed for the plausibility of human error caused by inlaid assumptions?"

The professor wiped his glasses with his handkerchief, the initials *D.P.* careful stitched in cursive with gold thread visible in the corner. He wore no wedding ring but was known to be married. His young wife was rumored to be barren and, growingly distressed over the last three years, was said to fill her days sewing beautiful children's clothes that she stored in her hope chest for a future that she willed to come.

"Ah, Ms. Williams. This is a quantum physics class. Perhaps you had better find your way across campus to the philosophy department where they spend their time on frivolous discussion for the sole purpose of hearing themselves speak."

A roar lifted through the room. Polly looked around sternly. She stood, and with a loud bellow of her voice, she retorted, "I only raise that the limitations of human ego may be our undoing in further scientific discovery if we refuse to address the possibility of our own fallibility."

"Class dismissed!"

Nobody heard her. Oliver gave a gentle tug to her sleeve. "Hey, it's okay. Don't let these hooligans bother you." His supportive tone softened her anger, as usual. She didn't know what she would do without Oliver at her side.

She rammed her books carelessly into her tote bag. "It isn't fair!" she muttered, her heart still frazzled with a sense of injustice.

The boy on her other side leaned in, whispering in her ear, "Life isn't fair. If you can't handle it, then go join the other women in home economics or go write some fairy stories. Leave this seat for a man who can make a difference."

The hiss in her ear burned and spread across her face. An electric pulse pounded through her body. She clenched her teeth in order to restrain herself from punching the boy square in the jaw. She stared at him with a fury seething from her that she hoped would make him cower.

Instead, he grinned, content with the reaction he drew. "Go ahead and cry, Paulina. It is what girls do, isn't it?"

"Leave her alone, Fred." Oliver leaned forward between them, his tone and his posture suggesting that he would pay back Polly's debt on the rugby field soon enough.

She placed the last book into her tote and curled her hand into a fist. Her face must have shown her next intention, as the boy's demeanor changed from mockery to worry as he looked at them both. "You ain't worth it, neither of you," he spat.

"Ms. Williams, please see me after class." Professor Proust's voice cut the tension and she uncurled her hand.

"We'll see who makes a difference in this world, you peon." Embarrassed by her childishness, she turned to escape the row of chairs the other way, bumping right into Oliver. "Excuse me!" Annoyed, she stamped past him to the front of the room, pinched with regret at her misplaced anger.

The professor's look was questioning. He glanced over at Fred, who stood smugly at his place. The professor gave him a nod of dismissal, a message of disapproval exchanged between them. The boy hung his head low for a moment, recollecting his thoughts before he defiantly stood tall again, jutted out his chin, and uttered, "Women are nothing but trouble," before storming out.

"You may go," the professor dismissed Oliver, who was waiting for Polly at the door. She nodded reassuringly that he could leave.

Polly looked back at the professor, slightly defeated. "Professor Proust, I did not intend to be disruptive. I only wished to convey—"

He interrupted her with a raise of his hand. "Your reflections were not uninteresting, Ms. Williams. From whom did you take them?"

"Nobody, sir. They are my original thoughts." She felt compelled to add, "I swear."

He studied her closely. Silence sat between them as she challenged his stare with her own scrutiny of his eyes.

"Original only in so much as the question of human imperfection is a new thought, and not one that has existed since we developed a sense of self-awareness." He was content. His words delivered the impact intended. Polly's slouched shoulders and downcast eyes let him know he had won.

"Why are you here, taking this class, Ms. Williams?"

His tone was intended to provoke her, she knew. It ignited the rage of survival in her that had long existed and been continually drawn upon in a world steered by men. Women were required to justify their existence anywhere beyond a place in the home. She raised her head. Her intense gaze startled him a little. "I am here to learn, sir." She grounded her feet on the floor, stabilizing her spirit.

"Perhaps, Ms. Williams. But what has allowed you to be here?" His voiced demanded an answer to a multiple-choice question for which the options had not been revealed.

"Because I am smart and curious, sir." She searched his face, unsure of what game he was playing.

"Who allowed you to be here?" His question made her feel small. She withdrew into her mind, searching for the right answer so she could escape this humiliating questioning.

"The dean gave permission." She qualified her answer by adding, "When he saw my test scores."

"And who arranged for those tests?"

"My father," she replied hesitantly, unclear of the intention of the conversation.

"Ah, and there we have it!" He laughed rather ungraciously. He leaned toward her. His breath smelled of coffee and cigarettes, making her want to recoil. She stood her place, bracing herself to receive whatever came next. "Humility, Ms. Williams. You would benefit from a dose of it. Don't ever assume that your being here has anything to do with your intelligence over others. Rather, if not for your father's friendship with the dean," he spewed with particular pleasure, "and the dean's fondness for your fetching mother, you would not be here."

Tears threatened to fill her eyes. Her mouth went dry. Her tongue stuck to the top of her palate as she garnered the courage to speak again. "Believe what you wish, sir, but I know the reality of my abilities and that I deserve a seat in these classes. And, as your lesson taught us today, I can know that to be true without you having to observe it directly." She knew she was being spiteful in her cleverness, which dimmed any satisfaction she may have earned.

She gave a slight nod of her head and wished the professor a good day. Head held high, shoulders back and taking confident long strides, she marched out of the lecture hall. She allowed the heavy door to naturally slam of its own accord, closing the discussion with definitiveness. She walked down the hall, brushing past Oliver.

"Polly!" he called after her.

"I'm fine, Oliver. Leave me alone." Not until she was around the corner did she allow herself to breathe. Oliver didn't follow her, and for this she was grateful. He knew her better than anyone other than Dorthey. She leaned against the cold cinder wall, no longer able to retain her tears. She forwent any guard against embarrassment should anybody happen to walk by, and let the tears fall.

Once she felt purged of emotion, she rubbed her face roughly with her hands. "Piss off," she muttered to nobody in particular, as she wiped away the last tear and picked up her bookbag with new resolve.

Paulina worked with exceptional focus that semester. In each class she sat in the front quarter of seats and continued to raise her hand whenever she had questions or answers, regardless of the fact that she was rarely called upon.

When they raised their voices in mockery of her— "Oh pick me, pick me, Professor! I know, I know!"—she did not relent to the intimidation. Beside her in every class was Oliver, steadfast in support. She valued his friendship and admired his own strength against the taunts and prods of his peers, when they insinuated that he was a pushover and in love.

Oliver stood several inches shorter than her now. His sandy hair was cut very short to help control the dense mane that flopped in his face otherwise. He still had a rounded baby face that highlighted his weaker chin, over which he grew a beard to compensate. He and Petar remained good friends but saw less of each other these days. Petar never took well to school and opted to go work in the quarry, to their parents' disappointment, whereas Oliver remained on an academic stream with aspirations of becoming an engineer.

It was very intentional that she and Oliver had many classes together. When she could select the same course slot as him, she did. Having an ally nearby gave her some much-needed courage. Particularly on those hard days when her detractors would leave brown paper bags on her seat containing female hygiene supplies. Or when she would arrive at her lab to find her station had been stripped of all its beakers and Bunsen burners, requiring her to begin the session by washing used ones at the sink accompanied by the chortle of, "At least she knows where her place is, washing dishes!"

Oliver gave her continual words of encouragement. "Don't let them get you down. You're smart, Polly. You deserve this just as much as any of us." In those moments she felt an intimate kinship between them. She could not imagine her life without him. Her mind would wander sometimes to that moment, racing to the tree, and what it would be like to properly kiss him. But Oliver was Petar's friend, and a kiss could ruin everything. Plus, she had to stay focused on her schooling. There was no room to be anything less than consistently exceptional if she was going to survive.

In addition to her attending university, her mother still expected her to maintain all her usual daughterly duties. This included helping around the house, and Mama did not relieve her of any of her necessary and unnecessary chores to allow fruitful time for study. She persisted with her daily two-hour violin practices and twice weekly lessons with Professor Randall. When she grew tired of studying and needed a break from her household responsibilities, she would escape at her piano. No longer playing just the music of others, she was composing her own pieces. She would give way to the etude of colors extracted from the notes. The formal structure and pattern of sonatas made them her favorite. Contrasting themes told and retold in different ways bridged together with familiar chains of notes until ending in a recapitulation. The music brought home to an elegant and satisfying end, like an answer to an equation.

On this particular evening, she completed her chemistry assignment early and was relishing in the free time garnered by Professor Randall's out-of-town performance with a symphony. Sitting at her piano, she trilled the upper octaves quietly, representing pensive and demure, obedient and delicate characteristics. The bridge offered an uncomfortable combination of flats, enough to set a tone of building conflict. She then dropped her hands to octave C3, playing a Spanish-style tune: bullish, strong, defiant.

Interrupted by her father, she startled. "Polly, that is a powerful piece. Did you write that?"

Registering where she was in space and time again, she nodded with pride.

"Beautiful! Have you shared it with Professor Randall yet?"

"No. I don't think it's good enough. Not quite done. Plus, he wants so desperately for me to progress on the violin so I can apply to the symphony next year. I dare not distract myself from that work."

"Oh, my Polly. Always worried about other people." He smoothed her long coarse hair, which she no longer wore in braids. At home, she left her hair loose to drape across her shoulders. It was a relief from the weight it had when in the proper bun she wore to school.

He picked up the book he had left in the room, and went back from whence he came, pipe in mouth, humming the tune of her music.

"*Minushka*, please come set the table for dinner," her mother called from the kitchen doorway.

"Can I finish this next section? It's almost ready. I just need to play it through one more time to—"

"I left you all evening to do your studies while I cooked away in the kitchen. The least you can do is help to set the table now!" A look of fatigue washed over her mother's face, as the frustration emptied from her voice. "You can return to the piano after dinner, darling. I shall enjoy hearing you play then."

The table was set for four as usual, though everybody was skeptical as to whether Petar would show up. He had taken to working overtime at the quarry to save enough money to buy his own house. He and Dorthey had officially been dating for a year now, and they were keen to get married.

A pot of *bigos*—Polish stew—sat in the center of the table. One of her favorites. As a little girl, she often worried that the smell of sauerkraut and herring would seep into her clothes and hair, and she would smell funny at school. To avoid the risk of being teased, she would sprinkle rosewater on her hair and neck each day. When her mom began to notice the rapid rate of decline of her special bottle, Paulina took to making her own. Soaking flowers in water did not garner the same effect. It was Dorthey who kindly let her know that the smell of decomposing flora was not appealing, and that the cozy smells of her home were much better.

"How was your day?" Her mother began with the usual question, as she served her husband a bowl of the stew.

"Quite good. The boys are really coming along this semester. The dean has asked if I would consider taking on an extra-curricular club as faculty supervisor of the *Queen's Journal*."

"The student newspaper?" Her mother would not be the only one perplexed by the offer.

Polly understood. Her father was a literary fellow in that he enjoyed reading a diversity of genres, but he was neither a journalist nor a politician. Both criteria of which would have satisfied the suitability of a faculty candidate to this position. What Andrew Williams had on his résumé that others did not was being the father of a daughter who, along with a small number of other women, attended the university and was the target of misogynistic commentary.

Though the dean and several of the department heads had publicly reprimanded such cowardly and ungentlemanly remarks, they were unable to identify the source of the submissions. The Board of Trustees and Senate dissuaded any further rousing of controversy, explaining it away as "boys will be boys."

Thick with guilt, Polly swallowed her boiled potato, feeling it stick in her chest. "Will you take it, Papa?"

He nodded with false joviality, tapping the tip of her nose with his index finger. "You bet I shall, Polly. It's time we started talking about some interesting ideas among the student body. Plus, this will be a new challenge for me."

Petar entered through the kitchen door, freshly washed after a long day at work. Even his fingernails were scrubbed clean and his hair, still wet, slicked back to satisfy Mama. He grazed the side of their mother's cheek with a quick kiss, thumped a large hand on his father's shoulder, and playfully nudged Polly as he sat down in his chair. The mood in the room lifted, particularly with Mama, who proceeded to spoon a double ladleful of stew to her son.

"What interesting things?" Petar asked while leaning close to his bowl to reduce the amount of time the food traveled from the bowl to his stomach.

"I was thinking, the popular news, jokes and editorials are fine enough, but there should be a return to the true *raison d'être* for the paper. Something to curate the literary tastes of the students, including publishing stories, poems and art created by the students themselves. Their reflections on the war. It is something that has and will change the human spirit forever."

"Sounds boring." Petar had finished his full bowl by this time and was being served again by Mama.

"What about a section for scientific debate?" Polly offered with enthusiasm. "It could have highlights from the current conversations from Bohr and Einstein. Perhaps highlight a new theory every issue. Even bring in differing points of view on science and religion!"

"That's a fine idea, Polly. I think we can make room for something like that. Would you like to be a contributor to that section?"

She jumped up, hugging her father around the neck and kissing the top of his balding head.

"Oh, Andrew, why bring in more trouble? *Minushka* is already looked at unwelcomingly by the community. People at church consider her an unusual child, her attention always given to books and lacking the common sense to stay out of adult conversations." Her mother drew her napkin to her nose to stifle a sniffle. Furrowed lines vertically drew between her brows in concern.

Polly's heart broke open with pity. She knew the burden that her mother carried from supporting her ambitions. Whispers followed her that they "should not encourage such contrary behavior in a young girl." Why could she not be like most girls? Why could she not be the traditional daughter her parents wished for? Petar was to go to university, and she was the one that should be thinking of marrying a fine man at this age. The guilt lasted but a moment. The softness in the room broke with the tossing of a napkin on a plate and the subsequent clatter of a knife to the ground.

"I shall not have it!" Her mother's voice was demanding, non-negotiable. "This has been going on too long. It was well enough when at thirteen, fourteen, we allowed you to dabble with your time in study." Her mother looked intensely at her, grabbing Polly's hands in her own. "*Minushka*, don't misunderstand. I am very proud of you and know you are very smart. But you must find a way to quiet your restless mind. You must start to think about your future, find a good husband. You mustn't intimidate them, my darling." She stroked her daughter's cheek gently.

"Mama, I must continue at school. I don't need to marry. I shall be able to support myself someday." She pleaded with her mother to see the world with different possibilities.

"Ta-ta. You are foolish, *minushka*. There is no career in academia or science for a woman. To survive, you must marry. To have children, you must marry. You alone cannot change the rhythm of the world." The imploring sadness in her mother's eyes, crested with tears not yet fallen, was too much to bear.

"Mama. Don't make me stop. I cannot just stay at home and be a simple housewife, wasting my time cooking and cleaning for a man and a family all day. I must be my own person!" Mortification at the disgrace she laid before her mother spread through her body before the final words were out. She had been unable to stop them, like a reckless driver drunk on self-pity.

Great restraint was evident in her mother's posture. She could not hide the combination of pain, sorrow and anger that twisted her face into an unrecognizable person. "Go to your room," was all she said.

"Mama, I'm sorry!"

Her mother stepped away from the table and walked toward the kitchen door.

"Kasia, she didn't mean it. Please. This is a difficult time for all of us. Please sit and we can talk this through." Papa's expression was heavy with regret. "Once she is done university, life will return to usual."

Her mother didn't halt for a moment. She strode through the kitchen, out the front door and did not return for several hours.

Paulina cleaned the kitchen and waited at the table.

"Don't worry, Polly, she'll get over it." Petar attempted to relieve her of some of her guilt. "Dorthey and I are going to see a film. Would you like to come?"

"No, thanks." Polly sank deeper into her sorrow as her brother shrugged and left.

Nothing would make her more unhappy then seeing Petar and Dorthey together. She already felt she'd lost her best friend to her brother. They barely saw each other anymore without him around. But also, it made her think that perhaps Mama was right. She was being foolish with her choices. In the end she would end up with a good education but no job, no husband, no family, alone and lonely with only the ideas in her mind to occupy herself. She dropped her head and sobbed, wishing she was like other girls. Why could she not be satisfied with a home and family?

She fell asleep at the kitchen table. Her face sticky with tears, her mouth parched. Awakened by a soft hug, she stirred.

"Oh, Mama," she called upon seeing her mother's face nestled in beside hers. The reverberation of those few words spoken and the echo of all that went unsaid between them hung in the air.

"Go to bed, Paulina. Tomorrow is another day." An exchange of a deep hug, and a gently placed kiss on her head were not enough to take away the pain of not being called *minushka*.

CHAPTER 4

1941

The *Journal*'s newsroom pulsed with the naïve optimism of youth. Under her father's tutelage, the paper had grown in both readership and frequency of publication. Promoting Henry to editor-in-chief was a risk. The brash, dark-haired boy with ebony eyes stormed through the room with his notorious red pencil locked into place behind his ear. It was always at the ready to scrawl a disparaging comment or draw a substantial line through a young journalist's submission.

"I swear he sleeps with that thing nestled against his pillow." Sadie laughed. "He probably kisses it at night, with platitudes of a day's work well done."

Sadie was the only other girl working on the university paper, relegated to writing the society pages and tracking the volunteer war efforts by the women's auxiliary that the professors' wives enjoyed. She never ceased to insert her own little bit of fun into each edition. "Bandage roll for Red Cross, scheduled at John Deutsch University Centre, Memorial Room, at 6 p.m. Sausage party with faculty to follow."

"Sadie!" Even after a year of spending time together at the paper, her comments still embarrassed Polly. "You can't actually print that."

"Oh, Polly, stop being such a prude. A sausage party and a barbecue are synonyms after all."

Their banter brought a stern look from Henry. "Time is ticking, folks. Let's go. Deadline is two hours."

"Watch. He's going to come over this way." Sadie rolled back her shoulders, accentuating her voluptuous curves. Henry's infatuation with Sadie was his most poorly kept secret. Her ruse of flirtation earned Sadie an appreciative audience from everybody but Polly, whose own feelings for Henry remained hidden.

"Hello, Sadie. What are you working on?" His eyes focused on her upper button that was straining against her inflated chest.

"Oh, you know, just the usual. Recruiting for the bake sale and fundraiser to support our men overseas." She cleared her throat, which stirred a little jiggle of her chest. "Henry?" She knew he was still fixated on her bosom. "34D?" she said.

"Pardon?" Henry's embarrassment read better than the front-page story. He looked back and forth between the women, his eyes finally landing on the page Polly held in her hand. "Pardon?" he repeated, pulling the sheet from Polly and whisking his red pencil from behind his ear.

"Section D, page 3 or 4?" Sadie sardonically stated.

"Yes, whichever you like." He busied himself with looking over Polly's report. "What is this?"

"I came across a very interesting German paper by Grete Herman, in which she offers a counterview to John von Neumann's 'no hidden variables' theory, essentially discrediting it." Polly's excitement was unmistakable, as was her undisguisable shock as Henry drew a large red line through the whole text. "But . . ." She started to follow after him.

"Paulina." He turned to look at her squarely in the eye. The pronunciation of her full name by him was like poetry to her. She halted, every part of her on alert for his next words. "Find something else." The paper shoved back into her reluctant hands, he marched back through the aisle.

"But this is exciting. Not too many people will be familiar with her paper as it hasn't been translated yet."

"How did you read it? Do you read German?" He did not wait for a response. "Come with me." He grabbed her hand, guiding her stealthily through the rows of tables eclipsed in clouds of cigarette smoke. "Here, sit. Can you read this?"

The intrigue of the moment was exhilarating. To Polly, the rest of the world blurred away. Only Henry existed. His cool scent from the peppermint gum he incessantly chewed lingered in the air. The dark wooly curls of hair on his arms called for her caress. She forced herself to focus, aware of his impatience. He placed before her what appeared to be an official German document handwritten on scrap paper. It touted the importance of restoration to order and elimination of the lurking threat of enemy power. It promised absolution of the populace to bringing balance back to the world by congregating all enemies of the state to work camps.

"You're brilliant!" Henry was aglow with enthusiasm. "Can you transcribe this for me? My cousin sends me these from Italy. Until now neither he nor I were sure of what they said. Before he delivers them to his boss, he always makes a copy for me." He spun around with excitement.

Not one to miss an event, Sadie joined their private party. "What? What is it?" Her eagerness to know and be included was vaguely hidden behind a mask of aloofness.

"Polly just translated this German propaganda letter for me. Amazing, isn't it?"

The significance of the event was obviously lost on Sadie, though the kiss Henry planted on her lips in the impulse of the moment was not. "Sorry. So sorry," he mumbled and quickly walked away. She giggled, amused with herself.

Polly tried her best to interpret the poor penmanship, hurried by the author's clandestine activity. The German her mother taught her as a girl lapped back in natural waves of ease.

"Oh, come on!" Sadie pulled the paper away impatiently, stuffing it into Henry's arms as she guided Polly out into the fresh spring air. Outside, they both lit cigarettes dipped in cinnamon or peppermint oil at the butt, as designed by Sadie to improve the tolerance of the flavor. She had learned that a cigarette and a cup of coffee were a good substitute for lunch and helped to keep Polly's naturally rounder hips and thighs slimmer.

Sadie was three years older and studying nursing. Her father was a dressmaker. Since her brother died at a young age from a septic wound after falling from a tree during an innocuous game of war, her mother remained in a quiet depression. Encouraged by the eventual need to support the family, her parents sent her from the nearby town of Belleville to Queen's University for school. Sadie once declared that her only educational goal was to marry somebody rich.

"Why don't you wank him?" Sadie asked casually.

"Wank who?" Polly sputtered, choking slightly on her cigarette. The word uncomfortable in her ears.

"Henry. I know you want him." Sadie took a long drag on her cigarette. Her eyes squinted against the sunlight gave her a malicious expression. "He's always here by himself late at night. Just come one evening in your sexiest dress. Nix that. I'll lend you something." Sadie smiled at the group of boys who walked by, noticing only her in the pair. She ignored them. This act made her even more appealing to them. The fellows could not look away.

"How do you do that?" Polly's mouth was agape.

"Do what?" Sadie was well aware of her sexual allure, and harnessed it well to get what she wanted. Polly hovered between awestruck with a slight tinge of envy and shocking embarrassment when it came to Sadie.

"I read about it. I practice." Her words played off her tongue salaciously.

Polly conceded, "Practice? With whom?"

Sadie leaned in against her friend's shoulder, the moxie drained from her. "Professor Randall. He and I have been in a relationship."

Astonished, Polly was flummoxed that Professor Randall, her austere music teacher with his long full beard, musty-smelling tweed jacket and queer musical tastes, would behave so scandalously.

"I have been wanting to tell you, but I promised I would keep it a secret. He would lose tenure and not be able to find work elsewhere if anybody found out." She blushed. "Oh, Polly. He makes me feel like a woman! His fingers play with me like a violin and send the most intoxicating vibrations through me."

Polly wondered if she would ever feel that way. She tried to imagine Henry, with his brusque manners and serious intensity, touching her in such a way that could muster up those sensations. An image of Oliver, his soft eyes drinking her in, fluttered into her mind. It had been a while since she had heard from him. His courses shifted more toward engineering, as hers narrowed increasingly in math. She missed him.

"But Sadie, he's your father's age!"

"You are such a prude." She stubbed out her cigarette on the bottom of her heel. "It is really all wonderful and I don't want you to ruin it for me." She linked arms with Polly and guided her back to the newsroom door. "You really should wank Henry and feel just how incredible it is."

"What about getting pregnant?" Polly was earnest. "I'm worried about you, Sadie. This doesn't seem right at all." It was these moments that Polly was grateful for Dorthey's wholesomeness. Dorthey and Petar rarely kissed when she was around, and never shared pieces of their romantic times together. Yet there remained a magnetic pull toward Sadie's confidence of which Polly could not get enough. Her two closest friends teeter-tottered Polly's expectations of romance.

"Oh, it feels very right. Very excitingly right!" She caressed Polly's right breast, and successfully elicited the embarrassed reaction she wanted. "Plus, I use a Dutch cap."

"A what?" Polly blushed. She pictured Sadie in a translucent night shirt printed with small lilac flowers. The shadow of her curvaceous body visibly naked underneath and a starched cotton white cap neatly tied under her chin. The provocative image stirred a desire in Polly. A yearning to be passionately loved and craved by somebody.

"Oh, dear Polly, I have so much to teach you." She kissed Polly on the cheek, and grabbed her hand, swinging it playfully between them, as they descended the steps.

The rest of the semester progressed with ease. Despite a full course load with accompanying labs, Polly kept busy with the newspaper and volunteering with the women's auxiliary to support the war efforts. Connecting with the other woman made her feel less alone. Today, the final edition of the *Queen's Journal* for this academic year would be released, with the first ever article published concurrently in the student paper and the *Kingston Whig Standard*. She waited, in great anticipation, for Petar and Oliver to return from the university with her copies.

Spring was warmer than usual, bringing an early bloom to the yellow, red, and pink tulip patches around the town. She lay on a navy-and-black plaid picnic blanket to protect her skirt and blouse from grass stains and stared up at the misleadingly calm blue sky. The subtle pulsing headache behind her left eye was indicative of an oncoming storm. Polly took a long pull on the tip of her cigarette, admiring the complimentary color of the glowing orange embers against the blue backdrop.

She knew smoking would shorten her lifespan. Though there was no science to prove it, she surmised from her observations that it likely wasn't good for her. Mr. Collins next door developed an incapacity to move the entire right side of his body and was now in a home for those with disabilities. Mr. Brown developed a terrible cough that echoed through the building corridors when he cleaned the school and struggled to climb the stairs despite his young age, while Johnny from the grocery store had part of his lung cut out due to a tumor. He grew so thin and pale that father had sent Petar to shovel his walk and cut his grass this year. They all smoked. Polly knew there must be a link. She enjoyed the quiet warmth between her fingers and the tingle in her chest. It was hard to give up, like a rude friend who you continued to spend time with because they make you laugh when you are feeling down.

"Polly," her mother called from the back door. "Polly? Professor Randall is here to see you."

She stubbed out her cigarette and hid the remains under a rock in the garden. She stood up from behind the garden bed so her mother could see her. "Coming, Mama!" she hollered.

Professor Randall had not been to the home in over a year, since it was determined that he had nothing further to teach Polly. Though she always held a deep affection for the man who fostered her enthusiasm for music composition and tempered her mother's worry about Polly's time spent on her music, since Sadie's revelation she felt conflicted about him.

She folded the blanket and placed it on one of the four wrought-iron chairs arranged around a table on the patio for later use. From her pocket she pulled a small tin of mints and a thin mister of lilac water, both of which she used before she entered through the back door into the kitchen.

"Paulina, dear, take this tray in with you," her mother directed, extending the silver tray upon which was a small vase with tulips, a plate of freshly baked oatmeal-currant cookies, and a pot of earl grey tea with four cups, sugar, and milk.

Reluctantly, she moved through the swinging door into the living room where Professor Randall sat on the couch. Her father sat in his usual armchair. Both men puffed on their pipes creating a swirl of aromatic smoke in which Polly hid.

"Ah, Polly, come sit." Her father gestured. He seemed smitten, ready to divulge a joyous secret.

Both men stood up to greet her. Her father took the tray from her, setting it on the table where it remained ignored.

"Well, say hello to Professor Randall," her father coaxed, obviously befuddled by his daughter's unwelcoming manner.

Polly answered with an obligatory hello, unable to meet his gaze directly.

"Paulina, I have some most exciting news to share with you. Earlier this year, I was on special instruction in Toronto . . ." the professor began.

"And when might that have been?" Polly knew Sadie had missed a week of school just after Christmas. An old aunt in Toronto apparently ill with consumption wished to see her while she was still alive. Sadie returned with a new scarf, purse and earrings, apparent gifts from her dying aunt.

"Ah, must have been sometime in January," the professor searched his memory.

"And did you enjoy your trip to Toronto very much, Professor?" she interrogated him.

"Paulina. You are acting rather peculiar. Please let Professor Randall continue. He has some very exciting news," her father interjected.

The professor proceeded cautiously. This time, Polly met his eyes unswervingly. A slight twitch gave way in his right eye, while her own headache was mounting further.

"Yes, I enjoy Toronto very much. I shared your concerto, A Winter's Tango in D Major, with the artistic director of the Toronto Symphony Orchestra. They would like to perform it as part of their fall repertoire and have invited you to the season opening!" He clapped his hands in rare jubilation.

"Isn't that thrilling, Polly! Imagine your work being played by a full orchestra!" Her father's enthusiasm elated her.

Polly rose slowly. Her quivering hand lifted to cover her mouth in amazement. "Oh my goodness, Professor Randall! I can't believe it! I simply can't believe it!"

Forgetting all decorum, she lunged toward him with open arms, embracing him with gratitude. He chuckled, all tension between them resolved for the moment.

"Oh, Papa! This is so exciting. I must tell Mama!" She placed a kiss on her father's cheek then bounded toward the swinging door, and stopped just in time before it clipped her shoulder.

"What is all the excitement?"

"Oh, Mama! My piece is being played in Toronto by the symphony there. And they are inviting us to attend the performance this fall! Isn't that just thrillingly splendid?"

A proud smile lit her mother's beautiful face. "*Minushka*, I am so happy for you!"

They embraced for a long time. Plans were quickly set that Mama and Professor Randall would be the two accompanying adults for whom the symphony would pay expenses. Plans for new dresses, lace and satin gloves, and repair of her shoes would need be undertaken for the trip.

Among all the raucous celebration, Petar's entry through the front door went unnoticed until he hollered, "What are you all up about?"

"Petar, leave those muddy shoes at the front door and hang up that wet coat," Mama muttered after accepting his kiss of hello upon her cheek. "You see how nicely Oliver takes care to not trudge a mess into my house?"

Petar shook his wet hair, spraying a mist of water over Mama, who couldn't help but laugh.

Oliver stepped into the living room behind Petar, his socks and pant hems darkened by the wetness. "It sure is starting to rain hard out there." A drip of water escaped his mass of damp hair, traveling along his temple and down his neck until it escaped, then disappeared on his shoulder.

"Great news! The Toronto Symphony will be playing Polly's musical piece at their season opening," Papa announced with pride. "Isn't that splendid?"

"That is thrilling news, and so well deserved." Oliver smiled then leaned in to offer her an awkward hug. "No surprise given how talented you are."

"Thank you," she said, and returned his hug with a simple pat on his arm. "Mama, I am sure I can borrow some elegant clothes from Sadie. You know Sadie, don't you, Professor Randall?" She watched for his reaction carefully.

"No, I am afraid not." Not a flinch at the mention of the name. There was no crack of the voice nor clearing of the throat Polly noted. "Well, I should be off. Congratulations again, Paulina! Well deserved, indeed."

As Papa saw Professor Randall to the front door and bid him goodbye, the others carried on. It was decided that as soon as the rain stopped, she would walk to Dorthey's house to share the news.

"And I must tell Sadie. She can tell me all about the things I should do in Toronto."

"Maybe you won't want to do that after you see this." Petar handed Polly the two newspapers he had tucked into his sweater to keep dry.

"The newspapers! I almost forgot."

Polly unrolled the *Queen's Journal,* reading the front-page title story. "The Women of Queen's Support the War," she enunciated clearly. The double excitement of the day, her concerto and now her article elicited an unusual confidence in her. Her eyes diverted to the byline in anticipation of seeing her authorship declared in print.

"By Sadie Johnstone," she read in shock. "But this was my story. I wrote it."

She quickly opened the *Kingston Whig* to the second page. "Queen's Women's Group Helping to Fight the War, by Sadie Johnstone."

The dismay deflated any excitement that had filled the day. "I don't understand. How could this happen? It was my story."

Her mother's arms were quickly around her. "Oh, *minushka*, perhaps it was just an error. Something you can get fixed."

"No, Mama, this is the final print of the year, and a one-time special contribution to the town paper. It won't get fixed."

"You were betrayed," Petar said theatrically. "I always knew that Sadie girl was no good."

"I'll check in at the paper tomorrow, see what happened. Don't worry, darling, it will be all right." Her father's words did nothing to settle her angst.

After a few more conciliatory comments, Polly stood up. "If you will all excuse me, I have some business to tend to." She marched to the door. Pulled on her goulashes and rain coat.

"Paulina, where are you going? It is pouring rain out. There is nothing you can do about this now. It can wait until tomorrow!" Her mother's voice transitioned from comforting to pleading to demanding.

Without another word, Polly stormed outside. The complex aromatic mixture of rain, grass, soil, and flowers set her thoughts alive. The pelting rain drops beating down on her only fed her anger. How could Sadie do this to her? She thought they were friends.

Angling herself away from the wind, her muscles flexed against the resistance. Fueled by anger and self-reproach for being so naïve, she trudged through the storm. Upon reaching the building, she found the front doors locked. Undeterred, she proceeded to check each door around the perimeter, pulling and jostling with determination. Finally, she found the side door near the janitorial closet to be unlocked. The smell of acrid sweat and ink pierced her nostrils and brought on a wave of nausea. A quick reminder that her headache was still present and throbbing more than ever.

"Polly? What are you doing here?" Only Henry was in the writing room.

"Where's Sadie?"

"I don't know. She's not here." Henry had a look of consternation. "Are you okay?" He gestured to a chair for her to sit.

Polly declined, preferring to stand with her arms crossed about her chest, a deep, unhappy scowl on her face. "How could you, Henry? How desperate are you to have her like you that you would reduce yourself to stealing my story to give to her?" Polly was furious. Even she was aware that she looked like a rabid dog with her nostrils wide and eyes narrowed, standing in a guarded posture ready for a fight.

"What are you talking about?" Henry truly looked perplexed.

"This!" She shoved the now drenched paper into his hands, which he grasped between his pincer and thumb. "My story on the front page with Sadie's name!"

"Polly, believe me when I say I had no idea. When she handed in the story it had her name on it. I took it for face value."

"Really, Henry? I find that rather inconceivable. You never questioned the authenticity of it? Sadie never reads anything but the gossip pages and society columns. Under what circumstances would you believe her to have interest in a philosophical debate about personal sacrifice for the greater good?"

Polly stomped in a circle, with her hands clenched into fists. A guttural grunt emanated from her diaphragm. Her anger had yet to dissipate, though she now directed it at the inanimate objects in the room, rather than at Henry—moving, shuffling, and banging anything that was around her.

"I am so sorry. I should have stopped to think. She was just so excited to have headline coverage, and I was taken by her . . . gratitude." His hands in his pockets. His feet scuffing on the ground. The idiocy of his decision evidently weighing on him.

She pulled out a chair and finally sat, her fuse fizzling. "We were both enamored and taken for fools."

Day after day, Polly returned to the newspaper room to help close the office for the summer. Sadie did not make an appearance. Polly stopped by her dormitory but never found her. The girls on her floor said she was already gone for the semester. A family emergency had taken her home. The well-crafted scenarios of their confrontation that she elaborately imagined never had a stage.

In the fall, Henry stood by his word and printed a correction on page ten. The *Kingston Whig* never returned her calls. She forbade her father to intervene on her behalf.

Henry gave her the science and debate events to cover that fall as a peace offering. Still, the hurtful betrayal by a friend was not easy to heal. Her mind often wandered to Sadie, wondering what had happened to her.

She welcomed the return of her challenging academic year. A mix of second- and third-year courses in exclusively math and science gave her no reprieve for fun. Her only solace was the approaching debut of her concerto.

Days prior to the big event, Dorthey repacked Polly's small blue suitcase, adding colorful scarves and matching necklaces to every practical outfit that Polly chose. Her style was simple, nothing to attract attention to her broad shoulders and generous hips. Colors were understated and hem lines modest.

"I hate being so small." Dorthey pouted. "If only I was as statuesque as you, we could share clothes. I have a perfect tangerine-and-cream-colored blouse that would be darling with this brown skirt."

"If only I wasn't so big and awkward," Polly retorted.

"You are beautiful and strong. Nobody ever misses you in a room. You draw people's attention." Dorthey moved over to Polly, who sat looking out the window toward the garage.

"That is the exact problem."

She gathered Polly's hair at the nape, and with a twist and a pin from her own hair secured it into a fashionable style. "Don't be shy. People may notice you for your height, but they remember you for your intellect."

"Boys just always seem so afraid of me," Polly thought of the valentines and notes that filled Dorthey's desk each year when they were in school together. Petar's devotion to her.

"What about Ollie? I think it no coincidence that his father happens to have business for him to tend to in Toronto this weekend."

"Oliver? Goodness. He has been Petar's friend since childhood. Teases me into a fury most times." Polly thought affectionately of the race by the creek, the dare, the kiss. She missed having him beside her in classes.

Dorthey smiled knowingly. "Exactly."

During the lumbering train ride, Polly's mood shifted from nervous excitement, when they boarded the train at the small Kingston station, to wide-eyed curiosity as they wound through the countryside. Polly had never been outside of her hometown. The uniformly open fields, interrupted periodically with patches of forest, distracted her. Mama and Professor Randall sat two rows ahead, both absorbed in their books.

"Are you excited?" Oliver asked, breaking the silence since their departure. He offered her a bag of nuts his mother has packed for him for the train ride.

"Yes. Nervous mostly. What if they don't like it? This could be the start and end of my career all in one day!"

He reached over and grabbed her hand in his. "They'll love it! I am sure of it."

"Do you really think so? I wish I was there for the rehearsal. I don't remember if I noted that the second phrasing should be played largo. It would be natural for them to continue with the diminuendo from the first repetition, but it won't create as much tension."

"It will be perfect, Polly. Don't worry." He squeezed her hand reassuringly.

She rested her head on his shoulder. "I'm so glad you're here with me." Having a friendly support, outside of Mama, calmed her nerves.

"So am I." His eyes scanned her face. Intensely, he stared into her eyes, appearing hesitant to say what was on his mind.

"What?" she tried to coax. "What is it?" She quivered, nervous of what he might say.

For several seconds he did not waver from taking in every freckle and blemish on her face with a soft appreciation. He shook his head. "Nothing," he said. He took her hand easily into his. "You are just a very fascinating woman, Paulina Williams." They sat like that, in comfortable silence, hands interlinked, for much of the trip.

Union Station unexpectedly smelled of wet barn. Ribbons of people walked by, clearly focused on where they were going. In singles and doubles, the streams of people seemed to move like a steady current. Professor Randall had gone ahead to secure a car for the evening to take them to Massey Hall.

"Well, come along." Mama pulled her through the cross-section of people. "The hotel is just across the street."

Mama belonged in the city. Her subtle beauty was amplified against the gray and brown colors of the city. The tightly cinched cobalt blue dress she wore, with squared shoulders and a curved neckline, accentuated her delicate collarbones and her beautiful vase-shaped torso.

Cars parked along both sides of the rode, intermingled with people and horses, gave Polly a sense that she was on the verge of a great evolution. Women in small heels with crocodile purses sailed by her. Their bright-colored dresses flashed out from under their drab coats. Red lipstick and curled hair declared a new practical style unmarked by the war. Men in suits, ties and bolero hats stood in clusters, smoking and doing business, along sidewalks bordering the wide street.

The hotel lobby soared multiple stories high. Gold paint adorned the ceiling, accentuating cascades of light bouncing about from the multiple chandeliers. Towering, wide columns acknowledged the important work they did to hold up the palatial hotel.

Pale and drained by her monthly cycle, Mama retreated to their room for a rest and warm compress. Oliver and Polly explored the downtown shops. The windows of the Hudson Bay Company had displays of polka-dot dresses underlaid with crinoline, complete with matching gloves and purses. Luxury fur coats, sophisticated suits and shiny shoes in red, black and white dressed the windows.

"That is such an exquisite dress. Look at the detailed embroidery on the bodice." Polly stared at the black gown with its crimson and jade roses sewn asymmetrically throughout the fine lace overlay. The full skirt created a wide perimeter. Polly imagined entering a grand hall, a path clearing before her through the crowd as the fine silk danced back and forth around her ankles.

"You would look lovely in a dress like that. Perhaps for tonight then?" Oliver chided.

"Goodness, Oliver, look at that price! My navy-and-canary tweed suit will serve well enough for this evening." She gawked. "Imagine spending such money on a dress that you might have occasion to wear only now and again."

"Polly, you are always so practical. Someday you'll marry somebody wealthy enough to buy you such clothes to wear as you clean or shop at the market, should you wish."

"I certainly shall not! Firstly, I'll make my own money and won't need a husband to buy me things. Secondly, there are many things in the world worth spending money on, the least of which is frivolous, expensive clothing, Oliver."

"You can call me Ollie, you know."

"I rather prefer Oliver, if you don't mind." She pointed to the male mannequin in the same window dressed in an elegant double-breasted jacket with three buttons and a long tail. "You would look rather dashing in that."

"Are you saying I need frivolous decoration?"

"Perhaps. A little something to liven up your serious character." She nudged him in jest, nearly throwing him off balance.

They stopped at a café for a cup of tea, scones, and finger sandwiches before heading back to the hotel to get ready for the evening's concert. Mama was already dressed when Polly arrived back at their room.

"Paulina, where have you been? We must be on our way in an hour. Your hair needs washing and combing. Hurry along." She gestured to the basin of water that had been brought to the room for the purpose.

Mama plaited her hair, then fastened it in a crown around her head, still slightly damp and smelling of rose shampoo. The new suit fit perfectly. Flecks of yellow woven through the fabric set off the highlights in her hair and imbued her complexion with a healthy glow.

Oliver and Professor Randall were already in the lobby when they arrived. They had a few minutes to spare before the car would be there to take them to Massey Hall. Behind one of the large pillars, Polly caught sight of woman staring directly at her.

"Excuse me for a moment, would you please, Mama?"

Polly held her gloves in her hand. She strode over to the where the woman stood. Her high-heeled shoes forcing her to move more cautiously than she would like. Standing before the woman now, all her practiced words escaped her.

"Sadie, what are you doing here?" was all she could muster.

"I read in the paper that the Toronto Symphony was opening tonight, and listed in the program was *A Winter's Tango* by P. Andrezej. I remember that was your pseudonym, so thought it might be you."

"Well, my pseudonym certainly wasn't Sadie Johnstone, as appeared in the *Kingston Whig* and school paper," Polly stated bluntly.

"Please, Polly. I am so sorry. I needed to bring something home to my parents. Something for them to be proud of before . . ." She paused and stepped out from behind the pillar. Her swollen belly was visible under the loose-fitting dress she wore. Its light fabric, worn collar, and slightly stained lapel contrary to Sadie's usual fashionable style.

"Sadie!" She couldn't help but cup the sides of her former friend's belly in her hands, the girth suggesting she was into her third trimester. "Does he know? He's here!"

"Who?" Sadie looked frightened.

"Professor Randall. He is here to accompany us to the symphony. Is that why you came? To see him?"

"*Minushka!*" she heard mother call gently from the entryway.

"No, Polly. I came to see you. I need help. My parents sent me away when they found out. I'm living in a home for girls . . ." She paused, staring at her fingers whose nails and cuticles were peeled and cracked. ". . . for girls of my disposition, until the baby is born and taken away to folks who want a baby or to an orphanage. But I want to keep it, Polly." Instinctively, her hands rested on her belly.

A gentle tap on the back of her shoulder startled Polly.

"Paulina, we must go." Professor Randall was standing behind her now. His voice infuriated her.

She stepped aside, removing herself as the obstruction between him and his responsibility. He tipped his hat and greeted Sadie with a kind hello.

"Is that it? Is that all you have to say to Sadie?"

Sadie tugged on Polly's sleeve, her cheeks flushed and her breath short. Polly regretted the embarrassment she caused her friend in such a public place.

"Perhaps the two of you have some things to discuss, while I excuse myself." Polly gave a stern bow of her head and began to turn away but Sadie held tightly onto her arm.

"Hello, Professor Randall. I'm Sadie Johnstone, a friend of Polly's from school. I won't hold her much longer."

"A pleasure to meet you," he said. His eyes roved to her midriff. "Please, not too long. We have someplace to be." He gave a slight bow before placing his hat back on his head and meandered back to join Oliver and Mama in the foyer.

"It isn't his, Polly. All that stuff . . . I made it up. It wasn't him." Sadie was unraveling before her. Like a loose sweater thread, if pulled anymore, the entirety of it would be lost.

Polly stood in shock. Again, another lie. "I must go." She opened her purse and pulled out the few dollars Father had given her for spending money. "Take this." She nestled the paper into Sadie's closed hand. "Be well, Sadie."

Avoiding her mother's inquisitive looks, she rode in the car lost in thought, using the excuse of nerves for her far-off stares.

Massey Hall's simple brick exterior hid a riveting concert hall inside. The dim lighting and musty odor gave a feel of grand history. Great things happened here; Polly could sense it. As the crowds began to enter, Polly and her entourage were ushered into the bowels of the hall. Long corridors dotted with white light sconces, peeling paint, and scuffed floors were filled with energy and activity of the performers. Flutes, violas, and cellos were being tuned, their clashing notes intoxicating to her.

After climbing a dizzying narrow iron staircase, they arrived backstage to meet the maestro. Professor Randall shook hands and engaged in a jovial dialogue with the conductor about their travels, the hotel, and the excitement of the evening.

"Allow me to introduce you to the composer of the brilliant piece you'll be playing tonight." Professor Randall gestured toward the group and coaxed Polly over with a wave of his hand.

"Jolly good to meet you." The maestro smiled, extending his hand to Oliver.

Slightly embarrassed, Oliver shook his hand. "Oh, not me, sir. This is Polly. Or rather, Paulina. I mean, this is your P. Andrezej." Oliver ushered her forward with his hand at the small of her back.

"Hello, Maestro. It is a pleasure to meet you." Polly held out her hand, then quickly retracted it and curtsied as her mother had coached her.

"But you're a girl!" His astonishment was etched with slight disgust and intolerance. "This can't be." He shook his head with disbelief.

Polly straightened out of her curtsy, taking advantage of her height. She looked slightly down at the man and said bluntly, "But it can. And it is. Sir."

Flummoxed, the maestro waved his arms in dismissal. "So be it then."

They were hastily guided by the stage manager to their reserved seats in the center of the third row, with the other guest composers of the evening, Robert Fleming and Healey Willan among them.

Bells chimed and the lights blinked three times. The rumble from the crowd transitioned from a buzz, to a whisper, to a hush. The curtains rose, sending out a whiff of mothballs. All was still. Applause erupted as the maestro entered stage right and took to the center podium.

"Ladies and gentleman, it is with great pleasure that tonight we pay tribute to this vast country of ours and celebrate our own Canadian composers. We begin with a piece that highlights the singularly complex beauty of the piano. I present to you *Sonatina for Piano* by a most promising young composer, Robert Fleming."

A handsome young man, not much older than Polly, stood as the spotlight moved to rest upon him. Confident and gregarious, he greeted the crowd's applause with broad-stroke waves. The piece was fantastical. Full of mystique and intrigue, such that it would be well suited as a score for a Bogart film.

Following a round of gracious applause, the maestro addressed the audience again, introducing professor and accomplished composer, Healey Willan. A small plump man with rounded wire glasses stood at his seat under the spotlight, taking a humble bow. A beautiful choral piece, accompanied by the ghostly voices of the St. Paul's choir, truly brought a quiet religious experience to everybody in the audience. For more than thirty minutes, not a person coughed or adjusted in their seat. They sat captivated by the sounds of the violin and the echoes of the fifty people who sang from the back of the stage.

As the requiem quieted, Polly grew nervous. Her impassioned tango-inspired piece was much livelier and more exotic than the others. Should she wave or curtsy when introduced? She forgot to ask Mama. Perhaps a bow was best in this situation. She dried her damp palms on her skirt. Mama placed a reassuring hand on her forearm and gave a slight squeeze of contained excitement. Though it was Papa who had always supported her musical development, she was thankful Mama was here to share this moment with her.

"And now, for our final piece before intermission. Composed by a student and lover of music, I bring you *A Winter's Tango.*"

Polly readied herself to stand, but the light did not come. The maestro had already turned to count in the orchestra. Oliver looked at her, perplexed. Mama rested her hand heavily on her daughter's leg to hold her in place. Professor Randall gave a quiet disgruntled snort. Polly sank low into her chair. Hearing the rapture of the orchestra bringing her composition to life and the raucous applause from the audience at its conclusion could not compensate for the feeling of being cheated.

Professor Randall excused himself during intermission to share a few choice words with his colleague, the maestro. Oliver exhorted his disgust at the unfairness of the situation.

"*Minushka*," her mother said, "do not let him take this moment away from you. Your piece, that you wrote when you were just fourteen years old, was selected to be played here tonight. Your name is in print in the program, giving you credit. The audience milling about you right now is murmuring about how wonderful it was." She took her sullen daughter's face in her hands. "Do not give them the power. Celebrate your accomplishment." She gave Polly a kiss on the nose.

"Thank you, Mama, but this still feels terrible. I am going back to the hotel."

"Please don't go, *minushka*. Enjoy the rest of the evening."

Polly shook her head.

"I'll call a car and go with you." Oliver began to search for his coat-check ticket.

"No. Please stay. I want to walk alone." She gripped her handbag and smoothed her skirt. "I'll be fine. Enjoy the rest of the evening." Her voice cracked.

She alleviated her mother's worries with confirmation that she knew the way and would stay to the well-lit, high-traffic roads. The fifteen-minute walk would do her good, she acknowledged. She protested when Oliver again offered to join her.

"I'm good," she said. With a kiss goodbye to Mama, she set off to let the cool air and anonymity of the city purge her of her ego-driven pride. By the time she reached the hotel, her sense of injustice had only grown. Sadie's revelation, and then the maestro's snub, had upset her sense of the world. The kaleidoscope through which she saw the world was beginning to lose a few of its beads.

CHAPTER 5

1942

Polly chose to wait at the back door of Grant Hall to allow the stream of boys to finish passing through. Books clutched to her chest, she reluctantly stepped over the threshold. She surveyed the empty spaces to find one that would fall outside of Dr. Proust's vantage point. Over the last several semesters, she had managed to avoid any of his courses. The rumor on campus was that his wife had grown ill, which accounted for a leave of absence the previous year. Others said he was found to be in a compromising relationship with Mrs. Wardle, one of the faculty members in the nursing department. When she, a war widow, was discovered to be with child, her dismissal was swift and silent. People whispered that the professor was transferred temporarily to assist with establishing the military engineering laboratory at the Royal Military College of Canada as penance for his misdemeanor.

The top-secret program recruited some of the most inquisitive and agile minds from Queen's, including Oliver. Neither she nor Petar had heard from him in months. A great sense of intrigue enveloped the work happening across the lake. People said the engineers worked in long shifts to create wireless radios that could send signals across the ocean without interruption, and built pilotless airplanes that could take photos of enemy territory for war strategists.

"I heard they have to work all day and night underground, and their backs have grown hunched over from arthritis," she overhead the boys coming down the stairs say. The tallest of whom, still unaccustomed to his growing limbs, bumped his elbow against her, sending her books toppling to the ground.

"Sorry!" he hollered back as he continued down the stairs to his seat. "Apparently, they're all losing their teeth and are pale and skinny, like a bunch of vampires, after not seeing the sun for weeks," he continued with a laugh.

Polly bent down to pick up her books. She added each one with a new *thump* to her stack. She straightened her skirt upon standing and marched down to the row of boys. "Were you not taught any manners? It would have been appropriate, after having sent my books tumbling to the ground, to have helped pick them up," she stated.

"I said sorry, Polly," the boy choked out. His cheeks flushed as his eyes met hers.

Polly immediately regretted her sarcastic outburst. "Sorry. Do I know you?" She was stunned and bit suspicious that he knew her name.

"I'm Walter." He stood, towering over her. His broad shoulders and striped shirt in the Gaels' colors a telltale sign of a rower. "We have had several classes together," he shared with a deep chivalrous nod of his head.

"Well, hello, Walter, I'm Polly. But you already seem to know that," she awkwardly mumbled the last part almost to herself. They smiled at each other for a few seconds, while his three friends extended chuckles and nudges.

"Would you like to join us?" Walter offered.

Just as the others gathered their things to allow her into their row, a familiar voice echoed in the hall, bringing it to a silence.

"Well, Ms. Williams, how nice of you to join us. It appears you are having difficulty finding a seat. Allow me to direct you to the vacant one at the front of the room here." Professor Proust looked at her over the top of his glasses. "Please, do come sit so we can begin. That is, unless you are trying to achieve your M-R-S degree instead of your doctorate."

Polly stood to the challenge. "Thank you, Dr. Proust." Aware of all eyes on her, she took each step down to the front of the room with care not to stumble. He watched her until she was fully seated. When she placed her stack of books gingerly on the table, she met his stare and announced, audible only to him, "Though I don't see those two things being mutually exclusive of each other. Being educated and being a wife, that is."

A small grin creased the corner of his cheek. "Touché, Ms. Williams."

"Okay, gentlemen and lady . . ." His intentional singling out of her made Polly squirm in her chair.

Through the course of the lecture, she kept her pen moving on her paper and her head down to give the illusion of learning. Mathematical paradoxes were games she and her father had played since she was young—spirited intellectual pushes of logic until the reasoning either contradicted itself or contradicted intuition. She always won by deferring to the "I am lying" statement, when her father trapped her in a thought corner. By default, if she was telling the truth, by declaring she was lying, she would be lying about lying. A circular thought that would send her into giggles each time.

"Let's discuss Russell's paradox. Who knows it?" Dr. Proust searched the room of raised hands.

After several selections and failed explanations of the scenario, there was a hush in the room. A pointer finger fell in the middle of the sketch Polly was making of her cottage home in the spring. "Ms. Williams, perhaps you would like to illuminate for us the barber paradox."

Slowly, she put down her pen. As her mouth grew dry and her armpits moist, her own paradox was not lost on her. "Russell's paradox is about a small town with a single male barber," she started.

"Louder, Ms. Williams. Your female voice does not carry well in these large halls. Perhaps you should stand up at the front of the room." He grasped her elbow, much more gently than she expected, and guided her to a spot in the center. "Now, try again, and this time project." His own voice carried to the back corners in example.

She cleared her throat to fight down the suffocating heat that rose in her body. "Russell's paradox is about a town with a male barber who shaves all the men in town who do not shave themselves or anybody else." She glanced at the professor, who stood with his arms crossed against his chest, one hand holding his glasses which rested against his upper lip. His eyes were soft, though intense, as they focused on her.

"Go on," he coaxed quietly.

"The question is, who shaves the barber?" At this moment, she gestured to the chalkboard. The professor's gentle nod granted permission and she stepped forward, quickly drawing logic statements beginning with "if" and connected with "then" statements. When the room looked back at her with quizzical expressions, she went on to Venn diagrams, outlining how the barber could not shave himself, since he only shaved those who did not shave themselves, and that nobody else could shave the barber because he was the only one in town who shaved other people. Hence, the paradox of who shaved the barber.

"Excellent!" Professor Proust gave a light clapping of his hands, and motioned for her to take a seat. "Very good, Ms. Williams. You see now why many have struggled over this puzzle for some time."

"Except . . ." she continued with the full enthusiasm she brought to such games as a child. "It is not a puzzle if the barber has alopecia. No hair."

The room exploded in laughter. A hoot came from Walter and his friends, which bolstered Polly's confidence.

"It was not meant to be a joke," she added, though she herself chuckled with a bit of pride at being able to join in the laughter rather than being the target of it. "If the barber has no hair, then he is not in the group that needs a shave. I think that is the lesson Russell was trying to teach us. We need to carefully define the details of the groups to which we are referring and account for any contradictions to the logic by checking our assumptions."

The students were still rowdy. Professor Proust banged his meter stick on the table to regain control of the room. "Thank you, Ms. Williams. That shall be all for today." He pointed the stick toward her chair, and with an uncompromising stern look, let it be known that he would not be calling on her again this semester.

Polly was flattered when Walter invited her to join them at the pub after class. Not a typical place for women to be, she was emboldened to accept the offer. She only hoped her mama would not come to know of it.

"Five pints please, Charles," Walter called over to the barman. Apparently, he and his friends were regulars in this place of clear social hierarchy. Two freshmen cleared out of the corner table as Walter approached without being asked. "Thanks, chaps!" He patted them on the back as they took their full glasses and stood against the window instead, without a break in their conversation.

"Polly, you were great in class today. You really stuck it to that conceited, arrogant Proust," said the smallest of Walter's friends, who had introduced himself as Brent. He was blond and slight framed, with black-rimmed glasses. His clothes smelled of mothballs and his teeth were stained with brown deposits, a side effect from an antibiotic he was given as a baby. He was the coxswain on their rowing team. His light weight and panache for drumming were advantages that helped the team excel.

"Speak of the devil." Walter gestured with his chin to the other side of the room, where Professor Proust was entering with a few of his colleagues.

Polly turned her back and pretended to study the room. Set in the lower level of a house, the back doors opened up to a small garden patio. A few small windows were draped with heavy-set fabric, blocking out any other natural light. Light pine floors brightened up the space, while the dark walnut tables and chairs cushioned with crimson velvet gave an old-world enchantment. The intricate carvings on the lower portion of the bar, with images of gargoyles, wolves, and trees, brought a haunting mid-18th century mood.

When the beer arrived, Polly graciously accepted it, then quietly asked the waitress for a soda instead.

"Come on, Polly, drink up!" Walter nudged the beer toward her. "This isn't class, and your parents aren't around. You can lighten up a bit."

"No thanks," she politely declined, and looked back for the waitress, anxious to get her soft drink.

"Go on! It's a good source of iron. You look like you could use some iron." He looked coyly at his mates. "Don't women need extra iron because of their monthly?" He laughed, again nudging the glass closer to her.

She grasped the glass, feeling parched after the stress of class, and took a sip. Just one, to hold her until her soda arrived. The cold liquid felt like a soft blanket on her throat. She didn't mind the bitterness on her tongue. Overall, she found the drink rather delectable.

"There you go!" Walter smiled a broad, enchanting grin. "To Polly, a very funny girl." He winked at her and clanged her glass.

She took another sip, then another. "You don't need to drink that," Brent whispered into her ear.

Polly shrugged. She enjoyed the joviality of the moment. Walter taught her to throw darts, and then to play billiards.

He doted on her all evening. Their five-person party soon grew to seven, then nine. With each addition came new interesting conversations, as Walter ensured she was introduced to everybody. By the end of the evening, the whole rowing team and many of Walter's friends from the rugby team had arrived. They sang the Queen's fight song, whose Gaelic chorus Polly did not understand. *"Oil thigh na Banrighinn a'Banrighinn gu brath!"* they repeated over and over, as they stamped their feet around in a circle, beer splashing out of their glasses. Walter never left Polly's side, and a smile never left her face.

Reluctantly, Polly noted the time. She knew she would already have to account for her lateness to her mother, uncertain how she would explain the smell of alcohol and cigarettes as being from studying at the library. Perhaps the walk home in the cool fall air would refresh her before she stepped into the house.

"I should go," she hollered into Walter's ear, trying to get his attention amid the celebration.

"I'll walk you home." Walter handed his beer to Brent.

"You know, Walter, I'm going anyway. I'll walk Polly home. You stay and have fun," Brent offered. His look was unsettling to Polly. A wary sensation drew her to alertness.

"No, no. I got it." Walter discretely entwined his fingers between Polly's as he said his goodbyes to his chums.

Outside, the smell of fallen leaves was captured in the breeze coming off the lake. Polly thought of the unspoken messages that nature sent through smells and sound to the trees and animals, signaling that it was time to begin storing food. The moon sat low in the sky, missing a rim of glow imperceptible to most people, but not missed by Polly.

Walter cradled her hand in his. "Let's take the path through the park. It's much more private." He took off his jacket and draped it around her shoulders. Polly accepted it, even though she wasn't cold. A giddy feeling tickled her head. Perhaps she should have declined the second drink.

Instinctually, she searched behind the trees for raccoons and skunks, as she had always done. She felt happy and tried to pay attention to every sensation, word, and action to later recount to Dorthey, who would not forgive her if she left out one tasty crumb.

Walter stopped, taking a dance step back, and twirled Polly under his outstretched arm. She spun, feeling beautiful and desirable for the first time in her life. Her mother would certainly approve of Walter. He was strong, handsome, and came from a wealthy family. His father, she learned, was a court judge. Walter planned to follow in his father's footsteps someday. Though he wasn't required to take any math courses after his first year, he continued to do so to build his skills in logical thought. "It will make me undefeatable in court someday," he had explained to her over a plate of fish and chips that they had shared at the pub.

As she twirled the second time, he drew her in with a strong tug. After a few beers and a few spins, she lost her balance and stumbled into him. Before she could regain her footing, he steadied her and leaned in with a kiss. Her first kiss. It was softer than she expected. The leftover salt from their shared meal of fish and chips at the pub still on his lips.

He grabbed her from around her waist and walked forward, guiding her to rest against a tree. "Did you like that?" he asked.

She smiled, giving a childish nod.

"Polly, was that your first kiss?"

She nodded again shyly.

"Well, it is my honor to be your first." He kissed her again, this time uncomfortably harder. His tongue pried open her lips and plunged into her mouth. The taste of stale cigarettes and sour beer made her want to gag. She tried to turn her face away, but he pushed into her deeper. His nose pressed against hers, making it harder for her to breathe.

She tried to push him away. This was no longer pleasant, and the wary feeling Brent had set off in her at the bar was alive again. He pressed against her and clasped both her wrists above her head with his left hand. The bark scratched against her wrists. With his right hand, he groped her breasts roughly. The pain caused her to wince.

She opened her mouth to him, letting him smother her. As she relaxed into his motion, he moaned, softening his pressure. In that moment, she bit down hard on his lower lip, tasting blood in her mouth. As he pulled away, she yelled, "Get off me! Get off me!"

"You little bitch!" He grabbed her face in his right hand. "You like to play rough? I thought you might, Polly. I knew from the way you stand up in class, the way you study so hard and are so intense, that all you really need, all you really want, is to be tamed by a man."

He let go of her wrists, using his knees to hold her in place, while his right thumb put slight pressure against her throat, restricting her ability to speak.

"Do you need me to tame you, Polly? Is that what you want? You just need a man to show you what it's like to be a desirable woman." His words were thrown out with scornful accusation, as if to douse out her fight like one does with domestic animals. "Polly, I'll show you what a man can do so you can stop trying to be like one."

His left hand went searching for the bottom of her skirt. She fought him with her hands, holding her skirt down tightly around her trembling thighs. She wrangled her right arm free to fight his away, while her left arm unexpectedly came up, clobbering him under the chin. He pulled away and rubbed at his chin. "You're not worth it. You're not worth anything, Polly. Just an ugly girl who's trying too hard to be noticed."

She heard a noise. Possibly a skunk. If she made enough fuss, perhaps it would spray and scare Walter away. The sound became clearer. It was whistling. Yes, somebody was approaching them, whistling.

Walter stepped farther back. He touched his lip, and then his jaw again. In an instant, he was transformed from a dark man full of fury and lust, to a boy caught with a broken cookie jar on the floor in front of him.

"I'm sorry, Polly. I am so sorry."

He looked over his shoulder. The whistling grew louder. "Please don't say anything. I didn't mean to hurt you. I thought you wanted me to kiss you."

Polly stood like a frozen soldier with her arms crossed across her chest, leaning against the tree. Her face remained stoic, not revealing the terror that still quaked inside of her. Walter looked over his shoulder again, fear stricken. He picked up his jacket that had fallen from Polly's shoulders. As he stepped back to walk away, he paused and looked at her with genuine care. Gently, he placed his hand against her cheek. "I'm sorry," he whispered.

Before he walked away for good, he looked deeply into her eyes, reciting words that would echo in her soul for years: "Nobody will believe you, Polly. Nobody."

She sank down the trunk of the tree, trembling. How could she have been so foolish? She should never have gone to the pub, never accepted the drinks, never let him walk her home. Brent had tried to warn her. The allure of romance and being a focus of desire was so tempting that it had silenced her inner voice. She was a fool. Pounding her fists against her forehead, she vowed she would never be fooled again.

The whistling grew closer. Polly straightened her clothes and smoothed her hair. She stepped out from beside the tree and began walking quickly toward the lighted path, searching for safety and escape from the approaching stranger. Ahead by four hundred meters was the street corner, where a cluster of students had gathered to share stories from their day before heading home for supper and more study. She picked up her speed, in hope of outpacing the approaching whistler.

"Ms. Williams?" she heard a familiar voice call from behind her. When she did not stop, the voice called again in urgency, with a quickened jog of footsteps coming up behind her. "Ms. Williams?"

She did not want Dr. Proust to see her like this. She could only imagine what she looked like: a silly, frazzled girl. With fortitude she slowed, took a deep breath, put a smile on her face and turned around. "Oh, Professor. I did not recognize you. How are you?" Her voice was weak, and her knees continued to quake. Her cheeks still throbbed in the aftermath from the pressure of Walter's tight squeeze.

He searched her face and scanned the integrity of her body. His eyes seemed to see deep into her soul.

"Oh, Ms. Williams." The sympathy in his voice was almost enough to crack her façade.

She remained resolute. She could not give this man an ounce of reason to further see women as vulnerable, weak, and misplaced at university. Only her eyes betrayed her embarrassment. She pushed down the regret and the grief of what had just transpired. His brown eyes absorbed the message, bearing witness to the crack that was newly formed in her soul. He crossed his left arm across his body; his left hand rested against his mouth, in his typical stance. The familiarity of it brought Polly comfort.

"You seem to have grown wiser this evening, Ms. Williams." His voice softened. "Emotions make our lives rich, but logic keeps us safe. You are a brilliant woman, Ms. Williams. A brilliant person. Careful not to let others take that from you."

Her soul refilled at that moment, for he recognized her as a person, a brilliant person.

"I happen to feel anything but brilliant right now, Professor." A single tear escaped her cheek that she was quick to brush away. "I must get home. I am already rather late."

"I happen to be heading to the rector's house, which I believe is near your father's home. May I walk with you? I could use the company."

She accepted his quiet gift. His kindness and grandfatherly demeanor were unlike the airs he put on in the classroom. He spoke of Eleanor Roosevelt's illuminating leadership in the human rights movement and the influential work of other women, like Ella Fitzgerald.

"You have not chosen a conventional path for yourself, Ms. Williams. It must not be easy for you." He looked down at the ground in contemplation. "Come see me tomorrow after class. I should like to speak with you about your thesis options."

Polly brightened. She was struggling to decide on a thesis topic that both interested her and was a suitable subject area for the small number of professors who might consider being her sponsor.

"Really? Thank you, Professor Proust." She knew they would never speak of this evening again, but were bonded by it in a new way.

Departing, he wished her a restful night, and welcomed seeing her in class the next day. Polly opened the front door, wincing as it squeaked. Darn that old door.

"Paulina, is that you? Paulina?" her mother demanded, with a tone of worry peeking through.

"Hello, Mama," she called, mustering an attempt at a brighter mood. "Sorry to be late. I was studying and lost track of time. I happened upon Dr. Proust on the way home and we were discussing my thesis options." She prayed that the partial truth would redeem her of the lies.

"Oh, *minushka.*" In that one statement, her mother divulged that she knew the true events of the night. It may have been her uncharacteristic disheveled hair or the tear in her stocking that told the story of the evening. Perhaps it was the bruise that felt like it was growing like a scarlet letter on her neck, or the telling scratches on her wrists. Whatever it was that revealed the truth, Polly was grateful. Her mother's arms wound tightly around her, offering reassurance that things would be well.

"Are you hurt?" she asked. She kissed the wrists which looked sore. "Did he . . . did the professor . . .?" Unable to say the words, the implication was clear. Her mother was visibly relieved when Polly shook her head.

"No, Mama, it wasn't Professor Proust! And I'm fine. Nothing terrible happened."

"Paulina, you must know that men only want one thing from women. You must protect your virtue, my sweet girl." She placed kisses all about her daughter's face. The memory of how vigilant and protective her mother was when they lived in the attic apartment, anytime the landlady's son approached Polly, came rushing back to her.

Still distraught, her mother continued. "I knew going to university would be too much. You are too young. Too gullible. You may think you are so smart, *minushka*, but you know very little of the world. Perhaps it is best that you stop this nonsense."

"No, Mama, this has nothing to do with school. I should not have gone out after class. I should have come straight home. Please, Mama. This has nothing to do with my studies," she pleaded. Again, Polly was overwhelmed with embarrassment at her stupidity. "Please don't tell Papa."

Her mother nodded in solidarity. "Ah, *minushka*, you will be the early death of me! How I ended up with a girl like you I'll never know. Your brother and Dorthey are planning their wedding. Soon they will have babies. Do you not want that?" Her mother's imploring expression suggested that all she wanted was for Polly to say yes.

Polly couldn't lie to her.

"No, Mama, I don't. I want to learn, to teach, to contribute to the world."

Her mother closed her eyes and gave a sigh so large that it felt like a rock for a tomb was rolled into place, sealing the two worlds apart forever.

"Go have a bath. It will make you feel better. I'll bring you a cup of tea. Tomorrow the sun will rise and it will set, and time will go on as any other day." She released her embrace. "Go on now, Paulina."

Polly started up the stairs, pausing to watch her mother move to the window. A deep pain settled on her face, like a stitch pulled too tight. It seemed larger than tonight's events warranted. She realized for the first time that perhaps Mama's reaction had nothing to do with Polly. That it might be framed by moments and memories of her own, from a time before.

Paulina knew she would be fine, certainly wiser, as Dr. Proust said. She hoped her mother would someday see her strength, understand she was made of more than just flesh and fragile emotions. And that her mother would learn how to unburden herself of whatever dark stories she carried within her.

CHAPTER 6

1945

Since her first visit to Toronto, Polly was enamored. Smartly dressed people bustled along the sidewalks, always appearing to have someplace important to be. With the war now over, a kinetic energy hummed about the galleries and tea rooms that Polly found intoxicating. The Grange was one of her favorite destinations. Once home to a prominent lawyer and his family, it was donated as the first site for the city's art museum. Polly adored the tea room. Year round it was warmed by the large hearth centered on the long wall, bracketed on either side by austere portraits of the original family. Sunlight emanated through the two parallel windows throughout the entire day, wrapping the space in a joyful blanket. Adorned with ornamental rugs, their geometric patterns and bold colors were mesmerizing.

Always accompanied by Petar, Oliver, or one of her parents on these many trips to the city, she would find any excuse to wander the streets alone. Surrounded by strangers, she reveled in her freedom from the claustrophobic supervision. With a notebook always in her purse, she would end up at some point in her meandering at the refuge of the Grange. It was often in this room, and among the adjoining hallways of art exhibits, that Polly would retreat on her own for musical inspiration. This time, though, she would be on her own. Nothing holding her back. Adventure and success were before her, she just knew it.

Though she never received the spotlight at Massey Hall, the Toronto Symphony had performed two more of her pieces. Each time, Papa ensured she had fare and hotel accommodations to witness the achievements of her work. Never able to afford much more than the back rows of the second balcony, the sound still carried to where she sat. With her eyes closed she would let the colors dance within her head, as vivid as the first time they visited her. The powerful feelings they conjured in her never ceased to delight. She always marveled at how depictions of little dots and lines on a page could manifest in music and repeatedly transport one to an elevated stillness with the world.

She was always in the city for such a brief time with so much she wished to do. Her dissertation was well underway. Trips to the University of Toronto library and guest lecture series were essential to her learning. Kingston, still locked in the post-war climate, was stagnant. Enrolment during the war was low, and recruitment of prestigious faculty was a challenge. The intellectual elite in mathematics were at Oxford, Cambridge, and Princeton. Only through occasional special series would they grace the lecture halls in Toronto. It was the closest Polly could get.

Now that Petar and Dorthey were married and expecting their first baby, Oliver was off to England to complete his post-doctoral work, and Mama was frequently confined to the house due to her migraines, having somebody join her on these trips was inconvenient. For months she pleaded, recruiting Professor Proust, Petar, and anybody else she could muster to support her request. After much research on faculty, living accommodations, and budgets, she finally received her parents' consent to stay in Toronto for one year to finish her studies.

"*Minushka*, one year, then you come home and prepare for the rest of your life. You are twenty years old now. Your time for a family is running short."

There was no point in arguing with Mama and Papa, neither of whom could see that this was the start of the rest of her life.

She cordially accepted the governing rules that granted her this release from the mind-numbing confines of her small town. She would live in a boarding house run by one of Mama's old friends from Europe, with three other girls. She would teach piano and tutor in math, German, and French to pay for her room, board, and tuition. She was not to mingle with any boys unaccompanied. She was to be home every day by supper and study in her room for the rest of the evening.

"Yes, Mama," she dutifully agreed. Excitement bubbled up so great in her she thought she would pop.

"Study hard, Polly. Continue to work on your music." Papa leaned in for a hug. "In a year's time, you will be back home able to teach at the university with me. We may even be preparing to celebrate a wedding. Both Henry and that Walter Brown have been asking about you." He winked at her.

The sound of Walter's name still revolted her. She would not let the memory ruin the day. After all, if Professor Proust had not come upon her that evening on his walk home, he may never have offered to be her thesis supervisor, and this step toward independence likely would not have happened.

Coming out of Union Station, Polly fixed her hat carefully and adjusted the cuffs of her gloves. She clutched her blue suitcase in one hand, strapped her leather tote bag across her bodice, and hung her purse over her wrist. Taking effort not to look like a vagabond, she began the two kilometer walk to the boarding house on Avenue Road.

Loose strands of hair fell from under her brim, and a blister was forming painfully at her heel when she arrived. The house was rather small and in need of a restorative paint. The front gardens were tidy and the iron fence draped with fragrant purple wisteria gave a welcoming feel. Before knocking at the door, she paused to catch her breath and pat the perspiration from the late August heat off her brow and neck.

Mama's friend was a startling beauty, just like Mama. Katarzyna had glossy, straight, long blond hair that she wore loose, and sea-green eyes that reflected the light like small twinkling diamonds. She refused to be called anything but "Kata," forgoing the formality of Mrs. Stone. Widowed, with three children, she lived on the second floor of the home with her daughter and two sons. The main floor dining area and living room were for common use, while the rest, including the kitchen, remained off limits. Kata was an excellent cook and preferred her kitchen spotless and undisrupted by those she housed.

She would board four young woman at a time to help cover the costs of raising her family alone. Kata's husband had taught at the university in the history department until he suffered a massive heart attack before the war. Educated herself, she was known among the faculty to host evenings full of jovial debate and lively music over snifters of Scotch and bubbly wines.

Polly shared an attic room and a single bathroom with three other women. Two of them, Mary and Margaret, also studied at the university, while the other, Charlotte, was doing an apprenticeship in the growing garment district. Mary and Margaret were sisters who mostly kept to themselves. Raised by a single father, who himself was a physician in their hometown, they had been sent to study medicine and nursing. Studious and devout, they spent long nights at the library and their weekends working with the church. They were serious but well-natured. Charitable to a flaw. Often giving their week's rations of tea and bread to others, while their own tummies grumbled at night in their sleep.

Charlotte was an orphan, her parents having died in a car accident only the year before. Unwilling to marry, as her guardian had contrived, she opted to take her small inheritance and move to the city. She worked part-time dressing mannequins for the Hudson Bay Company displays, while studying fashion design and pattern making under the tutelage of Martha. Madame Martha, as she was better known, was a couturier whose dresses could be found in the pages of *Mayfair*.

The girls got along splendidly. Between study and work, they still managed to find time to pass around romantic novels, and discuss marriage and sex late at night.

"Have you really never dated a boy, Polly?" Charlotte asked.

"Why, I think I had my first crush when I was five and would walk home from school holding hands with Nathaniel. We swore we would marry one day."

"What happened to him?" Margaret asked.

"Turned out he much preferred boys. When the headmaster at his school discovered him in the yard kissing another boy, his parents sent him to a special hospital. He returned cured, found religion and married the preacher's daughter."

Laughter echoed through the beams of the attic. Then it dwindled to a complete uncomfortable silence.

"I don't think that's actually right. Being that way isn't something you can help, and I don't think it's anything people need to be cured of," Margaret thoughtfully offered. She went on to share the disagreement she had with her medical professor on the subject, and his final response to her: "This is the type of problem we get when we let woman think." She finished her story in the mocking voice of her teacher.

At that, the girls laughed wildly, until they heard Kata tap the ceiling of her room with a broom handle to let them know it was time to quiet down.

"Polly, how is your thesis coming along? It's been three months and we still don't know what it is exactly that you study," Mary asked, evidently wanting to change the subject.

"I believe you can predict a person's response based on a mathematical formula calculated by the person's pattern of decisions." The quizzical looks that gazed back at her prompted further clarity. "If we were playing a game, I could predict what you were likely to do for your next move and, improve my chance of winning, based on the series of choices you previously made in response to mine. It's called game theory."

"What kind of games?" Charlotte asked.

"In theory it could be used in war to predict your enemy's next move, in chess or in cards."

"Cards? You mean you're spending all those hours studying to learn how to win at poker?" Charlotte bellowed.

The girls broke out into raucous laughter, with Mary having fallen on the floor in a fit. Even with the double tap of the broom handle it was hard for them to contain themselves.

The following morning, the girls all awoke later than usual. Sleepy eyed and quiet, they sipped their double-dripped, warm chicory beverages—the best substitute for coffee—and ate their oatmeal. Despite the war, living in Canada afforded access to maple sap, which they added to everything to make it palatable.

"Ladies, I'll be having some people over this evening for a bridge game," Kata shared. "Do any of you play?"

They all shook their heads.

"Polly plays poker," Charlotte stated matter-of-factly as she took a spoon of her oatmeal. The other girls began to snicker. Polly blushed.

"I do not play poker. I only study it." They all laughed harder.

"A smart *and* funny girl, just like your mother. She was something." Kata came around and refilled Polly's cup. "How I miss those days together. We knew how to make such fun."

Polly had a hard time imaging her mother young. "Tell me about her," she inquired.

"Your mother was always the life of the party. Singing, dancing. Every boy wanted to be with her. Every girl wanted to be her. Then the world changed with the first war, and ended all that." Kata looked off through the window, seeing a different world outside. The longing and sadness on her face accentuated the looseness of her skin and wrinkles around her tired eyes. She snapped back to the moment and a smile returned to her face. She continued to absentmindedly pour the roasted chicory into each cup at the table. "Hm. Then she met your father, and well, you know the rest."

Polly was thirsty for more stories about her mother. She really did not know much about her parents' romance or their lives before becoming parents. She wondered about the parties her mother may have gone to in pre-war Poland. She often heard her mother singing Polish songs in the kitchen when she didn't think anybody was around. Outside of those few moments when she would catch her walking through the backyard gardens, a slight dance in her step to a song that only she could hear, it was hard for Polly to imagine her mother having that kind of fun.

"I don't really know the rest." There was a slight pleading in Polly's tone.

Kata looked at her for a moment, then shook her head. "It is not my story to tell. You'll have to ask your mother."

Polly knew exactly what her mother's reaction would be to such a question: *"Pah, my children are my life. There is nothing more you need to know."* Then she would busy herself with tidying something up and send Polly off to do a chore that didn't need to be done.

While it was typically frowned upon for a widow to be entertaining in her home, Kata extended her occasional bridge game with the faculty wives to a regular weekly salon again. The war, now officially declared over, people longed for lively company. Wives began to bring their husbands, who missed Kata's cheese pitas and almond cookies. The professors soon began to invite some of their elite students. Fridays were met with growing excitement at the boarding house.

Kata would begin preparing on Thursday evenings after dinner. Polly changed the time of her piano lessons so that she could distract Kata's children from circling their mother's skirt with needs and dirty hands. She enjoyed hearing Kata sing in an unfamiliar language while she baked, the melody jolly and light. A flair of fashion was added to these events, as Charlotte would take remnants from the factory for napkins, tablecloths and other decorative pieces, consistent with a theme for the evening. Margaret and Mary, when not working in the hospital, would spend the evenings at the library studying in peace.

There were regulars who would come, familiar friends of Kata's late husband and other European immigrants. Politics, literature, travel, religion—nothing was off limits for candid discussion and gregarious debate after a few glasses of liquor. It was the first time Polly saw men and women gather in the same room and share in hearty conversation. A game of cards was usually happening in the corner for those who preferred, and pairs would occasionally break off to gossip quietly about the comings and goings of those in their social circle.

On the evening of the first of these gatherings, Kata came across Polly and Charlotte eavesdropping from the stairwell.

"Well, make yourselves useful at least," Kata had said, shoving a platter into both of their hands. From then on, they would serve the guests, grateful to be among these creatures of culture and class.

When the girls were back in their room after the party was over, Charlotte sketched outfits for each guest. "Did you see that peach scarf and blue jacket Mrs. Platt was wearing? The colors didn't suit her complexion. She would look much better in a pink pastel jacket with a cinched waist and petal bottom to hide those hips."

Polly nodded absentmindedly, distracted with wonder by the stories she had overheard. People who had met Winston Churchill during the war. Others who had been to Diaghilev's *Ballets Russes* in Paris, and heard Stravinsky perform *Petrushka* live. Things she only ever dreamed of doing. Excited by the vicarious connection to history and genius, she longed for the next evening before she had closed her eyes to this one.

"Did you see that man who kept staring at you all night?" Charlotte teased.

"Which man? You must be imagining things," Polly dismissed.

Men still paid little attention to her. She had dolefully conceded to the fact that she was usually invisible to them and would likely never marry. She felt unattractive being so tall, and then there was her small chest and broad hips. Her unruly frizzy hair and plain features, despite her mama's best efforts, never improved. At school, many of her peers were intimidated by her scholastic intensity. Others who had shown some interest eventually came to bore her.

"No, I am certain. That little man with the dark moustache. The one everybody calls Eli."

Polly searched the catalog of her memory. "Oh, yes, Mr. Rubins. He is an assistant professor of art history, just back from a year of study in Montreal."

"Is that why he has a bad French accent?" Charlotte gave a little eye-roll.

"I am sure his accent is just fine. And I don't think he's been staring at me." There was an appeal to the idea, though. Since the episode with Walter, she had distanced herself from any boys, except for purely academic reasons. Even her feelings toward Henry at the school newspaper had turned to a platonic exchange of work-only conversation. Perhaps, a new city was a new start, with somebody more mature and sophisticated. But she was still doubtful that anybody would be interested in her.

The following Friday, Polly took extra care to rosy her cheeks and borrowed a dress from Charlotte. It was a bit short at the hem and the sleeves. To compensate, she wore darker stockings and kept her hands busy with trays to minimize notice. Designed to be a loose-fitting style, the dress fit snugly across the back and pulled at the waist on her. She had opted to skip lunch and dinner that day, and wear a smaller than comfortable girdle to assist in the fit any way she could.

"You look pretty tonight," Kata noticed. "Be careful not to attract the wrong type of attention." Polly could hear her mother's voice channeled through her friend. Kata scanned the room, smiling as she made eye contact with her friends. "Now, perhaps you can go get the torte to serve."

After retrieving the beautifully decorated walnut torte chilling in the fridge, Polly carefully sliced perfectly equal pieces across the slab. Balancing the cake across her upper arms, she felt the tight strain across the back of her dress. "Stupid vanity," she cursed out loud, and swore to never compromise comfort for fashion again. She pushed through the kitchen door into the hallway, where she found a figure lurking in the dim shadows.

"Oh, you startled me!" She quickly regained the balance of the cake before it and she slammed into this person.

"So sorry. It's Paulina, right?" Eli stepped into the center of her path. The shadows of his thin face seemed more pronounced in the dark.

"Yes." Polly shied away, trying to edge around him to deliver the cake to the awaiting guests.

"Here, let me take that," he offered, scooping the tray from her arms and carrying it into the living room.

"Ah, Eli! You bring cake," one of the others called. "Will you bring some coffee too?" They all laughed.

Eli, in grand gesture, bowed and replied, "But of course. I shall return in only a moment." He disappeared back into the hallway leaving the laughing crowd. "Come with me." He handed her one of two glasses of red wine that she had not seen him scoop up from the living room. Firmly, he entwined his fingers between hers, and guided her into the kitchen.

Like an expert, he rolled up his sleeves, filled the small Turkish coffee pot with water, and intuitively found the sugar and coffee in the cupboard to the left of the sink. "Can you get the cups?" he asked, looking very at home in Kata's kitchen.

With the water set to boil, he picked up his glass of wine and held it up to the light. "What do you think of the wine?" He swirled the ruby contents with perfect concentric rings, and then sipped. She noticed him hold it in his mouth before he swallowed. "A perfect Bordeaux," he exclaimed.

Polly took a cautious sip, unsure what to expect.

"Have you never had wine before?" His words and posture oozed with a tincture of unflattering pomp.

"No, I really haven't," she said with an illusion of being unabashed by her confession.

Eli added a few tablespoons of sugar to the boiling water, then moved to stand right beside her. Their elbows touched. The smell of wine from his breath feathered across her nostrils. She noticed his large dark blue eyes, like midnight pools with dancing reflections of stars speckled in them. There was something dangerously alluring about him.

"Wine is a perfect artistic expression. It holds centuries of the soil's history and is infused with the winemaker's passion." His eyes never left her gaze. "A perfect love story."

She took another sip, barely able to swallow. The dark fruit flavors and velvety texture coated her tongue.

Once the water bubbled to a boil again, Polly herself felt the percolation of something inside of her. Carefully, Eli stirred each spoon of the powdered coffee into the pot, while he took her through a tutorial of French wines and wineries. Admittedly he had never been, his trip delayed due to the war. "Perhaps someday soon I shall go and take you with me. Would you like that?"

It was either the thought of traipsing through the French countryside drinking wine and eating delicate cheeses, or the wine itself that made her giddy. She was only able to nod, as she hid behind the indulgence of another taste. A blend of decorum and insecurity suppressed the urge to press up against him. She imagined a kiss, a touch, an embrace between them. She was sure it would be a balanced dance between passionate desire and mature delicacy, very unlike her experience in the park.

He poured coffee into the cups that were already on the tray and lifted it without spilling a single drop. "Come." He motioned with his head. She dutifully followed, almost running into him when he stopped abruptly at the door, only the tray between them preventing the calamity. He quickly leaned over and placed a kiss on her cheek. "*Merci pour votre belle compagnie*," he said, his eyes glinting mischievously. "Thank you for your beautiful company," he translated.

Though Polly understood French perfectly, she dipped her head shyly, playing into his flirtation. "Oh. You're welcome," was all she said.

Eli began showing up at the house during the week to drop off books of poetry he thought she might like to read. Loose pages tucked in of his own work. She initially transcribed them into her own journal for keeping. Eventually, she began saving the originals, and when he didn't say anything about them missing, she understood he had always intended them for her.

He surprised her after class with a special picnic in the park, followed by a walk through the art gallery where he shared with her his learnings of the great artists.

"Pol," he said, using this shortened form of her name as an endearment. "Would you like to come with me to the opera this weekend? I have tickets to *Romeo and Juliet*."

"I would love to," she replied, unable to contain her enthusiasm. "I have never been to an opera before and desperately desire an opportunity to experience it."

He took her hand comfortably in his, gently swinging it as they walked down the sidewalk. Polly wore flat shoes anytime she was with him and shortened her stride so he could keep up. As they stopped just in front of the boarding house, he turned her toward him, taking both of her hands in his own, and bringing them up to his lips for a kiss. "You are so enchanting, Pol. I wish I could just put you in a glass jar to study you. Hide you away from the rest of the world." She slouched to ease his stretch so he could kiss her. "You deserve the best the world has to offer, and I want to show it all to you."

Paulina had never been the center of somebody's attention this way. She felt as though she was orbiting the world like a bright falling star, floating and falling at the same time. Perhaps she wasn't as awkward and common as she once thought. Eli seemed to know so much about the world that she desired to see. Things she had never heard anything about before, like architecture and foreign cuisine, enthralled her. His big dreams of showing her the world dazzled her imagination. Everything felt like a possibility when she was with Eli.

She sensed somebody at the front window. The children made faces at them through the glass. Kata stood slightly behind with her arms crossed.

"I must go. I hope to see you tomorrow, at the salon."

"I shan't miss it." He waved to Kata, tipping his hat in respect. "Until tomorrow. *Au revoir*."

Paulina hurried into the house. She placed her hat on the hook and slipped her gloves into her book bag. She hoped to cool her reddened cheeks with the palms of her hands.

"You are late for the children's lessons, Paulina," Kata spoke sternly. Her eyes penetrated deep into Polly's heart. "It is okay to have some fun. Just be careful that you do not lose yourself. Men have a funny way of wanting to own what is yours."

Confused by the statement, Polly simply replied, "Please don't worry about me, Kata, I'm fine."

"Have you written to your mother lately?"

"No," she said, feeling ashamed about how little of the rest of the world she had paid attention to these last few weeks.

"Perhaps it is a good time to visit home. Reconnect with your family. Remember who you are." Kata gave her a pat on the back. "Men will derail you if you are not careful, Paulina. They'll make you play small to fit into their shoebox."

Polly straightened up. "I know who I am. You need not concern yourself." She walked past Kata, careful not to brush against her. "I'll get started on the lessons now."

Kata was wrong about Eli. He was not trying to squish her down. His repeat comments about studying her under a glass jar away from the world did rouse some unease in her, but surely, he only meant it in jest. He was opening up a whole world to her that she never knew existed. She tried to be incensed by Kata's accusations on his behalf, yet she couldn't. A niggle of doubt planted itself in the center of her chest.

The following evening, Polly kept her distance from Eli. Quietly she served brandy and wine, poured tea, and hovered around the card table.

Eli had grown quite comfortable at these gatherings, often sharing in jokes and conversation with the others. The most junior among them, he bore the brunt of being the target of their humor. He took it all with joviality, appearing to enjoy the attention. "It is a tribal christening to join the ranks of the cultured university elite," he once told her. Though at times she felt embarrassed for him, not confident that he was anything more than a jester playing the fool.

"Let me show you something." Eli stood and walked to the piano that sat in the corner. "Pol, come here." He beckoned her over in front of the others for the first time. "I want to play for you."

He began a playful show tune known to everybody in the room. Some joined in the song; others tapped their feet to the rhythm. At the end of the piece, he transitioned smoothly into a second and then another. When he finished his third song, the room graciously applauded and cheered.

Kata stepped forward, her presence filling the room as it usually did. "Bravo, Eli." She took a sip of her champagne and watched him carefully as she said, "Paulina, why don't you play something for us now."

"You play?" Eli asked, a slight look of dismay on his face. "I never knew."

"I do. But not tonight." Polly shook her head, her eyes pleading with Kata not to ask her again.

"Please play, Paulina," various voices called from the room.

"Paulina, play." Kata tapped Eli's shoulder to indicate he needed to move, and then guided Polly to replace him on the bench. "Play *A Winter's Tango*. It is my favorite."

Reluctantly, Polly placed her fingers on the piano. She had not played for anybody other than the girls in the house and the children, since coming to Toronto. Once her fingers played the first set of heavy chords, she closed her eyes, allowing the colors to sweep her away.

Her heart filled with joy, and she felt elated coming down from the last repetition of the final eight bars. Her fingers settled lightly on the final notes like fairy dust.

She turned bashfully to the room. Alarmed by the quiet around her, she looked quickly at Eli, whose face was aghast. She had been so enthralled in the music that she was uncertain if others heard what had sung through her head. Suddenly, the room exploded with applause and hearty accolades. Eli, meanwhile, bore a tight smile, and his tepid applause did nothing to reassure her.

"I heard that piece played by the Toronto Symphony. It was beautiful then, but had even more power tonight." A great compliment from the German history professor whose love of symphonic music was fostered from childhood.

"You play brilliantly," one of the women proclaimed.

"What talent," stated another faculty member.

"Play something else," somebody else requested.

At the urging of the group, Paulina played another piece. Her mind was aware that Eli had refilled his drink, notably removing himself from the festivity in the room. In response, the colors in her mind dimmed. He sat quietly at the now abandoned card table in the corner, and in turn, her fingers stiffened and her breath found it hard to inflate her lungs. Upon finishing the Stravinsky piece, she feigned a headache and excused herself to her room for the rest of the evening.

Eli sent a note the following day that he had papers to grade and gave the opera tickets to a friend. "Perhaps another time," he wrote.

Melancholy filled Polly, like a humid summer day thirsting for a thunderstorm. Drifting back and forth between the boarding house, school, and the library in a mindless trance, Polly, for the first time ever in her life, had difficulty mustering up any creative energy. Usually desperate to quiet her spirited bounces of thought, now she found inspiration impossible to conjure. It had been one week since she heard from Eli. In place of math formulas and music compositions, she recounted the events of the previous Friday in her mind. She ran through each detail of conversation, interpreted each look exchanged between them to try to understand where she faltered.

Polly coiffed her hair into a bouffant, the way she had worn it when Eli first spoke to her in the kitchen that night. She again borrowed Charlotte's bright red lipstick that he had previously complimented. She was restless. Torn between outrage at his easy dismissal of her and her yearning to see him this evening at the salon. She had grown so accustomed to his attention that she now craved it like a cigarette.

"Oh, Polly. Please settle down," Margaret demanded. She was studying on her bed for an immunology exam the following day. "Stop pacing. Sit." She closed her book with a *thud*, looked her friend directly in the eye and said, "I frankly don't even know what you see in him. He's simple and too short for you."

"He makes me feel special," was all Polly could muster.

Charlotte, who up until now had been quietly curling her hair in the corner, began, "He has that terrible phony French accent. He was in Montreal for only a year."

"Isn't he from a small town just north of here? Nobody gets a natural accent from a year abroad," Margaret stated.

"And why does he call you Pol? That is so peculiar. You have a perfectly lovely name in Polly or Paulina," Charlotte insisted.

"It's a pet name. Something I have with him only." Polly grew defensive. "You wouldn't understand."

Margaret and Charlotte stared at each other, vacillating between frustration and compassion. It was Margaret who stepped forward first, wrapped her arms around her newest friend and said, "It was interesting while it lasted, Polly. It's good for you to spend time with different people, but it's time to move on. There are better men waiting for you."

Polly shrugged out of the embrace, giving a big sigh. "Perhaps for people like you, beautiful and graceful." She gestured at Charlotte and Margaret. "You don't know what it's like wanting so badly to be seen, to be loved. Eli was the first man to ever really pay me any mind in that way."

Charlotte linked her arm through Polly's. "You are loved and admired by so many, Polly. Don't you see that?"

"In the end, it is only what you think of yourself that matters," Margaret added. She pulled Charlotte away and directed her toward the door. "You can be content in your self-inflicted misery, Polly, but we are going to go have some supper. Come join us when you're ready to re-engage with what matters in the world."

The two set off to join Mary, who was already downstairs setting the table, as was her chore most evenings.

The salon was cheery with discussion about cinema and literature. Many had seen *All About Eve* and were enthralled by Bette Davis's detailed performance. The women thought that the conniving Eve, played by Anne Baxter, was well cast, while the brief performance by the sensual beauty, Marilyn Monroe, had the men aflutter about why she didn't have a leading role.

There was no sign of Eli, and Polly was unable to mask her disappointment. Kata unexpectedly handed Polly a glass of wine. "Smile," she insisted. "Men will come and go, but never lose yourself with them." She broke custom as she offered Polly a chair in the circle.

Sipping demurely from the glass she was given, Polly observed the conversation politely, nodding and smiling. By the time she finished her first glass of wine, her mood had lifted and she felt eager to contribute to the conversation.

"I am concerned that with growing industrialization overseas, our dependence on trade and import is increasing. Should Canada not preserve some of its essential manufacturing nationally? Otherwise, we shall open ourselves up to global vulnerability. There are simply some essential products and skills that we must preserve to be a strong, self-sufficient country." Polly was animated in her discussion.

"Well, Ms. Williams. Are you doing your PhD in math, music, or economics? I can no longer tell," one of the gentlemen offered with a broad smile and jolly laugh.

"I do say, Paulina, with a brain like yours, you would certainly be an excellent candidate for a secretarial position in one of those big banks or law firms filling up Bay Street," his wife added.

Before Polly could comment on the narrow stereotype, Kata graciously intervened with a request for some more coffee. "Polly, please do go to the kitchen and bring us some." Her stare was intense, with one brow lifted, declaring insistence and the need to do it silently.

Dutifully, Polly excused herself to the kitchen where she rummaged loudly through the cupboards looking for the coffee, sugar, and the Turkish coffee pot. Her temper boiled with the water at the comment, followed by the heaviness of acknowledgment that being a secretary would be the easier and more likely route, if only the idea did not make her feel like she was drowning.

Lost in her thoughts, she was startled by a tap on the back window. Peeking just over the window sill were a pair of unmistakable almond-shaped eyes. The fingers motioned for her to come to the back door.

Careful to turn off the stove, she grabbed the wool shawl that hung on the hook to brace herself against the cold Canadian winter.

"Eli, come in." Her heart thrummed and a fullness enveloped her head like being disoriented in an impenetrable fog.

"No. Not tonight. I just wanted to come see you." He looked down at the ground sheepishly. "You hurt me, Pol," he mumbled.

Her heart softened, along with the intensity of the chosen words she had rehearsed for this moment. The accusations of rudely abandoning their night at the opera and obstinate lack of courtesy to call her this week. It all fizzled away. She raised her hand to his arm in comfort.

"I thought we had something special. And then you flaunted in front of everybody that you were better than me with your piano performance. I never knew you could play like that. It was wonderful. But it really embarrassed me in front of my colleagues."

Polly was confused. "I didn't mean to," was all she could say.

"You know how they tease me. I am still just being welcomed into the circle, trying to make my mark. And then along comes my girlfriend underscoring that I am not good enough." He pouted.

The word *girlfriend* popped out at her like a blinding light. "Girlfriend?"

"Yes, Pol. I thought you were my girlfriend. That's why it hurt so much. I felt betrayed. We're supposed to be a team."

Polly thought of a bird whose mama had left it too early, and as it tried to fly away it fell, hurting its wing. She cradled him in a hug.

"I'm sorry," she offered. "I shall try to be more considerate."

He offered forgiveness by way of a smile, followed by a hard and long kiss that threw Polly off balance. After a long minute he slowly pulled away, his eyes still closed, apparently relishing in something mysterious to her.

"You taste like cherries," he said, smacking his lips playfully.

Polly was lost. The whole scenario was novel to her. She was swept away into a foreign world, where she was living somebody else's life. Never sure what to say, how to act, in what manner to respond. This was a grown-up adult life she was embarking on. Finally, her metamorphosis from a small-town girl to an independent city woman was happening. Eli looked at her closely. His breath smelled of whiskey and cigarettes, with a slight hint of mint.

"You're becoming such a woman. My woman." He smiled proudly. He admired her face, her long legs that left her standing a few inches taller than him. He reached for her hair, running it through his fingers. "Though a new hairdo might suit you better," he said tearing through a hairspray-cemented clump.

Polly winced. He offered condolences with gentle kisses on her neck alternating from one side to the other.

"I think I could fall in love with you, Polly," he said.

Polly felt an unsettling urge to pull away. The nuzzling at her neck made her feel a bit claustrophobic.

"I should go back in. Won't you come?"

Eli declined. A series of stolen kisses left her airy. His adoration reinstalled a confidence to Polly. Back in the kitchen, she finished the coffee, trying to hum the tune that had found its way into her head earlier. It was nowhere to be found. She settled on a simple childhood melody and returned to the salon.

CHAPTER 7

1946

Spring blossomed early into a wet rainy summer. There was little to do outside except get wet. As it was, Polly's one pair of shoes was wearing quickly, as was her patience with perpetually damp stockings. Even a night by the fire never dried them out completely. Her mood matched the drizzly days, while her school marks were something about which to be even more miserable. She was barely passing Latin, and her Greek philosophy paper was returned with a notation that it was "not worth marking—try again."

"Don't worry about it, Pol." Eli petted her head like a child. "You're a mathematician, you don't need the Greeks."

She smiled to let him know she appreciated his effort. She turned her head to nestle into his lap again, hiding her expression of exasperation. *Ridiculous! Of course I need the Greeks. They invented math,* she thought to herself.

"Come on." He jostled her. "Let's go out. You need some cheering up."

"But it's raining, and I should really get back home to study." She started to get up when he pulled her back down onto the sofa beside him. "I should go." Polly knew this pattern well. They would kiss for a while until both their jaws ached. He would grasp at her bosom, over her clothes, while he rubbed up against her, moaning. Sometimes she would help him along. Usually, he would push her hand away, and other times he would hold it there forcefully in place, so she was cuffed like a prisoner in the corner of the couch.

The other girls at the boarding house were virgins. Margaret and Mary were too busy with their studies and the church to think about the complexity of boys. Charlotte, whose world revolved around the fashion industry, was surrounded only by women—or men who were more interested in each other than in her.

After these interludes Polly was left frustrated. There must be more pleasure in it than this, she mused. After all, the romance books Charlotte lent her were full of expressions about fireworks and rapturous bliss. Dorthey would never dream to mention it, and would be tormented with embarrassment if asked any questions. Polly was curious as to what sex really felt like. Was it like the "heightened vibration" Sadie used to describe? It was moments like this she missed her old friend. Sadie would know how to coach her on what to do and say, give her courage to try something else.

As her thighs began to chafe from the friction of his corduroy pants against her nylon stockings, she wanted to bring the whole affair to a quick halt, so she blurted, "I think we should have sex."

Eli stopped in mid-thrust, his belt buckle pressing painfully into her hip. "Pol, you can't be serious." The shock on his face made her feel like a tart. "Are you serious?" His face transformed into a hopeful grin. "If you're sure."

Polly caught a brief glimpse of the power Sadie harnessed when she offered the flirtation of sex. She was an independent metropolitan woman now. "Yes, I'm sure."

She stood up and began to unbutton her blouse.

"Wait!" He raised his hand and hurriedly moved around the apartment, searching for a nub of an old candle that he lit. Then he put a blues album on the record player. "Okay!" He returned breathless.

Thankfully, Mama always taught her that her undergarments needed to be clean and fresh each day. She took the initiative to strip down to her slip, her nicest white bra and panties underneath.

Eli stood across the room from her and hastily undressed. Though they had explored each other under and over clothes and in exposed fragments, this was the first time she had seen him raw. His slight frame and almost hairless pale skin, marked with dozens of dark freckles, shocked her. She felt large in his presence, as if she had drunk some of Alice's growing potion and before her was a fragile hairless cat.

Though Eli had said he had lost his virginity in high school, she could tell he was just as nervous as she was. While they lay on the bed, his hands finding their way clumsily over her body, the overwhelming smell of musk and sweat triggered a pulse of nausea. The small attic apartment smelled musty. She asked to open the window to refresh the room. With a slight sigh of annoyance, he stepped out of bed, his parts shrunk against the cold. Polly considered stopping the evening then, but Eli's eagerness and desire for her overruled.

After several false starts, they were finally successful, the event more awkward than pleasurable. The scratching sounds of mice between the walls distracted her. Even the throbbing pain between her legs was not a bother so much as the disappointment was. She resigned herself to accept that perhaps this was how it was really meant to be, and not how it was in the books. Perhaps pleasure was reserved for woman with sexual appeal like Sadie, and not somebody like her.

That night Polly and Eli joined Charlotte and some of her work friends at a dance club. A dark room that smelled of bourbon and cigars, hidden away in a back alley off Dupont Street, opened up to them behind a metal unmarked door. It was the type of place that if you needed to ask directions to get to, you should not be there. Swing music permeated the small room, making it hard to hear.

"Come on, Polly, let's dance." Charlotte whisked her away to the dance floor where they attempted the jitterbug and the jive.

Eli was reluctant to dance, spending the entire evening at the table drinking gin rickeys. Despite her best encouragement, he refused. "Well, I'm going to go have some fun." She refreshed herself between dances with glasses of minty grasshoppers. Charlotte's two friends, Tom and Matthew, were always on the ready to partner up for a dance.

After an hour or so, she settled in beside Eli to rest, her toes pinched in her kitten-heel shoes. Flushed and breathless from dancing she reached for her drink.

"Don't you think that's enough, Pol? Flirting with every man around?" Eli asked her, a disgusted look on his face.

"What are you referring to, Eli? I'm just having fun." She took a sip of her green drink and nearly choked when she heard him call her an "active crop."

"How dare you suggest that I'm promiscuous!" she cried. There was nothing more she could think of to say. The insult scalded her like a toppled pot of soup on delicate skin.

She crossed her arms and closed her eyes in disbelief. This could not be real. She must have had too much to drink. Perhaps she was actually asleep in bed already and this was all a dream.

"Come on, Polly. Enough sitting. Let's dance." Charlotte's eye darted to Eli, sensing the tension.

"I think I've had enough for tonight. I should be going now."

"Polly, are you okay?" Charlotte scowled at Eli. "Let me grab my things and we'll go." Eli stood up to pull out Polly's chair from the table. "I'll take her, Eli. You can stay. Or go home. Or whatever you want to do." Charlotte waved him away with her hand, then nestled into a quiet exchange with her friends. They nodded their heads while their eyes scrutinized Eli.

"Pol, I'm sorry," Eli whispered in her ear. His physical closeness repulsed her at that moment. "It is just that I love you so much. I was jealous seeing you out there with those guys, having so much fun without me."

Her heart softened a bit. "I was only dancing. I would rather have danced with you."

He took her face in his hands. "Forgive me," he said. It was not a request.

"Eli, what you said was terrible. Especially after today."

"Today was beautiful. You're beautiful." He reached up and took the two side pins out of her hair, releasing the loose waves around her face. "There. That's even better."

Their kiss was interrupted by Charlotte's abrupt tone. "Let's go. I think we've all had enough of things for tonight."

On the taxi ride home, Charlotte asked only one question. "Are you all right?" They said very little otherwise.

When the lights went out that night, and they each lay in their bed trying to fall asleep, Charlotte piped up with one additional notation, "He isn't good enough for you, Polly. You deserve somebody better."

Polly pretended to be asleep.

It had been several months since Polly and Eli had begun to sleep together. Margaret, who was now specializing in diseases of the blood, took on the responsibility of schooling Polly in the use of a diaphragm to avoid pregnancy.

"You're lucky you haven't gotten pregnant yet," she scolded when she'd learned a quarter of a year had gone by without the use of one. "What were you thinking, Polly?"

"I was curious," Polly sheepishly answered, upset at her own carelessness. Truly, it was curiosity more than anything. She had yet to experience the exultation that she read about in the romance books. Now she consented mostly out of boredom or to turn Eli's foul mood around. When her friends asked how it was, Polly embellished the romance. She shared none of the disappointment with them.

The fall semester was intense. She had already overstayed her time at Kata's, and her mother was pestering her to come home. "One year, then you were to come home and prepare for the rest of your life." That had been the agreement. Though Polly's living expenses were covered by her tutoring, tuition and books no longer were. She did not qualify to extend her scholarship due to her poor grades.

Papa only knew that a second year was not offered. "Hmph. Wait until your thesis receives critical acclaim, then they'll offer you a full scholarship to stay on, perhaps even teach."

Father was supportive of her staying on for a few more months based on her accounts of school success and endless music rehearsals. It troubled her deeply to lie to them. They visited once that summer—a day trip to avoid the cost of a hotel.

Eli had joined them for lunch. Both Mama and Papa had been quiet. They did little to engage him in conversation. After Papa paid the bill, he nodded at Eli and said, "Good to meet you. We'll be off now so Polly can show us the campus. Enjoy your day." It was clear he was not welcome to join them.

They walked quietly for a few blocks. Mama was the first to speak. "A first relationship can be very exciting, *minushka*. I am sure he is very nice. But he is not for you." The conversation now open, she peppered Polly with questions. "What kind of a career is art history? What do you know of his family?" Her mother was adamant that she needed to think about her children. "What kind of father do you think he would be?" She then added as if it held any relevance at all to love, "He's too short. It makes for an odd-looking couple."

Polly protested. In defense of Eli, she spoke of his intelligence, worldliness, and when she realized she was not making any gains, she downplayed their relationship to being simply friends, like Oliver. Her relationship with Eli was nothing like the easy friendship she had with Oliver. She swallowed back the words, which felt like a terrible betrayal to both herself and her kind friend.

"You can stay on for this year to finish your paper, but then it is home, whether it is done or not." Her father was stern. "Don't disappoint me, Paulina." He paused before finishing. "Also, there are two conditions to staying. You begin attending church regularly as we do back home. And, you do not see that boy again." His words were final.

"Fine," Polly agreed. She would concede to any request if allowed to stay in the city and salvage what she could of her academic career.

Time with Eli was increasingly routine. They would visit the Grange, which no longer held her interest like it used to. Her once favorite place that had made a splendid escape no matter the situation, now felt constrained. Even when she tried to go alone to recapture the allure of the tea room, Eli would find her there. Details on the ornamental rugs preoccupied Polly's mathematical mind in calculated geometric patterns while she awaited her tea and scones—a preferable pastime to making conversation with the man seated across from her.

These days, when they would wander the museum to view the art, Eli would again tell her stories about each painting as if it was the first time, annoyed when she didn't show enthusiasm for his lessons.

"There are plenty of women who would appreciate an afternoon like this, Pol. You seem to be getting rather full of yourself," he said to her during one of these times, in a show of bitterness.

Other days they would take picnics between her music lessons. He would surprise her with bakery treats and chocolate, telling her how much he loved her. They would discuss what life would be like in the future. Increasingly, though, she struggled to place him in her plans.

"You are my love, my lady, my lover," he would remind her. Speaking as if she was a possession, like an automobile.

Several times she tried to coax Kata into telling her more about her mama as a young woman. The few stories she knew of contrasted starkly with the serious Mama she knew, who always seemed to carry a bundle of worry around with her. Perhaps she was wiser than Polly knew. Men only wanted one thing from a woman, and a woman's best chance in life was to marry. She could marry Eli, couldn't she? He was unkind at times, but she knew she could be difficult and provoking. She was quickly losing her academic status. A future in academia was seeming less likely with each month that passed. Mostly, though, she had given herself to him. No longer a virgin, what was she to do? Other men would frown upon her if they knew. Poor Sadie, she thought. How was she surviving as a single mother in the city?

To salvage any hope for an independent life, she knew she needed to focus and finish the semester strong. No more dance clubs and cinemas with Charlotte. Eli would have to manage with less of her time. She was heading home for Christmas, and Dr. Proust was expecting great things from her, as was everybody else. Oliver would be home this holiday; the thought of explaining to him this terrible conundrum she had twisted for herself, threw her into a fit of worry. She was no longer confident she could find the path back, but she owed it to herself to at least try.

CHAPTER 8

1946

Lulled by the rumble of the train, Polly drifted into a shallow bout of sleep that was haunted with disturbing dreams. Polly willed the reprieve of sleep that never came, but only lightly grazed her mind at night over these last few months. It had been since last Christmas that she visited home, and months since the day trip her parents took to the city to see her. Letters to her parents had grown infrequent, and phone calls even more rare despite her parents having a new dedicated line installed. She sat through enough lectures at school, such that she avoided her mother's as much as possible.

Petar worked long hours at the quarry. They had hardly spoken since her annual holiday trip home last year. Dorthey remained as bright and cheerful as ever, with two children and a third on the way. Polly welcomed the weekly letters recounting Dorthey's daily tribulations of motherhood, town gossip, and nothing but admiration for her husband. Doubt had been in the mind of many, including Dorthey's parents, about the success of their marriage—many being convinced that she would tire quickly of being a poor man's wife despite the appeal of Petar's sculpted physique. To everyone's surprise, Dorthey remained ever enamored with her husband.

Eli was puckered with sourness about her departure, feeling unappreciated and disrespected by not having an invitation extended to him by the Williams family to join them over the holidays. His own family did not celebrate many of the Christian holidays. His father an atheist and his mother Jewish, he recounted Christmas Eve dinners listening to the radio, and holiday mornings that stopped being magical once his parents told him at the age of six that Santa Claus was not real. He opted to stay in the city and work on the winter curriculum instead.

Polly welcomed the time to herself. Between the boarding house, school, teaching lessons, and Eli, she had very little time alone. Her holiday wish was for endless hours of walks in solitude on the trails behind her house. Her previous evening with Eli had been tense.

Jostled awake by the man in the seat beside her, who said she was moaning in distress, she was relieved to be released from her recurring dream. Every week for months now she dreamed of being locked in a glass box with only enough room to roll over. The box often, but not always, in a white room with only a table and chair in the corner, had thirteen air holes punched into the top. In her dream she would maddeningly recount the number, driven to a panic by the odd number and random placement of the holes. Always she awoke gasping for air, surprised that she was still alive.

She graciously thanked the man, as hers was also the next stop. She looked at her swollen feet squishing out of the tops of her brown pumps. Her dress fit snuggly across the chest and back. The style looser under the bra line, giving her more room to breathe. She began to gather her small blue suitcase, her violin case, and her school bag filled with her dissertation papers. Her red wool coat gave her security in covering up her figure. She donned her black leather gloves and red hat with fur trim.

She descended the train steps, welcoming the frigid December air. The smell of snow and evergreens notable in contrast to the concrete and exhaust of the city.

"Polly!"

She heard her name called from down the platform. Dorthey ran toward her with outstretched arms, Petar following with his long strides behind her. The two embraced like magnets, holding each other tightly. An unspoken exchange of stories and missed moments caught up between them.

"You look so lovely! Your cheeks are rosy. And the color of that coat is astonishing on you." Dorthey admired her, while Petar gave her a brotherly kiss on the cheek and took her suitcase.

"Welcome home, Polly. Mama and Papa are so excited to see you." He smiled with that deep warm affection that they had shared since childhood.

"Look at those elegant stockings, and such a darling little bag! Whatever do you put in such a tiny thing?" Dorthey inquired.

"It really only has room for some change, and a few personal items."

"Seems hardly worth the hassle of carrying it," Petar added.

"Eli bought it for me." Polly directed her comment to Dorthey, knowing her brother would likely roll his eyes.

"Well, I think it is very fashionable and matches so perfectly with your attire."

They looped arms and strode slowly to the car, savoring each exclusive step together.

"And your hair! You cut it so short. It looks so stylish."

"It's a poodle perm. Eli thought it would look good on me. I'm still getting accustomed to it." She flattened the puff on the top of her head to take down its ostentatious height. "It's a lot more work than my usual simple wash, brush, and pin routine."

The lake, on the drive home, was angry. The gray waves peaked wildly, smashing against the rocks like cymbals. Clouds filled the sky in rapidly moving creamy layers. They were smeared thick like buttercream icing. Dorthey chatted the whole way home with updates on little Teddy, who was now talking and curious beyond his two years. Baby Sonja, who slept and suckled all day contentedly, was apparently in no rush to engage in the chaos of the big-people world just yet.

Petar had spent the last year building them a house in the new section of town. A two-story home in red brick with central heat, and a large backyard. Away from the core of the town, there was space for the children to run, plus enough for a sitting area, varietal fruit and vegetable garden, and one of those cement fountains adorned with cherubs that Dorthey admired from magazine pictures of Italy and France.

Throughout the drive, Dorthey had been running updates on the various comings and goings of the people in the town, to which Polly only half listened. Her mind drifted to another time, when solitary walks along the lake with her paper and pen to do calculations or score music passed many splendid hours.

"Did you hear about Walter, the handsome captain of the rowing team?"

The name ignited a roll of anxiety in Polly and stirred a fury inside her that she had tucked away in the cracks of her memory. Not even to Dorthey had she shared the details of that night in the park, vowing instead to keep the terror and humiliation to herself.

"He died. Car accident one night crossing a train track. Left behind a wife and a daughter." Dorthey took Petar's hand in hers in gratitude that such tragedy had not been theirs. "He was apparently becoming a big-deal lawyer in Toronto with plans to run for provincial parliament at the next election before his passing."

After the initial shock of hearing his name, Polly imagined a book closing in her mind. A story she could now end. The slight feeling of justice and lack of sorrow frightened her. Immediately, she pushed it away, thinking of his poor wife and daughter, hoping he only showed the best of himself to them.

"And his wife, where is she?"

"She's a society lady in the city. Comes from a wealthy family. Her father's a big steel tycoon. Apparently, after the mandatory six weeks of grieving, she was back at events and parties. Trying to return to the normal life of a twenty-four-year-old, I guess. It would be a shame if she played widow for the rest of her years." Dorthey stared at Petar for a moment. She released her hand that still held his tightly to stroke the back of his head like a mother would a baby. "Though if I ever lost you, I couldn't image ever being able to step out of my misery."

He smiled lovingly at her. Polly diverted her eyes, uncomfortable in witnessing their private moment.

Nothing had changed about her parents' house. The shutters still sat slightly crooked and were in need of painting. The doormat that once was a burnt-red color had been reduced to a worn-out amber. Rugs and furniture had been the same since the time they moved in. It all seemed quite dull and old. Encapsulated in a fixed moment in time, the scene brought both comfort from its predictability and sadness from its stagnation. At least the room smelled of cinnamon. Her mother must have baked her favorite cake.

"Polly!" Her father greeted her with warm hugs, the smell of his sweet pipe and his dusty tweed jacket making her feel like a little girl again. She remembered dangling her legs over the couch as she nestled against him while he marked papers.

After a slight banging sound in the kitchen, her mother emerged in her usual bright red dress marking the festive time of year. She still looked fresh and beautiful.

"*Minushka*, so wonderful to have you home." She gave Polly a long hug. After a scrutinizing moment she added, "You've put on some weight. What is Kata feeding you?" She pinched Polly's waistline. "That hair is not a good style for you. And that bright red lipstick makes you look like a woman who earns her living on the streets." She handed Polly a tissue.

"Kasia, please. Polly just arrived home. Come, darling. Sit. Tell us about your school. I know Professor Proust is waiting for you today to discuss your dissertation, but take a few minutes to join us," her father said in his usually supportive way.

Mama brought out tea with cinnamon cake already plated, the smallest slice of which she offered Polly. They discussed the boarding house: the attic too cold, never enough hot water to wash her hair, an ample supply of students to tutor, and reassurance that the responsibility was not distracting her from her studies. She avoided the topic of Eli, knowing her parents disapproved of him.

"And your music? Play us something new," Papa said excitedly, like a child about to receive a long-awaited gift.

"I don't have anything new, Papa." His concerned look pushed her to say more. "I am just so busy with my advanced classes that I have little time to myself to compose. I am usually so tired and the house is such chaos that even keeping up with my playing is a challenge."

"Well, play something for us anyway. I have missed so much the sound of music in this house since you've been gone." He took the violin out of its case, and with a worried look, brushed off the accumulated dust.

She finished her small piece of cake in one large mouthful, wiped her hands daintily on the napkin, and took the foreign-feeling violin into her hands. Slowly, she led into the joyful brackets of Mendelsohn's violin concerto, her tempo slower than the usual exuberant propulsion that made this one of her favorite pieces. She missed a few notes as she stepped into the quieter, dramatic contrast. Her fingers felt stiff. She scrunched her face, longing to find the bursts of orange color that usually filled her mind with this section. After several agonizing minutes she brought the piece to a close.

"I'm tired," she said, deflated.

Her family allowed her the excuse. To escape the forlorn worry on her parents' faces, she suggested it was time she meet Professor Proust. As her thesis supervisor, she sent him regular chapters of her work, and they met whenever they were in the same city.

"*Minushka*, you should freshen up before you go. Change and wash your face."

Polly ignored her mother's suggestions, less out of defiance and more out of frustration that this was her best dress that still fit her. She wiped off her lipstick with the tissue in her pocket and draped a black scarf over her head, the tails resting elegantly along her shoulders.

The walk through the park invigorated her. A semblance of strength and resolve returned with each breath of frigid winter air. Being home felt good. The echo of rambunctious lake waves trembled through the air, still warding off the looming freeze destined to come later in the winter. Soon people would venture out on skates and skis across the lake. Inevitably, a rebellious youth or daring fisherman would impatiently test the ice too soon, or longingly stay out too late in the season and fall through. Some survived, others were only surmised to have been swallowed by the water. "Penance for their recklessness" was the town phrase for when they lost somebody.

She paused outside of the professor's office, searching through her well-worn satchel, the one item she would not replace with one of Eli's gifts. Between fancy pastries and boxes of Laura Secord chocolates each week, it was no wonder she needed a new wardrobe. Her meager earnings barely covered her tuition and books, plus what she owed Kata each month. Charlotte did her best to alter what she could. Truthfully, her attire no longer matched her lifestyle.

"You deserve the most beautiful clothes," Eli would say with each small gift he gave. He never included her in the shopping but would ask the shop girls to try the items on for him. "The dress looked wonderful on the saleslady in the store. Really showed off her voluptuous curves," he would say. "I got you a few sizes bigger because of your wider hips and square waist." He would often add such unnecessary details to the story. He shopped in the Asian markets where clothes were cheap and the styles gauche, designed for petite frames. She disliked the embellishments on the clothes he chose—too many frills, the colors too bright, the skirts too narrow.

"Well, Pol, you can't expect beautiful clothes to do all the work. You have to try too," he retorted curtly when she made her opinion known. Then he would sulk. "If you don't like them, I'm sure I can find another woman who will appreciate all that I do.".

"I do appreciate them, darling. It's just that I prefer to select my own clothes. Find things that reflect me a bit more."

"No other man would ever treat you as well as I do, Pol. Nobody. I let you study and teach. I spoil you with gifts and treats. Any other man would have you locked in the house, cooking and cleaning."

They would banter back and forth like this for a little while, until eventually they ended up in bed reconciled and reassuring each other that they were loved.

She took a moment to realign her girdle and smooth her hair before knocking. Professor Proust remained the same man of stern demeanor, but kind eyes.

"Ms. Williams, please be seated." He wasted no time with pleasantries, diving directly into business. "You are months behind on your thesis still. I haven't seen chapters in weeks, and what you did send me in this last installment was rudimentary drivel."

Polly pulled her meager pile of papers from her bag and began her defense. He graciously accepted the pile, placing it at the corner of his desk to be ignored, and gently raised his hand to signal it was not yet her turn to speak.

"You have exhausted your postponement options for your thesis. If you do not complete it by the spring, all will be lost."

Polly hung her head. In her misery, she lost all ability to muster a defense. She had failed. There was no justification for her underperformance.

"Paulina, is all well with you? Perhaps it is time you come home, finish your paper here where you can focus and reconnect with your work in a significant way."

The grandfatherly compassion in his voice pulled at her. He looked at her with the same knowing expression of the night with Walter in the park. Desperately, she wanted to talk to somebody about how she had been feeling, a mixture of excitement at all the new things she was learning about the world, suspended in the heaviness of loss for all that she was once able to do but could no longer find within herself. She doubted whether she would ever again feel the excitement of new ideas or see the colors in her music. Perhaps she was only a precocious child who had now caught up with her potential, and was destined to simply be ordinary.

Stoically, she refused to attest to defeat. "I'll get it done, Professor Proust. My final draft will be to you for review by winter's thaw." The promise frightened her. There was much work ahead of her, she knew. He handed her back the papers from the corner, unread. She committed at that moment to not disappoint him. Though he was hard on her, he took faith in giving her an opportunity when so many others turned away. She would get this done.

The idea of going home suffocated her. She opted for a walk by the lake instead, opposite the direction of her parents' house. When she got back to Toronto, she knew she would need to make some changes. Focus more on school and less on Eli. Some space would do them good. Though she believed she loved him, she felt smothered. He always waited for her after classes. He got upset if she chose to go to the cinema with Charlotte instead of spending an evening playing cards with him. Even the salon evenings lost their intoxication as he whispered to her not to be so showy or flirty or pretentious.

"Proper ladies don't behave that way, Pol. You need to know how to get along better in society if you plan to be a success," he would scold her.

After an hour of walking, she planted herself on a rock overlooking the water. The delight of the powerful water crashing against the shoreline took her over. It was the clash of texture between the water and the sky that broke the illusion of endlessness created by the merging gray colors. Snow would be coming shortly; she could smell it in the air. Still, she couldn't bring herself to go home. Withdrawing a pencil from her bag and scribbling on the back of her thesis—the only paper she carried with her at the time—a song emerged for the first time in months. It held a darkness previously unfamiliar in her work. Today, it seemed fitting and brought her a comforting solace.

The initial hues of charcoal and navy that flashed once again in her mind gave way to a burst of yellow. That would be the moment a cymbal would clash in her symphony. She was overtaken by the guttural rumble of the tubas and brooding wails of the saxophones that played in her ears. A jazz-infused beat, inspired by the live music played in the run-down historic buildings turned dining lounges that she and Charlotte explored—found its way onto the page. Her heart filled with the same exhilaration that she felt those nights, dancing away with Eli, drinking cocktails, and getting to know people with whom she would never otherwise cross paths.

Oblivious to the falling snow until her pages began to tear from wetness, Polly huddled under her scarf until she finished the opening allegro. Flushed with new enthusiasm, she ran home, her stomach grumbling for her mother's goulash.

The two weeks in Kingston went by nicely. The music, though, did not return for her to continue working on the symphony. She did enjoy spending time with Teddy and Sonja. The angelic way her niece drifted to sleep as she played lullabies on her violin, and the exalted applause her nephew offered when she was done, reminded her how much she wished to have children of her own one day.

Eli phoned every night, sometimes twice, to remind her he loved her. He inquired about her trip and shared that the world was dull without her. Their calls were short due to the long-distance costs. Polly tried to be first to answer the phone, explaining to her parents it was Charlotte calling, or something related to school. Once when she was out, Papa answered and took a message, which he forgot to give her, sending Eli into a spin of angst. "He did it intentionally, Pol, because he doesn't like me. You know I love you more than anybody could."

Polly welcomed every opportunity to step away from Mama's watchful eye. Criticized that she had gained too much weight, that she was not getting enough sleep, or that she was wasting her youth weighed heavy in the house between them. Father accused her of being dishonest about Eli. If they were just friends, he was calling an awful lot. To escape she would walk by the lake alone, or find her usual corner at the university library to delve into her thesis with a renewed enthusiasm. On this day, a welcome voice roused her out of her deep concentration.

"I thought I might find you here." Oliver peeked his head around the corner of the bookshelves. "Do you have time to step away from work for a bit of a walk?"

"I would love that!" Polly had seen little of him so far since being home. Oliver had returned from England to visit his family for the holidays, but things between the two of them were stiff. They had both carried on with their lives in very different directions. She couldn't help but notice how handsome of a man he had become. His eyes, ever bright, drew her in. Even his recessed jawline had filled out, giving him an aristocratic air.

They walked among the university buildings, fondly recollecting their time there together.

"How is London? You must love it!" There was a longing in Polly's voice.

"I do, very much. My apartment in Fitzrovia is quite spacious. The library—"

"You have your own library?"

"I do. With big bright windows, just the way you like it. My friends are all Eton- and Oxford-educated men who come from long lines of wealth and royal linkages. When I share stories about us growing up here, they tell me I am recapping a storybook. They think it all rather bucolic. With you, they are all incredibly fascinated. A female genius, talented in so many ways."

"I am no genius." She blushed, feeling unentitled to the descriptor. "You tell them about me?"

"Of course. They hear about you all the time." He paused, staring down at the ground. "My work is interesting, though top-secret so I can't say much about it. You would enjoy working for the national defense department, Polly! It has all the intrigue of being a spy without any of the risk."

He knew her well. "A spy! Perhaps I could be a code cracker or, even better, a war strategist." She exhaled a large sigh that surprised even her.

Gently, Oliver looped her hand through his arm and held it against his bicep. "You seem unlike yourself, Polly. Sad."

"Oh, Oliver. I am just not sure any more about school, work, my music . . ." She let the sentence hang. She did not want to talk about Eli. "But let's not ruin a perfectly good day on my boring life. Tell me more about London."

With Mama watching the children, the foursome of Polly and Oliver, and Dorthey and Petar, had plenty of time that week to play cards and go to the cinema. They celebrated the new year at the dance hall, where Oliver and Polly showed off their well-practiced swing dance. The couples retreated to Petar and Dorthey's house in the early hours to open a bottle of real French champagne, compliments of Oliver.

"What will 1947 look like for you, Polly?" Oliver asked, topping up her glass with the enchanting crystalline pale-yellow drink. The solitary stream of bubbles escaping to the top fascinated her.

"I don't know. I hope to finish my thesis, then look for work, maybe."

Oliver looked at her with an intensity that stripped away all bravado and façade. "Hope? Maybe? These are not usual words in the vernacular of one Ms. Paulina Williams. What happened to words like, *I shall achieve, I can accomplish?*" He left the thought short, cautious not to intrude too far.

"Polly will do amazing things. Don't you worry. She'll finish her thesis and marry Eli. They'll travel the world doing all those exotic things she always talks about, like eating raw fish and going to exclusive art exhibits." Always the optimist, Dorthey sipped her ginger ale.

"Is Eli the bloke you told me about?" Oliver directed the question to Petar, who nodded. Petar's displeasure was ill-concealed.

Polly put down her unfinished champagne glass and excused herself to bed. Her tummy was a bit upset, she said, and she was going to go sleep in Teddy's room as planned, since he was with his grandparents tonight. Dorthey blew her kisses from across the room, where she was nestled on Petar's lap like a cat. Oliver gave her a kiss on the cheek and bid her sweet dreams.

Still fully dressed, Polly curled up under the blue-and-red-plaid bed cover. A cocktail of confusion and angst with a twist of fear bubbled inside her. After two gentle taps on the door, Dorthey let herself in and sat on the edge of the bed.

"Do you want to talk?" was all she said.

Until dawn they stayed up. Polly spoke through tears and anger until she had exhausted all the pent-up stress that had been eroding her insides. Dorthey, for the most part, listened.

"I don't have the answers for you, Polly,' she confessed. "I do know that you are capable of greatness, and it shall find you so long as you remain true to yourself. Sometimes things finish their purpose for being in our lives, and we need to know when to let them go so we can make room for better things."

On her last evening in town, Teddy was afflicted by a slight fever and Dorthey was exhausted from being up all evening with him and the baby. This left Polly and Oliver to go to the cinema on their own. *A Streetcar Named Desire* was a movie they had both previously seen but each adored for different reasons: he for Marlon Brando's brooding love of a woman, and she for Stella's tormented soul.

Leisurely, they walked home in the bright reflection of the moon. Large flakes of snow entertained them in a twirling dance, until they landed and melted against their warm coats. Polly linked her arm through Oliver's, as had become their custom. He placed his hand over hers, securing it into place at the crux of his elbow. Tonight, the gesture was filled with an intimacy that made her uncomfortable when she thought of her commitment to Eli. She casually withdrew, putting her hands in her pockets instead.

"Polly, are you really going to marry Eli?" Oliver asked self-consciously.

"Oh, Ollie, I don't know. He talks about it all the time, but hasn't officially asked me as of yet."

He laughed.

"What's so funny? Marriage is not a laughing matter." She was riled. "I have given this topic much thought. You have to think about what forever may be like with somebody."

"No, it is not that. It is just . . . you called me Ollie. After years, this is the first time you called me Ollie." He coaxed her hand out of her pocket and held it in his. As she tried to pry it away, he offered, "Don't worry, Polly. My intentions are purely platonic. I respect that you are with another man." He paused to decide whether to continue. "Though, I must admit, I always thought that you and I would someday marry. Ever since you deprived me of my right to that well-earned kiss, I swore that I would reap the reward one day, unqualified and not bartered. Simply because you wanted to."

She turned her face to him and looked wistfully into his eyes. "You know I love you so. I am not sure we are well matched, though. Your secretive work abroad and poor taste in music, and my stubbornness and poor sense of style. I would not fit well at all into your posh London world." She laughed, light and free.

"I know, Polly. Your beautiful piano playing lost on my tone-deaf ears. My wonderful cooking unappreciated by your mediocre palate."

They laughed and slowed their pace. Walking through the snowy streets of Kingston felt like the world had stopped, and only they existed together in that moment. Polly felt her happiest self in a very long time.

Right into the next morning, as she boarded the train, she smiled from a comforting peace that had generated inside of her these two weeks. The evening with Ollie was a perfect end to an enjoyable holiday.

Eli waited for her at the station, a bouquet of flowers and a box of chocolates in his hand.

"Thank you, Eli!" She gave him an obligatory kiss, offering words of consolation about how the trip was boring, how much she had missed him. He suggested they return to his apartment so they could make up for weeks of missed lovemaking, but she declined. Classes started the next day and she needed to prepare.

The frequency with which they saw each other remained sporadic. She had not shared her new class schedule with him yet, so was able to escape to the library for dedicated work time without interruption. He would seek her out at times, finding her in the hidden back corners. Between the stacks of books, he would steal kisses and grope her. At times, he tried to entice her to go further, hidden by the shelves in the theology section where few people ever came. The sense of intrusion into her world and sacrilege of conducting oneself in such a deplorable manner in public grated on her.

With a new focus on her work, she would often lock herself in her room on Friday nights to study. The stairwell, guarded by Kata's sharp eyes, prevented Eli from inappropriately wandering upstairs. Eventually he stopped attending the salons.

They continued to see each other on Saturday evenings for a movie or dinner. Soon accusations began that her diminished affection toward him, since returning from the Christmas holidays, was proof that her parents had finally turned her against him. "They never did like me much because I am not bourgeois. They never accepted me, Pol. You must see that their prejudice against me has turned you from my love. You're letting them control your life."

"I must get my thesis done by March!" she hollered, fed up with his constant sulking. "I cannot have all these distractions, Eli. I must get back to focusing on my work."

"For what, Pol? You'll never work. Women don't work." He bent down on one knee and took her hand. "Marry me, Paulina. Marry me, and we'll live happily together. I'll give you everything you need. You can write music and tutor our children."

"I *shall* work!" she said emphatically. "I shall work and become a professor someday. I just need to finish my thesis." Funneling all the frustration she felt in her suffocated heart into a strong grip, she squeezed tight to avoid the temptation of slapping his face.

"I ask you to marry me and your answer is *I want to work*," he retorted, hurt and bewildered.

"Eli, I just can't think about marriage until I finish my thesis," she replied in a measured tone.

"Well, say yes to marrying me. You can finish your thesis after the ceremony. We can have kids right away. That will give you great joy and distraction. You said you loved being with your niece and nephew." His words spun quickly, like Rumpelstiltskin.

"No, Eli. I am not ready yet. My work is important to me right now."

"Your work!" He grew hot. She recognized this tone and knew that the words that flew afterwards would be ill-considered and quickly forgotten. "Your work means nothing, Polly. You'll never amount to anything. You aren't nearly as smart as you think you are. The only reason you have gotten this far is because every man just wants to get into your pants. Is that why you came back from holidays so happy? Did that professor of yours find his way into the most private of your parts in exchange for promising you a PhD?"

She stood solid like a wall, letting the rotten words he threw at her drip down like egg albumin. She quietly grabbed her bag and stepped toward the door.

"Pol . . . don't go. I'm sorry. I didn't mean it." He stood between her and the door. "It is just that I love you so much. I feel you pulling away and I am losing my mind out of fear that you're letting all we have disappear." He began to sob quietly.

"Eli, I must go now." She nudged him to the side, clearing the door for her escape.

She stepped outside and walked two blocks before she slid into an isolated alley. Braced against a brick wall, she screamed. Her rage escaped through every crack that had formed over the years in her soul. The cats scurried away. Even the rats hid out of fear of this unknown animal who howled.

Several weeks went by during which she ignored all of Eli's calls and letters. His declaration of love turned to desperate pleading, and eventually to unforgivably vile and cruel words filled with hatred and despair, the self-loathing, evident to her now in his actions and gestures. Kata eventually began intercepting the letters, until she ultimately had a word with Eli, after which he ceased to try to contact her altogether.

Polly was busy working on the final chapters of her thesis. Late nights blended into long days until she was finally finished. Proud of her accomplishment, she couriered the 120-page document to Professor Proust one week ahead of schedule.

The following week, she spent most of her days sleeping, recovering from the exhaustion. When she noticed her period was late in January, she assumed it was from stress. She checked her calendar and noticed another two months had now passed without her monthly cycle.

"You used your protection?" Margaret was the first person she told.

"Of course. Every time. I insisted on it, even when Eli tried to tell me it wasn't needed."

"You're sure?" Margaret looked quizzically at her. "Let me see it."

"My diaphragm?" Polly felt this was beyond normal, an intrusion into her most intimate matters.

"I'm a doctor. I do this stuff all the time." Margaret read her apprehension.

Polly retrieved it from her purse and handed it to Margaret still in its container. She took it to the bathroom and filled it with water.

"What are you doing?"

"Checking for holes," she said matter-of-factly.

"Holes? How would a hole form in it?"

She lifted the diaphragm, now filled with water. They both watched as a steady drop fell from the small hole intentionally pierced in the center. Polly saw her whole world slide down the side of the sink and into the drain.

CHAPTER 9

1947

Absentmindedly, Polly stopped on the sidewalk in the midst of the busy pedestrian traffic of Avenue Road. She bumped by passers-by, who politely apologized before continuing on to their important destinations. She checked the address Margaret had written down in large block letters. Dr. Garrett was a colleague, and from the ease of their conversation over the phone, Polly assumed their relationship was closer than just work.

The office was on the top floor of a three-story house that had been converted into business spaces. The narrow stairwell allowed for only a single person through at a time. A woman, accompanied by an older lady, paused on the second-floor landing to allow Polly to pass. The woman's large belly and swollen ankles stuffed into a pair of high heels gave the impression that she might tumble straight down. Polly wondered if Dr. Garrett ever considered switching suites with the dentist on the first floor for the ease of his patients.

When she entered the office, the reassuring smell of antiseptic greeted her. It gave a short-lived comfort of cleanliness and order before her nausea was triggered. A small Asian lady with a heavy accent greeted her at the desk. Her poor annunciation and notably restricted smile, which conspicuously hid a mouth full of crooked yellowed teeth, made her speech difficult to understand.

A gentle gesture toward the waiting area was her best attempt to communicate.

Polly sat, as instructed, choosing the chair in the corner hidden from the waiting room entrance. A few fashion magazines were fanned out in a circle on the table, with a small thirsty plant at the center. She flipped through one carelessly, and then replaced it, careful to adjust it evenly in the wheel.

After a few minutes she was ushered into a room by the receptionist. Polly believed she was instructed to undress and cover herself with the yellow gown that was neatly folded on the examination table, though she couldn't be sure. Outside of receiving her smallpox and whooping cough vaccines as a child, Polly had not been to a doctor's office, and never by herself.

A rapid double knock on the door, and then Dr. Garrett entered the room in his white coat, a black stethoscope draped in physician fashion around his neck. He stood nearly six feet tall, with large hands, dark ebony skin, and a radiant white smile that immediately settled her nerves.

"Ms. Williams, a pleasure to meet you." His accent, perhaps Nigerian, expressed a cheerful but competent nature. After shaking her hand, he settled onto the stool by the desk. "Margaret told me about your situation. Unmarried, unintended pregnancy, and perhaps a little unhappy." His voice was soft, non-judgmental. His eyes sympathetic. Polly knew why Margaret liked him.

He examined her, confirming her suspicion that she was nine weeks pregnant, then excused himself to allow her to get dressed. In the few moments of silence, alone in the room with nothing but the nakedness of her body, she grieved. Hands resting on her bloated bump, she finally released the idea that, up until now, had held her strong. It was the remote possibility that this truly was only stress. Replacing it was a feeling of being a little bird with a broken wing, unable to fly, everything programmed into her natural instinct frustratingly unattainable. The world was very different from this vantage point, on the ground. Sadie entered her mind. She still thought about her old friend from time to time, looking for her face in the street among strangers. Sadie had been the one to teach her about adult things in life: fashion, sex, people politics, and owning your own power. She wished her friend was here now. She would know what to do, having been a pregnant single woman herself.

Two knocks. He kindly gave her a breath to compose herself before coming in. She turned off the light in her mind that illuminated the memories of the playful nights dancing with her friends at the jazz clubs, and late-night private conversations in the attic room. Buried were the dreams of thrilling new mathematical discoveries, symphony performances, and her professorship. They had no place in this broken-winged world.

"Ms. Williams, as far as I can tell, you have a healthy pregnancy." He paused to scrutinize her. Hesitantly, he proceeded. "You have options."

He began with keeping the baby and raising it as a single mother or considering adoption. He monitored her reaction to his words closely. Polly sat stiffly, playing with her thumbs. She did not look at him. She turned each option around in her mind, studying it with the same objectivity and calculated probability she would her logic puzzles.

"Miscarriage?" she asked, awash with immediate guilt. She could not meet his gaze horrified at her words of wishing her own baby away.

"About one-third of pregnancies do end in miscarriage in the first trimester. At this time, there seems to be no indication of that." He leaned in closer. "There is the option of abortion."

"I couldn't do that." She drew her line. Wishing for God to intervene and take this baby away was already on the brink of a raging river that she uncomfortably approached. Actively stripping away the life inside her was a fall that she did not think she could survive. She reached for the cross slung around her neck on a delicate gold chain that Margaret had given her the previous week.

He nodded. "I recommend you take one of these every day," he said and offered her a bottle of vitamins. "I shall see you again in a few months."

He declined any payment for the visit, for which she profusely thanked him. She stepped out of the dark wood–paneled building, into the bright sunlight. Spring was starting to peek through. Her heavy winter coat was not needed today. Her belly still did not show under the insulating layers of indulgence put on over the prior year. Still, she hugged her coat tightly around her.

Whatever became of Sadie? she wondered. The last time they saw each other in the hotel lobby, her sallow skin and limp hair were a shadow of her previous exuberant self. Her child would be near two years old by now. She had no way of finding her. How she wished she had her old friend back, and her old life.

With aching feet and tight calves, she continued to walk, her high-heeled shoes blistering her skin. The pain felt necessary. She walked to, and then continued past the Grange. Its usual comfort no longer appealed to her, sullied by memories of Eli. After two hours she found herself distractedly standing in front of the familiar house. The upper floor window had always been there. Today, it held a presence as if never seen before. She knew the view out to this street, to the very spot she stood. Staring back up from the outside for the first time, she felt a foreboding. The dank smell, tight quarters, and heavy air bringing on panic.

"Polly?" The voice was sweet and childlike. "I knew you would come back."

Eli ran his hand down her arm, and nestled his fingers between hers. "Is everything okay? You look . . . terrible," he said with genuine concern.

"Good. I'm good." Polly looked at the ground.

"Do you want to come in? We can talk."

Hesitantly she looked up, his midnight blue eyes glossy with tears. "I don't think I should," she said.

They stood like two statues in the middle of the sidewalk. To anybody who walked by, an array of possible stories could be unfolding between these two young people. Unlikely were strangers to think of the mythologic flavor of their relationship full of love, deceit, anger, pain, and passion that brewed in a deep chasm of their broken selves.

"I should go." Polly eased her hands away, hiding them in her coat pockets.

"I love you still and always." He dug her hands out, holding them both to his heart. "Please forgive me. I felt you pulling away from me and I reacted because I was so scared of losing you."

She scrutinized every detail of his face. Beyond the midnight blue eyes, she searched for what this child would look like. The slant of his nose slightly to the left, the thin, almost straight lines of his lips hidden by the too-small moustache. The thinness of his face and fragile bone structure. The dimple when he smiled, on his right cheek. The dark waves of his healthy thick hair. She saw him—every vulnerable piece of the little boy inside who wanted so desperately to be loved but felt so unworthy of it.

"I should go," she said again. Her eyes scanning over him one more time.

"Can we at least meet for lunch?"

She nodded without saying a word.

"Tomorrow, noon, at the Grange! Meet you there." He quickly gave her a kiss on the cheek. "We belong together, Polly. You'll forgive me, and I'll be better because of your love. We can be happy. Really happy. If we both try."

She felt sorry for him. In his earnestness, he revealed the lonely sad soul within him. Polly pulled her hands away forcefully, gave a silent wave, and headed home. The punishment of her wandering was no longer necessary. Home to rest was where she now needed to be. Before she turned in for the night, she called the phone operator to find the number for Mr. and Mrs. Johnstone in Belleville, looking for Sadie.

After a fitful night's sleep, Polly rose early. Quietly preparing toast with butter and jam, and a cup of chamomile tea, she was out the door before anybody else arose.

The address she scrawled on the piece of paper last night was in a neighborhood unfamiliar to her. It took two buses and a ten-minute walk to arrive. The palatial house supported by four majestic pillars was built on an elevation. Behind the iron gates that guarded the long driveway loop, Polly felt miniaturized. She checked again to ensure she had the right address.

Short of breath from exertion as she reached the front door, she raised the knocker and tapped it gently three times. Immediately the door was opened, and a house servant acknowledged that her mistress was expecting her, and was in the drawing room waiting.

Polly reluctantly gave up her coat, reprimanding herself that she should have taken more thought in her choice of attire. The simple turquoise-blue A-line dress with white edging that Charlotte had recently made for her seemed less fashionable in the immaculate rooms in which she stood. Each item was carefully chosen and placed. A consistent color palette helped to connect the distinct rooms. Lighting, pictures, statues, and flowers appeared at varying levels, naturally drawing the eye around the space.

The drawing room was welcoming, with a small fire burning in the hearth, light wood furniture, and sofas upholstered in fabrics of soft pastel colors. In the center stood Sadie, wearing a pink jacket and matching skirt. The classic interlinking double *C* denoted the designer's signature.

"Polly! I am so pleased to see you." Sadie embraced her tightly.

The house servant poured a cup of tea for them both and quietly left, as if she was barely there, closing the double doors behind her.

"Firstly, I must apologize for being such a cad. I was young and stupid. Will you forgive me? Now that we've found each other again, I am really hoping we can be friends yet again."

Polly barely knew what to say. Stealing somebody else's work was a deceit of integrity that Polly was uncertain she could forgive, or should. She forgave Eli too often for his wickedness and look where that landed her. She smiled, took a sip of her too-hot tea, and placed the cup back down without a word.

"Sadie. It is so wonderful to see you . . . like this." She raised her arms in acknowledgment of the space around her. "How?"

"Well, I actually must thank you, Polly. That day I saw you in the lobby, looking so beautiful and confident, you gave me the kick I needed to stop wallowing and get on with life."

There was a slight knock on the door before it opened. Another young woman in a house servant uniform entered with a chubby curly-haired blond girl in her arms. At the sight of Sadie, the little one scrambled out of her nursemaid's arms, and with unsteady steps toddled over to Sadie calling for Mommy.

"This is my little Florence," she said, picking up the beautiful girl with a swing onto her lap. She dismissed the woman, asking her to come back in thirty minutes to take the child for her morning walk.

After some playful kisses and tickles, Sadie ushered Florence to her play area beside the chair.

"With the money you gave me, I went and bought myself a proper dress, shoes, hat, stockings, and a handbag at the second-hand shop." Sadie went on to share how she spent the next several weeks looking for a job, carefully dabbing out stains and washing her stockings in the sink of her rooming house each night. "It took a while to not feel like a fraud. Pretending every day, with this one set of pretty clothes, that I was really worth something, and not just like the pair of torn and stained undergarments that were hidden underneath."

Sadie got a job as a secretary to a bank executive. Her fast typing skills, university degree, and excellent writing abilities from her time on the school paper were an advantage. She eventually saved up money and bought herself a proper wardrobe, moved into a nicer part of town, and was able to find a sweet grandmother-type who lived in the second-floor apartment to watch Florence while she worked.

"And all this?" Polly coaxed.

"I met Teddy at work. He held a big account at the bank. As an exclusive client he had private meetings with my boss regularly. He had been widowed for several years and was living in this big house by himself, his children grown with families of their own. After a few weeks, he asked me to marry him. I have been Mrs. Theodore Grange ever since."

"Grange? As in the Art Gallery of Toronto Grange family?" Polly was agog.

"Distant relation, but yes, that's the one." Sadie poured herself a top-up of tea.

"And Florence?" Polly watched the little girl, who looked so much like her mother.

"I told Teddy that I had been married. My husband dead in the war, left me a single mother." Sadie moved uncomfortably in her seat. "Well, I wasn't totally lying. Florence's father did die, we just weren't married."

Polly sat in silence for a moment, then went ahead and asked, "I realize it is not my business, but . . ." She stopped, not wanting to ask. If Sadie wanted her to know, she would have told her the truth by now.

"Walter. Walter Brown. You would have known him."

Polly was instantly transported back to the pub, the dancing, the scratches on her arms, the hurtful tone of his voice. She saw Sadie clearly now. A naïve girl, putting up bravados to be more than she actually was. In the end she ended up a discard in Walter Brown's own ego-driven game. Of course she forgave Sadie of her impulsive transgression.

"He wanted me to keep our relationship a secret. His parents were already trying to match him up with the daughter of wealthy friends, whose connections they thought would help his political career. He promised he would tell them as soon as we finished school and were ready to marry." Sadie looked at Florence stacking and restacking colorful rings on a stick until she got the order right. "When I told him I was pregnant, he said it couldn't be his because he had mumps as a child and was told he would not be able to father children. He accused me of being loose. Told me he never wanted to see me again."

Her eyes glistened a marvelous green color under the gloss of tears. Florence, who noticed her mom's sadness, stood up and crawled onto her lap, cuddling in as tightly as she could. "My parents wouldn't take me in, called me a whore. So, I lost myself in the city."

She hugged her daughter. "I don't regret a piece of it, though. If none of it happened, I wouldn't have this little darling to love, and give me so much love." She rubbed noses with her daughter, a gesture obviously familiar to them both—a secret exchange that only they shared.

"Love you. Now go find Nanny for your walk." She guided the little girl to the door, releasing her to the waiting hands of her nursemaid who quietly stood outside in the hall.

"After I married Teddy, my parents forgave me. They promised to keep my secret in exchange for being in Florence's life." Sadie looked at her expectantly. "You must promise to keep my secret as well, Polly. I can't lose everything again. I just couldn't survive it," she implored.

"I promise." Polly solemnly made a cross sign over her heart with her fingers. "I was pleasantly thrilled when I was able to reach your parents last night and they gave me your number. I would never have known how to find you otherwise."

"Enough about my life. Tell me about you and all your successes. I'm sure your life is simply glamorous and full of adventure—a composer, a mathematician, a single young beautiful woman living on her own in the big city. I am devilishly envious of your liberties."

Polly painted an exciting picture describing the intricacies of her thesis, the thrill of having her music performed by the Toronto orchestra, her cultured and varied friends at the boarding house. She flaunted the fun she had exploring jazz, dancing until the early morning, and endless hours of leisure time filled with art galleries and Kata's salons. The wide-eyed bemused Sadie prodded her for details. She said nothing of her repeatedly missed deadline for her dissertation, and the anxiety she had of still not having heard from her thesis committee. Nor the fact that she had not completed a piece of music in almost two years. She avoided the subject of boyfriends, and intentionally omitted anything about Eli or the baby that grew inside her.

"I am happy being a wife and a mother to Florence, living on the outskirts of the city. Sometimes I do need to remind myself that I am only twenty-five years old." Sadie's pink-painted fingernails fiddled with the buttons of her jacket. "But you will come regularly and tell me all of your excitement. I can live vicariously through you, can't I, my dear Polly?"

The world felt awakened that afternoon. By the time Polly left Sadie's, they were as comfortable as during the newsroom days. The damp winter dullness bloomed into spring's crisp, slightly sun-kissed warmth. Invigorated by her rekindled friendship with Sadie, Polly got off the bus two stops early to take in the beauty of the day.

People bustled around her on the streets, oblivious of each other. Polly wondered what their lives were like. She spotted a handsome man in a tweed suit and bowler hat taking his lunch on a park bench, and she wondered who made that meal for him. Had he made it himself? Was there somebody at home, a wife? Perhaps he still lived with his mother. Whoever it was appeared to love him enough to cut the crusts off of each equally proportioned triangle. The old woman at the bus stop, hunched over from years of picking up crumbs after her several children and grandchildren, she thought. What worries might keep her up at night? She passed a woman selling flowers from a cart on the street. Her sign, "Brighten someone's day, buy flowers," was ambiguous. Whose day would be brightened? Hers, the purchaser's, the one to whom the flowers were given? Her smile and laugh drew a regular stream of people to her. Was she truly happy? Polly wondered. Could it be possible to be that happy?

Her watch read noon. She stood transfixed at the bottom of the stairs of the Grange, awed at the realization that this building of immense history would forever be part of Sadie's story. Her family connection, a legacy that she could pass down to Florence. A twang of jealousy crept into her heart.

Inside, she knew Eli waited for her to join him for their lunch date. She had promised yesterday to come. She knew his desire was to rekindle a life together; he would not let her go. Her hand rested on the small paunch of her lower abdomen. Rather than mounting the steps, she turned and continued home.

Over the following weeks, her isolation began drawing the suspicion of everybody in the house, except Margaret. Breakfast times became less routine as the girls' schedules grew busy, each taking their meals at a time convenient to them.

Charlotte had found a new circle of friends. Mostly young models or clients who admired her feminine designs, refreshingly absent of boning, corsets, belts, or other restrictions. The fabric weights and cuts flattering to a woman's natural curves. With every free moment, after her usual work, Charlotte was busy at the sewing machine making her own unique garments.

Mary was now doing her practical nursing studies on the hospital wards, working overnight and evening shifts. Sleeping odd hours with ear plugs and eye masks to shut out the rest of the world.

Margaret was also busy at work completing her residency program. Dr. Garrett, who she affectionately just called Garrett, lived closer to the hospital. She stayed there when he worked an overnight at the hospital; sworn to chastity, she never stayed when he was home. Their affection for each other bloomed, grounded in their mutual passion for medicine and research. She claimed the racial differences would not be a problem between them.

"The world needs to change," she would preach. "I can handle whatever disparagement others may throw. He is a good man. Those that matter to me will see that and wish us well." For all her bravado, an introduction of Dr. Garrett to her sister still remained undone.

Polly agreed to any work that would keep her busy, marking undergraduate exam papers, taking on additional tutoring sessions, overseeing labs. Her growing belly was becoming harder to conceal.

One morning Charlotte found her overwhelmed with tears, still in her night dress, when she could not find a single spring dress that would fit her. She tried hard to console Polly.

"A few added pounds are flattering on you. A beautiful goddess in a Rubenesque painting." She offered to walk to work together, rather than take the bus, as exercise.

Polly could no longer keep her secret. "I'm pregnant," she whispered.

Charlotte was less surprised than Polly thought she might be. "Well, I figured it wasn't all just from chocolate and Kata's good cooking." She laughed.

Charlotte did wonders reworking all of Polly's dresses with extra panels, and snuck in time at work to make her new ones that carefully hid her expanding midriff.

Kata delivered the mail each day to the table at the top landing, outside the front door of the girls' room. Today she knocked on the door to personally deliver the letter addressed to Ms. Paulina Williams.

"I think you might wish to see this!" She handed over the letter with the Queen's University emblem in the upper left corner. Hurriedly she opened it.

"Dear Ms. Williams, we are pleased to inform you that your thesis has passed first approval. Your dissertation defense is scheduled for June 9, 1948," she read aloud. She hugged Kata, excited to share this moment with somebody.

"That is only a few weeks away. You won't be able to hide anymore, Paulina. You'll need to tell your mother." Kata motioned down to Polly's belly. "I'm sorry to have to say this, but you won't be able to come back here. I have a reputation to keep. If people think I am loose with my boarders, and allow unwed mothers in my home, I won't have a steady business much longer." She turned away, unable to bear the look of abandonment that settled across Polly's face. "I am so sorry, Paulina. I wish the world was different," she said before gently closing the door.

Polly crumpled to the ground. Beside her, the letter that once held so much anticipation as a key to a future of greater possibility now felt like her coffin. Early June, she would be twenty-one weeks pregnant. She lay paralyzed on the ground seeing her childhood dreams sail away into the sky like a helium-filled balloon. The string out of reach, unable to pull it back. Without a plan, her world shriveled. She thought of Eli, Sadie, and Walter. Ollie. He would forever be out of her life now.

Perhaps Dorthey would know what to do. Sweet Dorthey with whom she had kept up weekly correspondence and mentioned nothing of her predicament, ashamed and fearful that she or Petar might mention anything to Oliver. Her lifelong friend had also recently suffered through a miscarriage, and she knew the agony it was afflicting on her. She could not burden her with this.

With a suitcase full of new clothes, compliments of Charlotte, she said goodbye to her friends. Even Kata blubbered through tears of goodbyes. Promises of future visits, lengthy correspondences, and forever friendships were earnestly exchanged. Words of congratulations and best wishes were shared with confidence in her successful thesis defense. They clustered in the living room one last time.

"Soon-to-be Dr. Williams," Margaret announced bearing a gift. "From me and Garrett." Inside was a Mont Blanc pen with her initials engraved along the pin, and a silver Tiffany baby spoon. "You'll be a great mom," she whispered when they embraced.

Charlotte presented her with a chenille quilted baby blanket in a beautiful sunflower yellow. Even Kata gave her a blue box with a large white ribbon. "Open it later. Once the baby is born," she insisted.

Polly grieved the loss of her former carefree life. Unbound by restriction, open to any possibility. It was a brief but magical time back when, if she could imagine it, there was the possibility the dream could come true. So much was gained and lost in these three years. Her usual busy mind had been quiet for a long time. Getting out of the taxi at the station, she knew she was leaving behind so much of herself. When she returned to the city, she would be a different person with new circumstances.

Startled by a gruff arm that grabbed on to her as she reached for the door to the station, Polly turned around. She was met with a familiar face aflame with spiteful anger. Though accustomed to the intensity, it still frightened her.

"You never showed up to lunch. Did you think you could leave the city without seeing me?" Eli spat the words at her. Spittle landed on her cheek. She did not flinch.

He looked down at her belly, well concealed under her dress. He placed his hands around it. The shape evident now between his hands.

"Did you think you could steal my baby? I am the father, and I have legal rights. You can't just take it away from me, Polly." Fury oozed from him. His fixed tight eyes seemed disconnected from a soul.

She hoped somebody would interrupt them, need them to move to get through the door. Rather, they continued to walk on either side to doors farther away. The pressure of his hands on her stomach were like a vice, and she feared for her baby. Warm sweat dripped underneath her breasts.

"Don't deny that it's mine." He seemed to have read her mind. "I have been following you, Polly. I have seen it growing and wanted so desperately to be with you. I don't understand why you wouldn't have told me." He stepped closer to her, their faces only inches apart. "I knew it must be mine. You are so frigid, uptight. Having sex with you was like sleeping with a dead fish. I knew you couldn't be with anybody else. Besides, nobody else would want you."

Her heart sped up. Desperately she tried to hold back her tears.

"Eli," she said his name softly. A forced smile formed upon her face for survival. "I just needed time. I am going home to visit my family for a few days. We'll talk when I'm back." She kissed him on the lips, trying to hold back the bile that burned in her throat.

He stepped back, creating space for her to breathe again.

"We could be happy, Polly. If only you let us. You fight against us all the time." He grabbed the piece of hair that had strayed from her bun and wrapped it around her ear. She tensed, afraid that he would hit her. "You really are a very difficult woman, just like your mother always said you were. Stubborn to a fault." He looked at her, knowing he hit a chord. "It's okay. You'll grow out of it. I forget sometimes just how young you are."

"I'll miss my train. I should go." She moved toward the door again. He took a step forward, obstructing her way.

"Yes, you should go. Polly's famous words." He stepped out of her way, never diverting his gaze from her face. "Polly, if only you let me love you, you would see how happy we could be." He rubbed her belly like a man polishing a trophy. "A happy family."

With frazzled haste she boarded the train, which pulled away only minutes after she settled in her seat. She wished he had hit her. If he had hit her, she would know with good reason that she could never go back. That she would need to protect herself and her baby. But what if he was right? What if she was too selfish, too cold and unwilling to love, too difficult? Does a baby not need a mother and a father? It wasn't until the man beside her asked if she was okay, if she needed anything, that she realized she was crying.

Graciously she declined any need for support, telling her seatmate that her husband had recently died, a car accident. She was going home to live with her parents, to raise their baby. He offered condolences. They were both grateful when his stop came a few towns outside of the city.

Petar was working that day, and her father was teaching. She had insisted a taxi would do just fine from the train station. Fretting over her parents' reaction, and still haunted by the incident with Eli, she entered the house feeling she might collapse. Her dress too tight around her bosom, she could hardly breathe. Skin puddled over her ankle bones, deforming her legs. She wanted to disappear. There to greet her was her mother.

"*Minushka*, what is it?" Her mother's face immediately changed from joyous welcome to deep concern. She ushered her to the couch.

All affirming words about being an independent woman in a changing world, and having the ability to both raise a child and work, were lost. With gloves and hat still on, for the next hour, Polly rambled about the pregnancy, the romance, the arguments, and finally the threats. Exhausted and relieved, she braced herself for her mother's harsh words.

"Oh, my *minushka*." She delicately reached out to embrace her daughter. She rocked her soothingly in her arms, like she was five years old again. "You've ruined it. I thought I taught you better not to repeat my mistakes."

"Mama, what mistakes?" Polly grasped onto the little dropped phrase.

"Mistakes of trusting people you should not have." She brusquely stood to move to the window, the look on her face reminiscent of the night Polly came home from the pub. "You must tell your father." Kasia sighed.

Terror seared through Polly's body. The baby kicked wildly in her belly.

"No, Mama. I can't." Her voice assertive like the strong-minded young girl she once was.

"You must." Her mother joined her again, determination in her voice, clarity in her gaze. "You will defend your thesis. You will pass as I know you should. You will not throw away all of your God-given talents and deprive yourself of an intelligent life because of a small, simple man." Kasia stared intensely into Polly's face, declaring it with such confidence that Polly trusted it to be so. Her hands clenched onto Polly's arms. She shook her slightly, affirming it was time to wake from her desperate loneliness. "You will continue forward. You will teach, you will learn, and you will make the world a better place, *minushka*." She held Polly's face firmly between her palms. "You are not alone," she whispered.

Polly rejoiced in the surprise of her mother's faith in her. "Oh, Mama, I wish I was as confident as you."

"You have not chosen an easy path, Paulina. You never did." She grunted. "Despite my deterrents you always knew your mind and stuck to it. That annoying stubbornness will still serve you well." She placed her head against her daughter's forehead. "You will find music and love again in life. I know you will."

Wishful childhood dreams that she and Dorthey had of raising their children together surfaced. Perhaps their crafty ideas of how Polly could both teach and do research at the university while being a mother could be true. Her goals, however, were even more forsaken given the current conundrum that no university would hire an unwed mother. She pushed the rumors about Mrs. Wardle from the nursing department to the back of her mind. That evening she told her father. Mama had prepared a simple dinner and avoided serving any spirits before the meal. Polly offered him a quick kiss on the cheek, avoiding his embrace. Comfortably hidden by the table, she filled the conversation with speculations about her thesis defense. The questions they might ask, the preparation she still had ahead of her.

Mama began to clear the table. "Andrew, Paulina has some other news she needs to share with you." There was no further avoiding the unpleasantry.

Unable to find her voice, she pleaded with wide eyes at her mother. A brusque shake of her mother's head confirmed she needed to step forward on her own. For all her father's liberal attitudes he was a devout Catholic, and a staunch traditionalist at heart. An unwed mother was beyond what he could fathom. There would be no escaping his anger.

"Papa. I am pregnant with Eli's child."

Her father, who had spent the evening basking in his daughter's success, grew quiet. His face sank.

"I see." The disappointment in his eyes was too great for her to bear.

"Papa, please, understand. I thought I loved him. I took every precaution. I had no idea he would do what he did."

Confusion crept into his face. "What he did?" The moment of sympathy extinguished at the shake of his wife's head.

"Not that, thank God." Kasia placed her hand on his shoulder. "He sabotaged her birth control."

He stared at the empty chair across from him. For several minutes they painfully sat in silence. Polly studied his face— clenched jaw, focused gaze, curled fingers, and shallow breaths. He seemed to be bracing for battle against a forlorn enemy only he prophesied was coming.

Mama delicately placed the last dish in the sink, then slowly stepped to stand beside him, cautiously placing her hand on his forearm. "Andrew?" The subtle gesture was enough to dislodge him from his trance.

"Foolish, stupid girl. I told you to stay away from him." His face contorted into a combination of remorse and disbelief. "We granted you every opportunity, despite everybody's warning. And you what? Threw it all away for some idiot boy and lustful nights. I did not raise you to be common, Paulina. But here you stand, nothing but a grave disappointment to me."

"Please, Papa, don't say that. I'll find a way." Polly reached for his hand carefully. Skirting her grasp, he reached for his glass of water and took a small sip.

With a sniff and the clearing of his throat he regained his composure. "When shall the wedding to Eli take place?" His name spoken like a terminal disease.

"There won't be a wedding. I am not marrying him."

Fists slammed on the table, where they remained while he stood from his chair. The weight of the situation carried on his hunched back. "You must marry. You can no longer study nor teach. Nobody else will have you. This impish man, it pains me to say, is your only hope for a decent life."

"I shall not marry him. Ever."

They shouted back and forth for some time. He criticized her weak character and lamented the wasted years of attention and money that would better have been served on her brother, who lived a sensible though simple life. As for Polly, she challenged his contradictions. Raising her to be as free and independent as any man, then forcing her into the confines of traditional female roles.

Kasia stepped between them. "Leave us. Go to your room," she calmly instructed Polly. When Polly declined, Kasia replied with a single steady, "Go now."

Polly raced up the stairs, nearly tripping. Safely in the bathroom, she locked the door and lay on the floor. She listened to them arguing below. Subdued harsh tones escalated to shouts and then quieted again after a shushing from her mother.

On the floor, she remained frightened by her father's anger. She had never seen him like this. Not even when Petar declared he was leaving university. Surely, he would forgive her. She would find a way to make it right. The baby was still for some time. If only it did not survive, she thought, things could go back to normal. Then she crawled to the toilet to vomit, revolted at her own thoughts. She loved this baby; she knew she did. Her blood fed it. Her body nourished it. This baby was her love. At that moment, she swore she would see to it that it would have a good life, grow up in a happy loving home. "I promise," she whispered.

She did not see her father for the next few days. He left early, arrived late, and some nights slept on the couch in his office. Polly moved in with Petar and Dorthey to save him the agony of being in her presence. Teddy and Sonja had a calming effect on her. The simple joy of life in that home restored her faith that all would be well.

A week passed before Papa visited her at Petar's.

"Your mother and I have been speaking. We have decided it is best if you give up the baby after it is born. You can carry on with your work, and find a respectable man to marry. You can have other children under the proper circumstances."

The discussion extended well into the evening. She would remain in the outskirts of town at Petar and Dorthey's until the baby was born to reduce any risk of rumors. She resigned herself to the plan. Truthfully, she knew she could not do this alone.

"You are my sister, Polly. Dorthey and I will do whatever we need to support you." Petar dug his hands into his pockets in that shy way he had when emotions become too big for him.

Dorthey gave her usual big-hearted smile. "Sisters forever." She offered Polly her pinky finger.

Polly locked her finger into Dorthey's. "Sisters forever," she repeated, grasping onto the hope that things could be reconciled, preserved.

With enormity, she knew things were forever changed.

The day of her defense her nerves were unquenchable. She wore one of Charlotte's beautiful creations, a light green jacket with a ruffled bottom that extended from a high waist, falling long enough at the hip to cover the elastic-topped skirt. Nobody would tell she was pregnant.

She walked to the third-floor classroom in Grant Hall. The baby turning somersaults in her belly all morning, squashing her appetite. Her father's face, full of disappointment, still flashed in her mind. If she did not pass, then she truly would be the failure that he saw her as.

Upon entering the room, five esteemed mathematicians whose papers she had studied and careers she had followed, sat behind the table. All were men dressed in dark suits, with white starched shirts and black ties. Each had hair somewhere on a gray-to-white scale, at varying degrees of thickness. Their shoes were polished and firmly planted on the ground.

For two and a half hours she answered questions about why she chose to deviate from von Neumann's well-established theory. Had she collaborated with John Nash on her non-competitive game theory? When she answered that she hadn't, they questioned why. Who had influenced her thinking, and did she really come up with it on her own? They threw a variety of applications for her theory at her from simple games of checkers, to complex war and business strategies.

The baby continued to be restless. As her blood sugars dropped, and only water was available to her, she felt faint. The baby quieted. She worried if it was well. Perhaps the stress was too much for it. If only she could eat something. Regrettably, that morning her nerves allowed her to take in a small cup of milk and a few bites of toast with jam. She strained to balance the intellectual whirl in her head, testing the fascinating scenarios in which her theory proved true. She needed to be agile, to move through the fatigue and hunger. She volleyed from the exhilaration of being back in the academic excitement with all its potential, to the deep sense of shame and disappointment that she brought to her family.

At the end, she knew she had done well. Regardless of the committee's decision, she had given her work everything she had. With that thought, she would need to be content. When Eli called the following week, she lied, telling him that she had not done well and that Dr. Proust insisted she stay through the summer to focus and try again in the fall. She would be back well before the baby was due. In actuality, she received her doctorate, with honors, in July.

At the start of September, she went into labor, six weeks early. After twenty grueling hours it was over. She sent Eli a letter that simply read:

> *Lost the baby. Stillborn. It was a boy. Goodbye.*
> *P.W.*

She stayed in Kingston for several weeks to recover. The fresh lake air and long walks rebuilt her constitution. On the actual baby's due date, she boarded a plane to England, to start her junior teaching assignment at Oxford University. Somerville Hall was expanding its offerings. With a recommendation from her esteemed thesis committee, and a willingness to move on short notice, she was offered a one-year contract. Petar and her mother were the only ones there to see her off at the airport. Papa did not express congratulations. He no longer trusted her to make good decisions. "Do as you like," was all he said when he heard the news.

CHAPTER 10

1950

Oxford bustled with the cacophony of year-end examinations. Acrid stress emanated from the over-caffeinated, sleep-deprived undergraduates, inciting nausea in those who were not acclimatized to the odor in the student study rooms. Many boys swore off any leisure time with girls for the two weeks prior to final examinations to increase their mental performance. Some took to snorting powders of tea and coffee to help them focus and be alert longer. Graduating first in class was more than an honor to many here; it was their family duty.

Somerville Hall was not recognized as a college by Oxford, and hence, to Polly's infuriation, did not sit exams. The students in her classes were just as smart as any male resident of the university. In fact, their rhapsody for learning made them wildly unabashed to explore beyond the conventional. Still, she welcomed exam period. It allowed her unencumbered time to explore her own academic curiosities, while her professor colleagues throughout the university expanded office hours and scored exams for days.

The growing library at Somerville was impressive, but the economic papers of which she most had need were in Balliol. Morning walks along the university parks invigorated her mind. Some days she would lollygag to enjoy the only place on this end of campus where walking on the grass was permitted. She watched the birds play elegantly in symmetric and perfectly timed swooping arches, and squirrels chase each other aggressively to stock up their individual food supplies for the winter. Observations of nature like these inspired metaphors for the human psychology that fed into her latest work. Wage- and price-setting patterns to control macroeconomic stability were not much different than sharing and storing food for the winter.

Humbly, she crossed the threshold into the library, ceaselessly awed at the vastness of knowledge she would learn and forget, and much of which she would never know. The swirls of information she held in her mind did not compare to the volume of the yet undiscovered.

"Good morning, Professor Williams. Your requested stack of documents is already awaiting you in Area Two." The young librarian was always bashful and eager to help. She hid behind oversized glasses and equally large sweaters. She was rather pretty with her naturally curly blond hair that never seemed tamed, though she was too skinny by most standards. Polly guessed she was about her age of twenty-five, perhaps a year or two younger.

"Thank you so much, Sarah." The girl fiddled with the book cover in front of her, flipping it open and closed.

"Professor Williams? You go through so many papers and documents. Every day I pull a fresh stack for you of new items. You seem to eat them up like gumdrops."

"I'm sorry to make so much work for you." Polly subdued an impatient sigh. "I want to finish this paper before the next semester and don't have time to slow down."

Sarah blushed. Her wide eyes pleaded to be understood. "It's not that," she was quick to say with a wave of her hands to wipe away the accusation. "It is just . . ."

Polly glanced at the wall clock. Already 7 a.m. She needed to get to her papers. "It is just what?" she coaxed.

"Would you explain it to me one day? The work you're doing. I am not sure I'll understand it, but I'd like to try." Sarah's neck grew splotchy with a nervous rash. Polly recognized the intensity of insatiable curiosity written across her face. The way she chewed her lower lip. Her pupils wide so as to take in the entirety of the world. "I thought by working here I would be able to get at least some kind of an education. I read everything I can when I have a quiet minute. But it is all thoughts of people from the past." She searched for words to carry on. "I want to know what is yet to come. What things are people thinking about now!" Her uncontained excitement was infectious.

"I would be more than happy to explain my work to you, Sarah." Polly tapped her hand. "As soon as I finish this paper, we shall make time for tea and discussion. For now, though, I must not delay." She pointed to the clock, signaling it was time for her to go.

Polly set off to her work station. Always the same one, in the back corner to isolate herself from distraction. Natural light streamed in from the stained-glass window that overlooked the courtyard. For many days she would remain in this little speck of the world, lost in her work. All sense of time and place lost to her until the angle at which the sunbeams came through the window alerted her to the darkening end of the day.

Sarah was an incredible help that day. Without interrupting her, Polly found blank pages were replenished for scribbling. Tea and crumpets were brought to her twice despite the rule that no food or drink was allowed in the library. Lists of references to be pulled for tomorrow's work appeared, while those in the completed piles were swept away and refiled to clear space.

"Professor Williams? It is past dinnertime. I'm sorry, but I must leave to watch over my brothers and sisters so my mother can tend to her evening work."

"No need to apologize, Sarah. You were a tremendous help today." Polly rubbed her eyes and gave a broad stretch of her arms and back.

"Before I go, I overheard some of the others discussing a talk at the faculty club tonight. Somebody from the Cambridge Circus is the guest. I thought you might be interested."

Polly leapt from her seat. The Cambridge Circus members were the most eminent thinkers of economic theory of the time. She had tried to get an audience with them for months. Her correspondence never received a reply.

"Yes! Thank you, Sarah. I am very interested indeed." With the assistance of the young librarian, she hurriedly gathered her papers and stacked the journals. "What time?"

"I heard eight p.m., which is soon. I'll keep these for you behind the desk for tomorrow." Sarah competently lifted the tower of documents in one swoop. She crinkled her nose and pursed her mouth, pausing in contemplation. "Professor, you may want to . . ." She swirled her hand in front of her face and fluffed her own hair. "You may want to freshen up before you go."

There was no time to return to her dormitory to change. Thankfully, she always kept a few grooming essentials in her satchel. She rushed to the only faculty restroom in the building. She locked the door behind her, as was her habit, since there were no designated female accommodations. Having been trapped once behind one of the stalls waiting to come out while a series of men came in to use the urinals, she learned quickly.

Carefully she hung her blouse on the stall door. With cold water, she washed under her arms. Retrieving a linen handkerchief from her bag, she patted herself dry. She then wiped to soak up the moisture that had accumulated at the edge of her brassiere. After a few strokes with a brush, she replaced the bobby pins to hold her hair in a twist. She checked her breath and caught the warm brown sugar smell of her tea. Her signature red lipstick looked ghastly against her tired complexion. She blotted it to near extinction. Only a tint remained. She used the tissue against her skin to brighten her cheeks and the arch of her brow, as Charlotte had once taught her.

Her long, purpose-driven strides created an echo as each of her high-heeled steps hit the pavement. The cool evening breeze renewed her energy. She increased her pace. The faculty club was not far. Typically, these events were by invitation only. She had no explanation for her presence, but was confident she could contrive a way to get in.

Outside of the building she stood, rummaging through her tattered satchel. Withdrawing a cigarette, she lit it. The warm familiarity of the little glow calmed her. After three quick pulls on the cigarette, she stubbed out the embers, and carefully placed the remaining bit back into the package for later. She extracted one strong mint from her tin to freshen her breath before she entered the front door into an alcove of dark wainscoting.

Before the gentleman at the coat check could ask for anything, she walked past him without acknowledgment. Best not to pause for questions. A low octave thrum of chatter guided her up the carpeted stairs to a large open room at the top. Men milled around in groups of four or so. Snifters of brandy brandished in their left hands, cigarettes in their right. Leather chairs were clustered for intimate conversations about the periphery of the room. A curved row of three high-backed armchairs was at the front near the hearth.

Polly scanned the room. Not a familiar face to be seen. She accepted a glass of something from the waiter who was trading full glasses for empty ones. Some stared at her with curiosity, others with disapproval. She meandered around the uninhabited darker edges of the room, conspicuous as only the second woman in the room. Removing her coat, she stashed it at a corner table near the bar.

The guest of the evening, Piero Sraffa, modestly stood with his wiry gray hair and stooped shoulders, encircled by a boisterous group of Brits. Polly strapped her satchel across her bodice and strode to hover outside of the circle. Slowly she nudged closer. Mirroring, she laughed in unison with the others. Nodded in agreement. With each action she inched her way slowly to stand between the guest of honor and the gentleman beside him. Biding her time for a moment of pause, she capitalized on the distraction from the waiter offering brandy and cigarettes.

"Professor Sraffa, I was interested in your criticism of the theory of value." Before the gentleman beside her could interject, she continued, turning her back toward him slightly. "I have been working on a piece about stabilizing macroeconomics, accomplished by establishing staggered wage and pricing adjustments at microeconomic scales. I believe this would minimize the reactive nature of an economy and the large volatility that leads to recessions and depressions."

Piqued with interest, Piero turned his full attention toward her. "Your name, my dear?"

"Paulina. Professor Paulina Williams," she proudly stated. "I have been writing to your circle in hopes of engaging in some further dialogue on the prospect of my theory."

"Ah, yes. Ms. Williams." He turned back toward the crowd. "You must understand we receive many wishes for correspondence and cannot entertain them all, as we need to focus on our own work and teachings."

"Understandable," Polly deferred. "Respectfully, Professor, the world is growingly complex, and unless we academics learn to collaborate better, we shall stagnate. We'll never be able to move faster than the solitary intelligence of the most published of us."

The gentleman beside her guffawed. He took a large swig of his drink before bellowing in a larger than needed voice. "Ms. William, did you say?"

"Professor Williams. Yes," Polly demurred.

"Where is it exactly that you teach?" His tone taunted her.

"I am a professor of mathematics at Sommerville Hall." She braced herself for what she knew was coming.

He smiled broadly, with an air of assumption that he had already won the debate he was about to begin. "Sommerville is not even part of the university. It is a friendly place where we allow girls to indulge their eccentric ideas to a degree that their brains can handle until such time as they quiet down enough to do real women's work."

Laughter ensued among the crowd. Polly clenched her fists and felt her face grow tight. She narrowed her focus on the oversized talking gorilla beside her.

"The studies at Sommerville are comparable to any of those of the other Oxford colleges. Remarkable women around the world have made masterful contributions to academia and science." She tempered her voice, intentionally drawing on the lower octaves of her vocal range. "By relegating more than half of your population to scrubbing floors and washing the stains out of men's undergarments, sir, you are depriving the world of an intelligent and capable workforce."

Her adversary's face grew red. "Perhaps, Ms. Williams,"— he annunciated his choice of title for her carefully— "if you were to properly marry and fulfill God's intention for women to have children, you would find the necessary peacefulness to quiet your disruptive spirit."

An ache filled Polly's lower belly. She felt a tug on her breasts at the thought of a child.

"God gave women more than a vagina and a uterus for which to bear children." The brazenness of her word selection was meant to make the group feel uncomfortable. "Even Eve pulled man out of a immature state to truly be challenged with deeper philosophical thoughts of good and evil. Do you doubt that was God's omnipotent intention? Would He not have otherwise made Adam more equipped to resist the temptation of a simple apple?" Polly heard the words coming out of her as if put there by somebody else. "I am sure God grew tired waiting for man to do anything more than eat, sleep, and have sex. He created us with the ability for thought and exploration. Eve was put to the task of drawing man toward his full potential."

The crowd grew rowdy. Engrossed in this spirited debate, they neglected to notice the quiet departure of Piero to his seated position at the front of the room.

"You see, gentleman," her opponent continued. His arms were open wide. His voice full of artificial joviality like a circus ringmaster. "This is the alarming behavior that is the product of good intentions, when we allow women to be educated." He leaned in closer to Polly. Usually, she stood as tall or taller than most men. His height allowed him to gaze down upon her slightly. With a hushed voice he threatened, "Words like that could cost you your teaching position, Professor. I would be careful if I were you."

Polly held her tongue but made no motion to avert her eyes from his stare. She would absorb all of his hate and fear, if only to drain some of his power to fuel her own. Then she spoke a great untruth, "I am not afraid."

The rest of the room by now was settled into seats or standing in small clusters as Piero began a guided discussion with two of the local economic professors. Nobody stood within two meters of her; Polly was left alone in the upper right portion of the room, as if she were contagious. For the next hour she stood like a Roman statue, her feet planted comfortably apart. Ignorant of anything else around her, she was engrossed in the conversation of her esteemed colleagues. Her mind whirled with connections that supported or refuted her own theories.

When the presentation came to a close, she was overrun by a stream of intellectuals eager to have their name known to Piero. She stepped back to the bar area and requested a gin and tonic, double shot with a twist of lime on the rocks. Nudged to the left by the person stepping in beside her, Polly sank into a stool, exhausted.

From a small wrinkled hand that belonged to a simple pale-faced woman with intelligent eyes, came an offer of a cigarette. She was the only other woman in the room and had stood at the back throughout the session.

Polly willingly accepted both the cigarette and the lit match. "Smoking is rather unladylike they tell me," said the stranger, lighting her own cigarette. "Somehow, I don't think either of us care." She picked up her glass of amber liquid and clanked it against Polly's just-delivered drink.

"Paulina." She introduced herself, tipping her glass then taking a long sip.

"Joan," said the other woman. "I know it's exhausting," she continued on, gesturing over her shoulder at the rowdy pack at the front of the room. "Being just as smart isn't enough. We always have to be better. We can never be too loud or too quiet. Being pretty is a detriment but being unfeminine equally so. Our energy needs to be double to dedicate not just to our work, but to the fight."

Polly nodded. She was too tired to speak. The woman glanced at Polly's left hand. "Wait until you add marriage and children to the mix. It's a realm of balance that even the most seasoned yogis could not achieve. It is a heavy place reserved for women alone."

Unsure if this was helping or hurting her state of mind, Polly felt an overwhelming desire to escape back to the dormitory with a cup of tea and book. Even the idea of returning to the library tomorrow did not lighten her downhearted mood.

"Be bold. Be brave," Joan said. "We need to keep going for our daughters and our sons. It is the only way the world will change." She swallowed the last mouthful of her drink, and walked over to where Piero stood. He welcomed her warmly, then showed great deference as he encouraged her to share with the group. Polly marveled at how this innocuous middle-aged woman commanded the ear of one of the most highly respected economists. It was only after they had gathered their things and slipped out the door that Polly realized that she missed the opportunity to have a real conversation with Joan Robinson, the only woman in the Cambridge Circus.

Summers in Oxford lacked the oppressive humidity of Polly's hometown on Lake Ontario. After her sunrise walk each morning, she would replenish herself with a single cup of coffee and a sweet bread. With little teaching responsibility, she would spend her days in the library, taking periodic breaks to lunch outdoors and meditate during mid-afternoon walks.

Like many of the female teachers, she lived in the faculty portion of the dormitory. The accommodations were considered part of her meager compensation. Upon arrival, near two years ago now, she spent most of her days in her room, asleep or crying. Suffering still with what she left behind in Canada. Mustering only enough energy to go to her classes, she did little socializing. The label of shy introvert transitioned to arrogant foreigner, which translated into not having many friends. Loneliness was staved off by her commitment to work.

At the end of the summer, Margaret and Dr. Garrett were to be wed. She had been saving for this trip, having not returned to Canada since she left. Polly looked forward to her three-week trip. She could practically taste her mama's borscht, smoked and salty. She longed to see her nieces and nephew again. Teddy and Sonja would be much grown by now. She couldn't wait to hold baby Miriam in her arms. Both Mama and Dorthey wrote regularly, though the postal service was so slow that by the time the letters reached her, the events were already mere memories. Sometimes the letters arrived out of sequence, the ending to the dilemma revealed before the situation itself. "Miriam's arm is all better," came before the letter in which Dorthey wrote "Miriam has taken a tumble down the stairs while playing with Teddy and Sonja."

She never heard from Papa. When she was able to afford the oversees calls, their conversations were short and focused on her publications. He had little interest in hearing about her teaching; he no longer felt that educating women was a noble task. "They will disappoint you," he said on more than one occasion.

Polly had completed two papers over that year, "Product and Wage Control to Minimize Economic Volatility," and "Consumer Demand-Driven Price Setting." Both were novel ideas. Neither were well received by her colleagues.

After the Cambridge Circus evening, she sought correspondence with Joan Robinson, who willingly read each of her papers. A simple white comment card returned with her pages read: *Well beyond your years. Keep going. J.R.*

None of the respected journals would view her work. The *American Economic Review* was biased toward works produced in the United States. The *Cambridge Journal of Economics* wished to see what notable economists had supported her work. Even her own *Oxford Review of Economic Policy* declared the work still too undeveloped to warrant the cost of ink and paper.

Undeterred, she carefully pressed copies of both works into a brown folder placed at the bottom of her blue suitcase to share with her trusted Professor Proust. She would be leaving for Toronto tomorrow, and she wished to be ready.

Awaiting her at the airport when she arrived was Charlotte, barely recognizable in a short skirt and flouncy blouse. Her hair cut straight across at a level just above her chin. Being in the fashion industry suited Charlotte, or rather her self-assurance suited fashion, making her a trendsetter. She fell in love passionately with her creative whims, and was a walking advertisement for what was to come in the clothing world.

"You look so lovely!" Polly gave her a hug so tight and held on so long to make up for the two years of loneliness she had in England. "Did you design this yourself?"

"Of course," Charlotte said, doing a little spin in the airport to an admiring crowd of men and their jealous wives.

After retrieving her luggage, they strode with looped arms to Charlotte's car and straight to Kata's where she would stay the night. The following day she would take the train to Kingston for two weeks, before returning to Toronto for the wedding.

The evening was full of the type of laughter that only came with reminiscence among good friends who shared lives and deep affection. Kata prepared a delectable meal, and the girls indulged in wine. Mary's absence was notable, having moved back to her hometown after graduation to become a nurse.

"Will Mary be here for the wedding?" Polly broached carefully.

"She will. With Father's permission." Margaret looked sad. "One of the most important days of my life and neither of my parents will be there. Mother gone and Father simply cannot get over Garrett's race."

Polly knew how much Margaret had sacrificed to be with Garrett. Neither her father nor the hospital staff were supportive of their relationship. People left caustic notes in her locker about having gray babies, and worse.

"I just don't understand," Polly said thinking back to how kind and capable Dr. Garrett was during her pregnancy.

"I'm lucky they are letting me keep my job at the hospital, otherwise we may never be able to afford a house or a family."

"Surely Garrett must make enough money as an obstetrician to support you." Polly was flummoxed. "How will you raise a family and still work?" She yearned to hear Margaret's solution to the conundrum of managing both work and children.

"Oh, Polly, you may be a world-traveler but you are still very unexperienced. Garrett makes very little money. Few people refer to him. Did you not notice the grim conditions of his tiny third floor office? He couldn't afford anything more. After he pays his nurse, who blessedly is happy to be working at all—with her own poor English she is satisfied taking whatever wages he can offer—doesn't leave for much else."

"I just don't understand. I saw many women with swollen bellies coming and going at each of my appointments." Polly was perplexed.

"Did you also notice that most were of another race? Those who aren't are often destitute, unwed mothers or prostitutes."

Noticing Polly's reaction, she offered, "I'm sorry, Polly. I didn't mean to imply anything by that." She placed her hand on her friend's and gave a squeeze. "Most can't pay. He accepts what they have to offer. If I can't work . . ." She let her words fall away. Life's unfair struggles were apparently not Polly's alone. The evening ended shortly after, morphing into a fitful night of unrest. She was filled with dreams of being chased by Eli and giving birth to a stillborn gray baby deformed by a third arm. When she boarded the train the following morning for Kingston, she was unnerved and tired. It had been too long since she had been home. Much had changed and gone unaddressed before her departure. She was uncertain of the reception that awaited her.

Restless the whole way, she opened and closed her book several times, then paced the aisle until she was asked firmly to be seated and remain seated by the conductor. She stepped into a patch of sunlight beating down onto the platform. Welcoming the deep warmth to her bones, she sought a moment of stillness with outstretched arms to greet the day ahead.

"Well, aren't you fresh and chipper this morning?"

Polly turned toward the voice, shielding her eyes from the sun to see better. Dots of color flicked as she focused in the brightness.

"Ollie!" She resisted the urge to skip to him, as she had done so often in the past. "What a lovely surprise to see you here." She gave him a kiss on either cheek and then looped her arm through his, picking up her suitcase with the other hand.

"Petar is at work, and Dorthey has her hands full with the kids. While I was at your parents for a visit, I offered to pick you up." He gave her arm a squeeze and touched his head to hers. "It has been much too long, Polly."

She had not seen him since the holiday trip, before the pregnancy, before Oxford.

"An Oxford professor? Polly, why didn't you tell me? Petar says too little about your adventures. It was only through my mother that I knew. How could you be so close to London and not stop in to see me?" He seemed hurt.

She searched his face to see if he knew. "Well, it was all so sudden, really. Finishing my doctorate, and then starting the job. There was a bit of time between, here in Kingston but . . ."

"Yes, Mother told me you were bedridden for some time. Exhaustion, she said. I had images of you draped in a dark shawl, withered and decrepit." He nudged her a little, his big laugh filling her heart with splendor again.

"No, it was more like sleeping beauty, restoring myself before my next big endeavor." She was confident now that he didn't know. Petar would not have said anything; he was never one for chitchat or gossip. Mother had ensured that she did not wander farther than Dorthey's backyard once she could no longer hide her belly. Banished to Petar and Dorthey's, their home farther out in the country was a perfect hiding place. It was only the obstetrician who delivered the baby at the house who knew, and was bound by professional confidence to not divulge anything. It was plausible that Oliver was ignorant to it all. The comfort of believing that inspired Polly to place a kiss on his cheek.

"What was that for?" he asked playfully.

"For always being so wonderful, Ollie."

Dorthey, Mama, and the children were all at the house when they arrived. Papa was expectedly absent.

"Oliver, please stay for dinner," Mama requested.

"I am sorry, Mrs. Williams, I have a family commitment tonight, but I shall see all of you Friday as planned."

Mama had already prepared a platter of cold cuts and cheese sandwiches, sliced pickles, and potato salad.

"This is most unlike you," Polly said. "Usually, it's schnitzel or soup. This is very American." Polly laughed, making note of the first television set in the house.

"Children, come here and see your aunt Polly." Dorthey ushered the children into a row.

"I have some gifts for you," Polly said reaching for her satchel.

Teddy, who was now five years old, ran to her. He admired the little hand-painted wooden train car with rotating wheels. With his new train conductor hat on, he called out "Choo-choo!" while he rolled the train along the furniture.

Sonja stood peering out from behind her mother's leg. Only with the lure of the gift, and a push from her mother, did she approach. "Thank you, Auntie," she said sweetly. She seemed unimpressed by the doll with the frilly dress and eyes that opened and closed.

"Do you like it?" Polly desperately wanted to please her. She reprimanded herself for not previously thinking of the fact that Sonja likely inherited all of Dorthey's dolls. Knowing Dorthey, there were regular additions. "Perhaps, Sonja, while I am here, we can make a trip to the toy shop in town, and you can pick out anything that you like as a gift from Auntie Polly." Sonja looked at her skeptically. "Perhaps a rocking horse or a tea set?" Polly tried.

The little girl looked at her mother, who encouraged her with a wide smile and nod of the head. "Could I get a train too? Just like Teddy?"

"Of course!" Polly laughed, appreciating her spunk and preferences for the non-traditional.

"Where's the baby?" Polly asked excitedly.

"Still sleeping. Let me get her." Dorthey returned a few minutes later with Baby Miriam. Not quite two years old, she was delicate and small for her age. Her hair, still wispy tufts, set off her biscuit-sized hazel eyes and broad forehead.

"May I?" Polly reached for the girl, nestling her close to her chest. She dared not squeeze her too tightly, yet she wanted desperately to melt this child into her. The smell of lavender wafted from her hair. She looked at Polly curiously, then turned and reached for Dorthey who eased her into her own arms. "Oh, Dorthey, she is beautiful!"

"Do you have presents for Miriam too?" Sonja asked in the sense of fairness and perhaps out of a bit of curiosity.

"As a matter of fact, I do." Polly retrieved a box of delicate white knit sweaters, caps, and matching socks. A poufy dress with tiny yellow daisies all about it, complemented by a yellow satin ribbon about the waist that matched the crinoline. The absurdity of the outfit struck Polly at the moment. "It was so adorable, I couldn't resist it." She rummaged through her bag. "Wait, I have more." She pulled out a stuffed cream bunny with floppy ears, a series of children's books, and an abacus colored like a rainbow.

"Why does Baby get more than me?" Sonja asked her mom with a pout.

"Sonja, that is not very polite. Be grateful for what you have. Go on and play now." Dorthey apologized. "I do try to treat them all equally. She's too young to understand."

They spent the afternoon in the garden updating each other on life, and playing with the children. Mama shared synopses of the daytime series she was following on television. Dorthey made them laugh with stories about motherhood. First words, sleepless nights, and playing in the snow. Polly, careful to drape everything in a positive light, described life and work at Oxford. Before dinner, they returned to Dorthey's where Polly would stay. It was agreed to be the best arrangement so she could spend time with the children and catch up with her friend.

Friday dinner at her parents' house came quickly. Polly arrived early to help prepare. Compared to Mama and Dorthey she was useless in the kitchen, never having had to prepare anything more than oatmeal or a scrambled egg.

"*Minushka*, take the children and go play. Your father is in the living room. Spend some time with him." To soothe the angst Polly was emitting from every pore, her mother encouraged, "With time he will soften. Go. You can't avoid each other forever."

Polly draped her apron over the chair and took time to fix her skirt and wash her hands. The children burst through the door at the first mention of seeing Grandpapa. It was little Miriam who toddled over to him first. Her feet struggling to keep up with her excitement.

Papa sat in his usual chair, now faded across the armrest from years of wear. His pipe emitted the sweet smell that Polly remembered fondly. He brushed the little child away, "Not now, Miriam, Grandpapa is reading," and he shook his newspaper as if to prove the point.

Seized with sympathy, Polly scooped Miriam up and placed her on her lap at the piano. She played softly so as not to disturb his reading.

"This is middle C. If you can find it, the rest of the notes come naturally. You can then write any series of stories with music." Polly played a light version of Brahms' Lullaby.

"Have you composed anything recently?" Her father rustled his newspaper, which shielded his face. His voice was tight and gruff.

"Not since before . . . not since moving to England." Filled with regret and loss, she fought back tears. All she wanted was for things to be as they were before. She knew those moments of playfulness were lost, when the room would fill with father's pride and the unbridled enthusiasm of what was possible. Rekindling those feelings was growing harder as the memories stretched to scattered remnants.

Miriam placed her little hands on the keys and pressed middle C.

"Wonderful!" Polly applauded with merriment.

"I can play too, Auntie." Teddy rushed over and began pounding his fists up and down the keyboard.

"Teddy, no, stop!" She grabbed his hand before he could pierce the room with more noise. "Pianos are delicate instruments. You must respect them and treat them gently if you want them to make beautiful music."

"Teddy, you come here to Grandpapa!" The boy climbed up on the old man's lap, pulling his pipe from his mouth.

Papa looked much older than his age. A deep furrow had been carved between his brows, giving him the appearance of permanent worry. A significant weight loss caused his cheeks to jowl like a hound dog's. It was mostly the flat, distant look in his eyes that unnerved her. Her child self would have wondered what alien being had inhabited her father's body. She could not escape the deep regret of responsibility for this alteration.

"Teddy, tell Grandpapa what you are going to be when you grow up."

"A mine worker like my daddy," he said playfully, evidence that this was a game between them rehearsed many times. Papa gave a scowl. "No!" Teddy laughed arching his back, obviously very pleased with himself. "I am going to be an engineer just like you." This provoked a smile of approval from Papa, who then cuddled the boy tightly, until the boy's wiggles were too busy to contain.

"That's right. You need to study hard and follow the rules in life."

Polly wanted to speak up. Things had turned out well, had they not? Before she could craft her words, the doorbell rang. Polly stood to answer it. It was much too formal for Ollie to ring the bell. A quick knock and then letting himself in was his usual way. She wondered who it might be.

On the threshold stood Ollie, holding a bouquet of flowers, and beside him, a tiny speck of a woman with moss-colored eyes and blond hair set in large curls that cascaded over her shoulders.

"Polly, hello." Oliver stepped in, giving her an awkward kiss on only one cheek. Accustomed to the double kiss, Polly turned her head to the other side and her lips near landed square on his mouth. He moved back. "This is Lydia, my fiancée. Lydia, this is Polly."

Lydia leaned in and placed a kiss on each of Polly's cheeks with such grace that she seemed to waft through the air like a cloud.

Dumbstruck, Polly simply stood there, faltering over several words in an attempt to compose a sensible sentence.

"I take it Petar did not tell you?" He put his arm around Lydia. "That is why we came home, for Lydia to meet my family and, of course, for me to surprise her with the official proposal." Immediately, Lydia dangled her hand like a trained dog offering its paw.

"But you didn't say anything at the train station," Polly said, receiving no response. Oliver looked over at Lydia, who beamed at him with affection. "Come in. Welcome. What a lovely surprise to meet you, Lydia" Polly ushered them into the living room, introducing Lydia to everybody's surprise but Petar's, who had neglected to share this substantial news with anybody. He later confessed he did not think Ollie would go through with it, so didn't think it that important.

Mama played the ideal hostess, keeping plates full and conversation moving. Oliver had obviously shared much with Lydia about the Williams' household.

"How clever you are, Polly," Lydia began in her aristocratic British accent. The use of the familiar name itched Polly like a rash. "Oliver tells me you compose under a pseudonym to hide that you are a woman."

"Not really to hide," Oliver jumped in to her defense. "P. Andrzej was more typical of a composer name, and she wanted her music to be accepted for its quality and not create controversy over the gender of its composer."

Mama cleared her throat, quiet for the first time all evening. Lydia diverted the tension to questions about Oxford and academia.

"And what is it that you do?" Papa politely asked.

"Well, I studied ancient literature at the University of London. Right now, I'm teaching primary school until Oliver and I get married. Then I'll be his wife, and hopefully a mother soon."

Papa gave an audible grunt. "Your parents must be very pleased," he said with a note of envy. The others took to filling their mouths as an excuse not to speak. Polly just stared at Lydia, fork and knife poised in mid-air.

When the phone rang, everyone was grateful for the distraction. Petar took the opportunity to share a simple joke that played on a word pun. It was benign enough that everybody gave a chuckle.

"Paulina, that was Kata. You need to return to Toronto. Something has happened to Margaret." Her mother's voice quaked.

"Is it something to do with the wedding?"

"I don't think there will be a wedding." Kasia began clearing her half-full plate.

"We can drive you," Oliver offered. "We're heading to Toronto tomorrow for a few days in the city before flying back to London." Polly was grateful for his concern, and tortured by the idea of spending two hours in the car with Lydia.

"I don't think you should go." The words were non-negotiable. Papa spoke as if to himself. "Those women have ruined you enough."

Papa's words caused even Petar to set down his fork.

"I am not ruined." Polly glanced toward Oliver and Lydia, struck by both embarrassment and outrage.

Papa would not meet her gaze. An aura of pent-up anger oscillated about him, like a brewing thunderstorm.

She could not stay quiet. "I am a doctor of mathematics at the most prestigious university in the world. I am a published composer, a concert violinist, and pianist. I speak three languages fluently. I should say that none of that speaks of ruin."

Oliver attempted a truce. "Mr. Williams, if I may," he said in that non-threatening way that powerful and confident men have about them.

"You may not!" Papa stated firmly. His fist slammed on the table. Every piece of cutlery rattled. "You were ruined the day you arrived in this house unwed and pregnant." His eyes rimmed with tears. "The sacrifices we made for you, the plans for your future here. You ruined all of it."

Polly looked at Oliver quickly enough to register the shock on his face, while Lydia sat quietly with her head lowered and her hands in her lap trying to disappear.

"I was ruined the day I was a born into this world a woman!" She pushed her chair back, scraping the legs against the floor. "I have ruined nothing but the small-minded ideal of what a woman is and should be for you and men like you." Polly fiercely stared at each person around the table. Her persistence forced each of them to acknowledge her, to witness her vulnerability, her strength, her regret, and her fury knotted together like a dam. "Shame on you, Father," she continued, now directing her sole attention to him. "You told me I could do anything, be anything *I* wanted. You lied." The accusation, she knew, was a reach. "There was a qualifier to that. It was true only so long as it fit with your expectations, the dreams you dreamt for me."

She excused herself from the table with an apology to her mother. Without a word to anybody else, she chose to walk the eight kilometers to Petar's house. Her anger wore out through the streets of town before she reached home. Too sad for anything more, she climbed into bed fully dressed, removing only her shoes. The hollow space that had been carefully concealed over the years was ripped open again, weeping and fragile.

The following morning, Oliver arrived early to pick her up for the journey to Toronto. Nobody spoke about the evening before. Throughout the drive she often caught him looking at her in the rearview mirror. Kindly, Lydia filled the time with placid observations and quaint stories.

When Polly arrived at Kata's, the house had an ominous feel. All of the women were gathered in Kata's bedroom. Margaret was asleep in the bed. She looked pale. A hot water bottle positioned on her belly.

"What? What happened?" Polly rushed to her friend's side. Impatiently, she scanned their faces, waiting for somebody to tell her what was going on.

It was Mary who spoke first. Garrett had picked up Margaret after a late-night shift at the hospital, not wanting her to walk home alone. As they made their way through the parking lot, a group of four men—orderlies, they thought, from the hospital—attacked them. One held Margaret back while the other three began kicking and punching Garrett.

"They called him a thief. Said a black man shouldn't be stealing a white woman for a wife. She said they called him terrible names. Even the two colored men in the group joined in, saying he was setting back the rights of his people by choosing to be a slave to a white working woman." At that, Mary broke into tears and couldn't continue.

Kata picked up the story, explaining how they left Garrett bloodied and beaten on the ground. They then proceeded to rape Margaret.

"They used a beer bottle." Charlotte winced. "Said they didn't want to pick up any diseases from her." She mustered up the courage to continue. "Apparently, they continued to plunder her with the bottle, which broke inside her. Told her maybe next time she'd stick with her own kind. They left her there."

Polly did not flinch or blink. She needed to bear witness to this story for her friend. Each word brought a convulsion of disgust from her gut. Her face began to twitch and tears escaped silently along the channels of her face. The cruelty with which human beings could torture each other was inconceivable to her. Amidst her shock, a deep sorrow was birthed in her soul. How much hate could a person have for themselves that their only path toward survival was inflicting pain on another?

"Had somebody from the hospital not found her soon after, she likely would have bled to death." Kata sat on the bed beside Margaret, caressing her hair. "They ruptured her uterus. She had to have an emergency hysterectomy to stop the bleeding."

Kata said next what Polly knew to be true. "She won't be able to have children."

The greatest joys in Margaret's life were her love of her work, Garrett, and the prospect of being a mother someday. Polly was torn apart at the fragility of it all. A whole life taken away in one angry, impulsive moment.

"And Garrett?" she asked cautiously.

"Still in the hospital. Nobody is sure if he'll recover from the head injuries. We thought it safer for Margaret to be here." Kata's face contorted through a series of emotions and landed on sadness. "Oh girls, what kind of world do we live in? I thought my generation would change things for you. It seems we failed."

They sat in silence. No words. No tears. This irreversible trauma would change them, each in their own way. She prayed for Margaret's recovery, and with heavy guilt her mind wandered to those moments when she wished God to take away the baby that had been growing inside her. It was reprehensible then, and even more so now, Polly thought. God forgive her for ever having thought such things.

Polly spent the next week taking turns at Margaret's side. The rest of the time was spent mindlessly milling around the house, making simple meals or sleeping. A doctor from the hospital, a friend of Margaret's and Garrett's, came every day to check on her. Her strength recovered, but her agony persisted. She accepted tea and soup, nothing more. Her features grew darker and fiercer. She did not speak, except to the physician when answering his questions.

On the day that was to be their wedding, Margaret dressed with Mary's help. Together they went to the hospital. Later that evening, Garrett died in hospital from wound sepsis. Margaret remained by his bedside until he was taken to the morgue.

There were whispers around the hospital about the four men who were responsible. Nobody stepped forward to speak to police. After three weeks, the case was considered unsolvable.

CHAPTER 11

1955

Birds whistled in the yard, awakening with the sunrise. Finally, Polly was able to move out of the woman's dormitory to a quiet two-bedroom cottage just outside of the university core. She stretched her limbs, tight and sore from all of the gardening she had done over the weekend. She was tempted to roll back over onto the cool edge of her bed for just another few minutes of sleep, but the squirrels chasing each other across her roof would not have it. In their fun, they coaxed even the most tired people to rise from slumber and frolic with them into the day.

Polly donned a wool tunic dress with thick stockings. She wrapped the knitted blue shawl Dorthey had recently sent around her shoulders. English winters were damp. The cold rattled even a young person's bones like an old skeleton. She warmed her fingers over the kettle to loosen them up. At twenty-eight, her joints were increasingly stiff in the morning.

With her usual cup of Earl Grey tea and a slice of rye bread with butter and jam, she sat at the small two-person dinette and reread the letters she picked up at the post office the day prior. A series of birthday cards and gifts had arrived. As usual, Charlotte's was the largest. A new winter coat, designed by herself, ready to withstand any Canadian or English winter. Her design house was flourishing, she wrote. She loved New York. Sometimes she missed the mark on her prototypes, giving way to her natural tendencies of practicality and frugality over high fashion. This particular coat had not made this year's collection, replaced instead by a camel-colored wool full-length double-breasted one, adorned with leopard-print fur trim along the cuff and collar. A matching fur hat and leather gloves finished the outfit. The new design was featured in *Vogue* magazine—a clipping of it was included in the card. Polly was happy to take the cast-offs, leaving the fancy styles to the social elite.

Mama sent birthday wishes from her and Papa, and a dainty gold necklace with a music note charm that sat perfectly between her clavicles.

Margaret and Sadie both sent cards, short on words or updates. It was kind of them to remember.

The collection of work by P. Andrzej was growing in popularity. Her more youthful, lighter pieces were played less often, but were now notable with orchestras in parts of Europe. She had not been home since the trip for Margaret's wedding. Her musical writing had been prolific since her return. With nobody to help heal the wounds of grief and anger that she carried within her, it was through her violin she was able to purge all that festered.

This latest piece had been commissioned by a Sikh heiress with whom she grew acquainted during the girl's studies at Oxford. Upon hearing Polly play her newest piece—a dark, brooding violin soliloquy, full of tumultuous spins that set your head dizzy and your gut twisted—she insisted that she needed a composition just for her. She was soon departing back to her home country for her wedding to a man she barely knew. In lament of relinquishing her freedom for security and good business relationships between families, she wished for one festive piece, something that captured the joyous and high-spirited time she had spent abroad.

Polly played light strokes to capture youthfulness. The scurry of squirrels inspired quick rapid jumps from lower strings to higher strings for friskiness. Sparingly, she added the longer, deeper notes, which were now considered her signature. She tried hard to muster up beautiful colors of fuchsia and yellow in her mind, but the image of this young girl betrothed to somebody she barely knew kept pulling dark forest greens and mustard yellows instead. Polly would do her best to deliver what was asked, but commissioned work was not for her. Great music came when it did and could not be conjured on a whim.

Jasu Kaur Deol was as beautiful as any woman Polly had met. Her lustrous black hair was braided densely, like the surface roots of great majestic trees. Her ocher-colored skin was smooth and unblemished. Dark coiffed brows framed her cocoa bean eyes, giving her a permanent expression of curiosity. At just over five feet, she was still an imposing figure, exuding an aura of strength and wisdom, which humbled Polly in her presence. Like all foreign students she resided in the dormitory but was granted permission to construct a larger space by removing a dividing wall between two adjoining rooms. Payment for the work and traditional Punjabi decor were funded by her father, along with a substantial donation to the university.

"Please come in." Jasu sweepingly gestured as she fully opened the door. "It is an honor to welcome you, Professor Williams. May I offer you some tea?"

Polly put down her violin by the embroidered armchair and accepted the cup of tea. There was a sensual aromatic spice to the tea, unlike the traditional English style. It was surprisingly sweet. The complex flavors were satisfying and unlike anything she had drank before.

"You like it!" Jasu was pleased, offering a second pour, which Polly eagerly accepted. She then presented a plate to Polly, as well, which she politely declined. "I shall miss these tea cakes when I return home," Jasu said, placing two on her own plate.

They discussed final papers and festivities planned by the students to celebrate semester's end. The welcome return to warmer weather for Jasu, and the contrasting Canadian winters, which Polly reflected upon fondly.

"You have finished the music?" Jasu clapped her hands together in anticipation. "Play it for me." Despite being the senior of them by four years, and the teacher, Polly felt younger in contrast to Jasu's bold confidence.

Golden sunset hues and the complex secondary colors from the furniture in the room came alive with the sonata. Polly erred thrice during the demonstration, her fingers fumbling on the middle adagio movement, drawing a warm blush to her face. Damp with perspiration accentuated by the tea spices, she wiped the dampness from her violin with her cotton cloth, and her brow with the back of her hand.

Polly could see the perplexed expression on Jasu's face. "You don't like it?" she asked, disappointed, packing away her violin in its case.

Jasu bit her upper lip. Her eyes narrowed as she thoughtfully searched for her next words. "It was lovely. The beginning was simply perfect. The end . . . it seemed sad."

"Is it not sad, going off to marry somebody you don't know, somebody you don't love?"

Jasu laughed comically with her head thrown back. The statement appeared to be utter nonsense to her, which Polly attributed to her innocent view of the world. "Jasu, you are a smart woman. You don't have to do this. You could stay here, finish your degree, perhaps teach." Polly reached over and placed her hand on the girl's arm in gentle support.

"Oh, Dr. Williams, I am not sad about my future. I am optimistic." Jasu leaned forward, stacking her free hand on top of Polly's. "My father has chosen for me a kind man. A good man. Together our families are building the new capital city of Chandigarh, where my people will be able to have health in body, spirit, and mind."

"You are sacrificing yourself so your father and this man can be financially prosperous." Polly was unmoved.

"My father has sent me here to be educated, to learn how we can be successful in building this city. Father and Raj both believe in education. It is the great equalizer for any gender, race, or religious group." Jasu stood and walked over to the cherry wood writing table in the corner. She withdrew a small white box with a blue ribbon on it.

"Through education we develop tolerance, understanding, self-respect, and an ability to fulfill our greatest potential, however it be designed for us. Our city will have universities of its own so our people can learn, so our children and our children's children can continue to do better." Jasu took a sip of tea. Her gaze drifted off into a daydream. "Change takes time, and I am part of this next step. Someday my daughters and granddaughters will run countries and militaries. Today, though, I begin with my contribution to bring this opportunity to people through my father and my soon-to-be husband." She handed Polly the box. "Open it. A gift for you."

Inside was a thick iron bangle with simple adornments of varying ridges and lines traced around the circle. "This is a *kara*. In my religion we wear these as a symbol of our commitment to God. It is to remind us to do no harm by our hands, only to use our whole selves for goodness. It will protect you, ward off bad karma."

Jasu placed the bracelet on Polly's right wrist. "For you. To continue to create goodness in your work, and to allow nothing to stop you."

Polly cupped her wrist with her left hand. "Thank you, Jasu. I don't know what to say."

"Say nothing. Just do. Now, we both must go to class. And I thank you immensely for my song. I shall forever think of you and my time here when I listen to it."

That evening, Polly returned to the dormitory and slipped the pages of a new sonatina under Jasu's door. When Jasu would hear it for the first time upon her return home, played to her by her old music teacher, she would weep with joy. The spirit of the song filled her with not only optimism and celebration, but it also lingered with a feeling of a promise in the last few bars, whispers of more to come.

Winter semester had just ended. There were only three weeks until the spring start to recuperate. Joan had invited her to a preparatory session at Cambridge, an opportunity for female teachers and teaching assistants to share new ideas for the coming term. From there, she had arranged a trip to London for Charlotte's new store launch. She had agreed to lunch with Oliver and Lydia, at Mama's behest. Polly had declined to go to their wedding as a representative of the family. Mama was both embarrassed and disappointed that Polly, already being on this side of the ocean, had excused herself as otherwise committed to a performance of her latest concerto. Truly an event she could have missed had she had the courage to go.

Cambridge was splendid this time of year, with outdoor skating rinks and stands that sold hot cocoa right along the pond's edge. Girton College was not dissimilar to the familiar buildings at Sommerville. The dark wood paneling, decorative carpeting, and the musty smell of history emanated from each room.

Joan graciously introduced her to a few of the younger faculty, all of whom were closer to Mama's age than her own. Over whiskey and gin cocktails, the ladies discussed the challenges of teaching.

"The girls are so distractible—all they think about are boys," said the woman who taught Greek and Roman history.

"I am not sure why some of them come to school at all," said another. "They obviously are not interested in learning."

Most, though, praised their students' dedication to furthering themselves.

"It is our responsibility to break the pattern, create a new expectation for women in education and the work force. That's why we are here, to learn how we can inspire them to be more," Joan spoke. All the others in the room nodded their heads. Those who had spoken out in criticism bowed their heads in reflection. "We should redefine the stereotypes. Let's be so bold that they can no longer ignore us."

Those final words brought a rousing cheer from the room. For the next hour they discussed deficits in university policy, inadequate research funding, and laboratory space, all which limited their ideal work. Surrounded by this handful of accomplished women Polly sat quietly, filing away their stories. There must be a way. Her mind darted, linking together the ensemble cast of her life: Sadie, Charlotte, Dorthey, Margaret, even Mama and Kata. How their lives would be different if they were allowed grace to be their own full person, without preconceived traits or expectations. Each person allowed to be both feminine and masculine, compassionate and strong, thoughtful and smart. For the first time since Kata's Friday salons, she began to feel alive again. She could do more, be more, change more about the world.

"Polly, you've been quiet. You're among friends—please don't be shy." Joan gave an encouraging nod.

"I don't really have much to say. My classes are very small. Not too many women entering into mathematics. Most take it as a requirement for their programs in medicine or nursing." Polly looked about the room with held breath. She shifted in her chair and fiddled with her glass. For years, she had to deal with an array of obstacles. Their impact on her, she truly did not even know. For the first time, she had a group with whom she could share all of her agitation. "Publication is near impossible beyond some small economic journals in Canada and the Nordic countries. The larger journals will not pay me heed, as I do not teach at a college recognized as part of a university. None of my male colleagues will sponsor my work, even if I give them partial authorship." Polly threw up her arms and let the frustrations regurgitate from her soul. "The whole concept of needing a sponsor is ridiculous!"

The women offered nods of supports. Deep grumblings echoed in the room, as they discussed their own plights of being paid a pittance, if paid at all. Often consigned into a supporting role like proofing equations and marking tests.

"Your contributions are collaborative. For a woman, that is where you work best," one woman was told.

Another teacher of natural sciences was told, "We could not put too much responsibility on you, for what would the faculty do when you go off to have babies? Your brain will turn to raindrops and bonnets. We simply can't risk our reputation on that inevitability."

The evening wound to an animated close. Each person was energized to take on tomorrow's challenges. Polly lingered for a private farewell with Joan.

"Thank you for the invitation. I had forgotten how wonderful it is to have female friends."

"You're welcome, Paulina. Your freshness added much to our conversation this evening." Joan crossed her arms and looked contemplatively at Polly. If she could see inside Joan's brain, Polly was sure she would have an electrical storm of activity lighting up where all the synapses were firing off. "Why are you waiting?" Joan probed.

Polly was confused. Her own brain at this moment would have looked like a swirl of gray clouds. "Pardon?"

"Why wait for them to change the rules? What would it take to get Sommerville recognized as a college of the university? How hard could it be?"

The task Joan proposed was daunting. Time and energy were so precious already. The political repercussions could end her career instantly.

"Think about it." Joan embraced her with a mother's warmth. "Be an agent of disruption. Resist the equilibrium of playing small. Step into the largeness that is inside of you." She pulled back, her hands still clasping Polly's arm. Joan's eyes glinted with an energy that Polly wished she could bottle and take with her. "We can only succeed at things that we try."

The next morning Polly boarded a train for London. Joan's words percolated throughout her dreams all night. She arrived at the hotel recommended to her by Oliver. It was far posher than any she had stayed in before. She was certain she could not afford it. With only an hour until she was meeting Oliver and Lydia for lunch in the adjoined restaurant, she had no time to look for a different place. She would simply need to accommodate her discretionary spending over the coming months to manage, she decided. No point in worrying about it now.

Never before had she seen such soft white linens and a duvet so overstuffed with feathers that you disappeared into its folds. Refreshed after a shower, she luxuriated in the comfortable warmth of the plush complimentary bath robe. She took extra effort to hide the dark circles under her eyes. Sleep did not come easily to her anymore. A slight sparkle of pink shadow under her brow brightened them. The cornflower-blue and white tweed skirt and jacket, with gold embossed buttons—another of Charlotte's creations—brought out the beautiful flecks of gold in her hair and eyes.

After presenting herself to the maître d'hôtel, he ushered her through a large room in which everyone was much too attractive and seemed to be having a perfectly splendid, leisurely time. White wine and champagne poured at every table, served with oysters, salad lyonnaise and poached fish. A significant variation from the pot pies and stews to which Polly was accustomed.

Oliver was alone at the table that was set for three. He looked particularly handsome with his hair grown slightly longer than he recently wore it, allowing his natural curls to spring out again. He greeted her in their customary way, kisses on each cheek. She was still in disbelief that he was married. She knew so little of his life now. Sorrow draped over her shoulders as she sat down.

"Is Lydia not joining us?" Polly asked cautiously.

Oliver diverted his eyes and cleared his throat. "No, she wasn't feeling very well today."

"Oh. I see." After a further pause, Polly added, "I suppose she wasn't so keen to see me, given the unpleasantness of our last encounter."

"It isn't that," Oliver was quick to justify. He shook his head. A conversation was circling quietly within him. "She isn't well. Actually, a recent miscarriage."

Polly dropped her gaze in embarrassment. It was silly of her to assume that this was in any way about her. "I'm sorry." She placed a consoling hand onto his, herself feeling a longing tug in her heart for a lost baby. Pierced by the guilt that she had once wished for a miscarriage.

"Her second, actually." Oliver was quiet, his eyes misty. "How are you?" He tried to brighten his mood.

"Good. Better than the last time we saw each other." Polly took a sip of her water to quell her nerves.

"About that. Petar explained to me." He paused. "I don't know what to say. Other than, I wish I had known before. I could have helped in some way."

"What could you have done?" Polly was pointed.

"I don't know. Perhaps if this scoundrel and I had met, I would have scared him off before he hurt you." Oliver looked at her bashfully. "Maybe, if I had told you how I felt about you, you wouldn't have been with him at all."

At that moment, she wished she could rewind her life, back to that Christmas they spent together both home for the holidays. Maybe if she had allowed herself the honesty of her feelings, things would be different. She had mused about what life would be like with Oliver. He was one of the only people she ever trusted, always wanting to take care of her. She simply rejected the need to be taken care of. But that holiday she was pregnant already, and what would Oliver have done when it was found out.

"About the baby . . ."

"I do not wish to talk about it," she insisted. "It is never to be spoken of. What is done is done." They said nothing for a minute. Each sipped their water and pretended to review the menu. "You look tanned," she offered the placid statement as a peace offering.

"Skiing. A snow tan from the Alps. I go often in the winter." He smiled, signaling acceptance of the truce.

"I've never skied before. It looks fun, though I'm concerned it would be rather too dangerous for me, given my clumsiness."

"I'll take you sometime! With a good teacher, there is nothing to fear. You just need to learn how to fall softly."

"Falling at all doesn't sound fun!"

They ordered lunch and shared a languid afternoon together. When the waitstaff began to hover about their table as a signal to depart so they could prepare for the dinner settings, Oliver noticed they were the only patrons left in the restaurant. He suggested an afternoon walk.

"Don't you have to return to work, or Lydia?"

"I scheduled my afternoon off, and Lydia is with her parents. Her mother would prefer that I not be there. Prickly, that one is."

Polly updated him on work, the published papers, and current developments in logic models and economic theory. She shared stories about her teaching and humorous details about the students. He inquired about the *kara* she wore on her wrist. She was impressed that he knew what it was. As the evening grew near and the sky darkened, they found a bench near the hotel upon which to sit. As she delved into the details of Joan and the evening at Girton Hall, he listened with intense interest.

"You need to do it, Polly! If anybody can, you can." He took her hands in his. She noted the platonic affection between them. "Let's not be strangers, Polly. I miss us. Our friendship."

She nodded. This afternoon with Oliver filled a warm place in her, a feeling of home and security.

"If you can stay in town until the weekend, Lydia and I would love to have you join us at our home. A small gathering of friends for dinner."

She had plenty of time still left of the school hiatus. After these many years of teaching, there was little preparatory work required. She would simply recycle what she had previously used for lessons in the first week. The cost of the hotel, though, would be ghastly.

"I really didn't bring enough clothes."

"What you are wearing is perfect. My friends couldn't care less about what you put on your feet—all they will care about is where those feet have taken you."

It was decided. Polly extended the hotel room for three additional days. It meant frugal lunches, and new shoes would need to wait until later in the season. With the extended time, she agreed to meet with Charlotte on Sunday at the store instead. The final touches would just be in progress for the grand opening of the boutique the following week.

Each day, she explored a new part of London with glee. Alleyways and dark corners that inspired Shakespeare and Dickens. Hours in awe of the great masterpieces in the galleries. Quiet moments to read in St. James Park, or meander through the bookstores and shops. Invigorated again by the world, she felt fearless—and just the slightest bit reckless.

Despite Saturday evening being mild, she wore her winter coat, having brought no light jacket with her on the trip. The short distance from the hotel to Primrose Hill was hardly worth the taxi fare. Crossing those few blocks, she was transported to an entirely new world, where rows of white-washed stone and brick homes lined the streets. The upper class lived here. Polly sensed that behind each door was an exquisitely decorated home, in which lived beautiful people, who wore designer clothes and perfume. This assumption was reinforced when Lydia opened the door to No. 59, and Polly crossed the simple front threshold into a marble entryway. At the center sat a large round table crowned with a bouquet of fresh flowers in an elaborate vase. The entirety of the bouquet was larger than many lilac bushes. Vanilla and fresh burning wood scents wafted through the air. Everything was decorated in shades of cream, pale Tuscan yellow, and baby blues.

Lydia looked thinner and more tired than before. Not surprising given her recent misfortune. Perhaps it was the black color of her Chanel suit that make her appear aged. She graciously took Polly's coat.

"This is a beautiful coat," she said admiringly. "A Charlotte original," she said noting the label at the collar. "They must pay you well at Oxford."

Polly flushed. "It was a gift from Charlotte. We're old friends. This too." She gestured to the blue skirt suit she had worn the other day to lunch, the only fashionable piece of clothing she brought with her.

"Well. I hope you can introduce me to her someday!"

"I am actually seeing her tomorrow, at her new store."

She sensed that Lydia was awaiting an invitation to join, which Polly refrained from offering, to her hostess's apparent disappointment. She was still unsure how she felt about Lydia; they certainly were not close in such a way that she was willing to share with her this rare time with Charlotte. "Shall we?" Lydia gestured toward the party.

Guests flowed in and out of the rooms on the main floor. All appeared very familiar with each other and comfortable in the space they occupied. Waitstaff weaved through the guests with precariously balanced trays of champagne flutes or canapes.

For several minutes they toured the house, exchanging what her mother called "social niceties," during which Lydia pointed out the meticulous details and Polly feigned interest with words of admiration. Lydia snatched a champagne glass from a passing waiter's tray, handing it to Polly. She then escorted her to a group of women sitting in the living room, wives of Oliver's work colleagues. It took only a few words exchanged between them to decide that Polly was of another breed, and the conversation resumed around her. Polly knew it was time to go. She would find Oliver, say hello, and then head back to the hotel for an evening cup of milk and a read of her book before an early bedtime.

Her eyes scanned the room, mapping her escape. She graciously excused herself from the group, all of whom were oblivious to her. Before she could amble toward the door, Oliver was beside her with two glasses of champagne.

"For you." He offered her one. "I am so glad you came."

He ushered her by her elbow to the corner of the room, where they had a clear vantage of the entirety of this and the adjoining room. Oliver took her through the names, titles, and connections of each person at the party. Occasionally, he would drop a scintillating or salacious detail that made them both laugh. A slight British accent was forming, evident in the way he drew out his vowels.

"Who is that?" Her attention was drawn to a man in his late thirties. He stood over six feet tall, had a thin frame, and a laugh that could be heard across the room.

"Hans Nillson. He is a chemist from Sweden. His father is a teacher, his mother a housewife. Came here for work a couple of years ago. We do a lot of work with his firm. I think he does some teaching on the side at the University of London."

"Can you introduce me?" Polly felt a bit of unaccustomed excitement. Perhaps it was the week of freedom in the city, or the glasses of champagne.

Oliver made a brief introduction between Polly and Hans. He watched with piqued curiosity as they quickly fell into deep conversation, until a colleague drew him away to settle a point of contention between two friends.

"Wait . . . are you the same Paulina Williams who authored the economic theory of staggered cost and wage adjustments?" Hans looked intriguingly at her.

"Yes! You're familiar with it?" She was both shocked and flattered.

"It was a tremendous think piece." He paused and took in her expression. "You look surprised." He seemed entertained by her reaction.

"It simply surprises me that you know my work. Not many people do." She was spurred with a new confidence.

"I still have my subscriptions to my favorite journals from home forwarded here. It really was a novel and well-articulated theory. You should be very proud."

She appreciated his sincerity and repaid it with a coquettish smile. They spent the next several hours chatting about their work, their childhoods, and the peculiar behaviors of the English. He discovered she had not driven a car since arriving. She struggled with the idea of driving on the opposite side of the road to what was intuitive to her, and feared turning into on-coming traffic.

"Nonsense! How do you know if you haven't even tried!" He insisted she drive his car home. After much cajoling she agreed. Both thanking their host and hostess for a wonderful night, they slipped into the cool night air.

Windows rolled down to enjoy the fullness of the evening, she put the car into first gear. Not only had she not driven on the left side of the road, she had not driven in years. They chugged through the streets slowly, managing to neither stall nor cross to the wrong side. Both of which they celebrated with cheers and cocktails in the hotel lounge.

That evening she let herself be kissed and touched for the first time since Eli. The deliciousness of it was like a first taste of hot chocolate.

In the morning she awoke smiling, with welcome memories of Hans's arms wrapped around her. The boyish sweetness with which he kissed her. His lingering stare before he bid her goodnight.

Reluctantly she rose from bed, her head heavy from the champagne. Check-out would be soon, and Charlotte was expecting her. In the hotel lobby she waited her turn to pay the bill, discreetly counting the money she carried in her purse, fearful she would not have enough. The receptionist pulled up her account with confirmation that it had been paid and settled by a Mr. Oliver Baker.

Her dearest friend, Ollie, still looking out for her after all these years. Across town, she arrived at Charlotte's store for noon. Seeing her name across the sign, in her signature scrawl, was impressive. Until then, she hadn't truly realized just how successful her friend had become.

A cluster of congratulatory flowers she had purchased at a corner stall held in her hand, she rapped on the door to get Charlotte's attention. Striking in a black fitted dress and high heels stacked like a roll of pennies, her hair dried straight and left to hang loose to the middle of her back, she welcomed Polly with an excited flair.

"This is Isabella, my partner," she said. A petite voluptuous woman greeted her. Polly was drawn in by her large seductive brown eyes and radiant honey-colored skin.

"So lovely to meet you," she said with a Latin accent. "Darling, I shall leave you two to visit. I'll be back shortly to finish steaming the clothes." With a pleasant nod to Polly, she stepped over to Charlotte and gave her a short kiss on the lips. "See you soon!" she hollered as she stepped out the door.

"She is stunning," Polly gasped.

"That she is," Charlotte said appreciatively.

"Is she . . .? Are the two of you . . .?" Polly stumbled over her words like a toddler learning to walk.

Charlotte both blushed and glowed, like a dusting of sunshine had kissed her face. "We are figuring each other out." With a faraway look in her eyes, and the slight smile that crested her lips, Polly knew she was in love. "Does that bother you?" Charlotte asked, evidently guarding herself for the answer.

"We should all be so lucky to find somebody who makes us feel like our bodies are coursing with champagne." They both laughed, appreciating the levity Polly brought back to the moment.

They moved throughout the store with Charlotte describing the vision behind each of her new pieces. The Toronto store was now running smoothly under the direction of a savvy manager. Charlotte had decided to move some of her production to London to cater to the handmade-couture clientele in Europe, which was very different in taste and paid more meticulous attention to detail than the North American market.

Upstairs, she had a modern design office and elegant fitting area for private commissions. In the back was a spacious sewing area with reams of fabric, trays of fastenings, and mannequins at the end of each table. Two other management offices were positioned at the back, one with Isabella's name on the door, the title "Clientele Relations" underneath it.

Polly shared general updates about work. Most of the time she chatted about the last two weeks she had spent in Cambridge and London.

"I described to Hans my idea of having a group at Oxford, like they have at Cambridge, of women academics and professionals to work as a support network for each other. He called me a 'bluestocking girl.' A term for intellectual women who gather to discuss literature and art, I understand."

"It sounds like Hans has finally been able to break through and stir you up again," Charlotte chided.

"We simply kissed, nothing more." Her cheeks matched the salmon color of her scarf. "It was nice. He was nice."

"Will you see him again?" Charlotte asked, lighting a cigarette in her long slim holder. Polly lit one as well.

"He said he would come up to visit me soon. We shall see."

"Isa would kill me if she knew I was smoking up here. The smoke makes the fabric smell, she says. She calls it a dirty habit. Lectures me that it will make me look old quickly." Charlotte drew a long, slow pull on her mouthpiece, then let the smoke escape in a steady, controlled way that seemed so sophisticated.

"She's right," Polly said, trying to imitate Charlotte, but failing. "You can blame it on me, your uncouth friend." They both laughed, then lapsed into reminiscence about antics in the attic, exploring Toronto's music clubs, and Kata's Friday evenings.

They avoided any mention of Margaret until Polly asked, "Any word on how she's doing?"

"Last I heard, she was working in a women's health clinic in the poor part of town. She isn't living at Kata's anymore. I only hear bits from Mary but they don't talk much either." Charlotte sobered. "I don't know what I would have done if that happened to me."

The thought lingered quietly between them. It was enough to put the strongest of people in a coffin of depression. Time drew near three, and Polly needed to go. They agreed to stay more closely in touch. With Charlotte's jaunts to London, they would see each other more often. Before she left for the train, she had the cab driver stop at Oliver's house, where she left a thank-you note for Oliver with the housekeeper, as well as a pair of cuff links she'd picked up at a men's store near Charlotte's. For Lydia, she left an exclusive invitation to Charlotte's store opening the following weekend.

For the entirety of the trip home, she planned her "Bluestocking Club." She spent the last week of spring reprieve introducing her idea to other women faculty members, many of whom she had never spoken to before. Polly's passion for the cause and clear vision for change were contagious. By the time the spring semester began, Polly, Sarah from the library, and six professors from various faculties had begun work on making the women's colleges at Oxford equal to all others on campus.

CHAPTER 12

1958

Officially they had no title. Simply a group of women who met monthly to share ideas and support each other. Nobody thought much of them initially. Many assumed they discussed motherhood and crocheted blankets. The membership had grown over the last three years to include teachers, students, and other professional women from the community. As it did, the group was referred to sarcastically as the "Bluestocking Club," a derogatory reference to the female society of intellectuals from the 17th century.

The women themselves took silent pride in the nod to great female leaders of the past, humored by the whispers of their colleagues, as if they were an order of witches. Once they had declared their mission to petition that Somerville be granted equal status with the men's colleges, the volume of criticism increased.

Polly spent her evenings and many weekends speaking to groups across the university. Having equal status would create opportunities for broader publications and grants. As well, a woman would be eligible to become vice-chancellor or assume other leadership positions, along with having full debating rights in decision-making. Wanting equality of admittance to any of the colleges, not just the ladies', would allow for alumni patronage and scholarships. In the end, a broader exposure to diverse learning and a better experience for all students at Oxford.

"Our examination results are in the top five of all the colleges in the university. Matriculation rates are rising with more women interested in further education. Degree completion rates are higher than ever." Polly inspired the other women in the room to see a different future.

Monthly meetings moved to weekly, and most days over dinner in the dining hall it was the chatter around the tables. Those from Lady Margaret Hall, the other women's college, joined efforts. Soon the Oxford Union could no longer ignore this well-spoken resilient group. Early to the group was Lucy, a history professor who, upon hearing about Polly, sought her out in her classroom to inquire about joining.

Tall and slender, with an oblong face and austere nose, Lucy introduced herself.

"Yes, I know who you are. It is a great honor to meet you." Polly was humbled by the visit. Already at age fifty-three, Lucy had lived many lifetimes. She moved from her birth home in Australia to South Africa where she studied history. Coming to Somerville originally, she was enigmatic from the start. Being principal spokesperson to preserve the women's colleges back in the late 1920s, her legacy at the university was already established.

"I am quite impressed with the enthusiasm you have generated among the student body to stand up for their rights." Lucy stood with her hands clasped behind her back. The green suit she wore, with skirt falling mid-calf, jacket settling just below the hips, and high-collared white blouse, gave an aura of stillness. She seemed to belong any place she wished to be.

Polly shrugged. "Really, they were poised for it. Hungry for change. I simply started the conversation in a more formal way."

"You did more than that, young lady. Do not underestimate yourself." Lucy was the type of woman who commanded respect. The melodic tones of her unusual accent punctuated with strong annunciation, and the fixed gaze she held when she spoke, drew people to her. "You have started more than a conversation. An organized group of impassioned people, drawn together through a common manifesto, is a force. I would like to help."

Lucy and Polly spent many evenings mulling over by-laws and governance structures. They observed meeting procedures unnoticed at the back of the halls, taking vigorous notes. Polly's skills in economics and natural inclination toward observation, in synergy with Lucy's oratory skills and patient nature, made them wonderful partners. A magical inspiration infused a room when they were together.

Each person reinforced the strength of the group in her own way. Not since her school newspaper days had Polly sat in a room that was pulsating with a collective mission. Her writing skills polished up speeches and letter campaigns. Her spreadsheets reinforced the undisputable financial advantage to the university of adopting their recommendations.

Only Lucy could bring the room to attention, though. Methodically, she inserted pauses and inflections into her speech to draw the audience in. They had no choice but to follow along with the logical irrefutable story that was laid out to them. She met their emotional commitment to tradition with calm recognition, then used the great history of the university to continue the story of progress and legacy. When frustrations erupted, she allowed them to squabble among themselves, and after tension either roused to a piercing level or broke, she would demurely step in with a humble but practical solution that the group had prepared in anticipation.

One summer evening, they were interrupted by a knock on the door of Polly's cottage. They had been scribbling away on the plans for the next series of reports to the chancellor and committee for hours. Polly rose and opened the door to a surprise.

"Hans!" She wrapped her arms around him tightly, and kissed him six times about his face. One kiss for every week they had been apart.

Lucy excused herself to her office, taking the paperwork with her.

"What a surprise! I am so happy to see you!" She peppered him with further kisses until he laughed and picked her up. She wrapped her legs around his waist and allowed him to carry her to the chair where he promptly deposited her. "This isn't our usual stop," she teased.

"Polly, my love. Tonight, I came with something important to discuss." He looked somber. The usual playfulness that he brought to her world held in suspension. "Let's go for a walk."

Fear roused in Polly. Her instinct suggested this would be the end of their time together. She'd grown to love the weekend trips and school break vacations in London. Time spent with Hans was marvelous fun, full of concerts, theater, and trips to the countryside. She focused on her work without disruption through the weeks, and had plenty of time for the Bluestocking Club. Their magical interludes were always an exciting change that regenerated her energy for her return to work.

He held her hand as they walked along the garden path toward the park.

"Polly, I love you. More than any other woman I have ever met. You excite me in every way." She squeezed his hand in response. "But lately, I have been feeling like a common gigolo. Traipsing back and forth between home and here to catch wisps of time together."

She thought about the luscious mornings spent in bed curled into his embrace. It was the only time she slept past dawn and did not think about work. He would make breakfast for them both, while she played the violin for him. Each day together was an escape from the mundane routine of their real world. Losing that would leave an emptiness in her life.

"Are you leaving me, Hans?" Even she could hear the fragility in her voice.

"No, silly. I want to marry you." Hans stopped and turned her toward him. "Say yes, Polly. Say yes and let's start our life together, where we can be happy, always, together and not just in these bursts."

Polly stumbled over a small stone. Her ankle twisted. She buckled to the ground.

"Are you okay, my darling?" Hans pulled down her stocking to expose her ankle, which he gingerly examined, the intimacy of it drawing looks from others passing by. "Quite the dramatic way to avoid the question, don't you think?" His eyes twinkled mischievously.

"I'm fine," she said and pulled her ankle away to cover it again. She stood without accepting his hand for support and hobbled slightly for the next few steps. The pain was a reminder that life hurt. "I do love you," she said after a few quiet moments. The fact that he did not rush her for an answer spoke to their comfort with each other. "You in London, me here. How would that work?"

"Well, my company doesn't have any offices here. There is the London School of Economics or the University of London. I thought that perhaps you could get a teaching position there. In the meantime, you will have nothing to distract you from your research. Also, there would be plenty of time for your music." After a brief pause, he added, "You always love London when you come."

She had finally created a community here for herself. She had a revitalized sense of purpose to bring an equal voice for women to the university.

"May I think about it?" Polly was acutely aware that this response could blister their relationship. "I love you, Hans, and I do see us getting married someday," she added for reassurance.

He easily agreed to let her think about it. This steady, calm way he had was what she adored most about him. The remainder of the weekend was comfortably bland. Both spent time working, with breaks for walking in the parks and enjoying simple meals. She appreciated this easy symbiosis.

He did not bring up the proposal again that summer. It hung in the air like a scent that neither addressed but of which both were uncomfortably aware. At the end of summer, a message arrived from home. Her father was sick with cancer. Could she come?

It had been years since they had spoken. Mama mentioned nothing of him being unwell in any of her letters. Dorthey only gave updates about the children. She was not due back home for another year, still short a bit in her savings for the ticket.

Hans offered to pay for two tickets, citing, "It's time they met me, don't you think? Regardless of your decision, I would like to be there with you."

She took a three-week hiatus from the school, leaving her preparatory notes for her colleague to follow. Next steps in the Bluestocking Club were left in the competent hands of Lucy, with secretarial support from Sarah.

When they arrived two weeks after the initial letter, she found her father very changed. He remained mostly in bed, getting up only to sit in a chair by the window. The whites of his eyes and his skin were a sickly shade of yellow. His once thick hair was plastered by perspiration in thin white wisps against his visible scalp. At merely half his usual weight, the frailty was startling.

Eating was difficult. Mama fed him broth with ground marrow to strengthen him, to no avail. She helped bathe him and change his soiled clothing. Dorthey read to him on the weekends to give Mama a break.

Polly thought of the weekends she had spent galivanting through London to concerts and dinner parties with Oliver, Lydia, and Hans. Meetings of the club where they harped about not having enough female washrooms throughout the campus. All the while her father had been edging toward death, with Mama caring for him completely and exclusively as one would a child. Dorthey had become the daughter she should have been to him.

"Oh, Mama, why did you not tell me sooner?" Polly cried.

"There was nothing to tell, *minushka*. He complained of some digestive issues earlier this year. He had a difficult semester, the students more demanding, harder to control in the classroom.

He thought it was stress." She pushed away her tea. "Then things changed so quickly."

"I'm so sorry I've not been home more often. I should have. To see you and Papa." She lingered on his name. "And the children in particular. My heart has just felt so broken. I just didn't think I could."

"I understand, *minushka*." Her mother grabbed both her hands in a clasp. "This gentleman you have brought home. He seems lovely. Is it serious?"

"Hans. We have been together nearly three years. I mentioned him only briefly in my letters for my world back in England seems so separate to my life here."

"Tell me about him. Is he kind to you?" Kasia's tone was hopeful.

"Yes, Mama. He is very kind." Polly bit on the next piece, unsure whether to divulge anything more to her mother. "He has asked me to marry him. I told him I would consider it."

She felt her mother's grasp stiffen, then pull away. "You are not getting any younger, *minushka*. Soon your youth will abandon you and it will be harder. If he is kind like you say, why not say yes? Your time to have any more children will soon be gone."

"I am not sure I want children." She braced herself for what would come next.

"But you always wanted children. What woman doesn't—" Mama caught herself. Her expression softened. "Have you told him yet, about the baby?"

Polly jumped quickly. "No, Mama! Never!" She paced the room, desperate for a cigarette.

"What if someday you wish to . . ."

"There will be no someday. What was done was done. Petar and Dorthey and Oliver are the only ones who know, outside of you and Papa. We have all sworn to never speak of it again."

Her mother dismissed her with a swat of her hand. "It is not so easy to forget, *minushka*." She joined Polly at the window, both staring out to the garden. "Papa is hard on Miriam. She reminds him of you. Sonja, too. He has grown hard in his old age. It is only Teddy he wishes to be with." Mama let out a big sigh. "Petar and Dorthey say nothing. I see it is hard on them."

"Mama, I don't know what you wish me to say. There is little I can do." Polly was terse. Desperately, she wished to escape, to fly back to Oxford and lose herself in her work again.

Petar creaked open the kitchen door. "He wants to see you, Polly."

She followed Petar up the stairs, grateful she was not entering the room alone. Each floor board depressed slightly under her step; the runner carpet so worn that the pattern was no longer visible. The room smelled of a decomposing animal as nature did its work. It was unbearable. Petar's broad shoulders and large arms, strengthened from years of working at the quarry, wrapped around Father, and scooped him up like a doll. Petar transferred him to the chair by the window. As he walked toward the door, to leave them alone, she grabbed his arm to stop him. "Thank you," was all she could say. He nodded.

"It is good to have you home Polly," Petar said. "We all missed you."

"I'm glad to be home."

All was good between them, she could tell. She kissed him on the cheek, a promise that it was time to reconnect, though she knew it would never be the same as when they were young.

Papa looked at Polly with eyes so sad she turned away. She had been gone from this town, from this house, for too long. She had no idea what his life had been like. Had he found a new way to still love her?

Polly drew the wooden chest over and sat beside her father. They said nothing for nearly half an hour. Both just sat, side by side, looking out the window at the overgrown garden.

"Play something for me," he finally said in a barely audible voice.

"But I did not bring my violin with me," she said. She had put it by the front door of her cottage, planning to take it with her, but chose to leave it. This would not be a visit that would welcome music, she assumed. The piano was terribly out of tune, not having been played in years.

"Your old one is in your room." Papa looked at her with deep regret, the misery so evident in his darkened, dull features. His body resigned to rest in a pile of bones upon themselves without strength to uphold a posture. Desperately, he seemed to be looking for peace.

She retrieved the old violin given to her by Professor Randall all those years ago. Too small for her now, she took to tuning it.

"Play me *A Winter's Tango*." Then he added a meek, "Please."

She had not played that song in years. The memory of being dismissed at the Toronto Symphony for being a woman was still upsetting to her. The song was never lost to her, though. She played every note with commitment, as if it would be the last time. For the next two hours, she held her violin, creating music with such passion that through her tears the colors blended and merged. A kaleidoscope of a lifetime's missed memories was shared.

Her fingertips cracked. Joints stiff and aching, she placed the instrument down.

"I am sorry, Paulina." With effort her father raised his arm to caress her face. "All of these years I have let my anger keep you away. Forgive me."

"I do, Papa. I am so sorry to have disappointed you."

"I have only ever wanted you to be happy, Polly. To accomplish something exceptional in life. To marry, have children. Have a happy life." Grief wrapped itself about his face.

"Oh, Papa. I am happy. I have everything I could want, considering . . ." She let the word hang, not wanting to upset him. "And Hans and I are getting married." The words surprised her. They escaped so quickly, and brought such a joy to her father's face, that she could not take them back.

It was settled that day, to the delight of everybody. Since Hans's family was in Sweden and their friends in England, they would have a small civil ceremony in Kingston so her father could attend, followed by a reception when they returned home to London to celebrate with their friends.

The day of the wedding arrived. Miriam, a few days shy of her tenth birthday, was the flower girl. Dressed in a simple pink summer frock, she stood tall for her age.

"Auntie Polly, thank you so much." Unable to get the rest of her words out, she clutched her aunt in an embrace.

"For what, my dear, sweet girl?" Polly stroked her hair which smelled like lavender, just as when she was a child herself.

The girl pulled back, with her head upright and looking directly at her aunt. She possessed a wisdom beyond her years. "Your letters, your gifts, your books. They give me something to look forward to."

"Are you unhappy?" Polly asked with concern.

"No, Auntie, just restless. Mama and Papa are always busy with work and chores. Teddy is off with his friends all the time. Sonja and I are just so different. She fusses over trifle things that I find boring." Polly gave an appreciative chuckle. She understood wholly. "Grandpapa never seems happy with me. I try to avoid being in his sight so as not to irritate him too much. Grandmama is my only friend, but she is getting old and needs to spend all her time caring for Grandpapa."

"Oh, my dear." Polly gave her a large, enveloping hug, which the girl sunk into. "When you are a little bit older, there will be a new freedom you can capture. The world will be yours and nothing will be able to stop you."

Miriam looked hopeful. "I know you and Hans," she corrected herself, "Uncle Hans, will have your own family one day. Would it be possible, though, for you not to forget me? To still send me letters when you can?"

The quiet sorrow tore at Polly. "I shall never forget you." A promise was exchanged between them. "You can come spend time with us in England whenever you like. Perhaps even go to school there someday." The idea of it excited them both.

She was unsure if she was too old to have any children with Hans. His philosophy was to leave it in the hands of God. Polly imagined the three of them living in a home similar to Oliver's. She, teaching and continuing her research, Hans being promoted to vice-president at the chemical company, and Miriam studying at the university, setting off together each morning for the Underground with their lunch bags in hand.

Petar carried Papa downstairs and seated him in his usual armchair. The Justice of the Peace arrived a few minutes later. Polly, dressed in a white linen summer dress she found on sale in one of the downtown stores, and Hans, in the only suit he brought with him, were married in her childhood home that afternoon. It was not the wedding she and Dorthey had dreamed up as children. At the end of the day, they were married and that was what was important, she reminded herself.

Hans returned to London a few days later for work. Polly was granted an extended leave from her teaching due to father's health issues. They celebrated Miriam's birthday just after Labor Day. Polly took extra care in planning the event to make it as memorable as possible for her. She wanted Miriam to always remember her fondly.

Papa died, after weeks of pain and starvation, one early October morning. The funeral was well attended by the university community, where he was seen as a diligent and respected man. Only Petar spoke, his eulogy simple. A repast was held at the faculty club, as was the custom for any active staff member.

Mama said very little other than the customary "Thank you" and "He was a good man" statements as people offered their condolences. She did not cry.

Polly left a few days later. She offered to stay to help Mama and Dorthey refresh the house. It was undetermined if Mama would remain there or sell it. They both insisted Polly needed to get back to London and begin her life as Mrs. Nillson.

"It has been wonderful having you here," Dorthey said. "Miriam, in particular, adored your attentions. Go start the next part of your life. You deserve to be loved, and Hans obviously loves you."

Dorthey always had a way of calming Polly's tendency toward worry and gloom. They intertwined fingers, attesting again to their sisterhood.

Miriam cried the day Polly was to leave. The two of them had grown close over the last few weeks, taking walks, sharing ideas, reading books. She pleaded with her father, unsuccessfully, to allow her to join them on the drive to the Toronto airport. He rightly insisted that Miriam needed to attend school.

Polly slept for most of the flight, drained by the emotional exhaustion of the last couple of months. Hans greeted her at the airport, a large bouquet of flowers in hand. "Welcome home, Mrs. Nillson!" he proclaimed. He seemed to dance with delight at the words. Polly explained away her lack of enthusiasm as fatigue.

Hans's apartment was a modest two-bedroom. The second room was converted into a study for her. He had taken pains to polish the space up before she arrived. Even the bedroom smelled of lemon cleaner. She unpacked the clothes from her suitcase, realizing the limited storage space was already near full with only these few items. She slid the violin she had brought back with her under the bed.

After a long bath and a small supper of sandwiches that Hans made, they nestled into bed. The fresh sheets felt cool against her skin. They wrapped their naked selves around each other, only a top sheet covering them. The heat between them was enough to counter the autumn chill of London. She settled into a deep slumber, happy to be home in England with Hans. At three in the morning, she awoke with an inability to breathe. She bolted upright, her heart thumping quickly. She forced herself to take a few slow deep breaths. A tingling sensation danced around her lips and chin. Hans was still asleep beside her. She roused him and described her unusual symptoms.

"It's only jetlag. It will pass," he said and then rolled over again. "Try to get some sleep, darling."

After a few moments, the symptoms disappeared as suddenly as they had arrived, leaving her cold and shivering. Unable to return to sleep, she opted for a cup of tea. Waiting for the sun to rise, she settled in the study, scribbling out a new body of work that had been brewing in her while she was away. It was only then that she felt she could breathe comfortably again. This was the first of many such nights for Polly.

"Darling, is there anything I can do?" Hans would ask as he rubbed her back and brought her tea.

"No. I think I am still just so sad." The grief over her father's death blunted the joy and adventure of her new life with Hans in London. "I'm sorry. This is not what our first months of marriage should have been." Polly regretted the years lost between her and her father. She should have tried harder to bridge the gap sooner.

"Don't fret, Polly. We have a lifetime ahead of us," Hans would reply.

She returned to Oxford at the beginning of November to pack up her cottage, and tidy up paperwork for her resignation. Both Lucy and Sarah came to help. The Bluestocking Club had made excellent progress over the last few months.

"I can't believe you must go. It doesn't seem right," Sarah lamented. "We are just about to be granted an audience to plead our case with the university council, and you won't be here. This was your idea, Dr. Williams. You really should attend."

Despite numerous requests for Sarah to call her by her first name, she continued to show great deference and refer to her only as Dr. Williams.

"I am Mrs. Nillson now. The university, and others, think it lacks decorum that I should live and work away from my husband. My life is in London." She gave a little sigh that drew a knowing look from Lucy.

"This is why I never married. A man's ambitions always supersede a woman's, no matter who is the greater talent." Lucy sorted books into a box. "Are you really unable to take any of these?"

"There simply isn't room in the apartment. I have a few favorites already packed. The rest will have to go."

"It's a shame." Sarah shook her head. "I hope to find a man right here in Oxford, so that I can carry on with my work and remain with the club."

Both ladies gave a smile for Sarah's goodness.

"Sarah is right, Polly. The Bluestocking Club was your creation. You really should be there when we present to the union."

"That, I wouldn't miss." Polly was thrilled. "It will give me something to look forward to."

"What about your work on consumer behaviors? You have only just begun, but it sounds fascinating." Sarah always loved to hear about Polly's new ideas. Easily her biggest fan, Sarah behaved like an ingénue despite being only a few years younger than Polly herself.

"The psychology department has agreed to continue our collaboration on the piece. A trial in London will certainly be easier with its larger population, all of whom seem to adore shopping." Polly laughed. The contrast was unignorable between the simplicity at Oxford, where what one thought and said was important, while in London the most important topics included the latest royal trends and who was invited to which social parties that week.

"Well, that looks like all of it." Polly stood with her hands on her hips, appreciating the tidy space around them. Even with the furniture and kitchen dishes remaining behind for the new owners, the house looked larger.

"What about this?" Sarah asked, carrying the white box with blue ribbon that Kata had given her over ten years ago when she left Toronto on the train, pregnant and lost.

"That comes with me." Polly placed the gift in the box with her work papers.

"You haven't even opened it," Sarah commented inquisitively.

"It hasn't been the right time." Polly gave another small sigh, again garnering a look of concern from Lucy.

"I've reviewed those final documents for you," Polly said, handing Lucy a folder of pages marked with notations and lines. "I adjusted the assumptions of revenue, and extrapolated out to twenty-five years with the added student census. Anything beyond that exceeds the term served for any of the council members at the university, and would therefore likely be of less interest to them."

"Thank you. I expect you to be standing beside me, though, to deliver this report yourself." Lucy was adamant.

The following morning, Polly left with her blue suitcase, her violin, one box of books, and two boxes of her work. She loaded Hans's car and drove herself back to London. The dense fog that day made it difficult to see the road ahead of her. It took her twice the time to reach her new home. All the while she strained to see the road, her mind struggled to envision her future. Like during her flight to Oxford, she grieved what she was leaving behind and could not yet celebrate that which might be awaiting her ahead.

Oliver and Lydia's home was beautifully decorated for the holidays. Garland with pinecones and red ribbons framed the railing of the front steps. A matching wreath adorned the front door. Inside there were two Christmas trees, one decorated in shades of blue, the other in variations of orange, a nod to each of their favorite colors. Twinkling lights and golden candles provided an additional magical overlay throughout the house. The brocade drapes of blue and gold, with armchairs, love seats and chaises lounges in similar Tiffany blue and vivid cerulean shades elevated the room majestically. Carefully placed cream and butter yellow cashmere blankets softened the austerity.

Lydia insisted on hosting an official wedding reception for Polly and Hans. Most of the guests were friends of theirs whom Polly knew loosely from previous engagements at the home. Some people from Hans's work were there. With finals so close, nobody from Oxford was able to be present. Charlotte and Isabella were both in attendance. Discreet as they were, the sexual magnetism between them still had questions sailing around the room. Hans's parents were unable to attend due to a recent respiratory infection that afflicted them both. His sister was staying home to care for them.

Oliver graciously relieved Polly of the incessant small talk by stepping into the circle and asking to have a word with the new bride. He seemed weighed down in thought all evening, but when Polly probed him on the reason, he said all was well.

"I hope you're happy." He formulated it more as a question than a salutation.

"Hans is a good man. He cares for me."

"Hardly a recommendation upon which to build a life together," he chided, though a sincere undertone in his statement highlighted what Polly felt. Most people ascribed her subdued enthusiasm of being a new bride with the recent loss of her father. Only Oliver knew there must be more underneath.

"And how are you and Lydia?" She tried to change the subject. "She tells me you may be expecting again soon."

"Yes, though I am not sure it will happen for us. Four miscarriages, and neither of us getting any younger." He tried to conceal his despondence. "You must be looking forward to getting settled into London permanently, starting a family of your own." He toasted in Hans's direction, where he was presently engaged in jovial discussion with friends.

"I am not sure I want to have any children." She colored upon realizing the insensitivity of her remarks and added, "I too may not be able to have any, given my age." She took a sip of her wine. "Hans, of course, would have a whole football team if we could. I'm not ready yet to try. I still want to get established in London, try to find a job."

"Polly . . ." Oliver turned to her, his back to the room, the two of them cloistered in the corner. "You are a most incredible woman. Don't ever forget that."

She searched his eyes for meaning, but before she could begin her response, Lydia stepped between them, giddy with excitement. "Congratulations again, new bride! I hope you are having a wonderful time. Sorry that the room is a bit hot. The weather warmed up so quickly today, and with all the people in the house, I wasn't able to have it aired properly."

Oliver excused himself and Lydia clinked glasses with Polly. "Cheers," she said. "It's apple juice, not really wine." She whispered conspiratorially to Polly, "I am pregnant again. Just five weeks. I haven't even told Oliver yet. I didn't want to get his hopes up again in case, you know." She sipped her apple juice. "But I needed to tell somebody!"

Polly offered a quiet congratulations.

"Just think, our children may be able to grow up together just like you and Oliver. He speaks so fondly of his childhood in Kingston. It has always sounded so fun to me!"

The evening carried on well past midnight. Hans and Polly both collapsed into bed and slept late into the morning.

Two weeks later, Lydia miscarried again. Nobody but Polly knew. She remained at Lydia's side for two days and checked in on her daily for a week. There were no more parties after that.

Lydia remained mostly in her house dress, watching daytime television.

In the spring of 1959, the Oxford Bluestocking Club was finally awarded its audience with the chancellor and university council. Lucy delivered a flawless elocution on their case. She remained unflappable against the ridicule, counterarguments, and offhand insults, according to Sarah's letter.

Polly was not there. Flaunting her obvious pregnant belly before the committee was felt to be a potential detriment to their case. She was put on bedrest for the remainder of the pregnancy due to severe leg swelling and high blood pressure. She tried to work, but struggled to access the necessary library papers. Her own documents were now also packed away, having converted the study room to a nursery.

The Bluestocking Club was successful in its arguments, having Somerville recognized equally as a college within the university. Lucy was soon after appointed pro-vice-chancellor. Polly read about the news and celebrations in the campus journal, which she still had mailed to her.

She read the letter and article for the fourth time out loud so the baby could hear. "This was for you, little one, so you and your cousins could one day have a better life. Mommy is going to continue to work hard so you can have all the opportunities in life to be your best self." She sensed the baby was a girl and was thrilled at the idea of raising her to be a free-thinking, independent child like Miriam.

Polly went into labor earlier than expected. After several hours of contractions with no descent, she was eventually rushed into an emergency cesarian section. Fredric Hans Nillson was born August 7, 1959, to the delight of his father. Polly slept for the first seventy-two hours of his life from the effects of the anesthetic. She was roused periodically to nurse him at her request. She struggled with the nurses who insisted on bottle feeding. Her mother had breastfed them both, and recent science suggested it improved infants' constitution. She wanted to do the same, to give her son the best she could. When her milk did not come in, the hospital staff were satisfied and proceeded with formula. Polly felt that at her first duty as a mother she had failed.

CHAPTER 13

1963

Polly's papers were scattered about the small kitchen table. She glanced at the clock. Hans would be home soon. Breakfast dishes remained in the sink. Her stomach growled. Again, she had missed lunch.

The two-bedroom apartment encroached around her, as if she was stuffed into a packing box; little space to move, the stagnant air had been gradually suffocating her over the years. Reprieve was found in brief moments of hurried work. The product of years of work begun with many false starts and continued through frequent interruptions was spread out before her in the confines of this corner. It was the only place she had to work. Fredric often ate lunch in the living room while watching the television. Two-year-old Juliette spent much of her waking time propped in her high chair or playing on the linoleum floor beside Polly. By evening, the space needed to be cleared for family dinner. Everything safely stacked away in the corner of their bedroom, away from crayons and sticky fingers.

Fredric dragged a black case into the kitchen behind him. "What this, Mummy?"

She briefly glanced up from her work, her son's handprints distinctly visible in the dusty layer that coated the case. "It's a violin, darling." She strained to keep the exasperation from seeping through her voice. "Fredric, you need to stop getting into Mummy's things."

"What you do with it?" He fiddled with the shiny latches, pleased with himself when he discovered how they worked.

"You play it, darling." She flipped through various pages, looking for the data results that she knew she recently had in her hand.

At first, Fredric hit the violin like a drum, then found the strings and began to pluck at them. Terribly out of tune, the notes sloppily vibrated like whale calls.

"Fredric, no, your sister is sleeping. You'll wake her." Pulled away again from her work, she felt her anger rise. "Mummy needs just a few hours of quiet to focus on my paper." Her voice was tight. It had been months since she submitted anything to her partners at Oxford. Resigned to Polly's lack of delivery on anything interesting, they had unsurprisingly moved on to other projects.

"Mummy, play." He continued to thrum with the great enthusiasm of any pioneer who discovered new territory.

"Fredric, stop!" Her tone was harsh and non-negotiable.

Hans entered the front door quietly, the perpetual droop in his shoulders more evident than usual. His boots and winter coat created a puddle in the narrow hallway. Something else for her to clean up, she thought.

Polly grabbed the overflowing ashtray to empty quickly in the garbage bin.

"I thought we discussed this, Polly. No smoking inside with the children," Hans said, his voice flat, tired of the repetition. "You were supposed to quit."

"I know, Hans. I shall. But it helps me to concentrate when I'm working." She dumped the remnants in the trash hastily, creating a cloud of floating ash. "These days I would benefit from any help I can get," she muttered under her breath. A vibration of restlessness hummed inside. For years now, creative ideas sailed infrequently, always close to shore, never bold enough to fully release into the open sea of her mind.

She looked back to her papers at the table, transcribing columns from various data sheets onto a single sheet of graph paper.

"Papa, look . . . violin!" Fredric continued to play with the instrument, twisting the tuning pegs this way and that.

"Yes, Fred. A violin," he answered absentmindedly as he hung up his coat. Grudgingly, he moved into the kitchen and stared at the counter. "I take it dinner isn't ready either."

"I'm sorry, Hans. I was distracted. It was the first day in weeks that I had a chance to sit down and really get any of my thoughts in order. Juliette, bless her, is still napping."

Hans rolled up his sleeves and began to wash dishes in silence. After the last dish was rinsed, Hans replaced the violin into the case and closed the latches. "Fred, take the violin and put it back where you found it." He ushered him down the hall toward their bedroom. Polly cringed at the sound of the case hitting against the baseboards, and Hans's lack of assistance to correct it.

He sat in the only other chair at the kitchen table, feigning interest in the various pages he picked up. "It's been five years, Polly, and you're not close to finishing yet. Is it time to stop?"

"I can't stop, Hans. This is good work." She was frazzled. The idea of stopping felt like a vice around her throat that slowly reduced her air supply until she could no longer breathe. It was the fear, really, that if she stopped, the inertia would stagnate her ability to resume anything worthwhile. The sleepless months after Fredric was born drained her of any creative energy. Becoming pregnant with Juliette shortly after made things even more difficult. She had only recently been able to get enough rest to ignite any worthwhile thoughts in her new research. "You know I don't do well when my mind is idle." She continued to work through the chart she was drafting. "If you were home more, I would be able to take the time I need to focus on things," she snapped.

Hans was silent. He took to building an orderly stack of the papers on the table. "I didn't get the promotion." His voice was hushed with disappointment.

Polly exchanged her pen for his hand. "Oh, Hans. I'm so sorry, love. I know you had been working really hard for it." She launched carefully into her next words. "Perhaps I can begin inquiring at the university for a position. Since moving to London, I've not seriously explored the option of teaching, what with the children coming so quickly."

"I would love that for you, dear. But what about the children?" His frustration at the repetitiveness of their conversations was evident.

"Perhaps something part-time. I could look at faculty positions in music, if not mathematics or economics." She was hopeful that opportunities were changing for women in London.

Hans sighed. He began packing her papers into the cardboard box in which they rested when Polly was not working. "The amount of money we would need to pay for childcare would outstrip anything you could bring home part-time. Sadly, women just aren't paid the same." He opened the fridge and took out yesterday's casserole to reheat. "I was thinking you could teach. Music, that is. Piano and violin lessons in the evenings or weekends, when I'm home to take care of the children."

Polly's entire body deflated. Her heart sank. All their plans of owning an actual house, near parks for the children to play, seemed impossible now that Hans didn't get the promotion. She was to have some help so she could focus on her work . . . the dream of it all floated away. She longed for the day that they need not worry about having enough money to pay rent, or repairs for the car. Their time together had been so magical those first years. She looked back knowing it was partially because of the time they had spent apart, where they could each focus on their own interests, with loving holidays together interspersed between.

"The extra money could help with a new car. We always wanted to move to a neighborhood with more parks and better schools for the children," he said as if reading her mind.

Juliette began to cry. "I'll go to her." Polly carried her box of papers to their room. Juliette rested her head against Polly's shoulder. The smell of lavender reminded her that she was a mother now, a wife, Mrs. Nillson. Those needed to come first. She returned to the kitchen with the toddler in her arms. "Okay. I'll start looking tomorrow."

"Papa," Juliette said, stretching to reach for Hans as usual. His large hands tossed her slightly up into the air, always securely catching her as she gleefully squealed at the carefree fall.

"Really, Polly?" Hans looked both relieved and thrilled. "You'll see . . . it'll actually be fun, I'm sure of it. Something to get you out of the house. Break up the routine."

That night they were intimate for the first time in months. Polly spent a restless night hoping she did not get pregnant.

The following day, Polly summarized her progress on consumer spending, and highlighted the outstanding questions and next steps she would take to answer them. Through priority Royal Mail she sent it to Oxford, care of the post-graduate student who was working with her. The rest of the team should not be held back. They could move ahead on the work without her.

She spoke to some of the friendlier mothers in the neighborhood and teachers at the school. By week's end she had a roster of twelve students for music lessons. She was also able to secure some added tutoring in math and English literature at the preparatory private school in Oliver and Lydia's neighborhood. None of the work excited her but she would make the best of it; teaching was teaching after all.

The next two years moved along in a predictable humdrum manner. Hans would arrive home promptly at 5:30 p.m. Dinner would be laid out on the now four-person kitchen table in a clean apartment. Polly would leave at 5:45 p.m. and spend her evening traveling from one student's home to another. On Saturdays she would rise early before the rest of the family to begin her day. Sunday was reserved for family time. Polly stole what hours she could while the children napped, to maintain her reading of the latest economic and math journals. When their naps fell away, she lost that small window again, save for those occasional times that she arranged for them to play at the neighbors'.

With Fredric now in school full-time at the age of seven, and Juliette four years old, Polly began to have some more freedom to roam about the city during the day. Bundled up, she and Juliette would take the tube into the city center to visit Charlotte and Isabella. Often, she would wander the art galleries, pushing Juliette in her carriage until she fell asleep. At times, she would lunch with Lydia.

"Come here, my sweet Juliette." Lydia's fingers were dressed with rings. Her flesh seemed to grow around them, swollen and discolored digits that came to an end at fingernails forever painted a poppy red, and grown long from idleness. "Aren't you just precious like a doll." She would stroke the little girl's hair, cuddling her just a bit too tight. When Juliette would fuss to pull away, she would only hold her closer.

Eventually Juliette began to cry at the mere sight of her, and Polly continued their monthly lunch dates alone. They said very little. Polly would pick through her salad. Lydia would devour a three-course meal, with double dessert. Polly avoided discussing the children. Even discussion about the music lessons she taught to other children seemed to upset Lydia. An emptiness echoed from her. She would endure Lydia's updates on celebrity and royal gossip, which always focused on the terrible and imperfect. There was little conversation about Oliver, other than that he worked constantly and was rarely home.

Polly continued to see Oliver often. He would join them for a family dinner at their house on Sunday. Those evenings, he would play with the children and insist on reading them bedtime stories. Lydia never came; a migraine or back pain had her in bed. Lydia never mentioned missing dinner at their home, and Polly never drew attention to it for Ollie's sake.

Today, the January weather was blustery. Juliette remained with Charlotte and Isabella in the upstairs studio of the store, while she had her obligatory meeting with Lydia. She had decided she would call a cab to take them home, versus trudging through the Underground. A little luxury she rarely expended for herself. She worked hard for what little she could bring in and deserved an occasional extravagance.

The store was quiet when Polly arrived, not many people shopping on a day like today. The salesgirl greeted her as she made her way to the backstairs and up to the studio. She could hear Juliette giggling already. At the top of the stairs, she burst into laughter at the sight of her daughter dressed in miniature couture. Earrings bigger than her tiny fist were clipped onto her earlobes, and necklaces draped to her knees.

"You look beautiful, darling!" Polly laughed, remembering the many dress-up episodes they'd shared in the attic room at Kata's when Charlotte first began her fashion career.

Isabella greeted her with the customary double kiss and whisked Juliette away to get cleaned up. A look exchanged between her and Charlotte alerted Polly that something was awry.

"Polly, sit." Charlotte was elegant as ever in a black wool dress that clung perfectly to her never-altered-by-pregnancy figure. "We should talk." Her voice was stern but sympathetic. "What are you doing with your life?"

Polly was taken aback.

"You're wasting away gifts and talents to clean drippy noses and teach basic piano to tots."

"The kids need me. They're my first priority!" Polly was irate.

"Of course, they need a mother. But there must be a way, Polly, for you to return to your own passions." Charlotte spoke to her as only a friend with whom you had shared a lifetime could. "I think you're hiding. You've lost your way again. Just like when you were with Eli, and now it's Hans."

"Hans is nothing like Eli," Polly shouted. "He is kind and steady. He would never hurt me. He is a good father."

"Yes. That may be so. Is that enough?" Charlotte was prodding further. "You live in that tiny two-bedroom apartment. Juliette says you never play the violin, and she often hears you crying in the bathroom."

Polly was shocked at the revelation. She was always careful to turn on the water to drown out the dulled sobs she released into a clenched towel.

"I don't think you're depressed. Lydia is depressed." Charlotte searched her face. "I just think you're unhappy. You've turned out the lights inside of you."

"You don't understand, Char, what it's like to be a wife and a mother." She looked at Isabella, who was obviously eavesdropping from the glassed-in office.

"I may not." Charlotte did not flinch. "But I do know when my friend is settling for a life that is too small for her." She lowered her voice and leaned toward Polly. "I don't have the answers for you, Polly. But I know you need to find a way to shine again."

The words haunted her for weeks. Echoed in her mind as she traversed the labyrinth of feelings from anger to defensiveness to resentment. Polly felt it was rather an overstep for Charlotte to say such things. *How could she ever understand my life, as neither a wife nor a mother!?* She wrote in a letter only to Dorthey, too uncomfortable to raise the topic with any other soul, least of all

Hans. Charlotte sent periodic notes: *It is because I care that I spoke up,* and *When you are ready to talk again, my friend, I am here.*

Winter dragged along that year with the cold bleeding into April and even early May. Tulips were delayed, as was the usual return of Polly's energy in the spring. Her innate tendency to hibernate in libraries over the winter and peek her head into the sunshine once spring arrived was held over from her years at school. Still, in May, she clung to her heavier-weighted clothes and boots.

The brightest parts of her week were receiving letters from home. Both Miriam and Dorthey began writing about Dorthey's changing demeanor. Increased fatigue and bloating had the doctor put her on a strict diet, with restrictions on milk and red meat. By summer, things appeared worse. Hans agreed to use some of the money they'd collected for a down payment on a house to send Polly and the two children to Canada for a three-week visit. The house could wait a bit longer.

"Can you not come with us, love? Mama would love to see you," she asked Hans. "And I could use some help with the children while there."

"Oh, darling. Work is busy these days. I am well on my way to that promotion and don't want to miss any opportunity to prove my worth to the company." He embraced her tightly. "Plus, you don't need an old stodge like me around. You and Dorthey have lots to catch up on."

They kissed passionately at the airport, invoking embarrassment in those who wandered by. "I love you, darling," Hans whispered. "I shall miss you."

She relished in his love. Despite the restlessness in her soul, his steady devotion comforted her.

Travel by plane with two children was troublesome, particularly with Fredric. She was pleased to have arrived at Kata's where they would stay for a week before taking a train to Kingston. A divide of the legs of the trip was necessary for the children to manage the long travel. Fredric had many issues at school, difficulty sitting still and listening to instruction. Sometimes he took to tantrums in the corner when too much was asked of him.

Kata possessed an aloof mystery about her with age. Her hair, still dyed, looked coarser and drier. Her makeup, simpler now, settled into the creases, exaggerating the wrinkles she was trying to hide. Still trim in her figure, she stood with a straight spine and well-toned legs from the high heels that dressed her feet.

"Come in. You don't need to knock. This is always your home." She gave generous hugs and kisses to Fredric and Juliette, as if they were her own grandchildren. "Please settle in, then come join me in the kitchen for tea."

Each step creaked louder than she remembered. The walk up to the attic felt like a return home. Kata no longer took in boarders, so her usual room was empty. Four beds remained lined around the edge of the room. New bed coverings and sheets, along with a window air conditioner and ceiling fan had been installed. Otherwise, the room looked and felt the same. She placed Juliette in bed to nap, and took Fredric downstairs to run around the living room. She joined Kata in the kitchen for a cup of tea. They spent well into the late evening catching up.

The children slept late the following day, then filled their time with a visit to all of Polly's favorite places, including a walk about the university buildings. The campus sprawled now across many city blocks. She wandered past Dr. Garrett's old office. The dentist had moved upstairs, and a new cosmetic surgeon was situated in the main floor office. They ended up at the art gallery, which had also changed greatly with modern wings added and the tea room closed.

"Why do you look so sad, Mummy?" Juliette was an empathic child.

"Just pensive, my sweet. It is amazing how much changes over time."

Margaret and Sadie arrived for dinner that evening. Kata had made a delightful feast, and left her to be with her friends. She now ran a small catering company for private events and had a dinner party to oversee.

Sadie, who was now widowed, looked as young and dazzling as ever. Her daughter was studying business administration at the university. She spent her time overseeing a portion of the foundation set up in trust by her husband's estate. After he died, his children contested the will through years of legal proceedings. Finally, they agreed to a one-million-dollar annual allowance for Sadie, and rights of determination for a quarter of the foundation's donations each year. She sold the large house in what was once the open country surrounding Toronto, and was now a growing suburb of common-looking houses.

"I spend most of my time doing charity work, hosting donor events, and handing over money. It is great fun!" Sadie looked like she was cut out of a magazine and transposed into another picture. Her navy dress with white trim and sparkling diamond earrings contrasted against Kata's worn and dated dining room.

"Is there anybody new in your life? It has been seven years since . . ." Polly let her voice trail, unsure how sensitive the topic was.

"He died?" Sadie's bluntness was refreshing. "There is, but we won't ever marry. My contract stipulates an end to my allowance if I ever marry. Frankly, I don't think any man is worth that." She gave an open laugh and then sipped the champagne that she had brought with her as a gift for the evening.

Margaret, too, remained youthful. Beside them both Polly felt old. Her taller stature and wider bone structure made her feel manly. Her hair, never colored, looked dull and hung about her shoulders in a haphazard way. The attempt at a straight cut had no chance against the summer humidity, causing it to frizz and twist in unusual places.

"It took me a long time to recover." Margaret shared her story of assault and the loss of Garrett with Sadie comfortably, even though they had never met before. The ease of her words and reflections showed she was at peace with it. "I couldn't return to the hospital. Each time I tried I would start to shake. I couldn't focus. The mere thought of having a shift scheduled the next day would keep me awake with nightmares. After several repeat attempts, the hospital chief of staff and myself agreed it best that we part ways."

"That seems so unfair. How is it that you get penalized for what happened to you? Losing your job in addition to everything else!" Sadie was engrossed in the story and aflame with the need for justice.

"Forests regrow healthier after a fire," Margaret said calmly. "I started working at the clinic downtown, helping mostly the impoverished and the mentally unwell. Many new immigrants." She spoke with pride and commitment about her work. "Occasionally we get a well-to-do person, usually a woman, who finds her way into the clinic to slum with the poor and troubled. After a few visits, though, they usually offer a donation and go back to finding a doctor on University Avenue or in Yorkville." She looked at Sadie, hopeful she didn't insult her.

The government pay never matched the time that it took to do a proper job. Margaret lived a very modest life, investing most of what she made back into the clinic to buy supplies, pay staff, and even created an emergency fund for patients to draw from—a few extra dollars to buy food or other life necessities to tide them over.

Polly's experience in rallying for equality with the Bluestocking Club, and Sadie's experience as a poor single mother in the city, inspired the conversation about what more could be done. Before the evening was over, they concocted plans to develop a new program at the clinic to provide legal aid and add in a food bank. Polly found herself excited at the prospect, even though she would not be there to assist; she would support with ideas from afar. She added in recommendations for a financial educator and social worker, and eventually a childcare center, so women could return to work knowing their children were safely looked after. The evening ran late with a second bottle of champagne. Sadie insisted she have her driver take Margaret home on her way. Once they left, Polly felt uncomfortable being alone, unable to ignore the void in her soul that had been hidden with busy motherly tasks. It was an emptiness, a lack of purpose. She wanted a clinic, a project to take on as her own. Something of which she could be a part.

The following day was quiet. She played games with the children. When Kata ushered them into the kitchen to bake cookies with her, Polly roamed around the living room relishing in the quiet. Her hands stroked the brown wood of the piano. It had been years since she had played. Sitting on the bench, she shook off the nightmarish memory of Eli sulking in the corner of the room. Hesitantly, she depressed the first few keys in a simple scale. Her finger memory struggled. She misplayed a few notes. Frustrated with the stiffness in her hands, she stretched her fingers, then again placed her hands on the keys. Stepping into one of her songs, she played at a slower pace than usual. For hours she continued to play. Kata quietly took it upon herself to mind the children. Polly escaped, soothing herself with music.

"Mummy, you play so pretty," Fredric said with such sweetness in his voice. "When can I play like that?" He gently pressed a few notes on the keyboard.

"Would you like me to teach you?"

That is how they spent the rest of their week in Toronto. At Kata's well-loved, tuned piano, learning to play. It was the only time Fredric sat still for more than a few minutes.

Traveling to Kingston was arduous with the children. Neither was cooperative. She tried to hum and quietly sing to soothe them, receiving disgruntled looks from an unappreciative audience in the rest of the car.

Mama had moved in to Petar's to help Dorthey, who struggled to bend down over her growing belly. Surgery was scheduled for the current week; both ovaries were to be removed. As the taxi pulled up to the once splendid house, Polly grew fearful. Everything looked like an old sepia photograph. The grass had turned to hay, left unwatered throughout the hot summer months. Weeds filled Dorthey's garden where pansies and geraniums were usually craftily planted. Inside, the house was clean and tidy. It smelled of lemon and vinegar, certainly Mama's hard work.

Teddy, now twenty, was working at the quarry with his father. Sonja was engaged to be married to a young man from the Royal Military College once he graduated the following year. Miriam, now seventeen, was finishing high school and thinking about university.

Mama shared a room with the girls, while Teddy slept on the couch to allow Dorthey to have some privacy in his room. With Polly there, she would stay with Dorthey, giving Mama a reprieve and some time with Fredric and Juliette at her home. It was decided that Miriam would go with them to help watch over the rambunctious little ones, so Mama too could rest.

"I promise we shall make lots of time to talk," Polly said to Miriam, when she quietly asked if they could discuss university options. They had grown very close over the years through their weekly letters and occasional phone calls.

"I want to know what it's like. I really hope to go, but I'm not sure Dad can afford it." The despondency in her voice was heartbreaking. "I've been trying hard for a scholarship. If I stay at Queen's I can still live at home, and help Mom when she needs me." She rushed to spill out the pent-up words. "I haven't discussed any of this with Mom and Dad, though. There just hasn't been the right time."

Polly tucked Miriam's unruly hair, much like her own, behind her ear. She admired the girl's vigorous spirit. "We shall figure something out, I promise." She sealed the commitment with a long hug.

Dorthey's surgery was not a success. There were small tumors growing throughout her abdomen. Nothing more could be done.

The idea of a world without her tainted everything with bitterness. Nobody could eat, or entertain themselves with television or even a card game. They moped around the garden unsure what to do with themselves. Petar distracted himself at work, leaving Polly and Dorthey in her room like when they were girls.

"I owe you so much," Polly confessed. She encouraged Dorthey to take small spoons of vegetable broth. "I could never have gotten through any of it without you."

"Shush, silly. You were my sister from childhood. I was happy to do it all." She moaned then pushed the spoon gently away.

"It could not have been easy for you." Polly knew about the whispers about town when Dorthey had Miriam. They gossiped about her sudden pregnancy so close after her miscarriage, and the involvement of the obstetrician from the neighboring town. It was the local midwife, who had delivered Dorthey's first two babies, who started the rumors out of spite when she wasn't called to support this birth. Even Petar got jeers at work about it.

"I was so selfish. I ran away. I left you here." Polly's voice yearned for forgiveness and for punishment.

"You went where you were needed. Think of all the splendor you brought to the world through your music, your teachings, your research, your women's education cause. So many people," Dorthey emphasized, "*so many*, are better off because of what you have accomplished."

"I have done so little." Polly thought of the last several years of tutoring and basic piano teaching. "I have let you all down."

"Now that's enough of that talk. There is more to come, Polly. Your light isn't out yet." Dorthey looked pensive. Her gaze toward the window peered past the glass, seeing beyond to what was to come. "I have something for you."

She motioned Polly to the top drawer of her nightside table. Inside was the pink journal Polly had given her for her thirteenth birthday, the pristine cover unblemished by pen marks or fingerprints. The internal pages slightly yellowed and much used. Dorthey's elegant script filled each page in blue pen. Words carefully crossed out and replaced in smaller font above.

"It isn't anything special. Just some poems I have written over the years. Basic musings of a housewife." She took the book and thumbed through the pages, evident that each one was linked to a memory. "I want you to have it."

"Shouldn't you leave it for Sonja?" Polly declined accepting the journal.

"No. Someday you may share it with Sonja and Miriam. For now, I want you to have it." Dorthey extended the book again. "Sisters forever."

"Sisters forever." Polly swallowed the ominous burn of inevitability back into her stomach.

Polly spent the evening reading the entirety of the journal. Beautiful poems that spoke of joy, longing, and happiness. One stuck out so desperately, she marked it with a ribbon. She never asked about it, the content too raw and personal. Words that most women understood.

Hear me
I fumble through the days
Crawling over shards of glass
Saturated with the aftermaths of spilled milk
Do you hear me?

Mommy, what's for breakfast?
As always on the second day of the week
Eggs and ham, nothing new
Do you hear me?

Darling, are my shirts pressed?
Pristine rows of starched white cotton
Polished shoes and packed lunches
Do you hear me?

I scream, I cry in unseen silence
Slams and sighs fill the sounds of my day
I read in the paper today, I say
Do you hear me?

I rage into quiet madness
Perhaps only now will you hear me
My voice, my story, my thoughts hover
When will you hear me?

After the extended visit to Canada, they returned home for the start of school. Both children would begin late by a few weeks. Hans was finally successful in attaining his promotion at work, which afforded them a chance to move to a slightly bigger flat in a nicer neighborhood. Polly was pleased with the better local public schools, considering how much Fredric struggled.

Each child would now have their own room. Polly bought a small desk for the corner of the living room, at which she could work. Her legs barely fit under it. She did not complain; it was her own little space. In the midst of unpacking the children's clothes, she received a call from Petar. Dorthey had passed away that morning. Grief left him stunned, unable to speak more than a few sentences. She thanked him for letting her know, not pushing further. There would be time to come for more conversation.

Oliver returned home to support his friend during the funeral. Polly, having just returned a month prior, remained in London. She was there for the important part with Dorthey, she reconciled. All that needed to be said was said. They decided together— she, Dorthey, and Mama—that it was not time to share the past with the children yet.

She typed out Dorthey's book of poetry on her new typewriter so she could read it as often as she liked without worrying about scuffing the journal. Since coming back, she called Charlotte daily. She had missed her dear friend. For two hours each day after school, she would tutor Fredric, who to her embarrassment was significantly behind the other children in reading and writing.

Neither university in the city was recruiting new professors. It had been too long since she had published anything that made her credible as an academic. Perhaps a teaching assistant role, or a return to a post-doctorate program herself, was suggested by a well-intended lady in the human resource department.

She continued her part-time work to add to the household income. While the children were at school, she resumed her discipline of reading and practicing the violin. She even began composing small pieces of music for herself. Old friends from the Oxford Bluestocking Club welcomed her letters. They often sent her their work for review. Each day that she found such journals or draft papers in the postbox was a gift, the joy of which carried her through her otherwise dull week.

Just before the Christmas holidays, Oliver called. Lydia had been in a terrible car accident. Early Sunday morning, she had set off to the bakery at opening time for fresh croissants to take to her parents for a breakfast visit. Oliver had remained lounging in bed at her behest.

"Enjoy your morning. I'll be home soon," he recalled her saying to him. He was pleased that his wife seemed excited to be getting out of the house for a change. When she kissed him and said, "I love you, Oliver. Thank you for being a wonderful husband," he was overjoyed. It was a reminder of the woman he knew, possibly a sign that she was finding her way back. While he showered and prepared a coffee, he sang for the first time in a while, inspired by hope that the morning was a turning point for Lydia, for them.

Lydia's car hit a cement post on a bend at a presumed high rate of speed. The impact sent it into a spin across the road where it slammed into a nearby tree. The roads were clear. Her car had just been in for a tune-up and was deemed in good condition. There were no witnesses. She was pronounced dead at the scene.

CHAPTER 14

1968

Five years without Dorthey was like a fence with missing links. Things moved in and out of Polly's life unfiltered with little notation. Polly hadn't appreciated the levity that Dorthey's weekly letters and periodic phone calls brought. Mama tried to step in with reports on life in Kingston. Both Teddy and Sonya were married. Miriam was in Montreal for university studying literature. Petar seemed to go about his life in a rote survival mode of work, household repairs, chores, and some semblance of amusement during Saturday pub nights with a couple of childhood friends. Every letter gave the same mundane overview. Most of Mama's and Papa's friendships had been forged through the university, and many of these people had moved to temperate climates for retirement. Mama had moved in with Petar and Miriam so she had some company and people for whom to cook. Polly's childhood home was sold to a newlywed couple who were enthralled with the charm of the older place. Mama drove by weekly to watch the renovation underway.

"I barely recognize the place any longer. Garish siding placed over the wood, and cement everywhere. They haven't even moved in yet," Mama would lament. "You need to live in a place for a while before you decide what needs changing."

Hans found work at a new company, affording them the chance to put Fredric into a special learning school. At ten years old, he still struggled to write and lacked creative imagination. Everything was very literal to him. The doctors said he was born slow; nothing could be done. As a result of his struggle with nuances and social interactions, he was ostracized from any friends. Math, he fared well in. Polly capitalized on that, trying to teach him anything that was beyond his natural grasp in mathematical terms. Even basic social interactions were better understood if she presented a concept to him as a logic model with cause and effect, known and unknown variables.

They were sitting on the living room floor, Polly holding a towel filled with ice over Fredric's left eye.

"Mummy, I would have just punched those boys right back in their guts!" Juliette mimed her attack, with graceful kicks and punches thrown with sincere vengeance.

"I know you would have, Letti, but that isn't the right thing to do, is it?" Polly tried hard to restrain her desire to coax along her daughter and press upon her son the need to fight back. She wished Fredric would have socked the boys at least once.

What most children seemed to intuit, she needed to teach him. If you say this, or act in this way, then people will respond as such. He memorized these small formulas, storing them in his neural networks. He would search, pull, and apply a response from these files based on the situation, sometimes misguided by subtle mockery or changing societal norms.

When the phone rang, she excused herself, leaving Juliette to soothe her brother.

"I'll be late again tonight." Hans was bright. He seemed happier with work these days.

"It's Friday, though. Ollie is due by for dinner."

"Send him my regards. Not that he'll really notice my absence." His sarcasm was biting.

"Hans, stop. He's just as much your friend as he is mine. You simply aren't here much." Polly softened the accusations in her tone. "This new job is wonderful. I can see you're happier. We just miss you."

"Well, I have to work, Paulina. Another promotion would mean you could stop teaching evenings and weekends, be home more with the kids."

She gritted her teeth. "I'm barely teaching as it is with your long and unpredictable hours." The conversation stalled. "Freddy was picked on again today. A bruised eye."

"Poor kid. How did he handle it?" She could hear him moving things about his desk as they spoke.

"You know he doesn't understand. He joined in a game of monkey-in-the-middle and was obstructive to the play, insisting somebody needed to get a real monkey."

"Did he stand up for himself?" When she didn't reply, he continued. "He'll never learn if you keep . . ." He stopped and replaced the words with a small sigh. "I'll be home late. Don't wait up."

"Hans, I miss you. I miss us."

He was silent for moment. Polly was beginning to wonder if he still felt the same. The weekend picnics in the park with the children chasing balls and swinging so high until their squeals turned into shrieks of exhilaration were becoming rare. The exhaustion from the day usually allowed for an early bedtime for Letti and Fredric, and a reward of intimate time for Hans and Polly.

"Me too, darling." His words were wistful. "Enjoy your time with Oliver tonight. You and I shall arrange an evening out this coming week, just the two of us."

"That would be splendid, Hans. I shall arrange a sitter."

Polly prepared one of the few meals she knew how to cook well. Flowers for the room were a luxurious expense in which she indulged. There were no wildflower fields in the city from which to help oneself.

It wasn't often she was out of the house or had occasion to dress up. She took tonight to curl her hair and apply some makeup. "Sometimes you just need to feel pretty," she said to Letti when she asked why Mummy looked so different.

Ollie arrived with a large bouquet of flowers that took centerstage on the table. Her own bouquet moved to her desk to bring some brightness to the space. He looked modern in his turtleneck with jacket and slim-fitting pants. His hair grown shaggy made him look again like the young boy climbing trees and collecting worms along the creek.

He helped put the children to bed, including reading a story. As each child offered him a kiss and a "Good night, Uncle Ollie," she sensed his longing for a family of his own.

Settled onto the sofa with their glasses of Scotch, he asked about her work. She had resumed collaboration with colleagues from Oxford, writing opinion papers on the contribution of women in the economy as both the primary buying market and increasing talent in the workforce.

"It's so hard to get published, though," she lamented. "Nobody in academia is interested in pieces about women, and the lay press finds it too intellectual."

"You should publish it yourself," he said, his voice matter-of-fact.

Initially she laughed. "One doesn't just publish work! There are traditional publishing presses with long-standing histories and processes by which to do such things."

Oliver peered over the edge of the glass as he took a sip of his Scotch. He examined her like only an old friend could. He knew her better than anybody still living, the realization making her squirm in her seat. She took a long drink from her glass, the smoky scent calming, while the burning sensation distracted her.

"Why not?" he coaxed in earnest. "The Paulina I know can do anything she sets her mind to. Why not publishing?"

After taking another sip, she shrugged off his remark. "There is something else I have been trying to get published." Behind her, she reached for the typed copy of Dorthey's poems. "I am sure she wouldn't mind you seeing them."

"*Musings of a Simple Housewife*," he said, inspecting the cover with Dorthey's name on it. "Interesting."

"I have been taking it to various publishing houses throughout the city, magazines, lifestyle newspapers. Nobody is interested. They want sensationalism, sex, drama, crises. Day-to-day life apparently just isn't interesting enough."

Appreciatively, he thumbed carefully through the pages, stopping to read a poem every few sections. In all the time Polly had spent transcribing the poems and peddling them around town, Hans had not looked at a single one. He had simply nodded absently when she shared stories about the latest rejection.

"I think you could publish this," Ollie said. His confidence felt ill-placed to Polly. "You should do this."

Their evening moved on jovially as they spoke of books. She reading C.S. Lewis, and he F. Scott Fitzgerald. Both enjoyed the new music coming from the Beatles. They danced to van Morison's "Brown Eyed Girl" playing on the radio, trying hard not to wake the children. Polly even played him a rhapsodic composition she was experimenting with on the violin. Very far from traditional orchestral music and a bit more jazz in rhythm. Hans still wasn't home by the time Ollie left. Polly cleaned the kitchen alone. She grew weary and headed off to bed, unable to resist thinking about publishing works that needed a voice.

Weeks went by during which Hans continued to work late and on weekends. Their evening out never transpired. Though she enjoyed lunches with Charlotte, and hours of uninterrupted time to tend to her letters and music, the apartment, the ceaseless routine with the children, was all growing suffocating. Restlessness was a fertilizer for change.

Sadie had tracked down Henry, who was now working for the *New York Times* newspaper. He was more than thrilled to hear from the woman who enraptured his heart during their time at the university newspaper. Though not in publishing, he had many friends who were, and was willing to facilitate introductions for her and Polly.

Over the summer holiday, Charlotte had events to attend in New York for her fashion house. Thrilled at the prospect of attending elite social events, Sadie was fast to offer paid tickets for Polly and the children. She would meet them there. Her nanny, whom she no longer needed as her daughter was a grown woman with children of her own, but whom Sadie kept on staff, was to come along to mind the children.

"I am a bit nervous to go," Polly confided in Hans. "Robert Kennedy was just assassinated there a few weeks ago, and I understand there is looting and protesting in Harlem."

"It will be fine, darling." He drove the car swiftly, changing lanes. "A bit of a holiday will do you good. Maybe get rid of that growing irritation you seem to have with the world right now."

Polly furrowed her brow, her voice tense, "I wouldn't say I'm irritated, just worried. The world seems to be progressing but not in the right ways."

"Are you opposed to the rock-and-roll movement, free love, and marijuana?" His laugh held a flavor of contempt.

Ignoring his comment, she looked back at the children who were already napping with the hypnotic lull of the car. A car ride always soothed an irritable mood, except it seemed, for Hans.

"I mean, first Martin Luther King is assassinated, then RFK. The U.S. is in a war that nobody understands. The feminist movement is making ground on rights to birth control, but very little is being said about the strength and character of being a woman." She stopped her lecture and waited for him to reply. He said nothing. They remained silent for the duration of the drive, until closer to the airport Hans began again.

"I think it's good that you're going. I can focus on work without feeling guilty that I'm not home with all of you. Time with your friends will be nice." When she replied with her placating "I suppose so," he encouraged her to enjoy New York, perhaps break out of her comfort zone. "Live a little."

"I do have some meetings that Henry kindly arranged for me with some publishers." Grateful and excited, it was the sole reason she had accepted the tickets from Sadie.

"Always so serious, Polly. Play a little. Do some shopping, go to the theater." He wrestled with his jacket and pulled out one hundred American dollars.

"Hans, that is very sweet, but we can't afford it. I'll be fine with what I have saved from the extra lessons I gave last month. End of school examinations are a busy time for tutors." She laughed.

He shoved the money back in his pocket. They said little other than goodbye at the departure gate.

"You're right," she said, wanting to leave on good terms. "This trip will be good. I shall have plenty of fun. Please don't work too hard, darling." She pointed to his pocket. "When I get back, let's use that money to do something special. Perhaps a weekend trip to the country. Alone."

They kissed, bent at the waist, two feet between them, only lips pecking. "I love you," she said, her heart filling with endearment.

"And I you," he said before directing his attention to the children.

His reply left a hurtful feeling of emptiness within her. When she was back, things would be better, she thought. A little time away would do them both good.

Turbulence overtook several parts of their flight to New York. Both children became ill, and her only good pair of shoes were soiled with vomit.

Relieved to have survived the erratic driving and pungent smell of the taxi, the hotel was a welcome sight. Charlotte's tastes were exquisite. Though Polly insisted on staying somewhere more affordable, Sadie wanted to be close to Charlotte, and the Waldorf Astoria was where Charlotte wanted to be. Most of her savings for this trip would be spent on the room.

Before long, Sadie arrived at her door looking fresh and smelling of flowers. "A little extra perfume," she explained, "to stave off the putrid stench of the city. Enough to make you want to throw up."

The reminder prompted Polly to change out her shoes before they left for their excursion. Strict instructions were left with the nanny not to leave the hotel. They could play games in the room or read. Exploring the hotel was fine. Outside was too dangerous.

"I must say, for all the excitement about New York, I really don't see the appeal," Polly said. "It is very dirty and terribly crowded."

"Ah, where is your sense of adventure?" Sadie looped her arm through Polly's. "Toronto feels asleep compared to New York. London is stuffy. Here you can be anything, do anything!" She put a dollar in the hat of a man on the street corner. "Let's pretend we're in school again. I never had the full experience of nightclubs and dancing with friends. Help me catch up!"

With each day Polly grew more comfortable in the city, allowing the kids to venture out with the nanny to the museums and park, but only for a few hours, and with a pre-planned itinerary outlined the night before. Charlotte was occupied for the early part of the week with business, which allowed Sadie and Polly time to explore.

Lunch with Henry truly did bring them back to school days. Nothing had changed about him. His dark thick hair was untamed and bushy. Broad-rimmed glasses enlarged his brown eyes, highlighting the besotted look he carried whenever Sadie spoke. Twice divorced, he swore never to marry again.

"Unless you'll marry me," he qualified to Sadie. To which she simply laughed and ordered more champagne.

"I won't marry you, but I will let you take me dancing," she bartered, "if you promise to help Polly learn everything she can about publishing."

For the next several days Polly toured printing presses and publishing houses. She spoke with agents, copy editors, and typesetters. She learned about how to discern paper quality and the resistance of different inks to fading. Paperback books were growing in popularity due to their mass appeal and lower price point. Lighter-weight pages could be held in place with glue as opposed to the string binding still needed for hardcover books.

People were rushed and stressed everywhere she went in the industry. Some believed in repeat authors with common and predictable storylines that people could read with ease. A literary equivalent to television, she thought. Other publishers risked taking on new authors on whom they were gambling to become a Dickens or Hemingway one day. Staunch opinions on quality literature were ingrained in the culture of each office, with some only accepting hardcover publications as true books. All were worried about the growing conglomerates—larger publishers that took over smaller houses.

"Success will only come if you appeal to the masses. You gotta sell in this business if you're gonna survive," one man reported.

"Marketing is key," offered another. "You can get people to read anything if you have a good marketing team."

After another whirlwind afternoon, Polly needed some quiet time to process all the information coming at her. She chose to walk the several blocks back to the hotel, barely tolerating the unexpected dank heat that descended that afternoon. Getting lost would be terrifying for her. Nonetheless, she diverted to a side street for reprieve from the congestion of the sidewalks along the main route. So long as she kept heading toward the tall building in her sight, she knew she would reach the hotel.

A quaint series of small shops made her nostalgic for home. In the center of them was the smallest doorway she had ever seen, with a Ceylon blue awning. She admired the bright color, on which the store's name, Ya Ol' Dickens, was printed in white. She was proud that she now recognized the classic Baskerville typeface in which it was written. The allure of the simple window display coaxed her into the store. Bells on the door jingled a pleasant tune when she entered. Despite the cramped quarters, the books were neatly stacked on tables, and the shelves allowed for ample room to walk down the rows. A stained-glass window in the back dispersed ambient light to all nooks in the store.

Alone, without even an employee at the cash, she wandered the aisles, exploring the history and poetry sections. Only a small alcove at the front of the shop held contemporary fiction. The majority of volumes were written by authors from decades and centuries past, or translated into English from a multitude of other original languages in which they were written.

"May I help you?" A small man she guessed to be in his late seventies stood by a door labeled "Private." His straight-backed posture gave him a youthful vitality.

"Just browsing," she said.

"The best kind of time spent in a bookstore." He went about his business behind the counter, marking off books as he unpacked them from a large box.

"May I ask"—she approached timidly— "what you think makes a good book?"

He pondered the question for a moment. "I would say that a good book satisfies a need that you sometimes didn't know you had. It might fill you up when you're sad, remind you of something important when you feel lost, or teach you something new when you think you know everything there is to know on a subject." His laugh made him look even younger. "Mostly, though, you know a book's good when it lingers with you . . . changes you. When it's something you go back to every few years, like reminiscing with an old friend."

"Thank you," Polly said, and he shrugged and went back to his business. Frugal as she needed to be, she bought a sturdy leather bookmark and a book of poems by Emily Dickinson.

On her way out of the shop she turned to take in the space one more time. "May I ask one more question? Does it ruin it for you?" The old man looked at her curiously. "Does turning one's enjoyment into one's livelihood take away their appeal? Books, I mean?"

He offered a knowing smile. "Not so long as you never put profit above the magic."

She nodded. "Thanks again. I hope to come back here one day." On the sidewalk, she jotted down the name and address of the store in the front cover of the book so she would always remember it.

Tomorrow was their last full day in the city; already scheduled was a visit to the park with the children. They grew fond of helping the man on the bench feed the pigeons and wanted to share the experience with her. Then there was Charlotte's private show in her store for an elite clientele, which Sadie was relishing. Afterward, celebrations were to take place at the hotel. As such, she declined this evening's invitation for dinner and dancing, to Henry's delight. He would have Sadie all to himself.

Two blocks away from the hotel, Polly stopped to pick up dinner: a box of crackers, cheese, a couple of tins of tuna, several apples, a bunch of bananas, a lollipop for each of the children, and a chocolate bar for herself. She planned on spending a perfectly relaxing night curled up with the kids, reading poetry.

When she arrived at the hotel, a kerfuffle was underway at the reception desk. A group of four young men with long pale faces whom she recognized from television to be in an English rock band, *The Who,* were demonstratively pacing. An older man, puffed out and red in the face, was in heated discussion with the hotel manager. People gathered round at a respectable distance to watch. Accustomed to an audience, the band members rallied support for their cause, an apparent disagreement over their reservation.

Up in the room, the children were already eating from a carboard box, slices of greasy dough drooping from the weight of cheese and meat coins.

"I hope you don't mind," the nanny said, noting the grocery bag Polly carried. "I treated the children to a takeout pizza."

"Thank you. You didn't need to do that, though. Let me cover the cost." Polly rummaged through her bag for her wallet.

"No need," she insisted. "It was my pleasure."

"But I don't expect you to be paying for my children out of your wages."

"It's okay. Ms. Sadie pays well," she said, smiling

The words cued Polly, and she noted for the first time the mid-calf red boots the nanny wore with her short mini dress, and the matching clutch handbag with the initial of the classic designer embossed on the leather. To the left, she saw her own shoes by the door, scuffed and bearing remnants of her children's air-sickness.

Sadie certainly did pay well.

Polly did not look forward to the flight home that evening. They were all rudely awakened in the early morning hours by the band she had seen in the lobby—a smoke bomb they thought would be a funny prank gone awry. She was excited to return to the cooler English summers and streets less crowded with young people just milling about. A weekend away in the country with Hans would be welcome after this trip.

Charlotte had convinced a magazine editor-in-chief from her party the evening before to join her and Polly for one final lunch.

"Oh, I wish Isabella was here," Charlotte bemoaned. "She is so much better than I am at these things. London is in its buying frenzy right now for the new season so she couldn't leave. Overall, I think it went well." She underestimated her success. The fashion release had been a sensation. Representatives from various magazines clamored to snag the first photo spread for their winter editions.

As a handsome young waiter offered glasses of champagne with orange juice, Charlotte welcomed her friend from the magazine. He was from one of the biggest and fastest growing media conglomerates. Likely why he justified maintaining an air of sophisticated snobbery.

"You can't just open a publishing company." He smirked when she explained why she had come to New York. "What are you going to publish? Books? Magazines? Science stuff? You've mentioned it all." His condescending tone irritated her.

"Well, I don't quite know yet. That is what I'm here to figure out. I do know that I want to publish works by people who don't often get a voice. Things with messages that push people out of the formulaic scripts that mass media directs us toward." She could tell he found her amusingly naïve.

"You certainly have conviction. That'll serve you well." He hastily finished his meal in three successive large bites, barely stopping to breathe. "Give me a call in a few years when you're up and running. I'll buy you out, even let you keep a job in it." From his tone, she knew he was serious and attempting to be gracious.

"Thank you, sir, but it won't be for sale. There is a large enough audience of intelligent women and men who are looking for something different." She looked at Charlotte, careful to remain respectful and not disrupt her professional relationship with this man. Her friend simply smiled and offered a small nod as she sat back in her chair, casually smoking her cigarette. Polly continued, her tone confident, bordering on haughty. "You are welcome to come visit, perhaps even pick up some new hints, if you ever like." She toasted her glass against his, then finished its contents in one swig. It had been a while since she was so piqued about something. A welcomed fury bubbled inside her. The kind of hungry energy that comes from waking after a too long sleep.

Throughout the flight home Polly was unable to rest. Sadie was accompanying them back to London, and then was off for her own two-week holiday to the south of France. Fredric and Juliette slept in the seats beside them, the boy's head resting against the window as his sister's head was propped up against his shoulder. Polly wished she could take a picture to remember them like this forever. Soon they would grow out of needing her and be off, creating their own dreams. Where would she be? Still tutoring children on the basics of music and math, likely. She had been out of the academic world far too long to ever go back.

Polly explained the torrent of doubts that were rippling through her to Sadie. "Even if I could do this, I am doubtful any bank would consider financing me. The risk is too high. I have no collateral. A previous music composer, doctor of economics, and mother of two with no publishing background is not a smart investment. I would recommend against lending to myself!" She took down her glass of Scotch in a single mouthful.

"I'll back you, silly," Sadie said it as if this was a known fact all along. "It'll take us back to our university days. You can run the business and have full editorial privilege. I'll attend the promotional events and write an occasional piece, with your approval of course," she added. "You can pay me back over time. Or I can just remain the silent owner and you can remain in the position of president, in perpetuity."

"Sadie, I couldn't. What if I fail and all that money is gone?"

"You won't fail, Polly. I trust in you." She rested her head on Polly's shoulder. "Plus, it will be great fun. If we make no profit, I can write it off as a failed investment, and life goes on."

By the end of the flight, the details had all been agreed to and sealed with a handshake and a toast.

Back in London, the apartment was empty when they arrived home. The children settled right into bed, despite the nap on the plane. Even with the time change, the week exhausted them and they were happy to be settled between their own sheets.

She tried Hans at the office but there was no answer. A note was left on the table that Miriam had called. She was back in Kingston caring for Mama, who was growing frail. She had several fractures in her spine from osteoporosis. Pain seared down her back, right to her toes, anytime she tried to move about, essentially leaving her bedridden. Her fading memory was attributed to the strong medications the doctors prescribed to keep her comfortable.

Miriam took a leave from her studies to care for her. Their phone call was short due to the cost. She noted Mama's steady decline. The pressure ulcers on her heels and backside from lying in bed for so long.

"Auntie Polly," Miriam started, "she keeps saying I need to speak to you about the truth. She keeps saying you'll tell me the truth, and that I must understand how much my mother loved me."

Polly's mouth felt parched. Her throat tightened, keeping her mute. The phone crackled in the silence between them.

"Auntie?" The voice on the other end sounded young and pleading. "Are you still there?"

"I am, darling. I'm not sure what Grandmama is referring to. You are much loved, by all of us." She knew this conversation was not suited to a telephone call.

They promised to continue writing often. Miriam would continue her studies from home. The university had given her special dispensation to send her assignments by post, and to sit her exams independently, supervised by a local professor. Polly could not return home at that time, though promised she would get there as soon as she could. Messages of love were exchanged. "Miriam, please tell Mama I said I love her. And darling, thank you for all you have done to care for her.'"

Hans finally arrived with the smell of wine on his breath. A work dinner, he explained, otherwise he would have been at the airport to surprise them.

She began to update him on the adventures of the week, starting with the visits to the editors and ending at the conversation with the owner of the bookstore. He quietly listened while he poured himself a drink. After a big yawn he suggested it was late, that they should go to bed and she could tell him the rest tomorrow. He checked on the children before he went to sleep. The next day he slept late and hurried off to work. The rest of the conversation would be delayed for several days.

A few weeks later, Charlotte's barrister helped draw up a contract between herself and Sadie to open a publishing house. The following months were a rapid swell of activity. The business was incorporated, money transferred, real estate selected, and equipment and materials purchased. A small staff was hired.

In spring of 1969, the Bluestocking Publishing Company officially opened its doors. The first work published was *The Simple Musings of a Housewife* by Dorthey Williams. Copies were shipped to Kingston and Toronto, where Sadie oversaw the logistics and promotion. A few small London bookshops and friends in Oxford carried the volume of poetry. Polly sent a copy addressed to "The kind gentleman of Ya Ol' Dickens" in New York. The inscription on the front cover simply said: *I'll never let the stories lose their magic. Thank you. P.W.*

CHAPTER 15

1972

It seemed every person in London had the same brilliant idea of enjoying the unusually hot day at Hyde Park. Couples nestled together on blankets sharing a picnic, oblivious to the barking dogs and raucous of children. Groups of school chums played football, competitive tensions mounting beyond the friendly game they set out to have. Some people sat alone reading a book, while others napped easily with the comfort of strangers' watchful eyes upon them.

"Happy anniversary, darling." Hans presented Polly with a small box wrapped in red paper with a gold ribbon.

"What is it, Mum?" Fredric grabbed at the box with insatiable curiosity.

"Leave it, Fred. It's for Mum." Hans slapped his hand away.

"It's okay. Let's take a look together." Polly gathered Fredric next to her. He was small for his age, and fit into the crux of her side with ease.

"Me too!" Juliette climbed onto her mother's lap. "It is so pretty. Open it."

"I didn't get you anything." Polly always felt inferior when it came to gift giving. Hans remembered every special day, including less traditional commemorations like their first meeting, their first official date, and the day he told her he loved her for the first time. Polly remembered moments, and how she felt, but dates were not her fortitude. Days passed too quickly for her to keep track. Anniversaries and birthdays usually arrived between work deadlines and school crises, and gift buying fell somewhere on the to-do list between scheduling doctor's appointments for Fredric and dance class for Juliette. Her lack of preparation for such celebrations was now a humorous expectation between them.

"I know better than to expect anything." He smiled.

"Open it." Fredric pulled carefully at the ribbon. When the knot snagged and he could pull no further, his distress was evident by the way he knocked his knuckles against his temple.

"Stop that." Hans pulled Fredric's fists down and secured them tightly in his lap. He looked around to ensure others were not staring.

"It's okay. Let's try again." Polly gently released Fredric's hands and guided them to the other end of the ribbon, which they pulled together, easily unraveling the bow.

Hans stared at her with pride. "You are so good with him."

Polly squeezed Juliette tight, and placed a kiss on top of Fredric's head. "It is just practice. We spend a lot of time together, so know how each other works. Isn't that right?" She kissed both children again.

"Open it already," Juliette insisted.

"All right." Polly hurriedly unwrapped the paper, keeping it as intact as she could to avoid upsetting Fredric, who liked to fold the colorful paper and save it for a future use. He would get irritated if the edges were torn or the wrapping blemished.

Inside the box was a dainty gold chain that held a heart-shaped pendant. Along one edge were two small diamonds.

"It is beautiful, Hans. Thank you." She undid the clasp and draped the necklace around her neck. It rested below her collarbone, complimenting the musical note charm her parents had given her years before.

"Let me." Hans reached around, securing the chain in place. He gave her a kiss on her neck. "You deserve it. Two diamonds, one for each of our gems." He tickled both children.

"Stop it, Dad. We don't like tickles anymore," Juliette stated.

They spent the afternoon playing gin rummy, which Polly won each time. After eating their lunch of tuna salad sandwiches and chocolate-chip cookies, and after much prodding, Hans agreed to play Frisbee with Fredric, while Juliette napped on the blanket beside her mother.

Polly retrieved an article that she was overdue to review from her tote. She carried the bag with her everywhere, in order to capitalize on whatever time she could steal away to get some work done. She rested her back against a tree. With a red pencil she began making notations in the margin. To herself, she chuckled at the memory of Henry, and knew she was never as ruthless as he was at scoring out large pieces of people's work.

"Put it away, Polly." Hans sat beside her, slightly breathless. "It's Saturday. In some countries I am sure it is illegal to be working on a beautiful day like today."

"I do believe so," she chided, "however, I have no other time to get this done. Plus, it is wonderful for you and Freddy to spend some time together. You see so little of each other."

They looked over at their son, who was inspecting with great interest an ant that had crawled onto his leg. Hans sighed. "They need their mother. You are much better at this than I am."

"If you spent a bit more time with them you would understand them more." Polly ran her hands through Hans's hair. "They do adore you. They just don't see you much."

Polly rose early most days. She made coffee and breakfast, packed the children's lunches, then put in an hour or so of work before anybody else was awake. After dropping the children at their respective schools, she hustled to the publishing house where she spent the days working until school was let out. After preparation of a quick dinner, and assistance with homework, she reviewed layouts and manuscripts while the children passed time in front of the television. If Juliette had dance class, she would spend the time they waited role-playing different scenarios with Fredric, to help him practice social norms.

Hans often came home around bedtime and would settle the children to sleep, while Polly tidied the house. After an evening cocktail together and a chat through of their respective days, she would retreat to bed to finish what work she could until her vision blurred from eyes too tired to read any longer. Most Saturdays Hans puttered around the house doing small repairs, washing his car, mowing the lawn or, he would go into the office. Polly would bring the children to the publishing house if she was behind in work. They loved playing in the art department and would spend time writing their own stories, which they would print in a pamphlet style, using only the limited array of equipment that Polly allowed.

Today was a rarity. Polly set aside her work. "Hans, it would be good if you could pick them up occasionally from school. Take them to some of their activities. They would like that, and it would give me a bit of relief."

"Darling, the children are my main priority. As are you. You are just so much better at this than I am. They need you more." He caressed her cheek. "You are running yourself ragged. I hate to see you so tired."

She relaxed her head into the palm of his hand. Her eyes closed. It felt like a brief vacation from the busy days that blended from one into the next.

"You should take some time off. Slow down. The publishing house is going well. Perhaps let Sadie take on some more work, or hire some extra help. Something to give you a bit more of a break, more time with the kids."

She felt dejected. "But I love my work."

"I know, darling. The children need you now, though. I need you. I miss you. I miss us." He offered her a kiss which she willing melted into. She missed him too.

She was tired. Perhaps she needed to take a step back, reset her priorities. Her mother's words, "You're a mother now, Polly," rang through her head.

"I'll think of something." Her mind drifted to her father. He would likely be proud of her, married with two children and working. Not the profession he had hoped for, but she had made something of herself, hadn't she?

"Come on, join us." Hans grabbed her hand. They roused Juliette, who was already partially awake from her nap.

They spent the afternoon playing chase and Frisbee. Juliette flitted around like a butterfly. "Catch me!" she hollered.

"You run too fast, Juliette. Let me catch you, Letti!" Fredric ran after her, unable to predict her curving paths. "Letti, wait!"

Though she admired the simple pleasure of the moment, Polly felt an unease stealthily invade her spirit. There was a deep irritation scratching within her, that she should be somewhere else, doing something else.

Two weeks of continual rain and gray skies went by. The warm day at the park seemed so long ago. Bluestocking Publishing was releasing its next series of books for the summer reading season. Sadie nudged toward publishing more salacious novels. "Sales are abysmal. I am bleeding money, Polly," she would complain.

Polly had a good sense of emerging cultural topics. Her years of game theory helped her pick up on subtle cues about what people would soon be discussing. On the release list was a biography about a group of civil rights advocates, just in time for the congressional vote on the Equal Rights Amendment to the Constitution in the United States. A history of Northern Ireland's long conflict with the United Kingdom had already been released. The recent protests turned massacre in Londonderry, coined Bloody Sunday, gained the book some interest.

"People want to escape, Polly. They have too much of this dreary stuff in the news already," Sadie offered. In the end, she trusted Polly's vision. "You will make this into something, I know it."

Polly dreamed restlessly most nights. Her mind always preoccupied with worry about the publishing house. When Petar rang in the middle of the night, she was already awake and in the kitchen with a cup of warm milk. It was dinner time in Kingston.

"Mama died this afternoon." He was solemn. "Miriam and I were both there." Petar remained quiet on the other end.

"Oh Petar, I'm sorry I wasn't there." Polly felt a piece of her break away. Now an orphan, having lost both parents, she felt like an incomplete puzzle; the picture was evident but a few pieces were uncomfortably missing. Mama had been her greatest support, despite their quibbles over decorum. Polly rarely worried about what others thought. She dressed for comfort, particularly after the ludicrous outfits Eli had bought for her. Mama worried far too much about presentation and popular opinion. Somehow, though, she understood Polly deeply, and set her life back on course.

"She wanted me to tell you she was proud of you, Polly," he went on.

Polly swelled with the knowledge that her Mama loved her. She had adored Hans, and was happy to see Polly finally married with children of her own. Her work was a hobby in her mother's mind; something Polly did in her spare time to fill the day.

"Do you think he would have been proud, Petar?" She trusted her brother to be honest with her. No matter the answer, she needed to know.

He was silent for some time. "Petar? Are you still there?"

"I am." He sighed. "You broke Papa's heart, Polly. I knew I was always second to you with him. I was good with that. We all knew you were special, and we loved you for that." Petar went on. "He wanted you to work with him, at the university here. Teach beside him, get married, spend Sunday dinners together as one big family." Polly could picture the simplicity of it all clearly. "He used to talk to Dorthey and me all the time when you were in Toronto about being the first father-daughter professors at the university."

He wanted a legacy, perhaps even to become a legend in the halls of academia. He just wasn't willing to have her compromise the traditional womanly duties of marriage and motherhood. He must have known it was not truly possible—to be both herself and his version of her. Polly felt a peace settling within her. Arriving pregnant and unmarried, with her thesis still undefended, she was beginning to understand her father better.

"Thank you," she replied. The simple words were enough to end the weariness of shame and guilt she carried all these years.

She asked about the children and work. Petar gave updates on all the children, including the gratitude he had for Miriam. She cared for Mama over the last few months when her heart had failed. She grew breathless with the basic task of dressing or bathing. Her ankles so swollen they wept, and made it difficult for her to climb the stairs. Miriam was there through it all.

"I miss Dorthey," he said. Polly heard him sniff, and then begin to cry. Polly had never witnessed her brother volley through any emotion except quiet stoicism and playful humor. Oliver had shared that at the funeral, Petar endured the heartache with strength, holding the girls' hands while Teddy stood in front, leaning against him throughout the service. The small quartet, bundled close together, stood strong beside Dorthey's grave.

"I miss her, Polly. I miss her so much. Now Mama. Everybody is gone."

"Me too," Polly whispered. "I miss them both. Papa too."

"I don't know how to keep going without her any longer." His pain seeped through the phone and penetrated deep into her, rattling her confidence in the balance of things.

"The last poem in her journal. I never published it. I thought it was too personal. I think it was for you." He didn't want to hear it. The poems unnerved him. Made him feel that he wasn't enough for her, that she had kept something hidden from him because she didn't trust him to keep all parts of her sacred. "I think it might help."

Polly retrieved the journal from the bookcase and read:

Forever
When you kissed me tonight, I cried with a fullness of being
Your eyes saw me—I am here, frail and dying
In your world I am real, worthy

To others I am a clock ticking
Afraid to get too close should my decomposing body be contagious
But you embrace me with the faith of a saint

I live my last days on the marrow of your strength
My children think they know sadness; deep sorrow is yet to come
I have no fear—they have you

Remember the delicate way you twisted my hair, our intimacy
Relive the moments you cried upon by breast
Then, find mountainous joy to share with our children

Your tenderness granted me each day of our lives a miracle
An eternal sun shone on us in smile and slumber
You, my love, my forever, will carry on

Carry on
Until we embrace again

It was four in the morning when they finally hung up the phone. Through tears and laughter, they reminisced about the years together, and the memories formed apart: Dorthey's beautiful garden and inability to ever use profanity, Papa's habit of forgetting where he left his pipe, and Mama's failed attempts at Western cooking. She crawled into bed beside Hans, exhausted and grateful. She formed herself against the curve of his spine and reached her arm around him.

"I love you," she whispered before she fell asleep.

CHAPTER 16

1974

In London, January was a month of hibernation for most. Streets emptied shortly after the work day. Commuters cloaked themselves in wool and descended to the sooty depths of the Underground. People didn't speak to one another. No smiles were exchanged in passing between strangers. Most covered their noses and mouths with scarves to stave off as much risk as possible of catching a chest cold, knowing if they did, it would linger with them until the break into spring.

Polly usually did her best work in these isolated winter months, her office at Bluestocking brighter than the outdoors, with its enhanced overhead lighting to ensure she could inspect the finest details on finished products. The company was publishing a current events magazine, *Maat*, that opened healthy debate on international political tensions. Inclusive of economic reviews and social commentary, it was geared toward women. *Maat* was slow to pick up circulation. The notable absence of any reference to fashion or recipes, save for advertisements, was initially all people discussed.

Sadie's brilliant marketing, which included a cover photo of Charlotte and a feature story about her as a female entrepreneur, was a turning point. Free magazines were delivered to the universities, and speaking engagements by Polly at both Oxford and Cambridge to the Bluestocking clubs there were instrumental in raising the magazine's popularity. Their subscribership was growing exponentially throughout London and in the university towns. Newsstand sales suggested men were quietly purchasing the magazine to read tucked into their newspapers during their morning commute. The once quarterly journal was now distributed six times a year, with a double-sized edition in the late winter.

Polly was hunched over her light table, inspecting the photos for an architectural piece. She jumped, as always, from Fredric's unnecessarily loud triple knock on her door.

"Did I startle ya, Mum?" His question was legitimate. He still had difficulty assessing people and predicting their reactions.

"It's okay, dear, come in." She motioned for him to look through the eye piece.

"These are Denys Lasdun buildings," he said after a quick glance and handed the eye piece back to her.

"How did you know that?" Outside of the National Theatre, most people did not know the work of this British architect, never mind a sixteen-year-old boy.

"He always layers and tiers concrete this way. It makes it look sturdy but not cold," he stated.

"Did you study that somewhere?" He was a history buff with a near photographic memory.

Fredric shrugged. "Come on, we'll be late for din. Everybody's waitin' on the birthday girl. Forty-seven years young you are today."

Polly rarely ever celebrated birthdays. This year Charlotte insisted they do dinner at Simpson's with the family, plus Charlotte and Isabella, Oliver and his girlfriend.

Fredric pulled on Polly's patience whenever he was in the car with her. He scolded her for accelerating through yellow lights. His right foot planted against the floor mimicking breaking when he believed she was going too fast or getting too close to the car in front of her. Continually he would remind her to turn on her signal, mind the arrows and take inner street routes that technically were shorter in distance but took a much longer time due to stops and pedestrians. Conceding to his recommendation was often easier, and today was definitely a concession-type of day.

The restaurant was quiet as expected for mid-week in winter. They were the last to arrive. Everybody was already seated at the table, engaged in lively conversation.

"You're late again," Hans said. He motioned for the waiter to bring their menus.

"At least I'm consistent." She laughed, trying to ward off any tension that might ruin the evening.

Fredric pulled out her chair. She sat between him and Juliette, who was adorned in a ballerina-like dress complete with a set of faux pearls and tiara. Dorthey would have been so happy to see this, she thought.

Isabella looked more exotic with age. Nary a wrinkle to be seen. The gray streaks throughout her black hair appeared intentionally placed. She maintained her beautiful figure, still accentuated in the demure clothing she now wore.

"You look tired," said Katherine, Oliver's girlfriend of two years now. "You shouldn't work so hard."

Polly ignored the comment. She clenched her jaw instead, staving off her urge to snap back. Oliver quickly interjected with a toast. "To Polly, a celebration of not only her birthday, but also for now officially being the sole owner of Bluestocking Publishing. I knew you would do it." He raised his glass in salute.

Those that could reach clinked their glasses over the center of the table. After the initial sip, Hans raised his glass. "To Sadie, for helping fund the start, but knowing it was time to sell the entirety of the business to the true brains behind it all, my incredible wife."

Polly's smile felt forced. Something was amiss. The two toasts sat uncomfortably with her. She never was one for being the center of attention. "Thank you everybody for being here. I could not have done any of this without you." It was the obligatory statement, and truer for some around the table than others.

Laughter and stories circled the group all evening. Only Hans seemed to be out of sorts, squirming in his chair with frequent trips out to the hallway. His back was stiff, he explained. Too much sitting in one place today.

"I understand your niece is coming to live with you," Isabella inquired. "That must be nice."

"Yes. With her mother passed, and my mama now too, Miriam will be coming to join us. She has finished her literature degree and will be working at the office. I am thinking of expanding into fiction books and thought she would make a splendid editor."

"Isn't that nepotism?" Katherine asked.

Polly exchanged a look with Oliver. He gave her a slight shake of his head.

"She is my niece, true. She is also highly qualified for the job. So, no, it is not nepotism." Polly took a sip of her gin and tonic.

"And what does *Maat* mean again? I always forget. I know it is supposed to be something smart." Katherine sipped on her water.

To Polly it seemed that Katherine's big eyes never held any curiosity or indication that she was thinking, and with hair that curled around her ears, she vaguely resembled a poodle. Polly struggled to understand what Oliver saw in this woman. She had never needed to work a day in her life, living off her rich father.

"*Maat* is the Egyptian concept of truth, law, and morality that brings balance to the world." As Katherine opened her mouth to ask another question, Polly stood up. "I think I'm going to go outside for some fresh air."

"Mum, goin' out for a fag is an oxymoron for fresh air," Fredric said. He did not laugh but looked to the others to see if he successfully managed a humorous comment.

"Use proper language, please. Yes, I am going for a cigarette and when I blow the smoke away, I will refill my lungs with fresh air. Hence, going out for fresh air." She gave him a playful kiss on top of his head and mussed his hair, which she knew irritated him.

Isabella decided to join her, though she was not a smoker. They chatted about Juliette and her sole goal in life to become a prima ballerina, and Fredric's current preoccupation with the Spanish flu epidemic of 1918.

"Are you and Hans okay?"

The question really surprised her. Though they had known each other for years now, their relationship was casual and social. Charlotte was all they had in common.

"Yes. We both work plenty. Hans loves his work as much as I do. We ensure we have time together with the children." She thought for a moment. "We're good. Same as usual."

"I don't know how to say this. It may be nothing. But as a friend I thought you should know." She bit her red-stained lower lip with her perfect white teeth. "I have seen him a few times lunching with a woman. Nothing really." She hesitated, gauging Polly's reaction, who was wide-eyed at the accusation. "It's just, last week it was dinner, and it seemed more intimate."

"Intimate how?" Polly wanted details, facts to support Isabella's insinuation. She had little tolerance for loose perceptions.

"Sitting in close, cuddling, whispering in her ear." Isabella verged on saying more. "Perhaps it's nothing. I just thought you should know." The intensity of her eyes, the tightness across her lips, the slight angulation of her brows suggested she was confident this was something.

Polly's dropped her cigarette to the ground and stomped on it. "Thank you," she said, embracing Isabella. "You're a good friend."

For weeks she said nothing to Hans. A trained academic, she knew better than to jump to conclusions. Perhaps it had been a work event. More women were entering the engineering profession. A few too many drinks and Hans could get flirty. At parties in the past, she had seen it with other women. Maybe this time he'd just gone a bit too far.

As a game theorist she was trained to spot changes in behavior, patterns that were out of keeping with the usual. No receipts were found in pockets or lipstick stains on collars when she did the laundry. Last year when they moved into a home finally, she packed up the whole apartment and didn't find a single photo or letter that would have raised her suspicions. Yet, when she offered to meet him for lunch or step out early for a quiet dinner, just the two of them, he would inevitably say, "Don't be silly, it's clear across town. I'll see you at home tonight."

Eventually, she accepted that Isabella must be mistaken—her words a kind protectionism from a friend. Hans may lunch and flirt, harmless interludes to break up an otherwise ordinary routine. She wouldn't fuss about it. He accused her of the same preposterous notion with Oliver. "Ridiculous," she would always say. This wasn't very different.

Miriam arrived in the spring. It had been two years since they last saw each other. Pride filled Polly when she witnessed the patience that Miriam embodied as she took care of Mama. A quality Polly always lacked.

They embraced for a long time in the airport, oblivious to the streams of people who hustled around them. They had shared so much over the years through their letters and phone calls, and lost even more.

Hans was pleased to invite her into their home. The children even more so. She settled into the routine quickly. Unlike Polly, Miriam was an accomplished cook, and her meals were inspired by dishes from all over the world. She and Juliette read stories to each other with dramatic flair, each adding a mood to the characters through accents and intonation. She played chess with Fredric, losing multiple games in a row, stopping only after they played four consecutive ones—any other number left Fredric irritated.

At work, Miriam solicited manuscripts from women around the world. With an open mind she read through each one, picking up the most subtle of hints that there was something special buried between the pages. Her professionalism and hard work put an immediate end to the gossip about her only qualification being her relation to Polly.

"What do you look for in the writing that signals there is something worth pursuing?" Polly once asked as they finished their glasses of wine after dinner.

"I don't. It's more of a taste. It's an image or phrase that surprises me, something interesting that leads me to want more."

She reached over and twisted the bracelet on Polly's hand. "What's that?" she asked.

"It's a *kara*." She went on to explain the story of how it was gifted to her by an impressive international student. "It symbolizes a commitment to God to do no wrong by one's own hand." She twisted it around several times before removing it. "I wear it to remind myself to always do the right thing, no matter how hard that might be. Here, I want you to have it." She offered it to Miriam.

"No, Auntie, I couldn't. This is such a special memory for you."

"And now I want to share it with you. Please, take it." Miriam graciously accepted the gift. On her slender wrist, the weight of the metal appeared too heavy to carry. "I often wonder what became of Jasu. If her marriage was as ideal as she imagined. If she was able to create the community for education that she dreamed of, where women were considered equals."

She took a sip of wine. "And you, Miriam? You're twenty-five now. Have you thought of marriage or children?"

"I don't think I want children, so I really don't have to think about marriage. And I can earn my own living. Take care of myself. It's not like it was with Grandmama in Poland."

"What do you mean?"

"You know, how she left school to work in the performance hall as a singer as a way to take care of her family. How she married Grandfather after knowing him for just a few weeks, hoping that he was her salvation to escape Poland. She planned to bring the rest of her family over, but it never happened. The war set in and she lost them all."

"I had no idea." Polly buried herself in regret. She only knew her as Mama, the woman who took care of her and the family. She never thought of her as Kasia, a person independent of them with a history, desires, or dreams for a future. To ask about her youth, her ambitions, never occurred to Polly, save for those few moments with Kata at the boarding house.

"Auntie, don't feel bad. You were a child and children are selfish." She reached out and grabbed her hand. "I barely knew my mother. I knew she loved me. I just didn't know what she thought or felt about the world, until you published her poetry." She leaned in for a hug. "Thank you for that."

Polly's heart cracked. "You're welcome, darling. Dorthey was a special person. She loved, and was loved, by many," she whispered.

"I always felt like there was something between us that went unsaid." Miriam began to cry. "I tried so hard to please her. There was always a space between us . . ." She dabbed at her tear. "I guess I'll just never know."

Polly hesitated, trying to contain the urge inside of her to tell the truth. "Oh, my dear, dear Miriam." She caressed her wiry hair, scanning the familiar features on her face. "It may be time to tell you. For so many years we wanted to tell you. You were too young or the time never seemed right. Eventually, it was so far past that it seemed unnecessary, perhaps even cruel. It may not offer anything but confusion to you."

"What, Auntie?" The urgent pleading in Miriam's voice drew Polly to a precipice, a place from which if she took the next step there would be no return. "Is this what Grandmama was referring to, about you telling me the truth?"

Polly froze. She was unable to speak. The words floated in her mind like specks of dust suspended in the sunlight, unable to be grabbed. She felt herself falling from the sofa, unable to brace herself. A dark hood pulled over eyes. She could hear Miriam but could not speak herself.

"Auntie! Are you okay?" She heard Miriam speaking. "Auntie?" The sound echoed several reverberations in her head. "I'm calling an ambulance."

Hours later, they returned from the hospital. Hans doted on her, commanding her to walk slower, drink water, rest.

"What did they say?" Miriam had remained up all night awaiting their return.

"It was nothing. Just a spell. Probably too much wine." Polly waved her hand in the air. "Nothing to fret about."

"The doctor did say you need to slow down." Hans was stern. He exchanged a look with Miriam, suggesting he needed an ally in the mission.

"The doctor knows nothing of my life to be able to draw that conclusion," Polly snapped.

"Let's get you to bed," Hans encouraged.

"I'd like to take a shower first." Polly went toward the bathroom, knowing she was leaving the two of them to conspire. "A little rest might be good just for a day or two. Miriam, you can look after things at the office. I'm going to spend some time at home, to catch up on sleep." She seemed to appease them. The thought of slowing down again sparked anxiety within her.

Hans was already asleep when she entered the room. Polly returned to work the following day to close out the final decisions on the current issue, gave the team directions on what to do, and settled Miriam's role while she scheduled the following few days off. It would be her first vacation ever since starting Bluestocking Publishing.

She arose each day of her holiday with the rest of the family, rather than before sunrise as usual. Puttering and tidying about the house filled the first few days. On the third day she decided to surprise Hans at the office. Finally, a chance to go out for lunch. His secretary was flustered when she arrived. He was already out and she wasn't sure when he would return. Work lunches could be lengthy. Polly insisted on waiting. Against opposition from the young woman, she settled herself in his office.

At first, she wandered the room looking at the titles of books and reference journals on the shelves. Dusty photo frames with pictures of Fredric and Juliette on their first day of school were on his desk. She tidied the stacks of paper so their edges aligned nicely. She dampened a tissue with water from the pitcher on the table, to wipe away the dust.

Hans returned forty-five minutes later, clearly unhappy to see her there. "You should have called before you came." He gave her a perfunctory kiss on her cheek. "I see you kept yourself busy." He gestured to the more organized room, disrupting the perfectly stacked pile of papers in a hurried attempt to find something. "Paulina, I have work to do. Sorry you came all this way today. Maybe we can plan for something later this week."

She sat down in the armchair across from his desk. Memories of their youthful days back and forth between London and Oxford seemed only a short time ago.

"Are you keeping a secret from me?" Polly was calm and genuinely curious. There was no accusation in her voice.

"Like a surprise?" He smiled.

"Like an affair." No matter the answer she realized, she would not be surprised. Patiently she waited. Then came his sigh, the rubbing of his temples.

"Why?" The frustration in his voice was subdued. "Polly, I love you. I love our family, our life. Sometimes it is just too heavy." He sat upright at his desk, his hands neatly folded in the center as if he were in a conference. She let the silence hover. "These women, they don't expect anything from me. They just want to be told they're pretty, and be taken out for nice dinners and shows. It's simple."

"Women?" The plural was not lost on her. "How many?"

"Maybe six or seven," he said, seeming to relish in the freedom of truth. "Everybody does it. It means nothing." They stared at each other, waiting. "Say something," he said. "What are you thinking?"

"I don't know what I am thinking." Polly got up and walked toward the door.

"Polly!" He seemed resigned to a future that was now out of his control.

She stopped at the door, her hand resting on the knob to settle the trembling as she turned toward him. "Did you ever think I might just need nice dinners and to be shown that I am special to you, every once in a while? To be told I was pretty? Simple things to make it all not so heavy?"

His look of surprise angered her. Without another word, she marched out the door, passed his assistant and went out to the street in a daze.

She spent the afternoon walking through the park. Spring was in its bright transition to summer. A rainy mist lingered in the air all afternoon through a sunny sky. Alone at the bridge in St. James's Park, she watched the ducks putter around in broad figure eights. Her mind reeled with questions, bathed in an array of emotions from self-pity to contempt. Why did she have to been born with this temperament? Serious. Impatient. Driven. Cursed with a brain that never stopped and a craving to keep doing better. She was never satisfied. Lives of others seemed simpler, content with things as they were. She was tired, pushed herself too hard, she knew. Hans knew she was like this when they married. It was part of what he claimed made her interesting.

Clouds began to drape across the sky. Fredric would have finished school and picked up Juliette by now to take her to ballet.

Canopies of black umbrellas filled the space around her, as people jostled over puddles to get to the Underground stations.

"Ma'am, are you all right?" a gentleman in a bowler hat and trench coat stopped to ask. She nodded, confused when he handed her a clean handkerchief. She had been unaware that she was even crying. "A good cry on a rainy day purges the soul. Rest assured, the sun'll come up tomorrow, and a new day will shine a new light on whatever it is may be botherin' ya." His kindness touched her, making her cry even more.

She stopped at a café for a cup of tea and a warm scone. By nine o'clock her feet ached. Her bones were chilled from the dampness of her clothes. She fought off the urge to call Oliver in fear that Katherine might be there. Instead, she resigned to go home with a black cab.

"Where have you been? I was worried sick." Hans was at the kitchen table. Dishes were in the drying rack and a plastic-wrapped plate held leftover meatloaf and mashed potatoes with carrots. "You're soaking wet." He removed her sweater, to reveal her blouse, clinging and transparent from the rain. She quickly pulled back the sweater to cover herself.

"I'm going to take a warm bath," was all that she said. When Hans offered dinner, she declined with a shake of her head.

Even a long soak in the tub did nothing to warm her core. Steam filled the room, obscuring her sense of reality. She thought she might have another spell and welcomed the temporary state of disorientation. This limbo between knowing the truth, and not knowing where to go next was too much for her. It was too painful to linger on the memories of the past, but her mind could not hold on to an image of her future. At this moment she felt suspended in a black hole, a space-time continuum where nothing felt real.

After a short goodnight to the children, she escaped into their bedroom feigning a headache. Wrapped in her winter robe, she sat at the end of the bed staring at herself in the mirror. At first, she traced the landmarks of her face—the bump on her nose, the scar on her left cheek, the mole on her chin—confirming that she was still there. She disrobed. Her broad shoulders and wide upper arms looked unsightly in the dainty nightdress. Her belly, after three pregnancies, rolled upon itself slightly. She caressed the thickness around her midriff before pinching it at both ends between her fingers until she felt deep pain. She moved down to her hips and then her thighs, trying to remember the last time Hans had touched her in any gentle and intimate way.

"Are we going to talk about it?" Hans stood in the doorway. Hands in his pockets. When she gave no answer, he grew frustrated. "We need to talk about this."

"I have nothing to say." She lay down on the bed.

"Paulina, we can't just go on without discussing it."

"Did you love them?" She sat up abruptly. "These women?" She knew the answer could hurt. That once said it could never be unheard, and she would carry it forever.

"No." He turned is head, unable to meet her interrogating stare. "Maybe. But we're married. I made a commitment to you. I stand by my word."

That justification made her seethe. "Your word? To love, honor, and obey? Those words?" She walked to the window. "How many years of secrets, Hans? How many years was I toiling away, suppressing my dreams, my life, for you and this family, while you were off selfishly galivanting?"

"Secrets? What about your secrets, Paulina?" Hans raised his voice, his collar looking tight around his neck, and the buttons on his shirt revealing his aging belly. "You and Dorthey with your letters that you always tucked away in secret drawers. Oliver and you sharing stories that stopped as soon as I entered the room?" He waited for her to say something. "That box!" He pointed to the white box with blue ribbon still tied in a perfect bow on top. "You said Kata gave you that as a gift. You still haven't opened it yet, after what, twenty-five years?" She turned away. "What are you hiding, Polly? There has been something through our whole marriage that you haven't told me."

"I can't," she whispered.

"You can't? You can't tell your husband what's in this box?" He marched over to the bookcase and picked it up. He shook the package aggressively. "What is so important, Polly, that you have to keep it wrapped in an unopened box?" He began to tear at the ribbon and the paper while she pleaded for him to stop.

"Auntie? What is going on?" Miriam stepped into the room, distraught by the argument. Neither seemed to notice she was there.

"No! Stop, Hans, don't open it." She tried to wrestle the package away. To the floor fell an engraved silver spoon, a baby journal, and a christening gown.

Polly crumpled to the floor crying. She held each artifact against her chest to conceal it.

"What is this?" Hans was perplexed.

"It was a gift, for a baby I had when I was twenty-two." She was barely able to get the words out between sobs. The tension in the room was like a whistle to a kettle that was well past boiling.

Miriam crouched down beside her aunt. Her arms wrapped protectively around her.

Hans's initial shock moved to anger. "How could you have kept this from me?"

"I was unsure of your reaction in those early days. As time went on it grew harder, and then it seemed simply unnecessary to tell you."

Miriam eased her up onto the bed. "Auntie, you shouldn't be stressing yourself right now. The doctor said you need to rest."

Polly shook her head. She reached for a tissue from the box on the dresser, and dabbed at her tears, regaining composure. "It is time I tell this truth." Miriam moved to excuse herself, to leave them to this moment in private. Polly clasped her hands, and pulled her back beside her.

"I was so very young and still finishing school. I thought I was in love, at first anyway, but the relationship was . . . not good. I knew I needed to leave. Then I found myself pregnant. An unwed mother in the 1940s . . . I had no choice." Her voice was full of regret. "I should have told you, Hans. I should have told you both."

"Oliver knew?" Bitterness spat out with each syllable. Hans paced the room, his hands clenched tightly at his side.

"Yes." She hung her head. She knew how much that stung him.

"And the baby?" Miriam asked with gentle curiosity.

"She was raised by another loving family." She looked at Miriam, and then at Hans. "I knew they could give her a much better life, with a stable happy family. Not a single mother who would have been cast out by society."

"You just gave your baby away to strangers?" Hans was reproachful.

"No, I did not just give her away to strangers!" She was defensive. Hurt by the accusation. "I gave her to Dorthey." The words slipped out before she could stop herself.

Hans looked at Polly, then to Miriam.

"The secret Grandmama told me you would share. This is it." Miriam walked to the corner of the room.

"All these years and you didn't trust me enough to tell me." Hans shook his head. "I need to go for a walk."

Polly nodded in acknowledgment. She did not stop him. After the door closed behind him with a thud, she treaded carefully over to where Miriam stood by the window, afraid of her recriminations.

"I am at a loss for how to explain this. We wanted to tell you so many times." Cautiously she touched her arm. Miriam remained motionless. "Dorthey and Petar were your parents. They loved you and raised you, for which I am eternally grateful. I was able to watch you grow and support you in every way I could from afar."

"The tuition?" She turned toward her with openness, no hostility evident in her expression. "The books. I knew Papa couldn't afford all that. He told me not to worry. He told me an angel was always looking after me."

Polly began to cry. Her dear brother gave her the greatest gift in life.

"It all makes sense now. I was always a bit different from Teddy and Sonja." She choked on her tears. "And Grandpapa, that is why he never liked me as much as the others. I always thought it was because I was bad. Because I didn't deserve his love."

The two women embraced and allowed the lifetime of missed moments to whirl around them. So much that they had shared through letters and brief phone calls redefined now as mother and daughter.

Polly made cups of tea, and they spoke until the early morning. She shared with Miriam stories of Eli, careful to paint their love story with the forgiveness of time. Miriam asked questions about her life in a way a daughter might.

"I don't know what became of Eli. I truthfully haven't inquired. He was a part of my life that I needed to leave behind." Polly's voice cracked. "If you want to contact him, I won't dissuade you. I am just not sure you will like what you find."

"Today I got another mother. Somebody I have known and loved my whole life. That is enough for now." The heaviness in the room was lifting, like fog after a long rain. "What do I call you? My dad, is he still Dad or Uncle Petar now? If I call him Dad and you Mom, that would be weird. Plus, Dorthey will always be my mom." Her pragmatism was evident as she looked at Polly the entire time, not a waver in her voice once.

Polly shook her head. "You can call me whatever you feel comfortable with. Auntie Polly, or just Polly, is fine. No rush."

"This is like a bad acid trip. I don't know what's up or what's down."

Polly scowled at the comment. So much about her daughter's life she did not know. It was not her place, not yet anyway, to lecture or scold.

Hans did not come home that evening. They phoned Petar in those early morning hours, catching him before he settled into bed. "I'm glad you know," was all he said. "I couldn't have loved you more if you were my own."

The following day they discussed how to tell the children. Fredric responded without concern or even many questions, just a new fact to accept. Juliette was overjoyed to have a big sister.

For the first several months they kept the truth among the five of them, as Miriam gained more comfort with the situation. Many stories were shared over dinner about their respective pasts. Hans remained quiet or was absent during most of them.

Gradually they told their close friends. Soon, Miriam began introducing Polly to her new friends as her mother. Calling her mom began to feel natural to them both.

Six months after that day of truth, Polly asked Hans for a divorce on the grounds of adultery. She did not want to remain married to somebody who was there only out of a sense of obligation. The divorce, for the most part was amicable. In the greatest irony of her life, she was the greater income earner at that moment in time, requiring her to give Hans half of her savings and part ownership of the publishing company. They sold the house, and she and the children moved into a two-story on the upper east side. Miriam moved into her own flat. Hans took a three-bedroom apartment in mid-town so the children had a place to stay if they ever wished, though they rarely did.

CHAPTER 17

1980

Traffic was heavier than usual for mid-afternoon in spring. Polly carefully maneuvered the car into the right lane, then again turned on her right signal.

"Mum, where are you going?" Juliette was impatient in the passenger seat. "I'm going to be late. The theater is straight ahead."

"I am just trying to get around this traffic so you get there on time."

Juliette huffed. She took off her shoes and began stretching her feet. Tonight, she was debuting her dream role as the female ballet lead in *Romeo and Juliet*. To anybody who asked, she insisted it was whom she was named after, when in fact Polly named her after the British writer and politician Juliet Rhys-Williams. Determined to dance this role since she was nine years old, she worried that she was too old. At nineteen, she was still young by all standards except those of the Royal Ballet.

Polly turned left at the following corner and then again right.

"Mum! What are you doing? The theater is back that way."

"No, it's this way," Polly insisted. She looked in the rearview mirror and then again to the right, recognizing her error. "Now, wait just a second, where am I? I seem to have turned myself around in all this traffic."

"Ugh!" Juliette slipped her shoes back on. "Just let me out here. I'll take the walk-through." She hustled quickly out of the car, opening the door before Polly made a full stop at the side of the road. "You'll be here tonight, right? Performance is at eight p.m."

"Of course, I'll be here, love. You'll be splendid. I'm so proud of you." Polly blew her a kiss. "See you tonight."

She watched Juliette's blond ponytail bounce as she jaunted across the road. Awed by her grace and maturity, Polly expected to see the energetic, long-limbed thirteen-year-old who would come dancing through the living room, pretending to be on the stage. It still shocked her how much Juliette had grown into a young woman.

Finally, she managed with some luck to find a circuitous route back to the office. Miriam was now established as editor-in -chief, making the work much lighter for Polly. Fredric was also now working for her; his close attention to rules and details, plus his expansive memory, made him perfectly suited as fact checker and copy editor. A comma was never out of place once Fredric had reviewed a piece.

Polly developed a reputation for fickleness at the publishing house. One day she said the cover ought to be blue, the next she was certain she had said red. Miriam now ran the creative brainstorming meetings and team updates in the afternoons. Periodically, Polly would still attend, particularly at the beginning of the month, to give her opinion and final approval on the edition's theme and story ideas.

Today, when she came into the boardroom, storyboarding was already underway. Never a small person, her entrance into any room always drew notice. Demurely, she sat in a chair at the back end of the table, relishing in the pride of seeing her daughter command the room. Almost imperceptibly, everybody swiveled their chairs away from Miriam, toward Paulina. Rarely did she interject her opinion until the end of the meeting. Today, the discussion was on the growing tension between Iran and Iraq, and the shocking likelihood that Ronald Regan—an actor, no less—would be elected to run as the Republican candidate for presidency of the United States.

"The cover mock-up looks like this." Miriam removed the Bristol board from the easel to show the *Maat* logo in its traditional Baskerville font, done in multiple colors, and a Rubik's cube, with each square containing an image of a person from the stories inside.

"No, no, no." All eyes drew to Paulina who was muttering her disapproval.

"Pardon?" Miriam took a big breath and partially held it. "You don't like it?"

"No. It's too busy. The title needs to always remain classic and identifiable by our readers. I thought we had agreed on putting the images on post-it notes, not the cube!"

Miriam let out the rest of her breath. "No. You insisted on the cube. And since the images were going in the actual squares, you wanted the color scheme brought up and replicated in the name."

Around the room Polly saw nodding heads and quiet whispers.

"Well, now that I see it, I have changed my mind. The brand needs to be preserved. The post-it notes are more fitting. I want to see the mock-up by tomorrow morning on my desk." Polly stood up quickly. The room seemed to sway. "Excuse me, please."

Without drawing attention, she walked down the hall close to the wall in case she needed support. She brushed her shoulder pads against the glass walls of the office to steady herself. Pins and needles ran down her arm. In her office she fumbled with the glass pitcher, spilling more water on the table than in her glass.

"Mom? Are you okay?" Miriam had followed her down the hall after dismissing the team early to work on the new design.

"Fine." She sipped her water, dribbling some on her suit jacket. "I just need to sit down."

"Another spell?"

"I am fine." She made her way to her chair and sat down slowly. "Just a little tired today. Night sweats had me tossing and turning for hours."

"Maybe I should take you to the doctor, Mom. Get you a check-up. You haven't seemed like yourself recently."

"I'm fine, Juliette!" she yelled. The pins and needles had subsided, replaced with a slight tremble that she noticed when she reached to open her cigarette box.

"Miriam," her daughter corrected.

"Pardon?" Polly shook her head, then lit her cigarette.

"I'm Miriam. You called me Juliette."

"Oh, Miriam." Polly let out a sigh. "I am so sorry, darling. Just a little tired."

"Maybe you should go home and rest a bit before tonight."

"Tonight?"

Miriam eyed her suspiciously. "Letti's debut."

"Oh, right. Of course." She took an inhale of her cigarette. Her nerves seemed to have settled. "Yes. A little rest would be good." She stubbed out her almost full-length cigarette and gathered up her briefcase, into which she placed several manuscripts.

"Perhaps I should call you a taxi?" Miriam urged.

"Nonsense. I'm fine. See you tonight." She gave Miriam a quick hug. "I really do think the post-it notes will look better. More in line with the brand."

Once home, she changed out of her suit and blouse, and into a pair of high-waisted slacks with a simple knit sweater and cardigan. A cup of tea and the first manuscript in hand, she sat in her armchair with her legs comfortably resting on the ottoman.

She dozed a few times, no more than twenty minutes, into a dreamless rest. Leftover lasagna was reheating in the microwave when the doorbell rang.

Oliver stood at the doorway in a full tuxedo and top hat, complete with white gloves. He gave her a kiss on the cheek and stepped into the house. "Something smells good!"

"Lasagna, would you like some?"

He looked at her peculiarly, taking in her ensemble. "You aren't ready yet, Polly. We have to go. Curtain's up in an hour and we want to wish her good luck backstage."

"I'm ready," she said in embarrassment.

"Polly, you know you can't go like that. It is opening night at the ballet."

"Well, people can say what they like. I think this is quite fitting for today's fashion," she said, trying her best to cover up her error.

He looked concerned.

"Well, fine then, Ollie. I shall go change. I'll stick to convention for Letti's sake."

She hustled to her bedroom, her heart pounding. How could she have forgotten? Her dress was already laid out on her bed, selected by Juliette that morning. She wished she had time for a shower and refresh of her hair with hot rollers but things would have to do as is. A spritz of perfume and tease of her roots did the trick. The navy-blue dress had a long slit up the side, which accentuated the one benefit of being so tall. The off-the-shoulder design and asymmetric ruffles over the bodice gave her a youthful vibrancy to which she was unaccustomed.

"You look stunning," Ollie said, as he held her purse so she could put on her sling-back shoes. He was one of the few men over whom she did not tower in high heels. He stood behind her with an open shawl to cut the cool evening chill. As she twirled to allow him to drape it over her, he caught her exposed shoulder and placed a soft, slow kiss on it.

"Ollie!" She jerked around, startled. A sheepish grin on his face took her back to the day at the creek where he bet her a kiss that he would beat her at the race.

"I have wanted to do that for so long." His fingertips traced the edge of her face, down her neck and across her clavicle. They had been spending almost every day together for the last year, since her divorce was final. Katherine had moved out shortly after that, their relationship not progressing the way she hoped.

"I have loved you and admired you my whole life, Polly. After Hans and Katherine, I wanted to give us both enough time to reset. Tonight just feels like the right moment to say it." He grasped her hands bringing them to his chest. "I want to be here with you right to the end. If you feel the same way." His eyes did not shift their focus from her face. He would not allow her to be coy this time. Many intimate moments had been shared over the years, from which she often pulled back. She had thought at times about them being together in a romantic way surely, but between relationships and marriages it never seemed destined to happen. She thought their time had passed.

Feeling the reverberation of his touch made her come alive, and she saw Ollie differently in that moment. An aging man with a playful spirit and a kind, handsome face. He was a constant in her life since childhood, there for every major milestone. Tonight, he confronted her, declaring what he wanted.

"I don't know, Oliver. You know I am not an easy person. I would hate to ruin what we have." She wanted desperately for him to kiss her, to feel desired again.

"I am in no rush, Paulina. I have waited a long time, and can wait some more." He offered his hand to her. "May I?" She placed her hands within his like a key in a lock.

They held hands walking to the car, and from the car into the theater. It felt so natural that she had forgotten until they entered Letti's dressing room and everybody's eyes drew to their interlocked hands. Ollie let go only to shake Fredric's hand.

Miriam gave her mother a hug. "Good for you," she whispered.

In her usual dramatic way, Juliette threw up her hands and announced, "Finally!" as she congratulated them.

Juliette's performance was seamless. Every transition was fluid. Her energy intoxicating right to the final moment. At curtain closure the audience sat silently stunned by what they had just witnessed until Fredric began clapping. A crescendo of applause overtook the theater, and roused everybody to their feet during her curtain call. For weeks she would replicate that performance with force. Polly and Oliver would see it together four times in total. Every newspaper and magazine, including *Maat*, would write about the explosive new talent at the Royal Ballet.

A few weeks later, the honor of the graduation address for Somerville Hall was bestowed upon Polly. Carefully, she folded her favorite black suit and cream blouse, one of Charlotte's designs, and placed it in her suitcase. She opted for pearls over diamonds and practical pumps.

She relished in showing Ollie around the campus. It seemed like only a short time ago that she left one life to start another here. She visited Lucy, who, at the age of seventy-seven, was no longer teaching. Still sharp as a whip, she recalled stories and events with such detail, it was like rebuilding it all for Polly again. "You make me very proud, Polly. I am a better person for having known you in my life," Lucy told her.

Sarah remained at the university in charge of archives and special collections. When they met for lunch at the faculty club, she flattered Polly with compliments. "You inspired me, Polly. You inspired all of us—your students, the Bluestocking girls, even the other teachers. It just wasn't the same after you left."

Polly often wondered what her life would have been like had she stayed. Hans likely would not have moved, so there would have been no marriage, no birth of a Fredric or a Juliette. Nor would there be the Bluestocking publishing house or *Maat* magazine. "No regrets," she said, squeezing Ollie's hand.

After lunch they socialized with the other faculty, whose tradition of lamenting about the shortcomings of the graduating class and the fate of the world in their hands would soon begin over Scotch. Oliver was in his element. Outgoing and cheerful, there wasn't a conversation he shied away from.

"What is it that you do then, Mrs. Nillson?" Beside her sat a man with large ears and a small forehead, whose eyes darted around the table in assessment of the most interesting conversation he would like to interrupt.

"She is a publisher," spoke the lady who sat on the other side of Polly.

"Well, I am a publisher now, but I was a professor of math and economics here in the fifties," she said with pride.

"And what, per se, do you publish?" The way he annunciated his hard consonants irritated her.

"Books, a magazine and *PEP—The Journal of Politics, Economics and Philosophy.*" She turned to continue her conversation with the woman on her other side.

"I've heard of that. It's not really a journal, though. It's more of a news magazine, wouldn't you say?" His brows raised as if he was scolding her for telling a fib.

"It is a journal. We publish research papers, observational studies, and white papers on new areas of discovery." She turned her body toward him, prepared to hear his retort.

"But it's not a peer-reviewed journal. There is no formal adjudication, no rigor to determine the worth of what gets published."

Ollie smiled at her across the table in support.

"What makes you say that?" she posed the question back at him.

"Well,"—the man seemed unsettled, not expecting his statement to be challenged— "where is your panel of distinguished members? Those seasoned, experienced academics who can bring a sight of wisdom to the worth of the work."

Polly shook her head, then patted the man on the shoulder in a disarming fashion. "Oh, sir, how small the world would be, and how slow our progress, if we only allowed a small group of distinguished old men to curate what we read, what we saw, and what was deemed worthy." She leaned in toward him. "The point, sir, is to bring a diversity of voice and thought to people, rather than have everything filtered and judged by a single lens. Only then will we reach economic stability and justice. Humanity will find balance and peace in the midst of world turmoil, only once we understand each other enough to not have fear."

The man held out his hand. "Professor Perkins, Political Science. A pleasure, Mrs. Nillson." She graciously took his hand.

"Dr. Williams, actually. But please call me Paulina."

She turned to her table mate on her left again. "Bravo," she said, offering Polly a little applause. "You will do splendidly tomorrow."

Commencement ceremonies held an ethereal ambience of possibility. Students recognized for their years of hard work, finally brought to fruition at graduation, dreaming of careers and accolades yet to come. Parents celebrating their job completed. Their child now prepared for the world, and being sent off to independence. The commemoration address always went first, followed by the conferment of diplomas to the undergraduate lower classes, followed by first class, and finally the graduate classes.

The day was splendid, with a cloudless sky and cool breeze. Inside, the auditorium was dank from the perspiration and body heat of all the excited people. Polly paced backstage, rehearsing her speech.

"You have given hundreds of speeches. You will do amazing today, as you always do." Oliver gave her a lingering kiss of reassurance.

The paper in her hand was drooping from the moisture of her palms. "I have had this memorized for days, but this morning made some very necessary changes. I just hope I don't forget them."

She had marked her changes in red ink to draw her attention to the key words. She tried to reassure herself but could not curb her nervousness. Speaking to her alma mater was different than other speeches. Looking out at the four hundred female students made her so proud to have been even a little part of the progress made at this university.

Ushered to her chair on the stage, she slowed down her mind and absorbed the details of the moment, noting every face, scent, and sound. Usually, she moved through life at a fast pace. There was so much to do. In contrast, this moment held an eternity of hopefulness in which she relished.

When she was called to the stage, she stood tall and strode slowly to take her place at the podium. Her voice quivered at first. "Graduates of Somerville Class of 1980, you shall carry your days here with you always."

Soon she stepped into a rhythm, the words flowing easily from her without thought. She knew the next section held an edit, a key message about responsibility to not just oneself but to others, that she wanted to get just right. She looked down at her page. The words blurred, then spun. She kept talking, blundering through. Fear, then disappointment, overwhelmed her at the lost opportunity to eloquently convey her advice. The crowd seemed to be swaying like a boat lapping on the lake. She continued on in spite of a growing nausea, her own voice hollow and echoey in her head. Finally, she came to the end, having run through the speech as if in a dream.

Applause rippled through the audience. At her seat she stabilized herself. These spells always passed. What a terrible time for one to come on, she cursed. Beside her, the chancellor sat and was speaking to her. Words of praise for her speech, she believed, but was unable to piece them together with any sense.

It was customary for the guests to remain on the stage throughout the entirety of the ceremony. Part way through, though, she excused herself. Focused on Oliver, who was standing in the wings, she ambled her way to him, trying desperately not to fall. His face registered concern.

"Polly, dear, are you all right?"

"Fine, fine, I think." She tried to take a step and fell into him. "Ollie, I think I need to go to the hospital."

In the ambulance, she mumbled his name several times but said no more. Miriam drove from London with Fredric. They had not told Juliette anything. Polly's spells were becoming more frequent and often passed. They didn't want to disrupt her evening performance.

"She has been in with the doctors since we arrived. I don't know anything. They mentioned bloodwork and scans and were waiting for her next of kin before they told me anything." Oliver was distraught. At her moment of need, he was helpless to do anything.

Miriam presented herself to the front desk, and was ushered into the back behind the double doors.

In the bed, Polly lay asleep. Her face was pale. Her large frame positioned awkwardly in the small bed. The nurse informed them that the doctor would be around shortly.

Positioned in the seat beside her, Oliver grasped her limp hand. "My dear Polly. My love. All will be well." He kissed her deeply, like in a fairy tale, hoping it was the magic remedy to wake her. She opened her tear-crusted eyes; a partial smile came to her face. "Darling, you're awake!"

Miriam and Fredric rushed to the bedside. "Mum? You, okay?"

She turned to them and tried to speak, then her eyes fluttered closed again.

It was hours before the doctor arrived. He asked about her past medical history, anything recently of concern. "How long has she been having these spells?" he inquired.

"A few years. For as long as I've been in England, so maybe six." Miriam took charge.

"And smoking?" the doctor asked in rote form.

They looked at Oliver. "Since university."

"Has she been having any memory issues?" the doctor probed.

"Not really. Some usual forgetfulness with age. She's a busy woman with lots going on, so nothing I wouldn't expect from just being overworked and tired," Miriam reassured.

Oliver cleared his throat. "I would say yes. She seems crystal clear about the past, our days as kids and events that happened during school. But she seems to struggle with remembering basic things." Oliver quieted, searching his mind for more details. "She is a math genius, yet she struggled to calculate the square root of a basic number the other day. She often forgets plans and appointments, sometimes loses direction. The other day she could not describe the cover of the magazine edition going out next week—she says she drew a blank." His voice grew more adamant. "So yes, I would say her memory hasn't been as good. We thought she was just pushing herself too much."

The doctor gestured for them to sit. "It appears Mrs. Nillson has vascular dementia. On her scan, it shows that she has been having a series of small strokes. Individually they may go unnoticed but cumulatively can lead to issues with memory, thinking, language, and sometimes mobility."

"Is there a cure?" Fredric remained steady. Miriam hung her head.

"I'm afraid not. Our goal is to try to slow it down, reduce any more strokes from happening. The rest will just be time."

"Not Mom. This can't happen to Mom. Her mind is her gift . . ." Miriam couldn't finish her words.

"We'll figure it out." Oliver rose to sit on the bed beside Polly. "We'll figure it out, won't we, darling? Our life together is just starting. There is so much we have to look forward to, don't we?" He clutched her hand to his heart, as if his love could restore her strength.

Polly remained in the hospital for several more days. When she was finally released, she could walk with little support. Her right arm was too weak to turn door handles. She took a bit longer to find her words, and grew frustrated when the exact one evaded her. She said very little during the drive home, except a few words to Miriam.

"When we return to London, I am passing over the entirety of the publishing house operations to you." She did not look at her when she said it. When Miriam protested and Oliver suggested she delay any decision until after she had some time to recover, she only raised her hand to silence them.

The following week she officially retired from the Bluestocking publishing house. As owner, she still reviewed the financial reports and Miriam indulged her by asking for advice now and again. Oliver moved into her house, selling the home he had shared with Lydia and then Katherine. Juliette finished her season with proclamations of perfection, and was invited to become principal dancer for the Royal Ballet. She moved into an apartment of her own.

"Now what?" she asked Oliver one evening over a simple spaghetti dinner. "The children are settled. The company is running splendidly with Miriam at the helm, better than I ever did it." She was content. It appeared that it was another piece and phase of her life from which to move on.

Still clumsy with her right hand at times, her strength and verve had returned. They decided to spend time traveling, something they had always wished to do, but were restricted by work obligations. They visited Petar and their friends in Canada for three weeks. Then it was on to the United States, specifically the exotic island of Hawaii, where they walked the beaches and motorbiked up volcanic mountains. They returned to England early to attend Lucy's funeral in Oxford. In the later fall it was off to Europe with stays in Portugal, Spain, and Italy.

While dining at a seaside restaurant under the bright moon, Polly suffered another stroke. This one affected her right leg, which now dragged slightly, requiring her to use a walker. They returned early from their holiday. Oliver had hired a decorator to put up the festive Christmas decorations before they arrived, hoping the celebration would cheer her up.

In the center of the front room, typically reserved for entertaining, adorned with a large red ribbon, was a baby grand piano.

"Oh, Ollie!" she wept from where she stood in the doorway. He had ushered her carefully, trying to block her view. "But what are we going to do with it?"

"Play it, silly. You are a piano virtuoso. Or have you forgotten that too?" he chided lovingly.

"I can't." She limped to the closest chair, using her walker as support along the way. "I haven't played in years. And now . . ." she mimed doing a scale with her right hand, her fingers moving coarsely. Lost were the dainty, light movements needed for any proper playing.

"You still have use of your hands. Use them for good things," he said, presenting her with the open box that held her *kara* bracelet. "Miriam wanted you to have this. On loan."

She let him slip the bracelet over her right wrist. Without much sensation in her hand, she needed to see it to know it was there.

He guided her to the piano stool, raised higher than usual to assist her in getting up and down. Shifted slightly to the right, it allowed for her left foot to work the pedal.

"Play something. Anything, darling." He put his fingers over hers and depressed each key with his right hand.

Beginner children's songs were her first attempts. Even those were clumsy with missed and wrong notes.

"I can't," Polly cried. "The colors don't come to me anymore. I've lost it all." She pounded her fists on the keys. The deep echoing sounds swallowed her.

"They are just hidden. You'll find them." Oliver rubbed her back. Her head rested on his shoulder.

That evening they settled into their new bedroom, converted from the den on the main floor to eliminate any need for stairs. In the middle of the night Ollie was awakened by sounds of music in his dreams. He rolled over to find the bed empty. Anxiously he rose to look for Polly. Her walker and slippers were both gone. Guided by the music, he found himself at the front room entrance. There she sat in her nightgown, playing over and over again Brahms' Lullaby. She had transposed the right hand to play stable simple chords, training her left hand to play the melody.

Silently, Ollie stood in the hallway admiring her. His heart filled with the joy of knowing she would be fine. That despite everything, she would survive this too. He sat, unseen, on the stairway, listening to her, until the sun rose and she decided to go to bed. He hurried into the room before her, pretending to be asleep. He heard her bump down the hall, the walker knocking into edges and tables. He resisted the urge to go help. Finally, she settled into bed beside him, and they both slept late into the morning.

CHAPTER 18

1986

For all of her life, time had been her nemesis. Never enough of it to accomplish what she set out to in a day. Punctuality was a standard unattainable to Polly, as she swirled forward every day to make each minute count. Only now that there was little do but sit in a chair or lie in bed did time finally decide to relax its pace.

The years had not been the gentle ones that she imagined, where age brought with it grace and wisdom. Polly spent most of her time looking out the window of the living room into the garden where she would be taken between ten and noon each day. A small lunch was fed to her on the patio and then she'd spend an afternoon napping in her bed, with nothing but empty time in between.

Oliver would read to her each morning: the paper, a favorite book, one of her company's own publications. Before they could marry, her mind was ripped from her like a tear in a stocking. Everybody considered them husband and wife except the law, which meant she could not transfer any of her assets to him. Not that he needed them; he did well for himself in life. Her will still declared Hans as the beneficiary, an oversight in a busy life taken for granted.

They tried to change it once, but when Hans arrived with his lawyers, she did not recognize him. Not because he had grown old. He still looked handsome with his full head of gray hair and slight paunch. After a series of romantic interests, he had married again. A young hairdresser from the salon where he went for monthly trims.

"Polly, you're so different." He was shocked at the transformation. Her once bright eyes that continually scanned the world around her for something new to learn were dreamy. Her usually strong body had grown lax with inactivity. On her broad bone structure, the skin and muscles gave the impression that she was puddling from the loss of tone.

"Hello, nice man. Are you one of my students?"

"How could you forget me, Polly? I was your husband. We loved each other." The children could tell Hans was hurt. He interpreted her confusion as an insult, and grew resentful.

"It's the disease, not her," Frederic would clarify. Still, he had trouble reconciling how she could simply forget him after over a decade of marriage. The situation supported his claim that she was incompetent to make any legal decisions. The will stood. Eventually, he agreed to transfer Polly's remaining portion of the company to Fredric and Juliet in equal parts. He was able to support his new family well enough, and wanted to ensure his children with Polly were cared after as well.

Each child would take turns visiting her. Juliette arrived in the mornings, where she would do her stretches and core training in the room while Polly sat on a chair by the window, slurping her tea and nibbling on her toast with marmalade. Juliette took the opportunity to share the details of her life with Polly, uninterrupted and without criticism.

"That's nice, dear," was Polly's usual response.

Miriam would arrive in the evenings to discuss work. She veiled her commentary in questions to garner opinion and recommendations from Polly on the business. Polly would nod her head, sometimes pointing to the cover she liked best or the title that was more interesting.

For the most part, Polly would reply with, "I'm sorry, dear, I didn't follow."

Miriam never needed the advice about design or corporate politics. The world had changed so much since Polly had retired. "She needs a sense of purpose, something to look forward to other than the telly," Miriam would announce when the family met to discuss Polly's declining health.

In the evenings, Fredric would come to help her into bed. He would assist with repairs to the house, and try to keep the garden tidy for her late-morning fresh air breaks.

Polly would often be heard humming music. She no longer played. The violin, even if held up by Oliver, was scratchy. Out of frustration she eventually threw it across the room, breaking the bridge. Oliver had it repaired, hoping she would want to try again. After that first Christmas, the piano sat untouched. Oliver thought of having it removed, concerned that it was just a painful reminder. Miriam requested that it remain.

"It just seems fitting that Mum's house would have a piano. Whether she plays it or not, I think the music just needs to be near her," Miriam insisted. She held fond memories of her childhood in Kingston when Polly would visit, listening to her play the piano for hours. Neither Fredric nor Juliette could remember every having heard their mother play, not even during those trips to Canada.

Each of the three moved on with their own lives with marriages and relationships but remained close to each other and Polly. Slowly she began to forget more things, and then people.

"Petar, you are such a handsome boy. When are you going to marry Dorthey?" she had said to Fredric, which terribly confused him.

On her fifty-ninth birthday, the children gathered with Oliver for a small celebration. Only Juliette brought her new boyfriend, a professional footballer from the Manchester United team. Miriam was pregnant, her belly just starting to show.

Oliver greeted them when they arrived. "Where's your other half?" he asked Miriam.

"At home, doing some work. You know these evenings can be a bit unpredictable." Miriam carried the cake she had brought into the kitchen. "I see Sadie outdid herself with the flowers this time," she teased. Bouquets sat in several rooms, each with fifty-nine flowers.

Over the last year, Sadie had taken to sending fresh flowers each week. "I know she loves them. Always wished she could have more but would never justify the expense. She deserves to be surrounded by the things she loves," was her reason.

Polly sat in her usual chair by the window, dressed in a proper pant suit. It made for a nice change from the slip-on house dresses she usually wore; they were easier for Oliver to dress her in. A new CD player was placed on the shelving unit among the books, a row of disc cases lined up beside it.

"Where did this come from?" Miriam asked.

"Charlotte and Isabella sent it over. A series of live orchestral performances captured on these little rounds silver discs. Amazing!" Oliver placed down the tray of cheese and crackers. His hair was now fully white. He still stood tall and straight, except for the slight roll of his shoulders from fatigue. Caring for Polly kept him strong. In his early sixties, he was still handsome. An aura of sadness enveloped him, having lost so much already in his life.

"How is Paris for them?" Juliette took the celery stick that was actually the garnish on the plate. "I miss them. I remember the hours I used to play dress up with Isabella in the store." She turned to her boyfriend and wrapped herself into his arm. "We should go visit them soon." He willingly agreed.

"You like this girl very much," Polly said to the footballer. "She seems very nice. Be kind to each other."

"Mum, it's me Juliette. Letti." Her voice was whiny like a child.

Polly just smiled back at her. Oliver offered an empathetic look. He went into the kitchen to retrieve the wine, declining any help from the children. "This is your time to celebrate your mum. I'll take care of everything else."

Miriam selected a CD to play from the Vienna Philharmonic. She turned up the volume to cut through the weight of the silence. The three of them discussed the recent conversation they had with Margaret about a new clinical trial in dementia that was happening in Toronto.

"Would it be worth having Mum take the trip to try? Ollie would go with her for sure." Juliette looked over at her boyfriend who was engaging in chitchat with her mom about the weather and football training. Her customary "I see" and "That's nice" sufficient to keep him talking.

"She couldn't manage the flight," Fredric stated. "Maybe if we gave her a tranquilizer." Nobody thought that a reasonable option.

"My song!" Polly shouted, which drew the attention of the room. "This is my song."

"Lovely, Mum. It's pretty. I haven't heard anything like it before. Where's it from?" Juliette wandered over and sat on the arm of the chair beside her boyfriend.

"I wrote it," Polly said.

"You wrote it? I don't think so, Mum."

"I wrote it! I wrote it! It's mine!" Polly pounded her fists on the table beside her.

Miriam looked at the CD jacket and carried it over to Polly. "Look here, Mom. It is called *A Winter's Tango* by P. Andrezej."

"Yes. That is me." Polly was insistent.

"No, Mum, you're Paulina Nillson." Juliette began to cry. "Once Paulina Williams, not P. Andrezej."

"Yes! That is me." She was emphatic. Against her chest she pushed her right hand, which was formed into a permanent fist, a result of the stroke.

Oliver entered with a tray full of glasses. "What's all the commotion?"

Fredric explained the confusion of the song and its author.

"But that is your mother. P. Andrezej. Did she never tell you? Your mother was a composer. She has a dozen or so symphonies and concertos that have been played around the world."

"I knew she wrote music." Miriam shared the story of Jasu and the composition she had done for the girl. "I just had no idea she had written this type of music and to this extent."

Oliver shared with them the story of how P. Andrezej came to be. A more likely name to garner the attention of the judges and give the piece some credibility, versus Paulina Williams. "And so, the pseudonym remained for all these years. There was a reputation and history with that name that she felt she couldn't change after she won that initial honor."

"I had no idea." Juliette looked at her mother as if seeing her for the first time. "She is a stranger to me in more ways than I knew." She excused herself to the bathroom for a solitary moment to cry.

"My song." Polly hummed along with her eyes closed. "Oliver, Oliver!" she shouted suddenly, drawing everybody in the room to her.

Oliver bent down in front of her and took her hands. "What is it, darling?"

"I see the colors, Oliver. They've come back. Fuchsia and magenta." She swayed to the music, humming out of tune. Repeatedly, they listened to the song, each buried in their own thoughts.

"Oliver," she declared. "I have decided I shall kiss you. Even if I do beat you to the tree and back." A peaceful pleasure overtook his countenance.

"I always knew you would, Polly." He knelt beside her. The others in the room did not understand. Some turned their heads, attuned to the private intimacy of the moment. Others swallowed up the exchange of love between them, hungry to fill their own souls with the purity of this simple human moment.

"I wish to have a love like that one day," Juliette whispered to Miriam, cautious that her boyfriend didn't overhear.

Miriam wrapped her arm around her younger sister. The two nestled together admiring their mother. "You will. Someday you will."

Before dinner was even served, Polly fell asleep in her chair. Fredric carried her into her room and covered her with a blanket. She would be up again before nightfall, never sleeping for more than a few hours at a time.

"Did you not know about the colors?" Oliver looked at the unknowing faces of Polly's children. "I take it she never told you. Weren't you ever curious about who your mother was?"

At the behest of Juliette, he spent the evening regaling them with stories about her life. Oliver seemed years younger reliving the stories of her life as he knew it. They laughed at her obstinance in calling him anything but Oliver in the early days. Miriam and Juliette raged at the injustice of how she was treated at the symphony. He skipped most of the Toronto years—those were Polly's to tell. Fredric celebrated her great research, and even the boyfriend was inspired by her courage behind the Bluestocking Club.

With winter dragging into April, so too did the weight of Polly's illness on those closest to her. Her sleep cycle reversed. She wandered the halls unsteadily at night. Alone with nothing but time, Ollie would leave the music playing softly before he went to bed to keep her company. A magazine would be left beside the armchair with a glass of scotch on the rocks, usually quite watered down, and a snack of cheese, crackers, and vegetables with dip.

He woke several times to check on her, and when assured that she was well he would tiptoe back to sleep or try to guide her back to bed. She no longer read; the words nonsensical to her. It wasn't clear how much she understood of what was told to her.

During her morning visits, Juliette would spout off gossip about the royals, her favorite television show plot lines, and the details of her friends' lives. Polly would shout at her at times, "Go!" or "Quiet!" out of frustration with the topic.

"Where is my Juliette?" she asked one day when they were out in the garden, still bundled up against the spring frost.

"I'm here, Mum," she said confused. "I've been here all day."

"No, dear. My Juliette. My little girl." She looked affectionately at this unrecognizable girl beside her, even tugging on her ponytail.

"It is me, Mum. Why don't you recognize me?" Her voice cracked. She gathered up her things quickly into her tote bag. "I don't know. I'll see if I can find her." Juliette gripped on to the grief so tightly she felt it was choking her. She hustled into the house, leaving Polly in the garden. She struggled to drink some water. Oliver had to run some errands, and Miriam was not due to arrive until the afternoon. She called Miriam to come early, claiming she needed to be at the studio.

"How is she today?" Miriam looked tired. Her official due date was two weeks away. Still unable to decide whom to leave in charge at work while she took a few weeks to be with the baby, her worry was wearing her thin.

"Not good. She didn't know who I was." Juliette's eyes drooped. She looked like a lost child. "I don't know how much longer I can do this."

"I'll take it from here. You have a great day! Go. Be twenty-four years old for a change. Head out with your bloke tonight and don't worry about anything here." A deep sisterly hug handed over the burden of responsibility and Juliette walked out lighter.

Miriam stepped outside with her shawl tightly wound about her. "Mom, it's getting pretty cold out here. You should come in."

The only response was the whistle of the wind through the still barren trees. She stepped outside, calling her mom along the way. "Mom, I said it's cold out, we should go in."

Polly looked up, then placed her hand on Miriam's pregnant belly. "I had a baby once. I gave my baby away." She rubbed Miriam's belly. "Babies are magic. They fill your life and at the same time take it all away."

"Mom, we should go in. The clouds are coming in. Looks like a storm soon."

"I want my baby back." She looked up at Miriam wide-eyed. "Can you tell Dorthey I want my baby back?"

In tears, Miriam bent forward to guide her mother to stand. "I'm here, Mom. You do have your baby back."

She tried to urge her up but she was too heavy. A tight knot in her lower belly dissuaded her from trying again. "Okay, Mom, let's wait here for a bit."

They sat in the backyard, in two metal chairs with plaid fabric-cushioned seats. They said nothing. Only held hands and watched the clouds roll in. The knots grew into cramps and Miriam was sure she was having contractions.

"Mom, I think the baby is coming." Miriam stood up, joyous and scared. "You have to come in. I have to go to the hospital."

"Baby? My baby? I want my baby back. I want my baby!" Polly cried with her face buried in her palms, crouched over like a child.

"Okay. Let's go get your baby." Miriam eased her up and walked with her to the house, stopping every so often from the pain.

She was able to reach Oliver on his Motorola, and called her husband to pick her up to go to the hospital. That evening, Miriam gave birth to a baby girl that she named Dorthey.

Polly held her granddaughter only once in the hospital before she suffered her final stroke. Unable to move without assistance, she spent most of her remaining days in bed. Her mumbled words were difficult to comprehend. She smiled whenever she saw baby Dorthey, and any time music was playing.

She wept when Petar arrived. Time had not been kind to him either. Decades of hard labor in the quarry and the loss of his wife so young left him a sad and lonely widower. His hair had thinned. Deep wrinkles etched his face like hieroglyphics. He wore simple jeans, a heavy fisherman's sweater, and sturdy boots. He kept his hat in hand as a security blanket.

"Polly, my baby sister. It wasn't supposed to be like this." He hung his head, resting it on the bed. Her left hand lifted to rest on his head, curling his hair between her fingers. "You are so talented and smart, a true polymath." He looked up at her. "Why you? I would have taken it, Polly, all of it, from you. Most of my life after Dorthey isn't worth remembering. What do I have to offer the world anymore?"

She pointed her finger at him like a school teacher. A tight scowl on her face and fierceness in her eyes. "You," she managed to mumble, "kind, good." The effort took much from her. She closed her eyes for a moment to regain what she could to finish what she needed to say. "Thank you," she said.

They sat like that for hours, like only siblings could. Not saying a word to each other. Their history was like cement between them, bound together with a wildness that only a life shared of great disappointments, tragic losses, and deep love could bring.

EPILOGUE

My mother died September 2, 1986. Ironically, it was the first day of the new school semester. Her funeral was attended by nearly a hundred people. Close friends and family, of course, and in addition, dozens of her students. Many former colleagues from the Oxford Bluestocking Club also came.

Hans attended the funeral with his new wife and toddler. He turned over his portion of the Bluestocking Publishing Company in full to Fredric and Juliette. With the help of Oliver, they installed a board of directors, and hired a CEO to run the business. I remained editor-in-chief for more than twenty years.

I did search for my dad, Eli, tracing his career from Toronto to Montreal. He had been unable to earn a tenured position at any of the universities. Last I uncovered, he had married and divorced twice. Neither of his wives knew where he was living. I stopped searching after that, not sure I wanted to find him. Once I found the truth I could never unknow it. Imagination was safer.

Juliette remained with the ballet until the late age of thirty, after which she married her football-playing bloke. She took the dividends paid to her from the publishing house and opened a dance school. Like Mom, she had a kind heart and offered several dozen scholarships to pay the tuition for children who exhibited great potential, but whose families could not afford to send them to the school.

The design brand Charlotte was sold for 100 million pounds to a large fashion conglomerate. Charlotte and Isabella spent the rest of their time living all around the world. They were godmothers to my baby, Dorthey.

Dorthey's—my first mom's—book of poetry, sold more than 10 million copies worldwide in twelve different languages. It seemed people did care about the musings of a simple housewife after all.

Petar, who I turned to calling by his first name, remained in Kingston his whole life. He began going to church, and was a respected member of that community. He spent every Sunday with Teddy, Sonja, and their families. We still remain close, even with his few words and several time zones, plus an ocean, between us.

Sadie remained one of the most significant women philanthropists of the time. She traded in her champagne lunches and luxury goods to volunteer at Margaret's clinic, supporting women escaping abusive relationships. Invitations for her to speak as a keynote were plenty from large organizations and universities.

Margaret continued to work at the clinic, donating most of her earnings back to keep it running. She became an esteemed teacher within the Faculty of Medicine at the University of Toronto. Honored by the College of Family Physicians with an award named after her for her devotion to humanitarian efforts through the field of medicine, she remained unmarried and lived a simple life.

Mom's notes and boxes were cataloged by Fredric. He was able to identify the various published pieces of music that she had composed under the pseudonym P. Andrezej. Through records at the university, the Toronto Symphony, and attestation by the old maestro and Oliver, he obtained acknowledgment that the work was done by Paulina Williams. With dividends from the publishing house, he commissioned the London Philharmonic to record an album of a dozen of her pieces for posterity under her proper name.

Oliver continued to live in the home he shared with Polly. He remained very close with all of us. After Mom's death he returned to work as a consultant. He volunteered his time for the Heart and Stroke Foundation, through which he launched the first smoke-free campaign in London.

In 1994, John Nash won a Nobel Prize for his work in economics on game theory. It was the same topic in which Mom had completed her thesis. In 2006, Edmund Phepps won the Nobel Prize for the Golden Rule, a similar theory to the one Mom was unable to get published while at Oxford. Their names remain in history; Mom's remains in our hearts.

Sarah, the librarian at Oxford, compiled a history of Mom's life. Eventually she wrote a biography, *Paulina Williams: The Many Names of a Quiet Polymath*. Each section was headed by one of Mom's different names: Polly; Paulina Williams; P. Andrezej; Dr. Williams, PhD; Mrs. Nillson; and finally, Paulina. The book went on to be a best-seller.

I regret not knowing Mom better when she was alive. The mosaic of her complex life pieced together from her own stories, letters, and memories of those closest to her is a wonderful gift. I wonder if, in the way women do, she would brush it aside as "just life, nothing remarkable here," an expectation that this is just what people do. The sad irony of this gifted mind stripped away in her later years through dementia seizes my heart whenever I think of it. Wasted time of not knowing who she really was, I still grieve. My mother is my hero, a true genius.

~ Miriam Williams

DISCLOSURE

This book is entirely a work of fiction. Though some of the people named in the book are real, the situations, words, and interactions are all of my own imagination. Please do not draw any conclusions about these characters from this story. I encourage you to do further reading if you are interested.

The Grange was the first site for the Art Museum of Toronto. The home and estate were originally owned by D'Arcy and Sarah Anne Boulton. The home was left to their son William, and later to his widow, Harriet, who went on to marry Goldwin Smith. It was the Smiths who donated the house for the purposes of the art gallery. In the book, Sadie marries into the Grange family, to whom I ascribe the ownership of the building for ease of association for the reader. Please visit the Art Gallery of Ontario website to learn more about the history of The Grange and the Art Museum of Toronto, which are now part of the AGO.

The Cambridge Circus did exist with members Piero Sraffa and Joan Robinson. There is no record, of which I am aware, of a speaking event that took place at Oxford as was depicted in the story, nor of a women's group of which Joan was a part.

There are many accounts of women coming together to fight for equal rights to access education. For those interested in learning more, I share with you *Bluestockings* by Jane Robinson, as a book that was incredibly useful to me during the writing of Polly's story. Lucy Sutherland was a progressive educator at Somerville College Oxford and the first female pro-vice-chancellor of the university. Whether she led a movement of women at Oxford is unknown to me. The character in this book is completely fictional.

Finally, Robert Fleming and Healey Willan were both Canadian composers of the time. Their appearance in this book is again fictional. An evening at the Toronto Symphony, as is depicted herein, did not actually happen. Their names in this book are meant to celebrate their work.

ACKNOWLEDGMENTS

Writing is not a solitary craft. I want to thank my incredible group of friends for their encouragement and support. In particular, Mirka who entertained her children and mine so I could carve out uninterrupted time to write in the early days. Lori, for her optimism and reminder that life is yours to design. To my writing group for helping me shape Polly in the early days; especially to Sandy for offering your insights and historical fact checks right through to the end.

Thank you to Sam for being my beta reader, and to all the book club members for helping me learn what makes a great story. Of course, a huge hug of thanks to my own bluestocking crew of ladies: Sue, Sam, Paula, Lynn, Jen.

To the team at TellWell, Ben and Redjell for your guidance through the process. To Lara for being a supportive editor—both encouraging and enhancing the story along the way.

I also want to thank my family for always believing in me. To my sisters, who are always my fountain of courage and support through the hard parts of life. My parents who raised me with compassion, and understanding that we are each a gift to this world. For my children whose wisdom and courage amazes me. I learn so much from each of you every day. To my husband for being my biggest cheerleader and always believing in me. I love you all.

For Book Clubs and Reading Circles

1) How do you feel about the shift in support of Polly's parents through the story, from her childhood through to her time in university and afterwards? What societal norms and personal expectations influenced the change in Polly's dynamics with her mother and father?

2) Dorthey and Polly are very different girls. What do you think bonds their friendship over the years?

3) Polly's relationship with Eli confuses some readers. What do you think attracted her to him, and why did she stay in the relationship as long as she did?

4) For years Polly carried about her blue suitcase and the unopened gift from Kata. What is the symbolism behind that?

5) Surrounded by an equally interesting group of women, how did Mary, Margaret, Charlotte, Lydia, Dorthey, and Kata influence Polly? What struggles do you think each of those women would have had in their own stories?

6) Several times in the book, Kasia warns about men's expectations of women and her own mistakes. What do you think those may be?

7) Do you think Polly made the right decision about her baby when she left for Oxford? What other options might she have had? What would you have done differently in that situation?

8) Oliver is a consistent, positive person in Polly's life. Do you think their lifelong friendship created a great love, or was it the reverse? How might her life have been different if Polly and Oliver fell in love earlier?

9) Polly has a complex relationship with being a mother. In the book it is referred to as a birth of a life, and a death of a person. What has been your experience with seeing woman evolve into motherhood, and the balanced shift of priorities and ambitions?

10) A dominant theme in the book is the lack of awareness children have of their mothers as people with histories, dreams, and passions that are never known to them. What curiosity do you have about your own mother's life? Would you ever ask her about it? If not, why not?

Manufactured by Amazon.ca
Bolton, ON

34594777R00178